When she was at school, Julie Garratt always came top of the class for writing stories! In the early 90s Julie gained a City and Guilds qualification enabling her to teach creative writing and has since often been employed to take courses in the county.

Julie is the author of four published romance novels and claims that her holidays serve a dual purpose:- 'holiday *and* research trip!' She is married with two grown-up children, and lives at the top of a steep hill, which overlooks a valley dividing Nottinghamshire and Derbyshire. Her hobbies include photography, driving, antique book fairs and music. Julie also has a much loved garden where she can 'sit under the trees to write my novels . . . or play with my dogs!'

THE TROUBLE WITH TAMSIN

Tamsin runs away from love but soon discovers that 'out of sight' doesn't necessarily mean 'out of mind'. She likes men — she might even be in love with one of them. There's Patric, wonderful — until she discovers he's having an affair with her best friend; there's Vaughn — the man Tam loved and lost; and the attractively menacing Craig. Then there's Mark, who is always there for her. But he will only take so much from Tam, and eventually even his patience wears thin.

Books by Julie Garratt
Published by The House of Ulverscroft:

CHANGE OF HEART

JULIE GARRATT

THE TROUBLE WITH TAMSIN

Complete and Unabridged

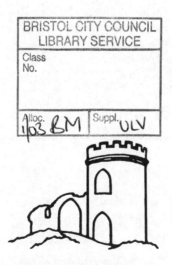

ULVERSCROFT
Leicester

First published in Great Britain in 1998

First Large Print Edition
published 2002

British Library CIP Data

Garratt, Julie
    The trouble with Tamsin.—Large print ed.—
Ulverscroft large print series: romance
    1. Love stories
    2. Large type books
    I. Title
    823.9′14 [F]

    ISBN 0–7089–4754–9

Published by
F. A. Thorpe (Publishing) Ltd.
Anstey, Leicestershire

Set by Words & Graphics Ltd.
Anstey, Leicestershire
Printed and bound in Great Britain by
T. J. International Ltd., Padstow, Cornwall

Prologue

'You're making the biggest mistake of your life, Tam.'

Mark Langham felt like shaking her, but he knew such an action would make no impression on her. Besides that, violence had never been a trait of his — but neither was he a man of infinite patience, he reminded himself.

He supposed he ought to be accustomed to her whims and fancies by now, as well as her mettlesome spirit and her prickliness where he was concerned. He'd known her for less than a year, but it had been enough for him to get to know her character, to grow to love her, and also to know that once Tamsin had made her mind up about something there was no going back. With hindsight, he might have guessed she'd spring something like this.

It was New Year's Day, and Tamsin's phone call had brought him speeding along the narrow lanes to the east coast village of Heronsea and swinging his beloved Porsche into the lighthouse car park, tyres squealing as he'd drawn up beside where she'd stood waiting outside her former home for him. He'd got out of the car and strode over to her.

She was wearing a leather jacket, with a soft moss-green scarf tucked high against her chin. Her legs were encased in cream cord ski-pants, and leather boots and gloves completed her outfit. She'd looked determined, and extremely self-assured.

Her phone call had been brief, and had left him in no doubt of her intention. She was leaving him. Leaving Heronsea. New Year's Day! A New Year resolution — to leave the past behind.

The sullen North Sea, churning up great waves and crashing them onto the beach so far below where they stood on the headland, was a fitting backdrop, he thought, to the scene. A storm was blowing up, and flurries of snow swirled round them in the early-morning air. And dominating the whole theatrical prospect, adding even more drama, was the majestic lighthouse — the place where all Tam's hopes and dreams had crumbled into heartache and wretchedness, and had finally disappeared into nothing with the tragic death of her business partner, Ava Thorne, only a few short weeks ago.

He couldn't blame her for wanting to get away, he supposed, but he had to try and make her change her mind. He stood in front of her now, aware that she was keeping her temper with difficulty as she replied in a tightly controlled voice, 'I knew, I just *knew* you'd go and put a damper on things, but you have absolutely no right to do that. It's *my* *life* we're talking about, and if I want to get away from Heronsea, then I'll do just that.'

'You'll propel yourself headlong into another pack of trouble,' he yelled at her above the sound of the thundering sea. 'You need somebody to look after you.'

'Meaning . . . ?' she asked pointedly, dashing back with one hand the riot of golden curls that the cold north-easterly wind was snarling around her face and swirling into her eyes.

Mark faced up to her. 'Meaning me! You know damn well I mean *me*. I want to marry you. I want to take care of you.'

'You want to wrap me in cotton wool,' she derided, her voice rising too now, above the winnowing wind and the sound of the sea. 'You want to be my keeper. You want me obedient and house-trained — just like Maggie's dog, Fudge.'

'That is ridiculous.' Mark calmed down a little as he pleaded, 'Tam — don't jump into anything, sweetheart. Just stop and think, will you? You're giving up everything — your home, your work . . . '

Her laugh was shaky. 'My work? I have no work to do now that Ava's gone. Ava was the foundation-stone in my life — she was the one who designed those dresses, not me. All I did was pretty things up with my flowers. And as for my home — well, they say home is where the heart is, don't they? And my heart is certainly not anchored in a dreary little one-bedroom flat at Heronsea. My life was here, Mark — at the lighthouse — at Ava's Ivory Tower. It was to be our whole life — and now look at it — abandoned, empty, looking for a new owner.'

He knew a moment of indecision; she spoke the truth. He took a deep breath and said, 'Look — I know you were put through a lot . . . '

She couldn't meet the steady look in his eyes. She turned her head away to glance northwards at the bleak and wintry coastline as she replied, 'It was a nightmare, Mark. I lost my best friend and my livelihood when Ava died. And I lost Vaughn Herrick's love — *and* his baby — in this place. I can't stick around here and be reminded of things I just want to forget . . . '

4

'Do you want to forget me?' he asked brutally.

Her gaze came back to him. She lifted her face and he saw tears glinting in her eyes. 'No,' she said, without even a moment's hesitation.' 'I shall never forget you, Mark — and it would be so easy to say yes, I'll marry you. But I can't do that.'

The cold was eating into his bones. A heavier coat and more windproof clothing hadn't been his top priority when he'd received her call this morning. He'd just grabbed a jacket — any old thing that was hanging in the lobby — as he'd raced out of the front door.

'Why not?' he asked. 'Why the hell can't you marry me? We fight, I know, but lots of couples do. The rest of the time, though, we seem pretty well suited.'

Calmly, she raised her eyes to his and said, 'I don't intend getting hurt again. Not ever, Mark.'

His expression held infinite tenderness, 'I wouldn't hurt you . . . ' He held out a hand to her. 'Tam — I worship the ground you walk on . . . '

'Don't,' she said quickly. 'Don't make me feel guilty or we'll say harsh things and that's the last thing I need. I want us to part as friends, Mark. I need to be able to pick up

5

the phone and talk to you when I want to. I can't risk us drifting apart like some couples do.'

In an incredulous voice, he said, 'You're moving two hundred miles away from me, for heaven's sake, and here you are saying you don't want us drifting apart. Tam — we're not just 'drifting' — this is a hatchet job. You're chopping us neatly down the middle and going off goodness knows where. Drifting . . . ' He laughed harshly. 'Drifting I could take — cold-blooded heart surgery without anaesthetic I can't deal with.'

She sighed and raised both hands to her head, trying to keep her dancing golden curls from whipping across her face and into her eyes again. She pulled up the collar of her leather jacket, and, holding it to her cheeks, she said, 'I knew you'd take it the wrong way. That's why I didn't tell you about my decision over Christmas.'

'I was looking forward to the New Year,' he snapped back at her. 'I thought we had something going for us at last . . . '

'It's done,' she said. 'Cass Fairburn is expecting me in Suffolk.' She waved a hand aimlessly at her little Beetle car, parked snugly up against the lighthouse base. 'I said I'd be there by lunchtime.'

'Who is this Cass person? You've never

mentioned her before . . . ' He flung his hands in the air in despair.

She fumbled in her coat pocket and held out a ripped-off page of a pocket diary to him. 'Here! This is her address and telephone number if you really do want to keep in touch. She's a girl I knew at school. There was a note in the Christmas card she sent me telling me her mother had died three months ago. She's on her own now and she invited me down to Suffolk to stay with her. It's just what I need right now, Mark — a complete break.'

The paper fluttered in her gloved fingers and he leapt towards her, fearful that the note might blow away. He clutched it firmly, holding it in both his hands in an attempt to keep it straight so he could read what she'd written on it. He looked up at her then. 'Well — at least you didn't go off without telling me,' he said in a disgruntled tone. 'I suppose I ought to be thankful for that.'

She pushed her hands into her pockets and her tense features relaxed a little. 'Maybe you could come down there and see me.'

His head shot up. 'How long are you intending staying?'

She shrugged. 'Indefinitely.'

He stared at her.

She said gently, 'I need a job, Mark. I'll

have a bit of money from the sale of stock from the Ivory Tower when it comes through, but it won't be a fortune.'

'Hell!'

'Suffolk isn't the end of the world.'

'Neither is Heronsea — but it was here I lost you to that damn race-driver, Vaughn Herrick.'

'That wasn't permanent.'

'No? You're not thinking of taking up with him again? This isn't some ruse so you can go back to him without me suspecting?'

'No,' she said, her voice steady. 'He's the last man on earth I want, and I wouldn't deceive you, Mark.'

'There are other men — between here and Suffolk.'

'Look,' she said, 'I'm not looking for romance. I don't intend falling into the arms of the first man I meet down there, if that's what you're thinking.'

He looked shamefaced. 'I wasn't really suggesting . . . '

'You should trust me,' she flared.

'It's difficult to do that . . . '

She stepped closer to him, lifted her face and kissed him gently on the lips, then said, 'It's not goodbye, Mark. We'll keep in touch. I just need some space.'

He bowed his head, wanting to sweep her

into his arms and hold her there for evermore, but he knew only too well that if he did that it would drive her even further away from him. She was like a butterfly. She couldn't be captured. She needed freedom just as much as she needed air to breathe. The only way to keep her was to give her that freedom, even though he felt he was dying a slow and painful death in the doing of that. He shoved a hand into his pocket, then muttered, 'Damn! I had something for you but I left it on the dashboard,' and swung round to his car. He raced across to it, yanked the door open and picked a small packet up, then hurried back to her. 'Here!' He glared at her. 'You wouldn't spend New Year's Eve with me, so I got you this instead of 'Auld Lang Syne' and all that clasped hands trash folks do when the clock strikes twelve.'

She stared down at the little box in her hand. 'What is it?'

'Open it,' he growled, suddenly embarrassed.

She glanced up. 'It's not a ring? Mark — you know how I feel about such things. It's not a half-hoop of diamonds or anything stupid like that, is it?'

He snatched the box out of her hands and pulled top and bottom apart. 'No.' He fished out a slender silver chain with something dangling on it. 'It wasn't expensive,' he said, his face dark as thunder. 'I know you're not impressed with worldly things.'

Her laugh was breathless. 'You shouldn't buy me any sort of things. There's no need — really there isn't, Mark.'

'It's just a little something to go with that flower brooch I gave you at Christmas,' he said. 'Heaven forbid that I should buy you something madly expensive — I know what you'd do if I did. You'd throw it back in my face. Heck, Tam, I daren't even buy you gold jewellery because I know damn well you'd think I was trying to buy you if I did that.'

'The lily of the valley brooch is pretty.' Her glance was soft. 'I'm wearing it now on the tunic underneath my coat.'

'Wear this too.' He held out the chain.

She caught at the pendant swinging in front of her. 'A dreamcatcher,' she said, her eyes alight.

'Some such thing,' he said. 'I didn't take it in what the jeweller was saying.'

'It's American-Indian in origin,' she said. 'See the filigree mesh? That's supposed to catch bad dreams and keep them away.' Her eyes held a faraway expression as she gazed up into his face.

'And the holes are to let the good ones through,' he finished for her, his voice low.

'Guess I did take in what that jeweller was saying after all.'

'It's lovely, Mark. I shall treasure it.'

He suddenly felt embarrassed. 'It's nothing,' he said dismissively. 'Just a bauble.'

'I don't have anything to give *you* for the New Year . . . '

Hungrily he stared at her. 'Just come back to me,' he said, reaching out and gently touching her face with one finger. 'Just come back to me, Tam . . . one day . . . and soon . . . '

1

It was impossible for the Beetle to pick up much speed on the twisty, narrow roads of Suffolk, but Tamsin wasn't worried. There was no hurry. Cass had told her on the phone that if she missed the turn to Alderwood after leaving the 'ten-sixty-six' road she'd probably never see civilisation again! Just at the moment, though, that thought didn't worry her.

The drive had been pleasant, the roads quiet and wooded, but now she was getting nearer the coast the trees were thinning, and she kept catching glimpses of wide open spaces with twisting creeks and vast sea marshes. It was a part of England she'd never experienced before, and it fascinated her.

She was looking forward to meeting Cass again, and hoping that Cass would be just the same as she remembered her from their school and college days. But, considering the fact that they hadn't seen each other for eight years, she knew there were bound to be *some* changes.

Something dashed out into the road and she jammed her foot hard on the brake. The car screeched and came to a crazy diagonal halt.

'Hell!' The rabbit was disappearing into trees at the side of the road. Relief that she hadn't hit it made her sit back in her seat, letting out a long hissing breath as the engine juddered, then died.

'Keep your mind on the road,' she scolded herself. 'That could have been one very sore rabbit if it hadn't had its skates on.'

The next signpost told her that Alderwood was two miles straight on, and there were sparse signs of population now — isolated pebble and flint houses, a duckpond, a red postbox on a corner.

'You have to go over the Borda river bridge,' Cass had said. 'It's the only way into the village. Then you can look for the Marsh Road, and Stride Common where I live, leads off it. On the sea side. The left.'

Tamsin smiled now. Well, she couldn't miss the river bridge; it had a black and white road sign, like a street sign, saying 'River Borda' beside it. It was one of the narrowest bridges she had ever seen — so narrow, in fact, that it had traffic lights so that only one stream of traffic at a time could use it. The lights were on green. She sped across. The road surface was bumpy and had a hollow feel to it, almost as if the superstructure was made of wood. Almost immediately she was over it, she spotted the road sign Cass had told her about. She flicked her car indicator, and then she was turning yet again — this time onto Stride Common.

It was no more than a cobbled track, lined with colour-washed houses, a time-defying assortment of windows, peg-tiled roofs — and Cass, in jeans and a brown woolly shift-type thing, leaping down two steps out of a doorway that led right onto the road. The girl was waving wildly to her, and prancing around, with her straight fair hair bouncing up and down, and her smile wide and welcoming.

Tamsin wore a big grin as she slowed the car, wound down the window and yelled, 'Where on earth can I park in a narrow street like this?'

'Pull right in — right up to the house — under the window.' Cass Fairburn was gesticulating, indicating the exact spot where Tamsin would not be blocking the road for other traffic. 'It'll be okay there for a while. Yellow lines haven't been invented down here yet, so you won't get a ticket. Alderwood wouldn't know what to do with a traffic warden if it'd got one!'

Tamsin did as she was told, then got out of the car, and the two girls just stood and looked at each other.

'You haven't changed a bit.'

Tamsin gave a grimace. 'Yes, I have. I don't try to dye my hair darker now. I got to thinking — what the hell! If God gave me hair the colour of a dandelion, and the texture of a dandelion gone to seed, there must be a reason for it.'

They fell about laughing, then grabbed at each other's hands and stood a yard apart, each one avidly taking in the sight of the other. Tamsin sobered and said, 'You're just the same, though. Level-headed Cass who kept me on the straight and narrow. Oh, Cass, it's so good to see you. So good to be here.'

'Come on in. The kettle's boiled a hundred times this morning. I was so determined to have a hot drink waiting for you the minute you arrived.'

Tamsin followed her friend inside the pink-washed house with two steep steps leading up from the roadside. It was still quite early, barely midday, and it had been a cold morning. The sun had, though, managed at last to fight its way out through the leaden sky, and, looking at it now, she was aware that winter had never felt so good in a long, long time.

Cass faced her in a room that was roasting from the heat coming out of a glass-fronted stove, and fragrant with the bunches of dried lavender tacked to a central beam. There was chintzy furniture and a computer and printer on a stand tucked into one corner. 'Take your coat off. Chuck it on a chair. I'll show you your room when we've had a cuppa.' She whirled away and went through an archway into the kitchen, switched on the kettle again, then abruptly turned and said, 'Or would you rather have coffee?'

'Tea's fine! A nice steadying cup of tea is just what I need. I nearly killed a rabbit a couple of miles back.'

Cass said, coming back to her, 'You'll find rabbits and pheasants littered all over the place down here on the roads. They seem intent on suicide. They're Suffolk's answer to lemmings.'

'It'd be kinder to motorists if they went and jumped off a cliff to achieve their mass destruction. Honestly, I nearly hit a tree avoiding that damn rabbit.'

Cass laughed again. 'We don't have any cliffs in this part of Suffolk. We just have marshes and creeks — and a nice shingly beach. I'll show you tomorrow.'

'Any night life?' Tamsin had deposited her coat on one of the easy chairs and stretched, easing her back, which was stiff from driving, and rubbing her hands over the hips of her cream cord ski-pants as she stood with her back to the blazing stove.

In the kitchen the kettle set up a wail. Cass sprang towards the arch in the wall again. 'No nightclubs. Pubs with quiz nights, and bingo once a week at the Institute, that's all.'

As Cass disappeared into the kitchen again, Tamsin followed her and stood leaning easily against the arch. The kitchen was the same size as the main front room, but had closed-in stairs leading up from one corner, she saw. The house felt warm, old-fashioned, and comfortable. She folded her arms, snuggled her chin into the bracken chenille of her sweater, and watched her friend pouring boiling water into the teapot.

Through the window, Tamsin saw a small enclosed garden with neighbouring ones alongside. Beyond a square of green lawn and herbaceous border were fields, the river, and mud-flats. The tide was out, and a winter sun sparkled on the low-lying water of the creek. It was a pleasant outlook. She began to relax after the long drive, and it seemed only natural that Mark Langham's face should drift into her mind briefly as she wondered what he was doing right now — two hundred miles away in Yorkshire. She pushed him back where he belonged. In the past. At least for the time being.

'You looked as if you were miles away.' Cass's voice broke in on her thoughts.

Tamsin didn't want to talk about Mark just at the moment. She turned her back on the view and said, 'Your house is nice. Friendly.'

'But lonely — since Mum died a few months ago.' Cass didn't look up from pouring tea into two stout mugs. 'She made me promise, though — before she died — that I wouldn't hang onto the past.' She glanced up at last, put down the teapot, then said, 'Okay! That's it. Now we can talk our way through the past eight years.'

'They were happy days,' Tamsin said, a little sadly, 'when we were all together. You with your parents, I with mine.' She sauntered over to the work-top and picked up a mug.

'You still have your father.'

'No!' Tamsin swished a spoon around in her tea. 'No. He went out of my life. He got married again and went to live abroad.'

'Yes. You said so in one of your letters.'

'I don't consider I have any family now.'

'Tam! That's awful . . . '

'No, it's not. We had a very bitter parting, Dad and I. He knew I couldn't accept Lucille, but he still went ahead and married her.'

'Tam!'

Tamsin scowled and sipped at her tea. 'Cass — you don't know the hell he put my mother through. He was seeing Lucille ages before the accident. It was Dad's fault Mum was killed; they were arguing about Lucille in the car when it hit that wall. Honestly, Cass. I shall never forgive him. I don't ever want to see him again.'

'What a tragic story.' Cass sighed and leaned against one of the modern units in the kitchen.

'Yes, I tell people now that I don't have any family. Even those I was closest to up in Yorkshire don't know the truth. It's awful when you're ashamed of your own father.'

Cass drank deeply of her own tea, then said, 'Come on, let's go back in the other room. It's warmer there.'

Cass couldn't get away that day to show Tamsin round the village; her computer had thrown a wobbly the day before, she said, and she was waiting in for somebody to come and put it right.

'Do you mind if I have a wander round myself?' Tamsin asked.

'Not at all. Don't get lost on the heath, though. You can easily wander onto the marshes and when the tide comes in it can be dangerous . . . '

★   ★   ★

Tamsin huddled into the wind, and strode out across the heathland that stretched for a couple of miles south of Alderwood, and half a mile inland too. Underfoot, the ground was uneven but springy, with coarse grass and brackish heather growing side by side, and frondy ferns and hawthorn in little patches here and there. The heath was dotted with spiky blackened gorse bushes that had been twisted by the wind into grotesque shapes. She could see the grey line of the sea in the distance, but the wind was keener here, and suddenly it was all too lonely for her, the way she was feeling. She wanted to be back in civilization, where life was a bit more colourful and people talked to you.

'Come . . . back . . . Tam . . . '

She gave a start, but it wasn't really his voice she heard. It was all in her imagination, in the whisper of the grasses and in the moan of the wind. They were all conspiring to convince her that the words were being carried down a two-hundred-mile stretch of coastline from where Mark Langham had been standing when she'd left him, on the headland at Heronsea. She could see him still, his thick fair hair all of a tangle in the morning's breeze, his eyes haunted as he watched her go . . . She felt incredibly guilty, and wanted him then, there by her side. Mark, who loved her. Mark, who always managed to put things right for her. Mark — the only man who really understood her.

She hunched her shoulders into her leather coat and shoved her hands deep into her pockets. It was freezing cold out here, and the afternoon light was fading. She trudged back towards the village, and once there gazed without any real interest into brightly lit shop windows bearing water-colour paintings and home-made bread. There was a tiny post office with a dusty remnant of Christmas tinsel hanging forlornly from a corner. The pub next door was called the Crown and Anchor, and its doors were open, spilling out noisy music.

A car was coming towards her up the village street. A black car. It was the only vehicle she'd seen since coming here. The road led nowhere, though. It ended where the heath began, with a broken down bit of fencing, overgrown hedgerows, and then that bleak and barren landscape.

For something to do, rather than any real interest, Tamsin watched the car. Then, from behind her — inside the pub — she heard the sound of raised voices, of glass being smashed, and as she whirled round again a mob of youths clattered out onto the pavement, yelling, jeering, jostling around two of their own kind who were in heated argument and aiming blows at each other.

She couldn't get the gist of what was being shouted, but she felt sickened listening to the obscenities that were being hurled between the two men locked in brawny combat.

She just wanted to run — to get the hell out of there. Alderwood had seemed on the surface such a quiet place, a place where she'd had hopes of licking her life back into shape.

The brawl was becoming nasty now. She flinched away from the sound of fists meeting jaws, and the howls of encouragement from the dozen or so spectators.

And then a knife flashed, and everybody except the two who were actively involved in the brawl melted away into shop doorways, flattened themselves against walls.

Tamsin became aware of the black car again. It had come to a standstill and the door was being pushed open. As the knife flashed again, she saw a man dive out of the car. He was wearing a navy blue business suit. He hesitated for only a moment, then rushed forward, yelling, 'Stop that. Stop it . . . '

The hand holding the blade was raised again. It came down like the silent swoop of a bird of prey. It scythed through the air, then struck.

She heard the ripping of flesh, and a tremor went right through her body. In that moment, the brawling man's scream of terror was the most hideous sound she had ever heard.

She pressed her hands to her ears, but her eyes were wide; they saw the knife being raised again — this time smeared with an ominous red. The man from the car was on his knees beside the victim. The assailant was aiming at the navy blue suit.

Her breath caught in her throat. The kneeling man was trying to stanch the victim's flow of blood. He'd done nothing to deserve a malicious stabbing himself; he was only trying to help. She felt her legs going weak. She gripped the wooden surround of the post office window and whimpered, 'No . . . '

But mere words weren't going to help!

She leapt into life, pushing herself away from the shop window and hurling herself towards the man in the navy blue suit. She screeched at the top of her lungs.

'Look out . . . '

And then she was in the midst of the commotion, acting instinctively, lashing out with her hands, knocking the assailant's arm upwards as he reeled back from her, surprised by the attack from such an unexpected quarter.

The kneeling man had swung round by now, and seemed to take in at a single glance the enormity of what had nearly happened to him. He grabbed hold of Tamsin behind the knees, and brought her smashing down onto the icy ground. Once there, he rolled her over and over, away from the two men, the injured one *and* the one with the knife.

'You fool . . . *fool* . . . ' he berated her. 'You could have been killed . . . '

The words were muffled in her ears. She was breathless and shocked, and her hair was tumbled across her face.

In the distance, the wail of a police siren could be heard. People started drifting silently away, unwilling to be called as witnesses to what had happened.

The man was heavy on top of her. She tried to shift him. He was crushing her into the ground.

'Fool!' he yelled, rearing up and over her.

'You could be lying there slashed and bleeding . . . '

He was no longer squeezing all the breath out of her body, but one arm was still locked round her, and he dragged her to a sitting position, hauling her away, back to the safety of the ground underneath the post office window.

People were rushing around now. The injured man was sitting up, his head in his hands, elbows resting on his knees. Somebody was with him.

Tamsin heard the scream of a police siren — nearer now — coming up the street.

The man with the knife heard it too; he acted swiftly, sprinting away towards the heath, and was soon lost from sight.

'Why?' the dark-clothed stranger asked, staring straight at her. 'Why did you do such a damn stupid thing as that?'

She gazed up at him.

He was smartly dressed, and well spoken. His black hair, short, wiry and thick, was brushed straight back off his face. He had heavy dark brows, a firm mouth.

Words came back to her. Words she'd spoken only that morning — to Mark Langham. She remembered them well . . . 'I don't intend falling into the arms of the first man I meet . . . '

Angrily she stared at him. 'I was trying to save you. He . . . he was lunging at you with that knife.'

The police car sped up and all was pandemonium. An ambulance followed, screeching to a halt, and paramedics raced towards the injured man.

The man in the navy suit sat back on his heels and glared at her, wrenching his supporting arm away from her. 'I can take care of myself,' he ground out savagely. 'I don't need a dame in shining leather coming to my rescue.'

'Well, thanks,' she said in a breathless but slightly sarcastic tone. 'Next time I'll leave you to it and see if you're still as complacent as this when you have a knife sticking out of your back.'

He seemed to relent a little as he scrambled to his feet. 'Look — I'm sorry.' He started dusting his suit down, then held out a hand to her. 'Here, let me help you up.'

Tamsin declined the offer of help and managed to get up under her own steam. Her jacket had come unfastened. The dark man grabbed hold of her as she teetered unsteadily in her high-heeled leather boots. She fell against him.

A police officer came running up. 'Hey — what's going on here?'

The dark man said irritably, 'This . . .
lady . . . tried to save me as *I*, in turn, tried to
help the injured man . . . '

Tam tried to pull away from the stranger,
but found that she couldn't. She lurched
against him again. Something was holding her
fast. They were locked together.

'What the hell . . . ?'

She glanced down and saw what the
trouble was. She yelled at him, 'Don't move!
My dreamcatcher — it's tangled round one of
your buttons.'

The young police officer stood back and
watched them, his face incredulous. 'Your
. . . what?' he asked.

'My pendant,' Tam snapped at him. 'Can't
you see? The silver chain's caught round this
. . . this . . . *person*'s coat button. Don't just
stand there! Get me free of him, will you?'

She heard a soft laugh just above her head
and glanced up into a pair of dark, cynical
eyes that were only inches from her own. 'It's
not funny,' she yelled. 'It's just not funny.'

They had to stand there, though, for
several more minutes while the young
policeman untangled Tam's slender silver
chain from around the navy blue suit button.
When they were free, the man asked, 'What
did you call it?'

'A dreamcatcher,' she said sullenly, glaring

at him with even more hostility.

'What does that make me?' he asked.

'Not a dream *man* — if that's what you're thinking!'

'These last ten minutes have been more like a nightmare than a dream.'

She hated men. All men, Tam decided. Once you met one, you always got tangled up in something you couldn't handle.

'The story of my life,' she said, more composed now.

'What is?' he asked, amused.

'Nothing,' she said. 'You wouldn't understand.'

The police officer moved away.

'We should introduce ourselves . . . ' the stranger said, proffering his hand, but before he could say any more she interrupted him.

'There's no need. I don't suppose we'll be meeting up again. Certainly we won't like this.'

And before he could object to the interruption, or grasp hold of her hand, she had resolutely turned her back on him and was running back down the village street.

She had the feeling he might have followed her, but, glancing back, saw he'd been waylaid by the police, who obviously wanted his account of what had happened.

Tamsin slowed down her headlong flight

then, and began to breathe more easily. She didn't want to know his name. She didn't want to get involved. Men were nothing but trouble, and she'd had more than her fair share of that just lately.

She had to admit to herself, though, he had gorgeous eyes — and more sex appeal than any man had a right to possess. And if she ever caught sight of him anywhere again, she made up her mind there and then — she was definitely going to turn round and run right away from him.

With looks like that, he could be a heartbreaker!

2

Cass said, 'I just hope those ski-pants of yours are washable.'

Tamsin twisted round, looked at the dirty wet patch that stretched from thigh to knee and muttered, 'Damn!'

Cass laughed. 'And you never even found out what his name was?'

'I didn't want to know.' Tamsin sighed. 'Look — I didn't ask to be dragged into a fight. I just happened to be there. Now, though, I'm glad to be out of it and back here, where it's nice and warm.'

It was true. She didn't even want to think about *him*, or be reminded of him. It had just been an incident, something that happened all too frequently nowadays. Brawls! Fights! Road-rage! Muggings! She wanted none of them. What she *did* want was a little bit of peace and quiet. All the same, he *had* been good-looking, and it *had* been rather disquieting when he'd rolled her over and over on the ground. She'd felt the strength in those arms of his, yet it wasn't the 'bully-boy' kind of strength. His voice had labelled him as well educated, his suit had been a one-off. She wasn't impressed with worldly things, however, but he had been nice . . . Heck — what was she thinking of? 'Nice' wasn't the word to describe such a hunk. He was gorgeous. And meeting him in such a way had been exciting.

Cass — practical, down to earth Cass — interrupted her thoughts. 'You need a bath. Come on — get upstairs and strip off. And throw those ski-pants down to me — I'll give them a soak.'

'I didn't come here for you to wait on me hand and foot.' Tamsin glowered.

'You're hardly the domesticated kind of animal, though.' Cass looked at her thoughtfully, her head tipped on one side.

Firmly, Tamsin pushed all thoughts of her mystery man aside and said, 'I can learn to be domesticated.'

'Can you type? Can you use a computer?'

'Are you joking? I never needed a computer to make bridal bouquets.'

Cass nodded vaguely, then said, 'I was just going to strike up a bargain with you. You do the computer work and I'll do the domestic stuff.' She shrugged her shoulders, 'However . . . '

'Computer work? You mean your journalist work?'

Cass gave a short laugh. 'Heck, no. I have to do that myself — as well as the photographs. But I'm working on something else — something you might have been able to help with. No matter, though . . . '

'You sound very cagey.' Carefully, Tamsin took off her leather coat and examined it for any damage it might have sustained when she'd been rolled across the ground in the middle of Alderwood that afternoon.

Cass grabbed the coat out of her hands and strode through the arch to the kitchen. 'Leave that to me — it's only icy mud. I'll see to it.'

Tamsin followed her. 'Come on then, tell me. What's all this mystery? This job you have all lined up for me?'

'If you can't type . . . '

'I didn't say I can't type. I can. I've never used a computer, though.'

'There's nothing to it. So how would you like to do a bit of typing for me — if I show you how to make friends with the word-processing bit of the computer? I'll be back at work next Monday — so that should give us plenty of time. I'm all yours till then, but after that it's sometimes an eighteen-hour-a-day job as far as I'm concerned.'

'What sort of typing am I likely to be doing?'

'The unpaid sort.' Cass laughed as she sponged down the leather coat, then hung it over the back of a chair and came back across the room to Tamsin.

'I guessed that.'

'Something to keep you out of street brawls,' Cass said.

'You're jealous because I told you that guy who grounded me was good-looking.'

Cass jerked her head up. 'You positively drooled about him,' she said, laughing. 'Anyway, why would I need a good-looking guy? I'm kept too busy for romance. And regarding the typing,' she went on, 'I've started writing a book in my spare time.'

'You have spare time after working eighteen hours a day?'

'It's just . . . something.'

'Something?'

'Something I feel I have to do.'

'Isn't that what *all* writers say?' Tamsin teased.

Cass laughed again, 'Call me crazy.' She threw up her hands.

'How long have you been writing your book?'

Cass shrugged again. 'Two — three years maybe.'

'Phew! That's dedication.'

'No. It's just light relief. I don't expect it'll ever get published; there's not much of it yet, anyway. Looking after Mum and doing a full-time job didn't leave a lot of time for it these past eighteen months.'

Tamsin suddenly felt sorry for her friend — sorry for teasing her too. It couldn't have been easy, taking care of her invalid mother who had died the previous year. She went to Cass and took hold of her arm. 'I'm sorry,' she said. 'I expect you needed something . . . different. Something to take your mind off . . . '

'Yes,' Cass said quickly. 'I did.'

'I'll do anything I can to help.'

'There are so many corrections and crossings out in it,' Cass said. 'The manuscript. It's handwritten. I used to write in huge notebooks at night when I couldn't sleep. It needs knocking into shape, and if it were double-space typed I could edit it more easily.'

'Leave it for me when you go back to work next week.'

'You're sure?' Cass brightened.

'Sure I'm sure!'

It was like old times, when they'd giggled and helped each other with homework after school. 'We're still just a couple of kids, aren't we?'

Tamsin laughed softly, and said, 'Yes, we are.' But deep down she knew that kids didn't throw themselves headlong into pub brawls, and then spend the rest of the afternoon cursing themselves for not even finding out a dishy guy's name!

★　★　★

'I need a job,' she said to Cass as they walked towards the fish-stall on the sea front a few days later. 'A proper job, I mean. Not just your bit of typing to fill my spare time.'

'You're not going back to Mark Langham, then? You've definitely decided against that?'

Tamsin had told her about Mark, and everything else that had happened at Heronsea in the past year as well. 'I need time,' she said now, 'to get things sorted in my mind before I make any decision about Mark.'

'Do you love him? Mark? He sounds nice.'

'I love too easily.' Tamsin smiled wryly. 'I loved a racing-driver — Rafe Thorne — or I thought I did. But he ended up with somebody else. Then I fell for another racing-driver — Vaughn Herrick — and I got pregnant, then lost the baby.'

'Could you have been happy with Vaughn?'

Tamsin shook her head. 'I would never

have got the chance. I told you the other night, Cass. He ditched me.'

'And Mark?'

'Mark picked me up. Mark always seems to be around to pick up the pieces when I go and do something stupid.'

'But do you love him?' Cass sounded exasperated.

They stopped at the fish-stall. Changing the subject abruptly, Tam said, 'Do we have to decide what we're having for dinner tonight right now?'

Cass shrugged. 'Not if you don't want to.'

'Let's walk on the beach. I might feel more like it when we come back.'

'You want to talk about your future?'

Tamsin scuffed at the sand and pebbles as they strolled down to the water's edge. 'I feel I owe it to you to be honest. After all, you are putting up with me. Me and my moods.'

'I love having you here.'

'I need a job, though. And somewhere to live. Are there any letting agencies around here?'

Cass said thoughtfully, 'There's an estate agent out on the Halesworth road. But you don't have to move. You can stay with me. There's plenty of room in my cottage.'

'I don't want to get in the way of your work. Look — I appreciate your taking the week off for me, but you *do* have a job, and it can't be easy with me around. You must have to develop or process, or whatever technical sort of thing it is that needs doing with your photographs, at home. You've got that computer set up in the living room too. I shall be in the way when you're working for the magazine people again. And anyway, I suppose I'll have to move away from Alderwood — there's nothing here that I can do, is there?'

'You could always start up a little business of your own. From what you've told me, you should have enough capital to do that.'

Tamsin shook her head. 'I don't want anything too permanent. At the moment I seem to be at odds with myself. I need to earn a living, but without immersing myself too much. Always at the back of my mind is Mark . . . '

'You're good with flowers, though. It seems a shame to waste such a talent.'

Tamsin was adamant. 'I have a bit of capital, but until I'm sure — absolutely sure . . . '

'You need a change of direction,' Cass said. 'Something maybe that doesn't remind you too much of your old life. Why not look in the Situations Vacant columns? You have a car — you could travel as far as Norwich —

maybe take a job in a florist's shop.'

'I don't know . . . '

Cass sighed. 'Well, why not have a look round and see if you can find a decent-sized self-contained flat or something, if you're determined to stand on your own feet. That would be a start, wouldn't it? There are a few holiday letting places in Alderwood — you might be able to pick up a long-term letting during the winter months.'

'Mmm. I'll look up this agency you mentioned.' She stopped walking and stood facing the sea, gazing broodingly at it.

Cass said, 'Now what's wrong?'

Tamsin felt infinitely homesick. 'It's the same sea Mark will be looking at,' she said wistfully. 'Higher up the coast, though. Two hundred miles higher up the coast.' Two hundred miles at that moment, she decided, was a hell of a long way.

'Do you wish you were back there with him?'

Tamsin hunched up her shoulders. 'I try not to think about him, and then something always comes and reminds me. If we were together we'd probably be fighting about something.' She gave a bitter little laugh. 'I tend to be always on the defensive when Mark's around, yet when I'm away from him I miss him. Perhaps I need a new interest in my life — a new man!' Even as she said the words, though, she knew that a man wouldn't solve her immediate problems. Men in her life had, up to now, meant complications.

'We'll have to find you some male company down here.'

Tamsin shook her head. 'I don't need anybody else. Look — don't go match-making, will you, Cass?'

'Come away from that sea, then — and stop looking so miserable.'

'I'm not miserable. Honestly, I'm not. It wouldn't be so bad if it wasn't the same sea, though.'

'Maybe you should move to the west coast of England, where it's the Irish Sea and not the North Sea.' Cass laughed.

Tamsin started to laugh too, then said, 'If only it were that easy.'

⋆ ⋆ ⋆

Tamsin sat in her car on the opposite side of the road to the small double-fronted shop, and leafed through the wodge of photocopies headed 'John Chambers — Estate Agent'.

Impatient, she discarded the 'sea-view' holiday flatlet type of thing, of which the meek-mannered little man had given her about twenty. They lay in an untidy pile on the passenger seat beside her. There was a holiday bungalow too, and a three-storey house — an 'excellent conversion' — in the middle of town.

And last in the pile was . . .

Tamsin drew in her breath. Long and grey, it nestled in a mess of a garden. The photo had been taken from above, looking down on it, so that front, back and sides were visible. There were clumps of golden-rod in the foreground, and lush green ivy clambering over a wall.

'Two acres!' She whistled silently under her breath, her mind already forming a plan. She stared in disbelief at a garden divided into neat squares with long grassy pathways between the beds. There were tall conifers and ornate stone pillars, oceans of lavender and rosemary, sage and foxglove. These were not herbs that had been planted purely for pleasure and on a whim, surely. There were too many of them for that. There was potential here. Maybe she could market the herbs, or turn them into creams and lotions, or herb pillows and dried arrangements. There was scope for making vegetable dyes too — that golden-rod for a start — and she could add to it with yellow marigolds, bracken for

41

green, sorrel and rose-hips for red . . .

She was out of the car and charging over the road, back to the estate agent's building, in seconds.

'I want to look at this property.' She placed the single leaflet back on the counter in front of 'John Chambers — Estate Agent'. 'I need you to make me an appointment to view this one. Its name is Herb House! Please — I need to see this property.'

'I can do better than that.' His glance was mildly surprised. 'I can let you have a key. The house isn't occupied, and what furniture was left when the owner died isn't worth much. The property is almost derelict, so if you can just let me have your own address — and show me some form of identification . . . '

'*Derelict?*' Tamsin's first rush of enthusiasm was dampened. 'But surely — it must be habitable? After all — it *is* up for letting. It *must* be in a fit state for somebody to live in?'

John Chambers pursed his lips, and gazed at her out of thick-lensed spectacles. 'It has potential . . . '

'I don't want 'potential'!' Tamsin placed both hands flat on the counter-top. 'I want somewhere to live. I want electricity, running water, and no leaks in the roof. I don't care two hoots for *potential.*'

He smiled. 'It's got all those things you mention.'

'Then I might just be interested.'

* * *

As they drove out of Alderwood, across the river bridge and right round the estuary and the mud-flats and the creek, Tamsin shot a glance at Cass and said, 'Why do we have to do this? Why the hundred-mile round trip just to get to the other side of the heath?'

'There's no other way. There's only the one road in and out of Alderwood. But it's only four or five miles, not a hundred, you goose. You have to go right back to the main road to get to the next village on the other side of the heath. And the roads are so narrow and twisty it takes an age.'

Tamsin sighed. 'Why don't they just *build* a road across the heath?'

'Because,' Cass said patiently, 'the other side of the heath is a marsh, and it's a wildlife reserve.'

'So I'm going to live in a wilderness? Is that what you're telling me?'

'Yes.' Cass laughed softly, then said, 'Take the next turn left and we'll have gone round in a big circle and will only be a mile from Stratton End.'

Tamsin asked tartly, 'Does it have pub quizzes and bingo?'

'Tam — I told you when you started on this hare-brained scheme. Stratton End has *nothing* except Herb House and a burnt-out church.'

'Sounds spooky.'

'It is.'

'Somebody must have lived there, though. Who planted all those herbs?'

'It's been there as long as I can remember. The old man who was last there sold herbs to Faulkener's Herbs and Spices.'

'Who is Faulkener?'

'Clare Faulkener. She has a factory just down the road from Stratton Village. She markets culinary herbs. Sells them to the posh places — big restaurants all over the world — or so they say — and pricey little shops up and down the country too.'

'So — Stratton End and Stratton Village are two separate places . . . '

'Turn left,' Cass shrieked. 'I told you back there — turn left.'

Tamsin swung the car in the direction Cass indicated. 'I didn't see the turn,' she apologized. 'All these trees and hedges . . . '

Cass was clinging to her seat. Her voice steadied as she said, 'Just keep below thirty, will you? This is not a motorway.'

'I can't wait to get there.' Tamsin grinned across at her friend.

'That,' Cass said, 'is obvious.'

★ ★ ★

Before she finally made up her mind about Herb House, Tamsin went to see Clare Faulkener.

The Faulkener Herbs and Spices 'empire' was impressive. At least, the reception area and Clare's office were impressive, with lots of smoked glass and chrome and highly polished floors. And Clare was impressive too, Tamsin found as she sat opposite a shapely goddess with sun-olive skin and sleek black hair pulled tightly back into a coiled waterfall away from exquisitely made-up features that consisted of direct brown eyes, delicate arched brows, and lips most men would describe as luscious!

Faced with such perfection, Tamsin also took note of the fact that Clare Faulkener was absolutely dripping in gold — heavy gold chains at her neck and wrists, gold-encrusted pearls in her earlobes, and diamonds, emeralds and opal winking across the desk from almost every finger. Surprisingly, her wedding ring was plain — plain and wide and obviously twenty-four carat! That wedding ring was solidly symbolic to Tamsin. Clare was obviously a woman who hung onto what she'd got — brains, beauty, and wealth, and, last but not least, a husband who must be reminded, every time he saw those hands across the table from him, that *he* had placed that ring on her finger . . . and there it was going to stay. Even before she spoke, Tamsin had summed her up. Clare Faulkener would make a positive and awesome adversary. It wouldn't be advisable to make an enemy of her.

'What can I do for you?' She leaned forward, hands clasped on her desk-top, a well practised smile on the *luscious* coral lips.

Tamsin came straight to the point. 'It's like I told you on the phone, Mrs Faulkener — I'm interested in the old Herb House, and I understand that at one time you had an agreement with the gentleman who lived there — an agreement to buy herbs from him.'

Clare nodded. 'I did indeed. Joshua Temple became a good friend. I could always depend on him. He never let me down. And what he didn't know about herbs wasn't worth knowing anyway.'

'I wouldn't let you down. I have been in business before — '

'The herb business?' Clare broke in questioningly.

'No. Flowers. And weddings.' Tamsin proceeded to give details of the type of business she'd been in with her partner, Ava Thorne.

Clare seemed suitably impressed. She nodded at times, and made notes in pencil at others, occasionally shooting in a question and jotting down the answer Tamsin gave.

The interview lasted three quarters of an hour, which Tamsin decided, was good news, because surely a busy woman like Clare Faulkener wouldn't waste that amount of time if she wasn't really interested.

At last, though, Clare looked at her office clock and said, 'Can we meet for lunch tomorrow? I'd like us to talk in more detail — but I have another appointment this afternoon at four. I like your approach, though. And I think we could do business — if we can come to an agreement on terms.'

Tamsin was elated. She agreed readily.

'Could you come to the house? Would that suit?'

'The house?'

'Aldwich House — Alderwood. It's where I live — on the seafront. A white, rambling place, with a red roof and dormer windows. Absolute hell in summer, when the beach is

47

full of screaming children.'

'Alderwood seems such a quiet place,' Tamsin said.

'Yes?' Exquisite eyebrows rose expressively. 'Well, maybe at this time of year you *could* say it's just about bearable. But my house at Alderwood doesn't even start to compare with my summer one.'

With interest, Tamsin said, 'You have two houses?'

Clare's burst of laughter held no merriment. 'It's essential, my dear. I couldn't stand it here in Alderwood in summer. How Patric, my husband, puts up with it, I just don't know. As soon as the first busload of day-trippers arrives, I'm away — away inland and up towards Norwich, to the house we bought when we were first married.' She shuddered, then her mouth snapped shut, almost as if she regretted saying too much and wasn't going to say anything more.

'I'll meet you tomorrow, then,' Tamsin said.

'Lunchtime. Any time after twelve.'

'I'll look forward to that.'

'I'll get my assistant — Craig Andrews — to show you out.' Clare Faulkener pressed a switch on an elaborate-looking telephone and said, 'Send Craig in, Frances.'

A clear voice answered, 'Right away, Mrs Faulkener.'

Tamsin wanted to tell her it really didn't matter — somebody seeing her out. She was quite capable of going down to the ground floor and walking through Reception to where her car was parked outside.

Clare smiled again. 'Security! They insist on it.'

Tamsin felt herself flushing. Could Clare Faulkener really read minds?'

The door opened and a young man came into the office — a man whose personality filled it.

'Craig — escort Ms Curtis to her car, will you?'

Craig's smile was more human than Clare's — quite disarming, in fact, Tamsin thought. He was obviously several years younger than Clare Faulkener, very tall, with chiselled classic features and direct grey eyes. His thick chestnut hair sprang back from a deep 'V' in the centre of his forehead. His shoulders were wide, hips tapering beneath the sleek silver-grey suit he wore. Clare Faulkener's assistant could have stepped right out of a Hollywood movie, Tamsin decided. He was most definitely *not* the kind of man you would dream of meeting in a sleepy Suffolk village. But then, neither had her mystery man been what she'd expected, she thought suddenly, and in that case she'd fallen right into his arms. It was strange how she hadn't bumped into him again since that day . . .

Craig was courteous and cool as he escorted her down to Reception and then through double glass doors to the car parking area that was ringed round with miniature evergreens and banks of heather — a lot of it the winter-flowering kind.

He went with her right to her car, then held out his hand and said, 'It was nice meeting you — *Ms Curtis.*' Suddenly there was a sardonic cynicism in his voice that made Tamsin's head jerk up to look at him sharply.

She shook hands with him, a bit surprised at his manner which had at first seemed somewhat old-fashioned but had now changed completely to arrogant. That emphasis on the 'Ms Curtis' could have been interpreted as slightly insolent, even.

'Thank you.' She turned away to unlock her car, not really wanting to enter into conversation with him.

He was not to be put off, however. 'Shall we be seeing you again?' he drawled.

She glanced sideways at him, and replied in a cool tone, 'I hope to do business with Mrs Faulkener.'

'Did you get a second chance?' One eyebrow quirked.

She stared at him, not comprehending. 'A

second chance? I don't know what you mean.'

'If she gives you a second chance usually you're accepted.' His lips twisted ironically. 'What I mean is — if she invited you to lunch, or dinner, or afternoon tea at 'the house', then you're over the first hurdle. Understand?'

Tamsin leaned her back against her car and studied him. 'Ought you to be talking like this? About your employer?'

He lifted his shoulders in a slight shrug. 'I just wanted to put your mind at rest — Ms Curtis. At a guess, I'd say she's taken to you. Am I right?'

Slowly she said, 'Mrs Faulkener invited me to lunch — tomorrow. That's all.'

His eyes stared coldly at her, but his lips smiled. 'Then you're in,' he said. 'But don't let it go to your head. She can cool off a person very quickly, and once you're out of favour, you're *definitely* out! No second chances.'

'I never let *anything* go to my head, Mr Andrews.'

'Neither do I — *Ms Curtis*,' he replied, ice-cool.

'Well, thank you for your advice,' Tamsin retorted. 'But I think I know how to conduct myself in a business deal.'

Pleasantly he replied, 'Just one more thing — a friendly warning, *Ms Curtis*. Watch it with the old man. Her husband. That's if he happens to be around tomorrow.'

'I — I still don't understand.' She didn't like the way this conversation was heading.

'Ogle him at your peril. She'll have you sliced up and cream poured over you for dessert if you even smile at dear Patric.'

'Look,' Tamsin said, becoming irritated, 'I don't think I need this . . .'

'Just trying to help. Just giving a friendly word of warning.' His gaze raked over her appraisingly.

'Does *Mr* Faulkener take an interest in his wife's business?' Suddenly she wanted to know more, realizing that if she was going to trade with this organization she might as well find out who was friend and who was foe.

'Patric?' He gave a slow, lazy laugh that chilled her it was so full of bitterness. 'Oh, no. Not him. He's away from home a lot of the time at the new circuit the other side of Cambridge.'

'Circuit?' Her heart gave a jolt.

'Racing-cars,' he said. 'You know? Brum-brum-vroom-vroom! Racing-cars. Noisy great things with long pointed noses.' His laugh was hushed, sinister almost. 'Our Patric put up a lot of the money for Bramsdown — or rather she did. Mrs Patric! Our own dearly beloved Clare Faulkener. She 'indulges' him — if you know what I mean. Buys him expensive prezzies — like a partnership in Bramsdown so he can set himself up as 'race control' — an expensive 'toy' to keep him sweet. Between times he fancies himself as a designer. A designer of those sleek monstrosities they call cars.'

Tamsin could have laughed out loud. She didn't. She just looked at Craig Andrews squarely and said, 'If Patric Faulkener has anything to do with racing-cars, then I can promise you I shall never even smile at him.'

'That's okay, then.' He stepped back, away from her, and inclined his head in what Tamsin supposed was a leave-taking bow. He said nothing more, and she slid into her car and drove away without a backward glance.

'Racing-cars!' she muttered when she was out of sight of the offices of Clare Faulkener and able to give free rein to her emotions. Racing-cars reminded her of past follies she'd rather forget. 'Racing-cars!' she muttered again. 'Would I really be fool enough to tangle with anybody in the racing car world again? Not likely. You can bet your sweet life on that, Craig Andrews. I just won't let myself get involved with cars or drivers ever again. And I mean that!'

As she speeded up the car and headed towards Alderwood, though, she had the feeling that Craig Andrews would still be standing there laughing at her, even though he couldn't see her now. The thought disturbed her. She shivered. And it was a crazy kind of feeling, but she believed in that moment that there'd be more run-ins with him. There had definitely been an undercurrent to the things he'd said to her.

Driving over the Borda river bridge, she still couldn't rid her mind of him — but she must do, she told herself. He'd disturbed her enough for one day already, without spoiling the rest of it for her!

3

Clare Faulkener put up her hands and gently eased herself away from the broad-shouldered man in front of her.

'Not here, Craig,' she whispered. 'Not here. You know what we agreed.'

Hard hands fastened on her shoulders and prevented her moving away completely. 'Why not? For heaven's sake — there's nothing to stop us. Your little *Ms Curtis* won't be here for another hour.'

Clare was well aware of that fact. She also knew that the housekeeper was around. 'There's Sal Pratchett in the kitchen. And you know what a tittle-tattle she can be.'

'But dear Patric will have to find out about us some time,' Craig Andrews said in a surly voice.

Clare looked at him sharply. 'No!' she said. 'Patric isn't going to find out. We've been too careful for that. I am not going to lose all I've worked for. And if Patric should ever suspect for a moment that we've been . . . '

'Sleeping together?' Craig Andrews shot the statement at her with destructive venom.

'Shut up,' she snapped, her eyes flashing a warning at him. 'Shut up and grow up, Craig, or we're finished. Do you understand? You're getting far too complacent and careless in your talk, and I don't like it.'

'But you *like* me,' he said silkily. 'You like the excitement, don't you? You like the things we do together . . .'

She gave him one last push and freed herself from him, then spun round and walked to the far side of the room, her breathing fast and shallow. He was getting too bold, too brash for her liking. And her whole way of life was at stake. Sometimes she wished she'd never taken up with him — and then, at others, she realized how much she needed him, wanted him, hungered for his touch and his closeness, his youthful adoration. He was eight years her junior, whereas Patric was thirty-nine years old, and just lately too immersed in his work to take a lot of notice of her.

'You take me too much for granted,' she ground out, whirling to face him with the safe width of the room and several couches and chairs between them.

'Not as much as dear Patric does,' Craig replied in a quiet, seductive tone. 'Just how long is it since . . . ?'

'You have no right to ask,' she broke in, her normally calm features twisting into a hostile sneer. In that moment she hated him for reminding her that her marriage was less than she'd like it to be.

'How long is it?' he asked quietly, starting to walk towards her, easing through the spaces between the comfortable and expensive furniture. 'How long since dear Patric made you feel like *I* make you feel — and how long is it since you walked down the aisle, my darling, a blushing bride who promised to love, honour and obey the master of this house.'

She squared up to him, her head high. It would never do to dissemble before Craig Andrews, she realized. If once he got a hold over her — a hold other than sex — she would be finished. 'You know how long Patric and I have been together,' she flared. 'My marriage has lasted for fifteen years, and it's going to last a lot longer.' She gave a bitter laugh. 'But as for Patric being 'master' of the house — well, if it hadn't been for me this house wouldn't exist — at least not for us. It's *my* hard work that's behind all we've got. Patric doesn't have a business mind. He would still be quite happy living in that little house at Stride Common with his parents.'

'Ah, yes,' Craig said softly. 'We all know who holds the purse strings, don't we?'

'I don't like you saying things like that.' Her cheeks were flushed. 'Me saying them is another matter altogether, and I suppose I was lucky when I started out in the herb and spice world. I just happened to be in the right place at the right time, and things took off . . . '

'But you were the one with the business acumen,' he said. 'You were the one with all the right ideas about running the show.'

She lifted her shoulders in an elegant shrug. 'I just have a flair for it.'

'But Patric does *not*. Isn't it time you woke up to the fact that he'll never make anything on his own?' he asked. 'He's too easily led — with *you*, my darling, doing all the leading.' He gave a bitter laugh. 'He's the child you never had. The babe in arms who has to be comforted when it cries — the wayward child who constantly whines 'I want . . . I want . . . ' And you give him everything he wants — and more besides. But what does he give you?'

'Patric's all right. Patric's my husband,' she defended. 'And when you're married it's for better or worse . . . '

'For richer for poorer? Is that what you're trying to say?'

'No!' Her reply was adamant. 'For better for worse. You stick together.'

'Even when it's *you* who has all the money, and only *you* who's capable of making still more?'

Cool as ice, she looked at him. 'It works both ways, you know. If I wanted a divorce, Patric could claim half of everything I own — *even* the business. And I don't want half, Craig. I want it all. It's mine. I've made it what it is, and I deserve it.'

He was standing right in front of her now. 'What would it take?' he asked in little more than a whisper. 'What would it take, my princess, to bind you to *me* for better for worse?'

Carefully, she chose her words. 'You know what it would take.'

He gave a dry little laugh. 'Money! Money's your god.'

'Life is empty without it,' she said flippantly. 'Don't try to kid me that *you* could manage without it.'

'Pay me a bigger salary,' he suggested with a nonchalant shrug. 'That way I might be able to keep you in the manner to which you've become . . . '

'Don't be stupid. I don't need another man. I don't need you. How could *you* ever give me a house like this, and jewellery and clothes of the kind I wear? That's what it would mean if I gave Patric up. I'd only have half of what I now own, so how could you make up the deficit?'

'I managed other things,' came the cutting reply. 'I managed to get into his bed — into his wife.'

'You are coarse! You are detestable!' A flush had sprung to her face.

'So you often tell me — usually when we are *in* dear Patric's bed.' His smile was cruel. 'Sometimes you like me being coarse and . . . detestable. You like me to make you submissive. It turns you on, doesn't it?'

A sense of shame raced through her. She knew he spoke the truth, though. 'You louse!' she spat out. 'You utter louse.'

'You love this pet louse, though, don't you, my sweet?'

He was so completely self-assured, and she hated having to admit to herself that, yes — she did love him, and she *had* grown to depend on him — in the office as well as out of it.

'When can we go to the cottage again?' he said softly, turning on his charm to the fullest extent.

'Lilacs?' She turned her head away slightly. Lilacs was getting to be a habit, and she didn't like habits. She wished she could break herself of this one, but knew in her heart that she couldn't. She never would. 'I don't know.' She prevaricated, and tried to think up a reason that was valid enough to keep both of them away from Lilacs. 'When the weather improves,' she said at last. 'Patric knows I hate it here in the summer. We can spend a lot more time there in the summer.'

His hand shot out and fastened round her chin, making her look at him again. 'When?' he wanted to know. 'If it's not going to be this weekend, I'm going away without you. There are other fish in the sea . . . '

'Where to? And who will you go with?' She knew there was fear in her eyes, even though the instant the tremulous words were out she tried to appear indifferent to him again.

'You care,' he whispered, bringing his face up close to hers. 'You care, and you are *frightened* of losing me. You know that I don't make idle promises, don't you?'

'No . . . ' The one word caught in her throat. 'I don't care what you do . . . '

'Lilacs! This coming weekend! Say yes, now.'

'I — I can't — not until I've talked to Patric. He might be bringing somebody home for the weekend. There's some race-driver he seems to have taken under his wing — somebody who wants to try out the new circuit . . . and Patric needs him to test the new car he's designed . . . '

'Cars! That's all your precious Patric is interested in . . . '

'At least he's *got* an interest again. At one time I thought . . . ' Her hands spread out helplessly, and she jerked her chin out of his hand and took a step backwards. 'Craig — be reasonable. If Patric says he's staying in Cambridge this weekend, then maybe I'll be able to get to the cottage.'

'I need to make my arrangements now. Today.'

'Surely not . . . '

'If you don't want me . . . '

'But I *do*, you know I do.' The fear was back again, this time in her choking whisper. 'Don't arrange anything yet. If it's at all possible, I'll get to the cottage.'

Slowly he shook his head. 'This has all got to change, my sweet. It's an impossible situation.'

'We've managed — so far.' Her eyes were pleading with him. She hated herself for doing it, but she couldn't bear the thought of losing him. Forcing herself to take a bolder line, she went on, 'Craig — you know how it is. I *need* my independence. I need nice things. I'd be absolute hell to live with if I had to exist on bread and cheese and love. I've done all that before. Patric and I — when we were first married — well, we had hardly anything, and it was a far from idyllic situation.'

'You stayed married to him, though — even though he never made anything of himself.'

'I loved him,' she said simply. 'And I realized from the start that he wasn't perfect. We were okay, though. Especially when the business started to take off. Patric needs somebody strong behind him. He's that sort of man. He works if you push him.'

'You don't have to push me.'

'But *you* aren't Patric,' she pointed out.

'You don't love him.'

She didn't answer at once.

'Admit it,' he said silkily. 'You know you don't love him.'

'I made a mistake,' she said in a husky voice.

'Marrying Patric?'

She looked up into his face, then shook her head. 'Putting the business into both our names,' she said. 'I'd lose it. And I couldn't bear that.'

'You would give up Patric without a qualm?' he asked. 'But you wouldn't give up Faulkener's Herbs and Spices?'

Her eyes hardened. 'Dead right I wouldn't.'

'You're real mean bastard material, aren't you?'

'Is that how you see me?'

'Real mean bastard, sexy woman material,' he corrected himself, with a gentle smile for her benefit alone.

She placed her hands on his shoulders. He had a lot going for him — looks, sex appeal, and a way with women that had made her sit up and take notice the minute she'd interviewed him for the job of her assistant two years ago. She couldn't let him go. He was like a potent, heady wine — a drug she'd overdosed on and was now hooked on.

'I could help you make this place a real goldmine.'

'It's already that.'

'But we're so *right* together, Clare.' He reached up and stroked her hair, and a shiver that had nothing to do with lust suddenly chilled her. 'We don't need Patric. If you got this far with *him*, think how much further you could go with *me*.'

'Prove it,' she said, wanting to give him a chance but hardly daring to.

'How?'

'Make some money,' she went on quietly. 'Make your first million, and then maybe . . . '

His eyes narrowed. 'You think I couldn't do it?'

She gave a breathless little laugh as his hands fell away from her. 'Ask me to leave Patric when you've made your first million, Craig. Then I might just take you seriously.'

'A million! Is that all it would take to make you turn your back on him?'

Suddenly she was impatient with him. He was still so young, so inexperienced in the way of the world — yet not in other ways that endeared him to her, she had to admit. Sex with Craig was something different. With Craig she could let herself go and indulge her fantasies. He satisfied her appetite for the unusual, the coarse, the erotic. It was a side of her nature that had been repressed, a side she'd never known existed until she met Craig and took him into her bed. And she liked it. She knew she had power over him, knew too that she couldn't ever imagine herself giving him up. But the carrot always had to be kept dangling in front of him. He wanted her completely. And the only way he was going to get her was if . . .

'A million pounds,' he said softly. 'It doesn't sound so much, does it?'

'You will never make a million, Craig.' Wearying of the conversation, she walked over to the window and looked out at the vast expanse of grey sea that was visible just across the road and beyond the promenade. She hated the sea. She hated Alderwood.

At Lilacs it would be so different. In the orchard, green spikes of daffodils would soon be starting to show through the grass, and already snowdrops would be clustered around the boles of the ancient apple trees. At Lilacs she could be young again — young and in love. Cherished. But not by Patric. All that was at an end. The struggle to survive had killed their love. Patric never went to Lilacs now. Patric said they should never look back. Patric would have sold the old house — except for the fact that it was in her name. She could give up Patric, but she would never give up Lilacs!

She knew she was safe — asking Craig to come to her when he'd made his first million. Craig would never do it. In many ways, Craig was like Patric. Craig needed a push now and then. Life wouldn't change. If they were careful they could go on in the same old way for all eternity — she and Craig. And Patric need never know.

He came up behind her and laid his hands lightly on her shoulders. He bent his head and kissed the hollow behind her ear. 'One day,' he whispered. 'One day I will give you all you ask for and more besides — I swear it.'

For a moment she believed him, he sounded so sincere. Reason told her, however, that this was just a line. 'How?' she said, twisting her head round so she could look into his eyes.

'I don't know yet,' he said. 'I have to get my brain round it. I usually get what I want, though.'

'Yes,' she said. 'I know you do. One way or another!'

★ ★ ★

Tamsin walked down through the village and onto the seafront. She'd taken care with her appearance, and Cass had been warm in her praise of the neat brown suit and clingy top underneath the jacket that she'd decided to wear for lunch with Clare Faulkener.

She'd used make-up sparingly today, and was happy with her appearance. Her hair she'd long since given up on. It went its own way and curled riotously no matter what she did to it, so she'd settled for an expensive trim as and when it needed it, and then allowed it to do its own thing. It seemed to appreciate the freedom she gave it, and consequently had never let her down. Mark had loved her hair . . .

'Go away, Mark,' she growled as she turned

her face into the wind and wished she'd brought the car. But she couldn't help wondering about him, and feeling a little guilty too, for not telling him about Herb House and all she was planning to do with it, when he'd rung her at least three times a week since she'd left Heronsea.

Already her plans were taking shape, and the house had forged its way into her heart. In every bit of spare time she'd had, she'd been there, walking in the gardens, along those dozens of little grass paths, pulling out weeds, making a bonfire of them — but not lighting it yet. That would come later — later today, probably — when she'd been over to 'John Chambers — Estate Agent' and signed the lease. First, though, she had to be sure that Clare Faulkener was definitely going to buy herbs from her. Life would be tough if not. Clare's contract with her would give Tamsin at least a modicum of support in the weeks and months to come, but she was tempted to sign the lease no matter what. She was convinced she could build up *some* sort of business around the herb garden, even without patronage if need be. It would be nice, though — to know that there would be an income coming in, a guaranteed income right from the word go!

She looked at her watch and saw it was

eleven forty-three. She had timed it nicely. Cass had given her exact instructions on how to get to the Faulkener house. 'But you can't miss it,' she'd said. 'It's right there on the seafront — at first sight you'd mistake it for a very large bungalow, then, when you get nearer, you'll see the little dormer windows set into the roof. It's a lovely place, or could be in the right hands. The Faulkeners have done away with the flowerbeds and hedges, though, so it looks a bit bleak.'

Aldwich House *was* impressive, however. When Tamsin saw it, she stood still, a little way off, and frowned. It wasn't what she'd expected. It was so clean-cut, so solid, with its twin white gables and half-hidden windows. It was open to the elements, no fences, no flowers, no trees — just a crushed shale courtyard in front of it, wide enough and deep enough to park twenty cars. There was only one there at the moment, she saw, a sleek silver-grey one, low and sporty.

Slowly she walked up to the front door that was deeply recessed inside a sterile, tiled porch.

Clare Faulkener herself came to the door and led the way inside.

'It was easy to find.' Tamsin smiled.

'I expect you'd prefer to see flowers outside, though.'

'I love them.'

'I hope you don't mind Craig being here,' Clare said as she pushed open a door and went inside a large sea-facing room.

'Of course not.' Tamsin acknowledged Clare's good-looking assistant with a smile and said, 'Hello!'

He came across the room. 'Lovely to meet you again, Ms Curtis.' He held out his hand with a show of politeness, and Tamsin shook it.

His glance raked over her with approval, and Tamsin felt she was being undressed by those steely grey eyes. She didn't like the feeling. Her head came up sharply and her gaze met his, asking him, without words, if he'd seen enough.

He obviously got the message and gave a quiet little laugh before sauntering back to the window-seat and flopping down on it, still watching her, lazily now, however, for Tamsin had caught the look Clare Faulkener had shot at him and obviously he had taken note of it.

For some reason she couldn't put her finger on, Tamsin found herself not liking Craig Andrews — or, more to the point, not trusting him. He was too sure of himself, there was an arrogance about him that didn't lie easily on his shoulders. 'Cocksure' was a word that sprang to mind. Tamsin didn't like the word, but it described him exactly. Cocksure and arrogant! She turned her back on him to give her attention to Clare, and could feel his steady stare burning into her. It felt like a dagger, imprisoning her like a squirming, fluttering butterfly held down by a pin. She wished he hadn't been here.

'My husband,' Clare was saying now, 'may be joining us for lunch. It was unexpected, but he rang about ten minutes ago and said he was bringing someone back with him.' She gave an uneasy laugh. 'It was totally unexpected, and Mrs Pratchett, my house-keeper, is very annoyed about it. She'd only planned on three being in for lunch today.'

There was a rustling behind her, and Craig rose to his feet and came over to them. 'Look,' he said to Clare, 'I'll go back to the office. It will make things easier here for you — *and*,' he added pointedly, 'Mrs Pratchett might be able to stretch lunch to four where she couldn't for five.'

The tense expression that had been on Clare Faulkener's face seemed to evaporate at Craig's words, but Tam saw there was a worried expression in her eyes as she gazed up at the young man.

'Would you mind, Craig? It would be a great help.'

Tamsin had the feeling there was some

71

hidden meaning in her response. It was as if a game were being played and she herself was a bystander who had wandered into it by accident.

'If it's awkward,' Tam said, '*I* could come at another time . . . '

'No, no.' Clare said. 'That won't do at all. I told Patric about you last night, and he wants to meet you. He does, after all, have some say in the company.'

'Oh!'

Craig said, 'The best thing is for me to go back to the office. You have everything here you need, Mrs Faulkener.'

Clare turned to him. 'All right. I'll be in about two o'clock, Craig.'

'Do you want me to come over and collect you in my car?'

'I'll ring you, hmm?'

He nodded and smiled. 'Okay. Bye for now, Ms Curtis.' He gave her a mocking half-bow and left the room.

Two minutes later, they heard the grey Jaguar doing a spin turn in front of the house and speeding away down the drive.

The air in the house seemed to lighten immediately Craig had gone, Tamsin thought, but within seconds there came the sound of another car. She looked questioningly at Clare Faulkener.

72

Clare smiled, completely at ease now. 'Patric's BMW!' She pulled a rueful face. 'I hope his client's not the usual sort — Formula One technical directors, or Research and Development boffins who talk about nothing but sponsorship, data processing and telemetry most of the time. And the drivers are the same . . . '

'To some of them, motor racing is a religion,' Tamsin said, completely understanding why Clare was so annoyed. She gave a little laugh. 'I was caught up in Formula One for a while.'

Clare gave a weak smile. 'It bores me silly — Patric's work.'

Footsteps were coming down the corridor outside the room. Tamsin knew she shouldn't be nervous, but she was. Motor racing had played a big part in her life — first with Rafe Thorne and then with Vaughn Herrick. It didn't hold many happy memories for her, and now here she was, about to be thrust right into it again when she met Clare's husband Patric. Well, she supposed she'd better look pleasant about it. She forced a smile to her lips and turned as the door opened inwards and a tall man came round it.

Clare went forward and pecked him on the cheek, then turned and said to Tamsin, 'This is Patric — my husband . . . '

Tamsin stared at him and felt her knees going weak. It had been a couple of weeks since she'd seen him, but she hadn't forgotten him. She'd been constantly on the look-out — peering at black cars when they passed her on the street, jumping nervously every time she saw a man in a navy blue suit . . .

'Well, well, well! The lady who saved my life!'

Tamsin just stood speechless and looked at him. He wasn't wearing navy blue this time; he was casually dressed in something beige, knitted and chunky, with corded beige jeans stretching tight across lean hips and a flat stomach.

Even married to Clare — he was still gorgeous!

Clare gazed mildly, first at one and then the other. 'Hey — what is this?'

'I told you about that fight outside the pub in Alderwood, darling . . . ' Patric Faulkener said, addressing his wife.

His wife! Tam could have choked. She'd been dreaming fond dreams, harbouring false hopes . . . She'd imagined herself halfway in love with her mysterious stranger.

'Well . . . yes . . . ' Clare swung her gaze towards Tamsin.

Tamsin quickly recovered herself — enough to say, 'Oh, please — don't bring that up again.' And, forcing herself to grin at Patric Faulkener, 'It was all in a day's work. It was my good deed for the day.'

'This,' Patric said to Clare, 'is the angel who came to my rescue when that thug was lunging at me with a knife.'

Tamsin laughed, and all hope of a romance — however trivial — with Patric Faulkener flew out of the window. 'I never imagined we'd meet up again.'

'Introductions aren't necessary, then,' Clare said a little stiffly.

'Oh, but they are,' Patric said, his eyes laughing. He looked straight at Tamsin again and said, 'You ran off without telling me your name.'

'But you do know it now, darling,' Clare said easily. 'I told you last night that Miss Curtis was coming over for lunch today.'

Tamsin found her hand grasped in a firm, hard, lean one. She looked up into Patric Faulkener's face and promptly fell out of love with him. He was just as good-looking as she remembered him to be, but he was a married man. And married men were taboo. It had been nice imagining that she'd one day meet up with her mystery man again, but this was one mystery man who was strictly out of bounds!

'It's nice to meet you properly,' he said,

gripping her hand in his and holding it longer than she thought was necessary. 'We only had a fleeting chance to get to know each other before — flat out on the ground, if I remember rightly.'

She laughed. 'All's well that ended well,' she said. 'I read in the newspaper that the man you were trying to help was only slightly injured.'

'Yes, thankfully.' His smile faded. He let go of her hand. 'I'm neglecting my guest, though — blocking the doorway like this.'

He moved aside, allowing another man, a smaller, slighter man than the six feet tall Patric Faulkener, to come into the room.

He was wearing steel-framed spectacles, and his blue-grey eyes were serious as he said, 'I thought I recognized the voice. Hi, Tam.'

And Tamsin stared, horrified and transfixed, at Vaughn Herrick, the man who had left her pregnant, the man who hadn't cared a toss about her — or about the baby she'd subsequently lost.

All the breath left her body as she stared at him. Then, knowing she couldn't just run out of the room — which was what she wanted to do — she forced herself to say quietly and calmly. 'Hello, Vaughn. How strange — that we should bump into each other like this again . . . !'

4

'How did it go?' Cass asked.

Tamsin flung off her jacket, descended heavily onto Cass's comfy sofa, leaned her head back against the cushions and looked at the ceiling before saying, 'Hell! It was absolute hell!'

Cass stared blankly at her. 'What do you mean? Isn't Clare Faulkener going to sign on the dotted line?'

'Oh, yes. She's agreed to do that.' Tamsin pushed herself into an easier position then, and said, 'But you'll never guess who was there.'

Cass shook her head. 'Who?'

'Vaughn Herrick! You know? The guy I told you I was mixed up with at Heronsea. The one I fell like a ton of bricks for. The one whose baby I lost in a miscarriage.'

'Oh, no.' Cass perched on the edge of the sofa and stared horrified at her. 'What did you do when you met him again?'

'We had lunch. We behaved like two

civilized people. And then we said goodbye.'

'But what was he doing there?'

'Vaughn — as I told you — is a racing-driver, and apparently he met Patric Faulkener at some meeting or other and Patric invited him to Cambridge to see the new circuit there, and to drive some prototype racing car that Patric has designed.'

Cass nodded. 'I knew that Patric had shares in the circuit,' she said guardedly.

'And that wasn't the end of it,' Tamsin said. 'I also discovered — on meeting him — that Patric Faulkener was my mystery man — the man I had a roll in the street with the other week. So what do you think of that?'

'Patric Faulkener?' Cass seemed agitated. She twined and untwined her fingers, making Tamsin look at her questioningly. 'Yes,' she said, 'that's Patric. He's a nice guy. He *would* go straight in to try and help somebody in trouble.'

'You know him?' Tamsin sat up straight and looked at her friend. 'You talk about him as if you do.'

Cass's expression became closed. She said curtly, 'I've known Patric for years.'

'Years?'

'He used to live next door — or rather his parents did — well, *they* still do.' It seemed as if the information were being dragged out of her.

'Next door? Here?' Tamsin stared at the fireplace wall — the one that was joined up to the cottage next door. 'They still live there?'

Cass said, clenching her hands firmly together in front of her now, 'Yes, they do. And Patric pops in regularly to see them. That's probably where he'd been the day you and he . . . met . . . He'd have been driving further up the road in order to turn his car round in a safer spot, and . . . '

'And he ran straight into trouble — and met me.'

'It's a small world,' Cass said, attempting a laugh. 'But now that we've got Patric straightened out, tell me more about your meeting with Vaughn.'

Tamsin had the feeling Cass didn't want to talk about Patric any more. She'd seen the spots of colour flaring in Cass's cheeks at the first mention of him, and suddenly realized that something was amiss. It wasn't for her to pry, though, she told herself. If Cass wanted her to know something, she'd tell her. All in good time . . .

'It was awful,' she said quickly, to cover up her hesitation, 'meeting Vaughn with no warning like that. I can't remember what I had to eat for lunch. I was completely gutted, having to sit there opposite him and say nice things to him. Well, I couldn't be anything other than nice, could I? Not when I was trying to impress Clare and get her to give me some business.'

'Is Vaughn still there? At the Faulkener place?'

Tamsin struggled to her feet. 'Yes! He's staying for a few days. I just hope I don't meet him head-on again.'

'Will he try to get in touch, do you think?'

Tamsin walked over to the arch in the middle of the room. 'I'm going to make a cuppa, if you don't mind, Cass. I need something to take the nasty taste of Vaughn Herrick out of my mouth — and in answer to your question, anything's possible where Vaughn's concerned.'

Tamsin disappeared into the kitchen and Cass followed.

'Oh, Mark rang while you were out,' she said, almost as an afterthought.

Tamsin spun round. 'You didn't say anything about Herb House to him, did you?'

'No.' Cass laughed. 'Though why you're playing this so close to your chest, I don't know.'

'He'll try and stop me taking out the lease. Mark always tries to stop me having fun.'

'I'm sure he doesn't.' Cass, more composed

now, leaned against a worktop and watched as Tamsin brought mugs to the counter and switched on the electric kettle.

Tamsin sighed. 'No. I'm not being fair to him. Mark's a great guy.' Her eyes softened. 'I think I'm only just beginning to see him for what he is — now I'm a couple of hundred miles away from him.'

'Not for long, though.'

Tamsin looked up slowly. 'What do you mean?'

'He's coming down to see you . . . '

'Like hell he is.'

'Tamsin — come down off the ceiling. He's worried about you.'

'I don't need anybody worrying about me. Did you tell him that?'

'Yes. I told him. Obviously he didn't believe me, though. He's coming.'

'When?' Inside, Tamsin was seething.

'Tonight! Tomorrow! I don't know. He didn't say.'

Tamsin leaned over the worktop and clicked off the kettle.

'What are you doing?'

'Going out.'

'Where to?'

'To see 'John Chambers — Estate Agent'!'

'But your appointment to sign the lease isn't until four-thirty.'

'By which time,' Tamsin said, looking pointedly at the kitchen clock, 'Mark could well be down here and persuading me not to go through with Herb House.'

'You can say no to him.'

'He can be *very* persuasive, can Mark. No, Cass, I'm going over to Halesworth and I'll wait there until four-thirty. I can't risk Mark getting hold of me before then. He'll point out all the disadvantages of me taking such a big step, he'll say that at twenty-six I don't know my own mind, and he'll also remind me that I'm a woman — meaning, of course, that a woman isn't capable of making a big decision like this.'

'I thought you said he was nice!' Cass pulled a face at her. 'He sounds like a real chauvinist to me.'

'He is. But in the nicest possible way. Mark *always* knows what's best for me.'

'Are you serious?'

'Perfectly.' Tamsin shook her head and ran her fingers through her hair to tidy it — if that were possible with such a mass of curls. 'I can twist him round my little finger in other ways, though.' She laughed.

'In bed?' Cass said, not beating around the bush.

'I don't know. I've never been there. Not with Mark.' Tamsin gave her friend a frank stare. 'And I mean that. I really do, Cass.'

'You've gone through so much with him and never made love with him?'

Tamsin nodded. 'I never went to bed with him.'

'Didn't he mind?'

Tamsin laughed again. 'He minded. Yes, he minded. But Mark's not the sort to push me into anything till I'm ready. That's why I like him.'

'*Like?* I note you don't say 'love'.' Cass pushed herself away from the worktop, flipped the kettle on again, then went back to leaning.

'In a way — I do love him.' Tamsin was quietly insistent now.

'I just don't understand you. I'm going to have a cup of tea, though, whether you are or not.'

Tamsin went over to the table and pulled out a chair. 'Okay — just a quick one. But I want to be out of the house before Mark can put a damper on this Herb House thing.'

'He hasn't got a helicopter — or a jet, has he?'

Tamsin shook her head and smiled. 'No.'

'Well, he can't possibly get here before four-thirty, then, can he?'

'No, I suppose not.' For the first time that day, Tamsin sat down and began to relax.

He arrived at Cass's house just after eight that night, and straight away Tam said, 'I'm glad you've come. I've got something to tell you.'

'I couldn't get here sooner,' he said. 'We had an urgent job to do on the old Buick.' Turning to Cass, he explained, 'I restore classic cars for a living.'

'Yes,' Cass said. 'Tam told me.'

They were all three of them sitting in the living room, and with Mark there it seemed oddly overcrowded. Cass stood up and said, 'Look — I've got some developing and printing to do before I go to bed. Do you mind if I go out to the wash-house?'

'The wash-house?' Mark said, looking horrified, 'Hey, you don't have to go outside on my account. This is January and it's snowing out there.'

'I had it converted to a tiny studio,' Cass said, laughing. 'The central heating reaches there so you needn't worry about me.'

He looked relieved.

'Do you have somewhere to stay tonight?' Cass asked as she reached the door.

'There must be a handy pub around here,' he said, 'or a park bench!'

'Stay on the sofa,' Cass invited.

Mark looked at Tamsin and she shrugged. 'Suit yourself.'

'Thanks,' Mark said to Cass, obviously relieved that he hadn't got to go out looking for a bed. 'I won't be any trouble. I promise.'

'He will,' Tamsin said calmly. 'He always is.'

He glared at her. 'You said you had something to tell me when I first walked in.'

'I'll be off,' Cass said quickly. Too quickly.

Tamsin raised her glance heavenwards and said, 'If you hear a bang it'll only be Mark exploding.'

Cass made a quick exit, and Tamsin had the feeling that if she'd stayed she would have collapsed laughing on the floor.

Mark leaned forward and grabbed at Tam's hand as she stood in the middle of the room; he pulled her down on the sofa beside him and said, 'What's all that about?'

She bounced down on the cushions, wriggled herself comfortable, then faced him. 'I'm staying here,' she said. 'And I don't want any argument. I've got myself a house and a garden and I am staying in Suffolk.'

His mouth clamped shut. She knew that obstinate expression well. She tucked a leg underneath her on the sofa cushion, sat up straight and looked him full in the face. 'Well, say something,' she stated. 'Rant and rave if you want to. It won't have any effect on me, though. I am staying here.'

His strong jaw relaxed only slightly as he asked, 'What kind of house have you got?' But there was no animosity in his voice, and his grey eyes were steady and watchful.

'Mark — are you feeling okay?'

'I made a New Year resolution,' he said. 'I'm playing a waiting game. I'm a reformed character — one who doesn't fly off the handle at the least provocation.'

'You are?'

He nodded.

'You're not angry? Not raving mad at me?'

'Not so you'd notice,' he said. 'I'll wait, Tam. As long as it takes.'

'As long as it takes for what?' she asked softly.

'For you to come back to me.'

She shook her head, bewildered. This was a new Mark, a Mark she didn't entirely understand. 'How do you know that I ever will do that?'

'I can't help loving you,' he said. 'I've loved you from the first time I saw you, and when you love somebody like that, something good has to come out of it.'

'But why have you come rushing down here after me?'

His face softened. 'I needed a fix of you. I was missing you and I just needed to see you again to remind myself of what you looked like, and felt like.'

'Liar,' she said softly.

'I'm always going to worry about you,' he said. 'So you might as well get used to it. When I want to see you, I'll turn up. I'm not after anything else — not till you're ready, Tam.'

She reached out and pushed her fingers through his thick fair hair. It was still damp from the snow that had settled on him after he'd parked his car up and come running back to hammer on the door of Cass's house.

'That's nice. Your fingers in my hair,' he said, closing his eyes and leaning back against the sofa cushions.

He looked tired. Her heart went out to him. After working at the garage all day, he'd cared enough about her to drive all this way down to Suffolk.

'Your hair's wet. You should get a towel.'

'It doesn't matter.' As she moved her hand away from him, he caught at it and raised it to his lips. Turning it palm upwards, he kissed it gently.

She felt tears welling up behind her eyes. She whispered, 'Mark . . . I've missed you . . . '

'Come here.' He released her hand and put

his arm round her, hauling her to his side so her head fell sideways into his shoulder.

It was comfortable there. And warm. She felt his lips against her hair and she pressed her face into the thick woolly-knit of his sweater, that smelled of engine oil and men's soap.

'So tell me about the house,' he said, just above her head.

And she told him.

'I'd like to see it,' he said when she'd finished.

'You'll hate it.'

'Why will I?'

'Because it's something I've done without consulting you first,' she said.

'Tam!' He eased away from her, inched round in his seat and let her flop back against the sofa cushions behind her. He perched on the edge of the seat then, and didn't touch her. 'Tam,' he said in a quiet voice, 'let's start again, huh? I haven't come here to make trouble.'

She stared at him, her eyes wide.

'Tam!' He was becoming exasperated, she could tell.

'What do you mean? Start again?' she asked.

'You were beginning to trust me at one time — in the not so distant past.'

'Yes,' she said, looking down at her fingernails.

'What went wrong?'

She lifted her head slowly and looked at him, but couldn't answer because there was a lump in her throat that felt as if it would choke her if she spoke.

'You can tell me.'

She swallowed, then looked away again and muttered, 'I can't trust my own judgement, Mark. Twice before I thought I was in love, but they both turned out to be the wrong man. You know darn well that I made a complete and utter fool of myself over Rafe, and then Vaughn Herrick.'

'Twice *before*? *Before* what, Tam?'

'Just . . . just . . . before . . . '

'Before *me*? Is that what you're saying?'

She nodded and hung her head. 'Something like that. Before I started to care about you . . . if you really must know . . . '

He got up and walked away from her. Then he spun round in the middle of the room and there was the old impatience back in his voice. 'Why?' he wanted to know. 'Why walk out on me when you say you'd started to care about me?'

He didn't understand. He *couldn't* understand. And she was furious with him for that. She jumped to her feet and faced him. 'I can't

89

bear the thought of getting hurt again,' she flung at him. There was Rafe Thorne, who I loved — and he treated me like I was nothing but a kid sister. And then there was Vaughn Herrick, who I would've died for — except that he didn't want to know me after I got pregnant.'

'He was an absolute swine,' Mark yelled, coming back to her and grabbing hold of her shoulders so he could look deep into her eyes.

'I know he was. Now. But saying that doesn't make it any better, does it?'

She stared at him, willing him to understand. Wanting him to do something or say something to wipe out the past so she didn't have to remember it any more.

But he said nothing. He just stood looking down into her face, and then he pulled her towards him and kissed her hard and ferociously on the mouth, till it felt as if her lips would stay bruised and battered for a month or more.

She was breathless when at last he let her go. 'Is that what you want?' he said, holding her at arm's length then. 'Do you really want me to hurt you like that? Just to prove I'm no better than the rest? Does it make the past simpler to cope with if *I* behave like that Herrick bastard?'

With a sob in her voice, she said, 'He didn't

hurt me physically — not like you just did.'

'No,' he said. 'He hurt you with soft words and his hard body. But don't blame *me* for what he did to you, Tam.'

'I'm not blaming you,' she said, blinking away the unshed tears. 'I'm not blaming you. But there was Rafe, and Vaughn, and before them there was my father, who killed my mother and then told me to go to hell when I couldn't accept the trollop he married.'

He thrust her away from him. 'I've had it with sympathy, Tam. I can't give you any more. There's only one thing left and that's my love for you. I'm sick of pussy-footing around you, picking you up when you've been hurt, being a friend to you . . . ' He uttered a harsh laugh. 'Hell! Friendship! What am I talking about?' He threw up his hands despairingly, then looked at her again. 'Come here,' he said in a voice he'd never used to her before. 'Come here.'

She took a step towards him.

'I wouldn't hurt you. Not ever.' His voice was hard and exasperated.

She tilted her head back and looked into his face.

He didn't attempt to take hold of her; he just bent down and his lips touched hers, gently, reverently almost, as her lips parted and she gave herself up to him.

Still he didn't try to hold her.

'Hold me,' she whispered against his mouth.

'No,' he growled back at her. 'It's your turn now. Hold *me*. Give *me* something back, Tam. Even if it is only friendship.'

She rested her hands on his shoulders. 'I've got nothing to give.' Her lips found his again. The kiss went on for ever. He kissed away the bruising he'd inflicted earlier, and she tasted the sweetness of him, and clung to him until his arms went round her and held her, rocking her against his body, swaying her gently, this way and that.

It was getting late. The coal settled on the open fire, sending sparks crackling into the chimney.

'Come and see my house tomorrow,' she said quietly when they parted.

He nodded. 'I'd like that.'

'Don't kill it for me?' Her eyes were pleading.

He groaned. 'Tamsin — oh, Tam. Will you never trust me?'

5

'You've let yourself in for a lot of work.'

Mark stood looking out of a bedroom window at the two acres of snow-scattered land surrounding Herb House, and frowned.

'I didn't invite you here to tell me that,' Tamsin said easily. 'I want to know what you think of the house.'

'Well . . . ' He turned away from the window and faced her. 'At least it's furnished — in a fashion. It's pretty old stuff, Tam. Can you be happy with it?'

'I need a new mattress. I don't think I can bring myself to sleep in that bed without one, do you?' She laughed as she cast her gaze in the direction of a great wooden monstrosity, with carved head and footboard and a lumpy striped flock mattress. 'It must be a relic from World War II — I've seen better specimens in museums.'

'It's so lonely here, Tam.' Mark's expression was serious. 'There's no other houses around for half a mile at least. And I don't like that burnt-out shell of a church just up the lane from you.'

'You can't see that from any of my windows, though.' She stood, hands on hips, still looking down at the bed. 'And anyway — ' she looked up at him at last ' — I'm not scared of spooky churchyards.'

'The house is okay. As I say, though — it's in a lonely spot. That's all I don't like about it.'

'I'm used to loneliness — I used to live in a lighthouse, remember? At Heronsea?'

'You had Ava for company there, though. And there was all the town around you.'

'Yes.' She felt a cold shiver run down her back. 'Yes. Don't remind me of Heronsea, though, Mark. Ava died there — shut out on that high lantern platform in the middle of winter.'

'It was an accident, love.' He came over to her, took hold of her hand and squeezed it.

'Was it?' she asked quietly. 'Or did she go out there deliberately and shut that door because she knew it wouldn't open again from the outside?'

'Ava was ill, Tam. Perhaps we'll never know exactly what happened.'

'Mark . . . ' She faced him fully. 'Mark — I don't think I'll ever want to go back up to

Yorkshire to live. There are so many memories.'

'Are you trying to tell me something?' His eyes were brooding, yet filled with a deep understanding.

'Are you ready to listen to something like that?'

'That you don't want to come back to me?'

She nodded, let go of his hand and went over to the window herself, to look out over the gardens. 'This is what I want. Just at the moment, this is all that I *need* — all that I can cope with, in fact.'

He stood on the other side of the room. 'Then go for it, Tam.'

She twisted her head round to look at him. 'You sound as if you mean that.'

'That heart-to-heart we had last night,' he said awkwardly. 'I meant what I said. I'll wait for you to come to me. I'll wait as long as I can.'

Her glance was questioning. 'And if I can't come to you? In Yorkshire? Where I was so unhappy? What then?'

'I shall have to come to terms with that. I shall have to try and forget you. It won't be easy, though.'

'Oh, Mark . . . '

'I won't wait for ever, Tam. There are things *I* too want out of life — things like

95

companionship, kids . . . '

'Mark . . . don't . . . ' All at once she knew she couldn't bear it if he found those things with another woman. Her life seemed to be falling apart. What had she done? she wondered. She realized she'd risked everything when she'd signed the lease for this house. She hadn't stopped to figure out how he'd take it. Now she knew, though. Now he'd spelled it out for her. He wouldn't wait for ever . . . And who could blame him for saying that?

'Don't keep looking at me like that,' he said.

'It's just the place, Mark. Heronsea! It's not you . . . '

'Places don't make unhappiness,' he said softly. 'We make our own heaven or hell.'

'Places hold memories, though.'

'Memories fade.'

'Do you have a damn answer for everything?' she asked, turning round fully and forcing a laugh.

Slowly he shook his head. 'I don't have any answers. I just have a lot of questions that — unfortunately for me — seem to be the unanswerable sort.'

★　★　★

They went out into the garden. The snow of the previous night hadn't settled to any considerable depth, but there had been a hard frost overnight, making the grass pathways slippery.

'How many herbs will you be selling to the Faulkener woman?' he wanted to know. 'Will it be enough to give you a decent standard of living?'

'That's still to be decided,' she said. 'I haven't had time to take stock of everything that's here, and Clare Faulkener only wants the culinary kind of herbs, not the medicinal or the cosmetic.'

'I wouldn't know the difference.'

'I could teach you,' she said softly. 'Come along — let me show you some of them. I want you to know what I'm doing when you . . . go back to Yorkshire, and I'm here alone.'

The rest of the morning was taken up with Mark making a rough plan of the garden for her on a large notepad, while Tamsin carefully identified what herbs were there, and pegged wooden spiked name-boards firmly into the hard ground. There was a good selection of culinary herbs — mainly, she supposed, because Joshua Temple before her had been a supplier to Faulkener's.

Clare had told her she needed various kinds of mint, parsley, rosemary and sage.

Tamsin was amazed now, though, at how many other herbs she would also be able to provide for Clare's industry.

Mark came over to her with the sketchpad and held it out for her approval. 'Will this do?'

She rose to her feet, a wooden mallet in one hand. She was snug in boots, jeans and woolly jacket, with a chunky scarf wrapped round her neck and tied in a huge knot at the back. She looked interestedly at the notepad, her eyes taking in the squares and diamond patterns that Mark had painstakingly measured out and drawn to a rough scale. Her gaze came up to his. 'Hey, that's really good.'

'I thought I'd work on it when I get back home, and send you a sketch that's wall-chart size, so you can put it in your office — wherever that's going to be — or else pin it up inside of one of those big sheds beyond the conifers.' He jerked his head towards the trees alongside the northern boundary wall. 'You can keep a check on what's planted where then.'

Her eyes were warm as they met with his. 'I thought you would wash your hands of me when you knew I was taking this on,' she said softly. 'Yet here you are, helping me to plan the garden out.'

'What else would I be doing?' he asked in a

solemn voice. 'Tam, even shivering in this god-forsaken place beats working in a nice warm garage two hundred miles away. I'm with you, dammit. And if this is what you want . . . '

'It is,' she stated firmly.

'You're going to be lonely, though.'

The silence of the walled garden was infinite. Not even a note of birdsong could be heard on this bleak January day. 'It won't always be like this,' she said, her breath puffing out on the still air. 'It will soon be spring.'

He closed up the sketchpad and shoved the pencil he'd been using into the top pocket of his zipped polar jacket. Then, tucking the pad under his arm, he crouched down beside a bed of slender green stalky plants and asked, 'What are these?'

'Angelica,' she said, going down beside him.

His head twisted towards her. 'It sounds like a girl's name.'

She reached out a gloved hand to him and grasped his wrist. 'Come and look at this next bed,' she said.

They got up and walked further down the path, till, coming to a standstill again, she said, letting go of his hand, 'Now, feel that one — crush it between your fingers.'

He bent down and did as she said, then stood beside her.

'Sniff it,' she said.

He obeyed, and his head jerked up and his eyes met hers. 'Hey — that's nice. It's like one of my favourite aftershaves.'

'In the old days they used it to treat flatulence, coughs and shingles.'

He laughed out loud. 'Gee, thanks. That's enough to put me off aftershave for evermore. What's it called? Just so I can avoid it from now on.'

'Thyme!' She frowned slightly. 'And it ought to have been pruned before now. In winter it could do with protecting from the frost too.'

'You really know what you're talking about, don't you, Tam?'

She faced him. 'I'll have to, won't I? If I'm going to make a living from these herbs.'

She watched him scuffing at the grass with the toes of his shoes, then bending down to look at herbs alongside the path they were on. Another one caught his eye; he reached out his hand to it.

She sprang forward. 'No. Don't touch it.'

His head jerked towards her. Slowly he uncoiled himself from his crouched position and stood up. A scowl marred his good-looking face. 'I wasn't going to steal it . . . '

'You can get a nasty allergic reaction to it,' she said. 'I know — because I once did when I was a kid. I came out in big blisters and red weals all the way up my arms. It's name is rue!'

He gazed down at the bushy green plant. 'I thought it was giant parsley,' he said, with a sideways grin at her.

'It has rounder leaves than parsley,' she said, leaning forward over the rue and carefully inching a sprig towards him.

He looked worried. 'Hey — ought you to be doing that? If you're allergic to it?'

'It's not so bad at this time of year. Anyway, I'm wearing gardening gloves, and I shall make sure I always am when I'm around rue. Strong sunlight in summer makes it secrete an oil that can burn skin, though. I was just showing you the leaves so you'll know next time you come across it. Look at them — each tiny one is club-shaped — like the playing card suit of clubs.'

Nervously, he said, 'Well, okay. But come away from the damn thing. I don't want you breaking out in lumps and things.'

'I won't,' she said.

They faced each other, and an expression of deep concentration was on his face now, she saw. He was going to give vent to misgivings again; she just knew it. On

101

impulse, she whipped off one of her practical cotton gloves and placed a finger to his lips. 'Don't!' she said. 'Just don't go pointing out all the disadvantages, Mark. Do you think I haven't had second thoughts? Second, third and fourth if the truth be known.'

His hand came up and fastened round hers, and he drew her towards him, pulled her gently into his arms and kissed her.

She didn't struggle or attempt to pull away. It was a good feeling, being there in his arms with his ice-cold face and lips pressed up against hers. She allowed the old wooden mallet she'd been using to slide through the fingers of her other hand and fall to the ground. Then she used that free hand to steady herself against his waist.

They were both so wrapped up against the weather that there was no question of actual bodily contact. She snuggled up against him, feeling the dampness of the path creeping through the soles of her boots and up her legs. Inside, though, she was warm, with a heat that touched her heart and sent a glow of pure joy swirling through her veins. She was glad he hadn't tried to dissuade her from her purpose. He seemed to be taking a genuine interest in her little venture, and it pleased her that he could do that, and that they could still be friends.

The kiss had to end, but to her surprise she knew a moment of sadness when it did. It would be so simple to take the easy way out — to say to hell with Suffolk, and return to Yorkshire and marry him.

His lips still very near to hers, he said, 'That was good . . . '

'Don't follow that with a 'but' — will you?' She gazed up at him with candour.

'I wasn't going to.'

'No?' She tilted her head and drew away from him a little, so she could see the expression on his face more easily.

He grasped hold of her shoulders and bent his head to kiss her again, this time, though, holding her so she couldn't snuggle up to him. She had to be content with no contact except for his hard hands on her shoulders, his even harder lips on her mouth.

At last he let her go again, and she said, gasping for breath, 'Wow!'

He stared thoughtfully down at the ground, rocked back and forth a few times in his winter trainers, then lifted his head to look at her, and said, 'Okay — let's get on, shall we? What's next on the list of this morning's chores?'

Uncertain of him in this new mood, she hesitated a while, then said, 'You are one strange guy, Mark.'

'I've been reading up on the New Man. No more chauvinism.' He gave her a quick grin. 'No more telling you what to do. Seems I've been going wrong for one hell of a long time. It seems also — from the gist of that article I read — that a) women are no longer being chained to the kitchen sink; b) they make better bosses than men, and c) they expect an orgasm at least three times a week.'

She started to laugh, softly at first, then couldn't stop. It was the first time he'd ever spoken to her like that. He was laughing too, and when they'd both sobered a bit, he said, 'Well — was it right? What I read in that book?'

She nodded, her eyes bright and her mouth already twitching into silent laughter again. 'Dead right,' she managed at last.

'When do we start, then?'

'Start?' Still bubbling with merriment, she almost choked on the words. 'Mark — what are you up to? You can't possibly have changed this much. You were always such a sobersides.'

'On the three times a week,' he said, watching her wickedly. 'That's what I'm talking about. When do we start?'

Teasingly she replied, 'We can't. I haven't got a mattress, remember?'

'I'll buy you one.'

'No.' She shook her head. 'You can't do that.'

'Why not?' he wanted to know, entering into the spirit of the game.

'Because it'll look for all the world as though you've got a vested interest in the bed.'

'As if we're sleeping together?' he asked. 'Is that what you're scared of? But nobody will know, Tam. This is between you and me.'

'It's not the sort of thing a man usually buys a girl, is it? A mattress?'

'I never do buy you the usual things,' he said. 'You'd read something sinister into it if I started showering you with bouquets of flowers or expensive jewellery.'

Her hand flew to the slender chain she wore around her neck. 'You bought me this,' she said, fishing it out from beneath her coat-collar and the constricting scarf.

He walked over to her and rested one hand on her shoulder. 'A little silver trinket,' he said. 'A dreamcatcher. It's nothing, Tam — it has very little value. It cost no more than filling the car up with petrol would have done.'

'It doesn't matter how much money it was,' she protested. 'I love it, Mark, because you thought about me enough to . . .'

He gave a short laugh and turned and

walked away from her. 'You used to have bad dreams,' he flung back over his shoulder. 'That's why I got it for you.'

She hurried after him and grabbed at his arm, and with a sigh he stopped walking and faced her again. 'Look,' he said, 'I'd give you everything I possessed if I thought you'd accept it. But I know you wouldn't. You're not impressed with all that sort of stuff, are you? Even though — '

She broke in. 'I know what you're thinking. You saw me as a gold-digger when I was out to get Rafe Thorne — and then, after him, Vaughn Herrick. They were both of them rich men, and for a while it was a heady thought that I could move in the same circles as they did.'

'Racing-drivers are exciting people,' he said, looking away from her, over her head across the bleak garden. 'More exciting than somebody who restores old cars for a living.'

'Racing-drivers are *rich* people,' she said. 'But I made two bad decisions, Mark. I don't want to make a third.'

'Well, I'm not made of money, for heaven's sake.' He shook off her restraining hand.

'No — but you're not exactly a pauper, are you? You have that lovely house up in Yorkshire, you're a partner in Brand Motors . . .'

'Big deal!' he scoffed.

'It would be easy to lead you on . . .'

'So lead me,' he challenged, staring down at her.

'No, Mark. We don't have that kind of relationship — you and I.'

'I'm not made of stone.' His jaw tightened. His voice dropped, 'I want you. You know I want you.'

'I'll buy my own mattress, Mark.' She gazed steadily at him. 'Okay?'

He threw up his hands. 'Okay!'

* * *

He stayed on Cass's couch for the next three days.

Waking him with a mug of tea on the third day, Tam said, 'You don't *have* to hang around, you know. I'm perfectly capable of moving into Herb House by myself.'

'I want to make sure you don't go lugging a great heavy mattress upstairs by yourself,' he said, struggling to a sitting position and shivering as he pulled Cass's loaned sleeping bag up around his shoulders.

'The delivery lads will do that,' Tam said. And, looking pointedly at the mantel clock, added, 'Speaking of which — I'd better get off to Stratton End, because they promised to bring it around eleven this morning.'

Mark's gaze followed her own. 'Hell! Is that the time? Why didn't you wake me earlier?'

'Just take this mug of tea out of my hands, will you?' she said, with as much patience as she could muster.

He reached up and took the mug out of her hands, yelping when the heat burnt his fingers. 'Hell's bells! This is hot . . . '

Cass peeped through the archway from the kitchen. 'Freshly brewed tea is supposed to be hot,' she said.

Mark scowled, and sipped at the tea. 'I suppose I've missed breakfast?'

Tam went to join Cass. 'It's under the grill. Keeping warm for you. Cass and I are going to the house now.'

'What about me . . . ?'

'You can follow later,' Tam said.

'When the mattress is in place?' he asked pointedly.

Tam said, 'Beds are very personal things.'

'Yeah,' Mark said. 'So I'm finding out.' His teasing look was directed at Cass now.

Sweetly she said, 'Don't look at me! Tam's spare room bed is big enough for two. It was up to her in the end where you slept.'

Tamsin's grin was wide. 'I like a big bed,' she said. Then added, 'And I prefer it all to myself.'

6

Cass dropped into the passenger seat of Tamsin's car and said, 'Okay! Let's go, shall we? Do you think you've got enough food to stock up your cupboards, though, when we get to Herb House?'

'There's only me.' Tamsin grinned across at Cass as Cass fastened her seat belt.

'Unless Mark decides to move in with you instead of going back to Heronsea today.'

'He won't be moving in.' Tamsin was adamant. 'He's got to go back home. He has a job there. People depend on him. Anyway, Mark's house is a lovely old place; he wouldn't want to swap that for my draughty little abode.'

'But he's a partner in Brand Motors, isn't he? Surely he can take a holiday any time he wants to if he's a part-owner.'

Tamsin started up the engine. 'It doesn't work like that, I'm afraid. Mark and Edgar Brand are 'working' partners. It's not a very big affair, and as Edgar's confined to a wheelchair Mark won't leave him in the lurch. They do have a mechanic called Jack-O, who works for them, so Mark might be able to get away for the odd weekend or two to see me.'

'I see.' Cass twisted round in her seat as they drove away from her house, checking with her hand to make sure the boxes of provisions on the back seat were secure. There were a couple of carrier bags against her feet too, and as she moved one of these toppled over. 'Oh, heck.' Cass shot forward to save a tin of salmon that had rolled under the seat, and her knee caught the catch on the glove compartment, flipping it open. Both girls laughed as a scattering of papers, car park tickets and petrol receipts flurried onto the floor of the car.

Tamsin slowed the car. 'Do you want me to pull over so we can tidy things up a bit?'

'No. It's okay.' Cass laughed breathlessly as she scooped up the contents of the glove compartment and stuffed them back inside, then slammed it shut again. 'Do you *need* all that stuff?' she wanted to know. 'There must have been a year's petrol receipts in there.'

Tamsin sighed. 'I tend to use the glove compartment much as I would a dustbin,' she confessed. 'Honestly — I keep promising myself I'll clear it out, but I've always been like this.' She glanced across at Cass. 'Anyway — there can't be a year's worth of receipts in there. I don't think I've had the car for a year yet.'

'You don't *think?*' Cass asked, exasperated with her friend. 'Don't you *know* when you bought the car?'

'I don't have a tidy mind,' Tamsin said. 'It goes with the hair.'

'How do you mean — it goes with the hair?'

'My fuzzy mind. Fuzzy mind, fuzzy hair. I never could keep either in order.'

Cass wasn't laughing any more as she said, 'You're going to have to keep things in order dealing with Clare Faulkener, my girl.'

Tamsin heard the sharp note of criticism in Cass's voice, and glanced at her. 'I get the feeling you don't like Clare Faulkener. I've noticed you've sounded a bit stroppy before when you've mentioned her.'

They were at the bridge now, and the traffic lights were on red. Tamsin stopped the car and pulled on the handbrake, and turned her attention to Cass.

Cass's forehead was tensed up. She said on a note of pique, 'I've never said anything against her.'

'You don't have to actually put it into words, love. Things like that come over even in minor topics of conversation.'

'As a matter of fact, I've never met her.'

Tamsin relaxed back in her seat. 'But you *don't* like her,' she said. 'Oh, come on now, Cass. It's not like you to harbour grudges or anything like that. What's going on? How can you dislike somebody you've never met?'

Cass looked uncomfortable. 'I've *heard* things about her.' Her mouth snapped shut.

'It's not like you to listen to gossip either,' Tam replied in a firm voice.

'Her in-laws are my neighbours, remember?'

'Ah, yes.' The light dawned — if only a little. 'Patric Faulkener's mum and dad.'

Cass nodded, but said nothing.

'It's not unheard of for a man's mother to dislike her daughter-in-law, you know.'

'It isn't like that.' Cass's voice was tight.

The traffic lights changed to green, and Tamsin drove over the bridge. 'It always sounds as if this bridge is going to give way — it's so hollow and rattly,' she said, searching her mind for something neutral to say, and attempting to change a subject which seemed to be getting dangerously charged with some sort of antagonism.

She was concentrating on the road, not looking at Cass, when she heard what sounded like a muffled sob at her side. Swiftly she glanced at Cass, and with horror saw that the girl was crying quietly into a paper tissue.

'Hey . . . what is this . . . ?'

'Nothing!' Cass averted her face and looked out through the side window as they left the village behind.

Tam was worried. At school she'd known Cass for years, and never once had she ever seen her cry before. She drove steadily on until the road widened, then she pulled in to the side, close up to a banked-up hawthorn hedge, and stopped the car.

Cass turned to her. 'It's nothing. Just drive on, Tam. I'm just being stupid about this.'

'No.' Tamsin shook her head. 'It's not 'nothing'. Tell me what it's all about. You're obviously upset about *something*. Is it anything *I* said back there?'

Cass shook her head vigorously. 'It's not you, Tam. But I can't tell you.'

'You can. I'm not moving the car again until you do.'

'No . . . '

'Yes. I mean it.'

Cass blew her nose, then stuffed the tissue away in her pocket. She hunched into her seat and stared, red-eyed, red-nosed, out through the windscreen and clamped her mouth shut.

'You look awful.'

Cass turned her face towards Tamsin and said, 'It's Patric.'

'Patric?'

Cass nodded. 'I'm being a fool, I know, but . . . '

Tamsin closed her eyes briefly, then opened them and stared at her friend. 'Oh, no. You're not in love with him? This isn't an 'eternal triangle' situation, is it?'

Cass tried to laugh, but failed in the attempt. 'Would it be the end of the world if it were something like that?' Her eyes were hostile now.

'You *are* in love with him! Is that what you're trying to say? Or is it just infatuation?'

'It's gone a bit further than that,' Cass said miserably. 'And Clare will never give him up.'

'It's gone further than that, you say?' Tamsin raised her eyebrows. 'Just what does that mean, Cass?' This was worse than anything she had expected. She was silent for a few minutes as Cass didn't answer, then she said, 'And Patric? Is he in love with you?'

'I — I think so.'

'You only think so . . . '

Cass rounded on her, eyes blazing. 'He says he is — and I believe him.'

'Heck! What a mess.'

'Yes.' Cass slid further down in her seat, until her coat-collar was up round her ears.

She looked lost and lonely, and incredibly young.

Tamsin turned sideways in her seat. 'Why didn't you tell me before? Are you going to be all right on your own? I can stay with you a bit longer. I don't have to move into Herb House right away.'

'I'll survive.' Cass drew in a deep breath and seemed more composed now. 'I'll have to. Clare Faulkener eats bigger fish than me for her breakfast.'

'Yes,' Tam said, remembering Craig Andrews' warning. 'Yes — her PA said something of the sort to me when I went to visit her.'

'Craig Andrews! That creep!'

Drily, Tamsin said, 'He has that effect on you too, does he? He's very good-looking, though.'

'They're having an affair, you know.'

'Who?' Tamsin stared aghast at Cass. 'Clare and Craig?'

Cass nodded. 'Patric knows about it. He says he's biding his time.'

'What,' Tam asked directly, 'does that mean exactly?'

'I don't know.' Cass sat up straight again, and said in an angry voice, 'He ought to divorce her, but . . . ' The words tailed off.

'Is Patric having an affair with you?' Tam said bluntly.

'It didn't start out like that . . . ' Cass made an agitated movement with her hands.

Tamsin sighed. 'It never does.'

Cass glared at her. 'You're going to blame *me*, aren't you? You see me as the home-wrecker, the marriage-breaker, but it's not like that . . . '

'Isn't it? He's a married man, Cass.' Tamsin tried not to sound as if she were being judge and jury, but secretly she was shocked. Cass had been brought up by strict parents, she knew. This was the last thing she would have expected of her.

'I know he's married. *I know* it's wrong.' Cass stared straight out through the windscreen again and her expression was haunted. 'Do you think I'm proud of myself?' she whispered. 'I'm not, Tam. But Patric was so — so caring, so good to me when Mum died. It was a bad time for me — and I really needed that shoulder to cry on . . . '

Tamsin let out a long, low breath. 'What a mess.'

Cass said, 'What shall I do? What would you do if you were in my position?'

Tamsin tried to convince herself she would never willingly put herself in such a position. Married men — in her book — were

116

definitely a no-go area. Remembering, however, that she too had been attracted to Patric Faulkener, she couldn't really blame Cass for falling for him when she was at a low ebb in her life. She started up the car again, and as they began to move said, 'Up to now, I haven't been able to organize my own life, but you're playing with fire, Cass. I think it's time to call a halt.'

'The right thing would be to give him up. Is that what you're saying?'

'I'm hardly the one to give advice, but . . . '

'It's wrong. I know damn well it is.' Cass sat brooding for some seconds, then said, 'But why shouldn't he have some happiness? Clare's obviously grasping hers with both hands, so why shouldn't Patric?'

'Clare? *Happy*? With Craig Andrews?' Somehow Tamsin couldn't imagine Craig making any woman 'happy', except in one department perhaps, but she had no desire to dwell on Craig's sexual prowess just then — or at any other time. Craig had come across as totally self-centred and arrogant when she'd met him. But maybe, she thought, giving him the benefit of the doubt, maybe he did have a weakness where Clare was concerned. Clare was very beautiful, and . . .

'It's her money he's after, of course. Craig!'

'Maybe.'

'I can't understand why Patric doesn't just give up on her and divorce her. He won't, of course.' Cass was full of despondency. 'He has firm beliefs about marriage. His mum and dad would be devastated if he was involved in anything seedy or sordid.'

'If he loves you ... ' Tamsin was concentrating on the narrow road in front of her ' ... it shouldn't matter what his parents think about him, should it?'

Cass broke in, 'He *does* love me. We're right for each other. And I get on well with his parents ... '

The last little statement sounded so sad, so pathetic, that Tam had to swallow a lump in her throat. It wasn't right — Cass and a married man. But she couldn't keep harping on about that, could she? It would make her sound like a right old sermonizer if she did, and just at the moment she realized that Cass needed a friend — somebody she could talk to and confide in. And there seemed nobody else on the horizon who *could* help, except herself. It wasn't a role she relished, though. She was no agony aunt, and she was honest enough to admit to herself that she was no saint either. She'd made bad mistakes in her own life. When love got in the way of reason,

118

logic flew out of the window. She said as much to Cass.

Cass gave a weak smile and mopped up her remaining tears. Quietly, she said, 'Let's leave it for today. I've said more than enough. Don't think too badly of me, though. I only want what everybody else wants — to be happy.'

* * *

When they'd unpacked all the groceries into kitchen cupboards at Herb House, Tamsin told Cass she could take the car back to Alderwood if she wanted to.

'Mark said he'd come over this afternoon. He can bring me back to Alderwood. Why don't you go into Norwich and treat yourself to something nice?'

'Does that work?' Cass pulled a rueful face, then laughed. 'Spending money on yourself? When you're hopelessly entangled in a no-hope love affair?'

'It can take your mind off it — temporarily,' Tamsin said. 'Especially if you buy something madly exciting and horrendously expensive on your credit card.'

Cass looked puzzled. 'How does that work?'

'If you do that, you have to spend time

worrying how to pay the bill at the end of the month,' she said drily. 'And love is the last thing on your mind.'

Cass burst out laughing. 'I think I might just try it,' she said, in lighter spirits now than she'd been all morning.

Just then, there was the sound of wheels on gravel.

'My mattress!' Tamsin raced to the kitchen door, then whirled to face Cass. 'Oh, go on,' she said, tossing her the car keys. 'Take the car. And show me what you've bought for yourself when Mark brings me back to your place tonight.'

A light snow began to fall again after Cass had driven away in Tam's car. The new mattress was swiftly put in place on the old bedstead, and Tamsin started tidying up the room, rolling up the large plastic bag it had been wrapped in, and then picking up staples and bits of cotton thread off the floor.

She took the rubbish down to the kitchen, then decided to keep the plastic. Maybe it would come in useful for covering some of the more fragile herbs if the weather got really wintry. She shoved it into a cupboard in the kitchen, then went and looked through the window at the garden. She was pleased with what she saw, and found herself thinking she couldn't wait for the better weather, so she could spend as much time as possible out there.

She made herself a cheese sandwich and mug of coffee, and had her makeshift lunch still standing there and watching the snow-flakes drifting down. It was quite mild outside so the snow wasn't settling. She looked at the clock. Mark wouldn't be here yet. She wondered if today might be a good time to light her bonfire out there, and decided she'd give it a try. If the snow did become heavier, all the rubbish piled up in the garden would get to a point where it was too wet to burn. She pulled on her jacket, remembered she'd seen a couple of old newspapers in a drawer and, tucking them under her arm, picked up a box of matches and went outside.

She'd sited the bonfire heap as far away from the house as it was possible to get it, at the end of the main grassy path and near to a tumbledown greenhouse that had lost most of its glass. It was a good hundred-yard walk to it, but Tamsin didn't mind. It was a still sort of day, so there would be no danger of any breeze fanning the flames towards the sheds or the rest of the garden.

She crouched down beside the heap of rubble and weeds that was almost as tall as she was herself, and pushed single sheets of newspaper as far inside the bottom of it as she could. When the two newspapers had been disposed of in this way, she took out the matches, and, lighting one, held it to the nearest bit of paper.

It was away in seconds, smouldering at first, then belching out grey smoke and starting to crackle. She backed away from it, and moved round one side to see if the paper was lit right the way through. It was, so she stood facing the house, at the back of the bonfire. That way she knew she'd be able to see Mark when he arrived, so she could wave to him and let him know where she was.

It wasn't often she saw the house from this angle, she realized. She was surprised, too, that she could see part of the ruined church from here. It was a good quarter of a mile away, with her own land and a field between it and her. She felt a sudden shiver rush through her as she looked at it; it was decidedly creepy on a dull grey day such as this one was. The fire that had destroyed it must have been intense, for there was only a jagged half of the square tower still left standing. The windows were black holes, and the space where the clock would once have been was gaping like a mouth wide open in a silent scream.

She pulled the collar of her coat up round her face, suddenly feeling very cold, although the snow had stopped now and a watery sun was trying to break through the clouds. As she poked at the bonfire with a blackened length of garden cane she'd found on the ground, she couldn't stop her gaze from wandering back, time after time, to the church. It was as if something was demanding her attention — yet there was nothing there, she told herself, nothing except a heap of grey stones and rotting timbers.

'Stop it!' she said sharply to herself, as for about the tenth time in as many minutes she looked in the direction of the ruined building. 'Stop it . . . ' The words ended on a gasp. There had been a brilliant flash of brightness from one of those gaping windows, but now it was gone. She looked up at the sky. Of course, that must be it — the sun was stronger now. It *must* have been the glint of sun on glass . . .

But then she felt goosebumps all the way down her back.

Those windows had no glass in them to reflect sunlight!

A sudden sound of hooting almost had her leaping in the air with the shock of it. But with relief she saw it was only Mark — pulled up at the side of the house in his car and trying to attract her attention. A long, drawn-out sigh escaped her lips, and then she was running lightly up the path towards him as he slammed the car door and came hurrying towards her.

He caught her in his arms and hugged her. 'I knew you wouldn't resist lighting that bonfire for much longer,' he said, laughing down into her face.

She felt tense and on edge. She flung her arms right round him and squeezed him tight.

'Hey!' he said. 'You're trembling. I don't usually get that sort of response from you. Is my sex appeal working at long last?'

She tilted her head back and looked up at him. 'Kiss me,' she said breathlessly. 'Kiss me and hold me tight.'

He bent his head down to hers and kissed her long and lingeringly on the lips. She relaxed in his arms.

Afterwards, he said, 'I don't usually get this sort of welcome, Tam.'

She pulled away from him a little and said, 'It was a bit scary — down there on my own, and . . . '

'And?' he prompted, frowning at her.

'Oh, it's nothing.' She let go of him and grabbed at his hand. 'Come on — come and see my bonfire.'

'Your hand is shaking,' he said. 'And it's clutching mine much too tightly. What are you scared of, Tam?'

'It's just my silly imagination,' she said. 'I didn't realize I could see the old church from the bottom of my garden like that. I was just looking at it, and something flashed in one of the windows.'

He too looked up at the sky now. 'Maybe it was the sun,' he said, as he walked beside her down the grassy path.

'I thought that too. But there's no glass in the windows.' She gave a tremulous laugh. 'So it couldn't have been that, could it?'

They'd reached the bonfire now, and Mark was screwing up his eyes against the smoke from it and gazing out across the garden and the field towards the ruined church. 'You're right,' he said. 'There isn't any glass.'

'It might have been a bird.' She wanted to think it was. She knew, however, that it hadn't been.

'Could have been. You get a flash of white with those collared doves I've seen around here — and you've also had magpies in the garden, haven't you?'

'Yes.' She was easier now Mark was with her. She was beginning to relax and think it had all been in her imagination. But Mark was still looking worried.

'I hope you're going to be all right on your own here.'

She managed a laugh. 'If I decide to stay, I'll get a dog for company.'

'I thought you didn't like dogs.'

'I'd like a dog that was all my own.'

'It might be a good idea, Tam.'

'And maybe a couple of cats.'

He nodded, then said seriously, 'I was reading the local newspaper at Cass's house. There's some talk of demolishing the old church. Apparently parts of it are unsafe. The land surrounding it is up for sale as well. Did you know that?'

She shook her head. 'I can't see anybody being interested in it. It's so far out from anywhere, and I suppose it's only agricultural land anyway.'

'It's a real eyesore — that church,' he said, frowning.

Tremulously, she said, 'I'd certainly feel better if they did pull it down.'

Still holding her hand, he spun her round to face him. 'You really were worried when I arrived, weren't you?'

'A tiny bit scared, that's all,' she admitted.

'It's only a pile of old stones.'

'Yes,' she agreed, but in her heart she just knew that somebody had been watching her.

And why would anyone, she asked herself, be interested enough in her to do that?

7

It snowed for a week and a half after Tamsin had moved into Herb House, and she was virtually imprisoned there. It didn't worry her. She'd covered the more fragile of the herbs in the garden with heavy plastic sheeting held down with bricks as soon as she'd heard the severe weather warning on her radio, and daily she shovelled snow away from the path to her coal store — a sturdy stone-built place just outside her kitchen door.

Cass telephoned her two or three times to see that she was all right in her isolation. She too had been partially housebound, but not quite to the extent Tamsin had. At least the streets of Alderwood were regularly cleared of snow, so Cass had been able to drive her car and get to work after a few days, and make sure her assignments for the various magazines she worked on were ready on time.

Stratton End, though, was completely cut off.

Back in Yorkshire, Mark rang her up, worried.

'How are you coping?'

'Fine,' she replied. 'I had a good store of tinned vegetables in the cupboard, and my little freezer was full too.'

'How the hell are you filling the time?'

'By working on Cass's book,' she said. 'Cass lent me a typewriter.'

'Cass's book?'

'I forgot,' she said. 'You didn't know about it, did you? Cass is writing a book, but it's only in the early stages so I'm transferring her handwritten notes onto the typewriter.'

'You're a sucker for punishment.' There was laughter in his voice. 'How's the garden, by the way?'

'It's disappeared,' she said, 'under all this snow — but the herbs will be warm underneath it.'

'Will you lose any of them?'

'Just listen to you,' she said, grinning into the phone. 'Anyone would think you're really worried about those poor little herbs.'

'I am,' he said, and she could imagine him frowning at the other end of the line. 'I got quite green-fingered when I was down there with you, learning about their names — and their horrible reactions if you touched some of them.'

'They don't affect everybody the same way,' she said. 'I must be the one person in a million who gets a severe reaction to touching rue. Anyway,' she laughed, 'it wasn't lethal. It just brought me out in red lumps.'

'Will the herbs survive this weather?'

Sobering then, she said, 'I hope I won't lose any of them. I covered some with thick polythene before all this snow descended on me.'

'You're sure you're okay?'

'I'm fine, Mark,' she said softly.

'No more scares with the old church?'

'I can't see it from the house. It's only when I'm right down at the farthest end of the garden it's in view, and I haven't been down there since you left. It's not really the sort of weather for bonfires.'

She heard him give a sigh of relief. 'That's okay, then. I'll call you again towards the end of the week, huh?'

'Look forward to it.'

'Call me, though — if you're worried about anything. Any time. Promise?' He seemed reluctant to ring off.

'Yes, Mark.' And, gently then, she said goodbye and replaced the receiver before he could start getting intense.

The thaw set in and the garden became a quagmire as snow turned to muddy water and the once green pathways took on the appearance of miniature black rivers.

It would be impossible to do much work on the garden, she decided, so she thought she'd take the opportunity to drive over to Alderwood and take Cass's book back to her now that she'd finished the typing up of it. Her pantry, kitchen cupboards and ancient freezer needed replenishing too, so a shopping trip was also on the cards. She didn't bother telephoning first, knowing that to do so might disturb Cass in her little converted out-house where she developed and printed the photographs for her magazines. And if she wasn't at home Tamsin knew she could always just pop the manuscript through the letter box.

But Cass *was* at home, and she seemed flustered when she opened the door to her and awkwardly asked her inside.

Once inside the little front sitting room, all was made clear.

Patric Faulkener was there, knotting his tie. His jacket was slung across one of the easy chairs, and Tamsin could see at a glance that she had picked the worst possible time to visit.

'I'm sorry,' she muttered to Cass. 'I ought to have just pushed the envelope through your letter box.'

Cass weighed up the brown-packaged notes in her hand and gave an uneasy little laugh. 'I doubt you would have got it through. It's gone into quite a lot of pages, hasn't it?'

'Two hundred and sixty four!'

Patric Faulkener said, 'Hello, Tamsin. We meet again.'

'We seem to be making a habit of it,' Tamsin said, trying to ignore her conscience and natural antagonism and sound as polite as possible — in the circumstances.

'I'd better be off,' he said to Cass, and Cass nodded, still clearly agitated.

'Yes. Yes. Okay, Patric . . . '

'I'll be in touch.'

Cass said quickly, 'Tam — put the kettle on, will you?'

Tamsin took the hint and went through to the kitchen, not switching the kettle on, however, but just making herself invisible and gazing out of the window across the fields and mud-flats whilst inwardly seething. Just what was Cass up to? she wondered. Couldn't she see the mess she was getting into?

She heard Cass and Patric murmuring against the front door, then she heard it close, and Cass came back through the sitting room and into the kitchen to her.

She whirled away from the window. 'Are you mad?' Her cheeks burned with indignation. 'Don't you realize what you're getting into?'

Cass placed the manuscript on a worktop and said, 'Don't start, Tam. Just don't start on me. I can't take it.'

Tam held out both her hands. 'Please . . .' she begged. 'Get out of this while you can. You know what you're doing is wrong.'

Cass slumped into a kitchen chair and gazed at her friend. 'Yes,' she said. 'I know it is, and I've told him we're through. It's difficult, though. We've known each other a long time and . . .'

'Let him run home to his mummy next door,' Tam said, hardening her heart against Cass's pinched and worried expression. 'Let him go there if he wants sympathy.'

'His mother knows how unhappy he is . . .'

'Tough!'

'Tam, you're heartless,' Cass cried. 'You just don't understand.'

'I understand the worry he's causing you, and it's tearing you apart,' Tamsin said, going over to the table and leaning her hands on it. 'I understand that none of this is making *you* happy — so why keep on seeing him?'

Cass shook her head and clasped her hands together in front of her. 'I don't know — I suppose I'm lonely. I don't have many interests — not since Mum died — and I've never been one to make friends easily . . . '

'But he's *using* you. Can't you see that?'

'He's not.' Cass's voice wavered. 'It's just that . . . well, I'm always here for him, aren't I? He comes to visit his parents, and then he pops in to see me too. And one thing leads to another, and . . . '

'You don't have to spell it out,' Tamsin said in a hard voice. 'It's perfectly obvious what he wants.'

'No! You don't understand. Often we just talk . . . '

'And he takes his tie off to do that, does he?'

Cass's eyes flashed dangerously. 'He can relax, can't he? It doesn't always mean we've been . . . '

'Your lipstick's smudged,' Cass replied curtly. 'I don't suppose it got that way eating cornflakes for your breakfast, did it?'

Cass reddened, and scrubbed at her face with her hand.

'Point taken,' she said, then, sharply, 'Now let's get off the subject, shall we?'

Tamsin straightened and said, 'I liked your book. When you've written up some more of it, I'll continue typing it for you.'

'Thank you.' Cass got up and walked over

to the kettle, lifted it and swished it to see if there was any water in it, then switched it on. 'We'll have a drink, shall we?'

'No, thanks,' Tamsin said. 'I've had it with tea and sympathy, if you don't mind. You said to get off that subject and I did. You should concentrate more on that book and less on Patric Faulkener. The book is *good*,' she said. 'I've never been to Northumberland myself, but you brought it to life for me with your description of the place.'

'I've never been there either,' Cass said, more at ease now, 'but I found it easy to write about — and the people . . . somehow they just came into my mind, and it seemed as if I knew them intimately.'

'You need something like that to take your mind off . . . '

'Patric,' Cass finished for her.

Tamsin let out a deep sigh. 'Look,' she said, 'I don't want us to fight. Okay. I think it's best if I go now. I do have quite a lot to do. My cupboards are almost empty, and I really do need to start clearing up my waterlogged garden.'

'And I have to get off to Cambridge,' Cass said.

'Cambridge! That's where Patric Faulkener has his racing circuit . . . ' Tamsin was immediately suspicious.

'Tam. Stop it. Patric's arranged for me to do a piece for a magazine on it, and take whatever photos I like, and my editor's told me to get on with it.'

'Okay.' Tamsin held up one hand. 'Okay, Cass. Don't let me interfere.'

The matter was at an end. And Tamsin left soon afterwards.

★ ★ ★

She had a visitor that afternoon.

He parked his car on the track at the front of the house, and came picking his way round the mud to her back door in his immaculate shoes and silver-grey suit.

She opened the door to him, being forewarned who it was because she'd caught a glance of him from her front window when she'd heard the car. Her eyes were wary. He was the last person she could have imagined coming to call on her.

Craig Andrews held out an envelope. 'Mrs Faulkener asked me to put this in the post,' he said, 'but it wasn't too much out of my way to call round with it, so I did just that. May I come in?'

Tamsin took the letter and looked at the envelope. It was franked first class. 'First class,' she said, raising her gaze to his face. 'It

135

would have reached me in the morning. Is it so urgent that you had to rush round with it?'

'No,' he said patiently, still standing on the doorstep. 'It's just a list she said she'd give you — outlining the herbs she'll need at certain times of the year.'

'Not urgent, then.'

'I said it wasn't. I was curious to see the place where you lived.' He rubbed his hands together and gave a mock shiver. 'Well, do I get invited in?' he asked, 'It *is* absolutely freezing out here.'

Tam opened the door to its fullest extent. He stepped inside the kitchen. 'I rang the front doorbell,' he said. 'Obviously, though, you didn't hear it.'

'It doesn't work,' she said, closing the door behind him. 'I think there's a wire gone amiss somewhere.'

'Nice little house.' He gazed round the large kitchen approvingly.

'I would've thought you'd appreciate something more modern than this.'

'For myself, yes, I would,' he said. 'But it suits you. You have such an air of rural charm about you.'

She didn't think much of his chat-up line. 'You make me sound like a milkmaid.' She tossed the letter onto the table and said, 'Would you like a drink of something hot?'

'No,' he said. 'I'm not a tea and coffee freak, and if you're thinking of offering me a whisky, don't. I can't afford to lose my driving licence — much as I appreciate the finer things of life.'

She found him vaguely amusing but a little unsettling. She must be getting desperate for company to be offering him hospitality, she decided.

She said, 'The finer things of *your* life being hard drink . . . ?'

'Fast cars and wild women,' he finished for her, with a completely disarming grin. 'I'm not so different to other men.'

'Sit down if you want to.'

He perched on a corner of the table.

'There *are* chairs,' she pointed out.

'That would put me at a disadvantage — me sitting down, you standing up,' he said softly. 'And I don't like to be at a disadvantage. I always like to be — on top.'

The slight pause before he said the last two words was deliberate, and suggestive in the extreme. She tried to convince herself that those words had no sexual connotation, but at heart she knew they had been meant to convey the very thing she was shying away from. She felt a little sickened by the thought of him and Clare Faulkener together, and hoped she was not giving anything away by the look in her eyes or the expression on her face.

'You know what I mean . . . ' He hesitated before saying softly, 'Of course you do. You wouldn't be human otherwise.'

There was no answer she could make. She was uncomfortable in his presence now. She picked up the envelope and ripped it open, taking out the single sheet of paper and studying it, but seeing nothing of what was written there.

He eased away from the table and came over to her, and her eyes flicked up to watch him. There was a look on his face, calculating, knowing, as very gently he took the sheet of paper out of her hand and turned it round before handing it back to her.

'It reads better,' he said, his voice sounding like a caress, 'if you have it the right way up.'

She was trembling. She was frightened. He was so cool, so polite, and yet there was a cunning, an insidious slickness about him that made her feel very naive and helpless. She mustn't let him see that he was worrying her, though. She slapped the letter down on the table, giving him a haughty glance, then turned and walked over to a cupboard. She came back to the table with a bottle and two glasses, and placed them in front of him.

'If you don't want one yourself, perhaps you'll open the bottle for me,' she said. 'I'm cold. I haven't been back home long and my stove has burned out. I was just going to light it again.'

He laughed softly. There was no amusement in his eyes, though. He picked up the whisky bottle and unscrewed the lid, slowly, deliberately, and all the time those cool grey eyes watched her.

'Do you want *me* to light your fire?' he asked, pouring a measure of golden liquid into each glass before putting the bottle back on the table.

She was more in control again now. She picked up her glass, looked steadily at him over its rim as she lifted it to her lips. Fight fire with fire, her brain was telling her. And don't let him see that he's rattling you.

'I doubt you could manage it,' she said, giving him back stare for stare.

He tossed back his whisky in one gulp, replaced the glass, and said, 'Try me, *Ms Curtis* — you might be pleasantly surprised at the things I can do.'

She kept her cool. She placed her whisky glass on the table, then went over to the mantelpiece and took down the box of matches she always kept there. Without warning, she spun round and tossed them to him, taking him so completely by surprise that he almost dropped them.

She stood aside from the fireplace then, and said, 'Be my guest — the old ashes need rattling out of the grate. You'll find firelighters in the cupboard under the sink, and coal is in the out-house just beside the kitchen door.'

He held onto the matches for only a moment, his face darkening. Then he glanced up at her and said in a voice like silk, 'Maybe some other time, Ms Curtis, I don't really think I can spare the time today.'

'Making a good job of something always takes time, Mr Andrews.'

He dropped the box of matches on the table-top, then moved towards the door, turning abruptly when he reached it to say, 'Did your racing-driver always do a good job? Or was he always in a hurry to get to the end . . . ' A slight hesitation again, and then he said, 'Of the track, I mean. I hope you didn't think I was hinting at anything more . . . '

Her heart gave a leap. 'My racing-driver, Mr Andrews? And who might that be?'

He laughed softly and savagely. 'Mrs Faulkener said it was quite extraordinary, you and Herrick meeting up at her house for lunch that day. It was a great pity I'd gone back to the office. I would have liked to meet him.'

'He isn't *my* racing-driver, *Mr* Andrews.' She stood her ground and tried not to let him see she was intimidated by him.

'But he was *your* racing-driver not so very long ago — or so I believe.' He stood by the door and watched her with those cold eyes of his. 'I made it my business to find out. You and he were . . . very *close* . . . close enough for you to be thinking of playing mummies and daddies.'

'You've been checking up on me . . . ' Suddenly she was furious, and her eyes blazed at him.

'It's company policy — checking on customers and suppliers alike.' He gave an elegant shrug of his wide shoulders and his voice dropped ominously as he said, 'Don't let it worry you . . . '

'It doesn't,' she snapped.

'Doesn't it?' His lips drew back in a smile — the smile of the tiger before it sprang — but almost immediately he was civil and courteous again. 'Don't let me keep you from your chores, Ms Curtis,' he said.

He opened the door and let himself out, closing it very quietly behind him.

She stood still and listened as he walked up

141

the side path and round to the front of the house again.

And she was so shaken she didn't dare draw a breath until she heard his car start up and roar away.

8

Tamsin couldn't settle in the house when Craig Andrews had gone. Her eyes kept darting to the window, and her ears were alert too, listening for the sound of his car returning. Why was it she couldn't bring herself to trust him? she wondered. She picked up the sheet of typed paper he'd brought and looked at it more calmly now. There'd been no need for him to come over with it, she reasoned. There wasn't anything in a list of summer herbs that needed her urgent attention.

She took it through to her small front sitting room and placed it inside an oak bureau that had come with the house. Without the ugly split in the wooden base of it, and stripped of its many and vari-coloured coats of varnish that had been applied over the past century, she supposed the bureau might be of some value. It would take an awful lot of work, though, to make anything of it.

She ran her hand over the worn, rutted surface, grimaced at the old black telephone standing on top of it, and made a mental note that she'd get that, at least, replaced with a new one that she could programme numbers into. It was a laborious business, fumbling through the haphazard entries in her diary for a number every time she needed to make a quick phone call. And, when somebody rang her, the tone on the telephone was loud enough to wake all of the demons from hell and bring them rushing to answer it.

As if to remind her the telephone shrilled out now, making her jump and half leap away from it. It was a piercing shriek of a ring, and she grabbed at the handset as the first shock subsided and got ready to curse him if this was Craig Andrews again.

It wasn't Craig, though. It was Clare Faulkener.

'I need a favour.' Imperious as usual. Tam also detected a note of agitation in the woman's voice.

She replied guardedly, 'A favour, Mrs Faulkener?'

'You remember my husband talking about that race-circuit when you were here for lunch the other week?'

'Yes.' Tamsin was puzzled at Clare bringing this up.

'Well, it's a bore, really, but I have to go with him down to Bramsdown tomorrow, and I was wondering if you'd like to come too.'

'Me? You want me to come and see the new race-circuit?' Tam was taken aback by the invitation.

'Well, you did say you'd had some interest in motor racing.'

'Yes, but . . . '

'Look, I'll come straight to the point — I'm going to be the odd one out — one woman with two men . . . '

'Two men?'

'Patric and Vaughn Herrick. It was Vaughn who suggested I ask you to come. I know you two have had your differences, but I really believe he wants to make it up to you, and . . . '

'Vaughn!' Tamsin let out a long, slow breath. 'I might have known.'

Clare said, 'Now don't be angry with him. I had a selfish reason for inviting you too. I thought you and I could discuss our own little business deal — the herbs you're going to supply me with. I hope we're going to be friends, Tamsin.'

The meaning was obvious. Clare wanted her along so she wouldn't be too bored — and she was now employing a subtle form of blackmail to get her own way. If Tamsin wanted to keep on the right side of her — well, she'd better fall in with tomorrow's plans. She hated being put on the spot like this. Hated, too, being bullied into something she didn't want to do. But she wanted Clare Faulkener's orders for those herbs, and the initial contract had only been for twelve months.

'It was nice of you to think of me,' Tam said, resigning herself to the fact that she would have to put up with Vaughn's company again, but knowing it wouldn't be for long, and that she wouldn't be alone with him. Anyway, there was no problem. It was all over between her and Vaughn, and she had no intention of taking up with him again.

'We'll collect you,' Clare said in a crisp, no-nonsense voice. She was accustomed to being obeyed, that much was obvious. 'Nine in the morning, if that's okay.'

When she'd replaced the receiver, Tamsin felt she'd just been used and tricked into this, and she cursed herself for letting that happen. She glared at the phone, and in the absence of anyone else to blame said, 'Now look what you've done; look what you've let me in for. Yes, I shall definitely replace you with something more modern — probably an answer-machine so that I don't get into a tight corner like this ever again!'

The journey was tense, but thankfully not too long, with Vaughn trying his hardest to win Tamsin over with small talk as he sat beside her in the back of Patric Faulkener's large and comfortable saloon. She was jittery and uneasy at his closeness to her, though. She cursed herself for not realizing she'd be thrown together with him like this. If she'd stopped to think about it, she'd have known that Clare would be in the front seat with her husband, while she and Vaughn . . . She gave a huge sigh and decided to make the best of things. There was no point doing otherwise, she reasoned. What was done was done. She *could* have said a firm and polite no to Clare Faulkener yesterday. It was her own fault, and nobody else was to blame.

Clare seemed uninterested in any conversation going on around her. She was preoccupied for a while, talking on her mobile phone to her office. And when she was off the phone it was obvious that her mind was still there. First and foremost Clare was a businesswoman, and this little trip today seemed to irk her. Tam wondered why Patric had wanted her along at all.

When they reached Bramsdown, Patric parked the car and they walked across the paddock so that Patric could give them a running commentary on all he'd achieved since taking over as a partner. Clare and Patric were a little way ahead of them, and it seemed obvious to Tamsin that Patric wanted to show off a little to his wife. Maybe, she thought, he felt daunted by her success and needed to let her know what *he* could do.

Vaughn whispered, 'I think Clare's under the impression we had a lovers' tiff — you and I. She's been hinting all weekend that we should 'kiss and make up'!'

Tamsin stiffened as he tried to take her arm. 'Let go of me,' she breathed. 'Don't you realize? I never wanted to see you again in the whole of my life.'

Vaughn was swinging a large sports bag in one hand. He looked questioningly at her. 'You really hate me, don't you?'

She relented. Seeing him there, striding out at her side, looking so young, so utterly charming and unassuming in close-fitting jeans and a thick bomber jacket, she couldn't help but remember what he had once meant to her. His soft brown hair was shining with health in the morning sun, and his blue-grey eyes gazed seriously at her from behind those steel framed spectacles he always wore — except when he was racing. She knew in that moment that she couldn't hate him.

He'd been her lover, the father of her child which had never drawn breath. No, she couldn't hate him. Not when they'd once been so close.

Clare saved her from answering his question. She spun round to them both and called, 'Stop lagging behind, you two.' Her easy laughter rang out. 'I know you must have lots of gossip to catch up on, but . . . '

Patric, at her side, stopped to light up a cigarette, then, blowing out smoke on the still air, said, 'Cool it, Clare! You'll embarrass the pair of them.'

Having had time now to compose herself again, Tamsin said, 'It's Patric's long legs — and yours too, Clare. You were leaving us behind, striding out like that.'

'My husband,' Clare said pointedly, 'can't wait to show me the circuit, and his office, and the plans for the new car; he thinks I shall fall in love with motor racing, but I rather doubt it myself.'

'You might get the racing bug, you know.' Tamsin fell into step beside Clare, leaving Vaughn to talk to Patric now.

Clare grimaced. 'Not on your life! Race-tracks don't interest me — but I felt I had to humour Patric and come and look the place over.'

'You might yet find out you get hooked on

racing. It can be very exciting.'

Clare shook her head, 'Oh, no. I don't think so. It will be interesting seeing Vaughn drive round the circuit, though. I've only ever watched motor racing on television.'

'Vaughn's going round the circuit? Today?' Tam asked.

Vaughn and Patric came up beside them and Vaughn said, 'Did I hear my name mentioned?'

'Tamsin didn't know you were going to try out our new track,' Clare said.

'Circuit, darling,' Patric said smoothly. 'Call it a circuit, please — especially in front of the TV cameras and the press.'

'Hey,' Tamsin said, 'what is all this? I thought it was just an ordinary day.'

'We need as much publicity as possible,' Patric said. 'That's why I wanted Vaughn here — you know, the new Oscar-Jade hopeful? The guy who is being tipped to win the big-time — maybe not this coming sea-son — ' he grinned at Vaughn ' — but hopefully . . . '

'In ten years' time?' Vaughn said, pulling a doleful face.

'You're racing for Oscar-Jade?' This was news to Tamsin. She stared at Vaughn. 'Your father's team?'

'My *late* father's team,' Vaughn said. 'Dad

left it all to Rafe Thorne, you know.'

'Yes.' Tamsin frowned. 'Yes, I know that. But you were with Blanchard's, the last I heard.'

'Blanchard's!' Vaughn gave a dismissive shrug as they walked on, nearing the pit garages now. 'I walked out on Tom Blanchard — or else he threw me out. I never knew which. Either way, it was by mutual consent. I didn't want him and he didn't want me, so we parted company — *not* amicably, however.'

'I'm glad you're with Oscar-Jade — at last,' Tamsin said. 'It's where you belonged. A pity, though, that your father isn't still there.'

Vaughn's voice was caustic as he answered her. 'Tam — you know that Dad and I had always been at daggers drawn. I would never have driven in his team — not while he was alive. He wouldn't have had me — and I wouldn't have made up that quarrel, not even if he'd gone down on his knees to me and begged me.'

'What a pair of obstinate hot-heads you two were,' Tamsin said.

'Yes.' Vaughn's reply was curt. His mouth set into a grim line then, and he changed the subject abruptly. 'I hope the weather keeps fine. We need some good photographs — and

151

not just stills like the ones your local girl shot yesterday.'

Tamsin glanced at Patric, wondering if he'd pick up on what Vaughn had said and mention Cass. He didn't, and the moment passed. They skirted round transporters and motor homes, colourful reminders to Tam of the times she had been at circuits in the past. And then Patric led them to a garage near the end of the pit lane, and they followed him inside. A computer was set up there, mechanics were swarming all over a white racing car, and engineers were collating data from screens and conferring together. Tam loved the atmosphere of the pit garages, but the sight of stacked tyres, trolleys, jacks and instruments all served to remind her of Monaco last year — and the race where Vaughn had almost lost his life when his car had gone up in flames.

It was a sobering thought, and looking at him now, as he and Patric headed towards the car, which was still in bits and pieces and taking up all their attention, Tamsin felt a surge of all the old feelings she'd tried to suppress during the last few months.

She wasn't being fair to Mark. She knew that. And yet Vaughn could still work the old charm on her. She only had to see him, be near him, to remember how it had been between them. But she wasn't going to be caught again, she decided. Vaughn wasn't the faithful type. Vaughn couldn't resist temptation where pretty women were concerned. She was better off without him . . .

Clare kept out of the way of everything that was going on, and Tam moved to her side. 'Do you think they'll even notice we're here?' Clare asked in a droll voice.

Tamsin gave a little laugh. 'No way,' she said. 'Women can't compete with cars — not these kind of cars anyway. You must admit, though — they are something special.'

Clare pursed her lips. 'It doesn't look much as it stands, does it?'

'But it will.' Tamsin's enthusiasm was bubbling now. 'Just wait till the wheels go on and the nose — they're beautiful, really.'

'Do you think they're extensions of a man's sexuality?' Clare was gazing at the car again.

Tamsin said, 'They're a turn-on for some girls. I do know that. But I think the drivers have a lot to do with it,' she grinned. 'Don't you?'

'I don't know many. In fact, I don't know *any* — except your Vaughn.'

'He's not *my* Vaughn,' Tamsin insisted. 'He never belonged to me in any sense of the word. He was always married to his car.'

'An interesting argument,' Clare said. 'Is it

the car that makes the man sexy, or the man *and* the car together? You know — the high-speed race, the sleek, long lines of the car, the engine thrusting it forward?'

'A bit of everything, I think.' Tamsin suddenly realized Vaughn was missing, and looked round for him. He was over by the monitors, looking at graphs and lines and things. He was fastening himself into his racing gear — white Nomex with a green slash across each sleeve. It was the first time she'd seen him in Oscar-Jade colours. The white suited him. It made him look lean and virile. In contrast to it, his face and hands took on a darker hue.

He glanced across at her and lifted his hand.

Her stomach churned. Those grey-blue eyes behind the spectacle lenses were worrying her with their absolute look of longing.

She closed her eyes briefly and turned away from him. No. This couldn't be happening, she told herself. Not again. She couldn't trust him. She'd done that once before and he'd let her down badly. She couldn't trust him. Wouldn't trust him.

'Hey, look at the car,' Clare said at her side. 'You wouldn't think they could get it ready in a couple of minutes like that, would you?'

Tamsin smiled. 'You should see them at pit stops during a race,' she said. 'Ten seconds to fill up with fuel and change all four wheels is four seconds too long for most drivers.'

'Really?' Clare's eyes widened.

Vaughn was getting into the car. He'd taken off his spectacles now, and a mechanic was standing to one side holding the steering wheel while Vaughn slid down into the seat. Somebody handed him his helmet, then his gloves. Then he clipped the steering wheel into position.

Clare said, 'Is that thing safe? The steering wheel — just popping on like that? Oughtn't somebody to tighten it up with a spanner or something?'

'It has to be like that,' Tamsin said. 'There's so little room in the cockpit that the driver can't get in and out of the car unless the wheel is easily removable. There was an accident at Monaco last year, and Vaughn's car caught fire. He was trapped inside it because he couldn't get the wheel off. If the steering wheel had happened to be a *permanent* fixture, it could have caused no end of trouble.'

Clare shuddered delicately. 'Oh, no.'

'The man he works for now — Rafe Thorne — he got the wheel off and dragged Vaughn out of the car.'

'He sounds quite a guy — this Rafe Thorne.'

'He's nice.'

'Is he here today?'

'No. We would have noticed him. I think this is just the test team. Rafe's recently got married — he'll have more important things on his mind, I suppose.'

Just then the starter motor was applied to the car and the engine sprang to life. In the confines of the concrete-sided garage the noise was deafening, and Clare gave a little scream and pressed her hands to her ears. Patric came across to her with some ear defenders and offered a pair to Tamsin too. 'Sorry about that,' he yelled. 'I forgot you two were here.'

Clare waved him aside and stumbled to the back door of the pit garage. Tam stayed where she was, though, and watched Vaughn roar out into the pit lane in the test car. She moved out onto the pit lane herself then, and watched as he disappeared round the first bend in the track.

Patric came up to her, put his hand under her elbow and said, 'Do you want to come onto the pit wall to watch? He's doing a couple of laps. The TV crew are out by the grandstand.'

Eagerly she nodded, and together they

crossed the smooth tarmac and went up the steps onto the wall.

★   ★   ★

'It went well.'

They were having lunch in the drivers' dining room part of the circuit restaurant. Clare was looking bored. 'It was noisy,' she said. 'My ears are still ringing.'

'You get used to it,' Patric said, hardly glancing at her as he and Vaughn talked across the table at each other — about graphics, chicanes, slipstreaming, Hill's strategy at the 1996 Suzuka which had won him the world championship, and then back to slipstreaming again.

Clare yawned as she pushed her plate away, the meal unfinished. 'I think I've had enough,' she said. 'What about you, Tam?'

Tamsin said, 'They'll begin testing again in half an hour . . . '

Vaughn broke in. 'We're boring you silly, aren't we?'

'Yes,' Clare said, and Tamsin broke into a laugh.

'Let you into a secret,' Vaughn lowered his voice. 'The photographers are waiting outside. How about a picture of two gorgeous girls — you and Tam.'

'Count me out,' Tamsin said quickly. 'I am *not* getting involved with motor racing again.'

'Sorry,' Patric said, 'but we've let you in for it. I promised those lads out there that if they let us have lunch in peace, we'd pose for them afterwards.'

'It's Vaughn and the car they want,' Tamsin replied with obstinacy.

'It's Vaughn, the car, and a *girl* they want,' Patric corrected her.

'Clare . . . ' Tamsin turned to the older woman.

Clare put up one perfectly manicured hand and said, 'No. Not me. I'll look like his older sister.'

Vaughn was sitting back in his chair, amusement all over his face as he watched the scene being played out before him. 'It's no use protesting, Tam,' he said at last. 'They'll start flashing their cameras the minute we get out of here so you might as well let them have a picture of you all smiling and serene, rather than with your mouth wide open and screaming at them to stop. You know what these bods are like — if they can get a gorgeous woman looking at her worst they will! And you wouldn't want to be plastered all over the tabloids looking like a shrew, would you?'

'I don't want plastering all over the

tabloids, full stop,' Tam stated. And it was true. All at once she thought of Mark, and made the decision there and then to phone him that night, tell him of the spur-of-the-moment trip to Bramsdown, and the possibility of her being caught on camera there. Then she stopped panicking and reasoned things out logically. Mark didn't *own* her, did he? Why should she have to account to him for her whereabouts? And why shouldn't she spend the day with Vaughn if she wanted to? She'd left her former life behind. She hadn't asked for Vaughn to come back into her new life. It had happened. This was only one day. And after today, she wouldn't be seeing him again.

She sighed. 'Okay,' she said. 'But nothing intense. No kisses. No arms entwined or that sort of thing.'

Vaughn spread his hands expressively. 'Is someone likely to be jealous?' he asked in a teasing voice.

Tamsin felt her face flushing, and she answered angrily, 'My life is my own.'

'Then,' Vaughn said, 'there's nothing to worry about, is there?'

9

Tamsin decided to walk over the heath into Alderwood a couple of days later, as January was drawing to a frosty close. Snow had been forecast again, but as yet there was no sign of it. It was too cold for snow, she thought, as she pushed her gloved hands into the pockets of her warm quilt-lined jacket and strode out along one of the many narrow paths through the bracken.

There was precious little in the way of life braving the wintry weather, but she halted for a while to watch a hen-harrier flying low, swooping slowly, its soft grey body almost merging with the ground so that only the paler underside was visible as it twisted and turned. Gracefully it glided upwards into the air again, silver wings lifting it high on a current of air blowing inland from the sea. She followed it with her gaze as it drifted and dived, searching for prey, until the last she saw of it was a flash of its underside again and the black wing-tips disappearing into the point where stunted black gorse merged with purple moor grass at the edge of the dunes.

She realized, from the cold creeping up off the ground into her feet and legs, that she had wasted far more time than she'd intended. With a last look towards the long grey line of the sea, some distance away, she turned and headed towards Alderwood, seeing the huddle of grey and red rooftops half shrouded in silent misty stillness, half a mile away.

A shiver crept over her, a clammy hand of ice trickling its way down her spine, as she had that feeling again — the feeling that somebody was watching her.

She stared all round her before she began walking again. There was nothing. Nobody. Unless . . . She whirled round to face the way she'd come. There'd been a sound. Something had made a noise. Her breath froze in her throat as she listened. It came again, this time from the direction of Alderwood. Her head jerked round. A figure was coming towards her out of the murk and the mist. She wanted to turn and run, but couldn't. She was too cold, too scared. She knew the real meaning then of being *rooted* to the spot.

'Ta-a-am!' The figure was huddled up in dark clothing. One arm was waving back and forth now, though. It was a man, and as she watched he started to run towards her. And then she caught the glint of the sky reflecting on something above that muffled-up collar.

She let her breath out in a long sigh. 'Vaughn!' Vaughn with his steel-framed spectacles. She began to laugh softly, and heard the frost crunching under his booted feet as he came up to her.

'You scared me.'

'That's why I yelled and waved,' he said, puffing out clouds of breath as he stood in front of her. 'I thought you might have heard of the headless horseman who's supposed to haunt the place.'

'You're joking!'

'No.' Laughter burst easily from his lips. 'I am not joking. Clare Faulkener's been giving me all the jokesy-folksy tales about this part of Suffolk, and the headless horseman is definitely our local ghost.'

'I don't believe in ghosts.'

'Not even in me? A ghost from your past?' he wanted to know.

'You're not a ghost.' She grinned at him. 'You're a bad penny, but not a ghost.'

'Ouch! I asked for that. Are you always going to look on me as something bad in your life that keeps turning up?'

'I hope not. I hope you won't keep turning up. I came to Suffolk to stay with a friend and

162

try and get my life straightened out. I can't do that if my past keeps catching up with me, can I?'

He came straight to the point. 'I was a fool to let you go, Tam.'

'Look — I'm cold. Do you think we can start walking towards Alderwood? I need to do some shopping,' she said. 'And I'd appreciate it if you'd keep off the sweet talk — it just doesn't work with me.'

They turned their steps towards the town and walked, side by side — Tamsin on the path and Vaughn in the bracken.

'Why are you walking there? To Alderwood?'

'They said on local radio this morning that we were going to get some snow,' she said, 'and I hate driving in snow.' She gave a little grimace of distaste. 'I was cut off at Stratton End last time it snowed.'

'I'd like to see your house.'

'Oh, it isn't mine exactly. I'm only renting it for a twelve-month period for a start.' She glanced across at him, wondering how much Clare Faulkener had told him about her. 'It seemed a good idea at the time, taking it on with that herb garden attached. I might yet make a bit of money from selling my herbs to Clare Faulkener.'

'She mentioned that you and she were

doing a deal,' he said conversationally.

Cautiously, remembering what Craig Andrews had said about checking her out, she said, 'Just how much does Clare know about us, Vaughn? Have you told her any of the gory details?'

'No,' he said. 'I don't go bandying details around — gory or otherwise — regarding my private life. It wouldn't do me any good — career-wise — to do that.'

'Would she check up on me, do you think?'

He looked at her, puzzled. 'Why do you ask that?'

'Oh . . . ' She lifted her shoulders in a shrug. 'Just something somebody said. Nothing important, really. I just like to know exactly what bits of my life are common property.'

'She could have run a credit check, I suppose.' He was frowning now as he glanced at her.

'Oh, well — my credit's good.'

'You're scared somebody might get to know that you and I were a bit more than just good friends, Tam?'

'Somebody has already come to that conclusion.' She met his gaze as he walked beside her. 'I don't want it getting around that I'm anybody's for the asking, though.'

'You were never that.'

'No!' She uttered a harsh laugh. 'I was crazy about you. I didn't need much persuading, did I?'

'It was mutual.'

'No,' she said in a determined voice, 'it was never that. I was just available. You never cared for me like I did for you.'

'I was a fool,' he said. 'I didn't recognize gold when I'd got it — right there in the palm of my hand. We could start again, Tam.'

His words hit her like a bucketful of cold water. She shivered, pushed her hands deeper in her pockets as she tramped at his side, and said, 'Why are you staying here? At Alderwood? It's a dead-end place for somebody like you.'

'I'm looking for somewhere to settle down,' he said. 'It came as a bit of a shock when Dad left me sweet nothing in his will. I'd always assumed one day that I'd go back to live at home in Northampton.'

His words bothered her, and made her nervous. 'You're not thinking of putting roots down here, are you?' She didn't want that. Didn't want him on her doorstep. She was done with the past.

They were almost at the end of the heath now. Through the mist she could see pale lights gleaming out from shop windows.

Beneath her feet, the springy turf was turning rough and the pathway was widening out.

'I doubt I'll stay here.' He kicked at a boulder, his shoulders hunched and his jaw thrust out. 'I like somewhere a bit more lively than Alderwood.'

As they walked across the last bit of green and onto the High Street, he stopped and said, 'Tam — I meant what I said. I'd like for us to start again. I've really missed you these past months . . .'

'Yeah! I bet you have.' She didn't need this. She just wanted to get on with her life now.

'Tam, I swear . . .'

'No,' she said. 'Don't swear *anything*, and don't promise anything either. I'm not looking for an affair, Vaughn. I don't want to get involved with you again. When are you leaving Alderwood?'

'Tam!' His hand shot out and fastened on her arm. 'Tam — are you made of stone? Have you forgotten what was between us? We could have had a kid by now.'

'Sex,' she said. 'That's all there was between us, Vaughn. And as for the kid . . .' She gave a harsh laugh. 'It wasn't to be. I had that fall, and that was the end of my pregnancy. If I'm entirely honest, I can't say I was broken-hearted.'

'But the baby . . .'

166

'You never knew about that until it was too late,' she retorted. And he wouldn't have cared anyway. 'You never came back to pick up the pieces of my life — or even help me put them together again, did you? It never entered your head I might need somebody to give me some support over what had happened.'

'I've told you,' he said. 'I was a damn fool. I've come to my senses a bit more since Dad died.'

Knowing she was sounding unfeeling and bitchy, she said, 'It's taken you all of two months, then?'

His face flushed a dull red, but he still kept hold of her arm. 'You don't know what it's like,' he said. 'You can't even begin to know how I feel because I never made up that quarrel with Dad before he died.'

'I don't want to know,' she said. 'I don't want anything to do with you, Vaughn.'

'They said you were glad when you lost the kid . . . '

'Did they?' she said angrily. 'Well, if that's what you've heard, that's what you must believe.'

'Were you glad?' His gaze was fixed on her face.

She stared back at him. After a few moments' hesitation she said, 'Yes. I was glad.

167

I didn't want anything around that reminded me of you.'

'I never dreamed you could be so hard.'

She laughed out loud. 'Me? Hard?'

'Not to care about my baby . . . our baby.'

'I hardly knew it was a baby,' she said. 'I was only a few weeks into pregnancy.'

'All the same . . . '

'All the same?' She raised an eyebrow at him. 'Are you shocked because I had no maternal feelings? Or are you shocked because it was *your* baby? Something you'd made — something you could chalk up on your scoreboard as if it had no more meaning than the winning of a race?'

'You hard bitch.' His hand fell away from her.

'Yes,' she said. 'As far as you're concerned, I *am* a hard bitch. You ditched me, Vaughn. You used me and then you walked off and left me, and I'll never forgive you for that.'

Dully, he said, 'I won't take no for an answer. I want you, Tam. I want you like I've never wanted any girl in my life before.'

'And you've had plenty, haven't you?' she said mildly.

'I'm not denying it. But I'm going somewhere now, Tam. I'm with the Oscar-Jade team and Rafe Thorne has plans for me.'

'I wish you luck,' she said, and knew she

really meant it. Racing was his life. Girls had always taken second place to it, and she knew he was at a low ebb just now. Oscar Herrick, his father, had died, and he was suffering pangs of guilt and wanted her to smooth them away. Well, she wasn't going to. She couldn't. And she didn't even want to try.

'I won't let you go — just like that. Not this time, Tam. There's nobody else in your life, at Alderwood, is there?'

She thought of Mark, thought long and hard, then found the courage to look Vaughn in the eye and say, 'No. There's nobody else — at Alderwood.'

'You'll let me see you again, then?'

She shrugged. 'Look — it's too cold to hang around like this.'

'I'll call you.'

'If you like,' she said, just wanting him to go, and feeling glad that she had been on her way over to Alderwood when she'd met him. If she'd been at home, at Herb House, he would have found her there, and then they would have been closeted there, nice and cosy, and . . .

And — *nothing*, she told herself. It just wasn't on any more — a friendship between her and Vaughn. It wouldn't stay as such. Friendship. It would have to move on, either one way or the other, and she didn't want a repeat of heartache like she'd experienced at Heronsea last year.

'Just go,' she said softly.

'Can I kiss you?'

Her head jerked up. 'Why?'

He hunched his shoulders up. 'Old times' sake?'

'Forget it,' she snapped.

He took a step towards her, fastened his hands on her shoulders and bent his head down to hers. The kiss was hard; it took her breath away and made her dizzily aware that she still had some fond feelings for him. She was glad they were out in the open, with shoppers around. In that moment it would have been so easy to respond to him, to put her arms round him and feel his hard body up against her. It would have been easy, in a more intimate place, to evoke the past and say to hell with the future. The kiss was over in seconds, though, and then he spun away from her and left her standing there, tingling all over at his touch, and watching him jogging at a gentle pace through the few shoppers that had braved the cold morning.

She fought down all the old feelings that kiss had rekindled, let out a long sigh and looked around her. Then she stiffened. Standing over by the post office, where she and Patric had had their first encounter, someone was leaning lazily against the wall watching her.

He gave no sign of recognition, even though she could feel his gaze fastened on her. And for some reason that had nothing to do with the weather she felt chilled to the bone.

She turned away and hurried to the bread shop. And when she came out a few minutes later there was no sign of Craig Andrews anywhere.

She was shaken, though, and knew that nothing on earth would persuade her to walk back home across the lonely heath on a morning such as this while he was around.

'Cass,' she muttered under her breath. 'I wonder if Cass is at home.' And, trying to forget all about Vaughn and all about Craig Andrews, she set off towards Stride Common.

★　★　★

Cass was at home. 'Like you — ' she grinned as they sipped steaming hot coffee ' — I decided not to risk the car. I heard the severe weather warning on the radio this morning, and I have plenty of work to keep me busy here — three films at least that have to be processed before the end of the week.'

171

'I've seen Vaughn.' Tam sat down in a straight-backed chair at the kitchen table.

'He's in town, isn't he? Staying with the Faulkeners. I've seen him and Clare Faulkener walking on the beach. He must have something going for him — she's never done that before. She hates it here, you know.'

'I was conned into accompanying them to the Bramsdown circuit . . . '

Interested, Cass asked, 'What did you think of it?'

Tam glared at her. 'Look — what does it matter? Vaughn's here and that's a problem for me. I don't want him in my life again.'

'Is he bothering you?'

'His very presence bothers me.' Tam slammed her mug down on the table. 'What am I supposed to do when I meet up with him — accidentally, I might add — on the heath, and he walks me back to Alderwood and then kisses me?'

'Did you enjoy it?' Cass sat down opposite her and looked at her over the rim of her coffee mug.

'No!'

'That was said a bit too quickly,' Cass said. 'You could have thought about it for a couple of minutes.'

Tamsin realized her friend was taking this all too lightly. 'You're perky this morning,' she growled. 'I take it your grand passion is still blossoming?'

Cass put her mug down slowly and said, 'No. It's over.'

Tamsin let her hands fall into her lap as she leaned back and said, 'Oh, hell! Trust me to put my foot in it.'

'You had to know some time. And you were against this particular grand passion right from the start.'

Quietly, Tamsin said, 'You can't grab your happiness at someone else's expense.'

'Oh, come off it,' Cass said impatiently. 'Clare doesn't care two hoots about him. Patric. You don't have to go all holy and righteous on me. Haven't you ever done anything wrong?'

'Yes,' Tamsin said. 'You know I have.'

'Well, we're all human.' Cass fiddled with the handle of her mug and looked down at the tablecloth.

Tamsin reached across and laid her hand on one of Cass's. 'I'm sorry,' she said. 'I know you cared for him.'

'I *loved* him, dammit. I didn't just *care* for him.' Cass's eyes were blazing as they met Tam's across the table. 'I *still* love him. But there's no future in it for either of us. I put an end to it. I couldn't go on like that.'

'We're a pair of . . . '

'Clowns!' Cass said, holding up one hand. 'Don't go and label us as something utterly evil. We're just two misguided fools.' She pulled a face. 'How about Mark?' she wanted to know. 'When are you going to see him again?'

Tamsin shrugged. 'I don't know. He phones me regularly. I'm getting the herb garden into shape, though, and I think I'm going to be okay there.'

'Just so long as you keep on the right side of Clare Faulkener.'

The words were bitter. Tamsin pulled her hand back from Cass and picked up her coffee again. 'I have to do that,' she said. 'I can't survive without Faulkener's Herbs and Spices.'

'And if you don't survive?' The question was loaded with meaning.

'I don't know. I honestly don't know, Cass.'

'Between us, we both need the Faulkeners.' Cass gave a wry grimace, and Tamsin could see she wasn't far off tears.

'Can I stay?' she asked. 'I've got some bread. We could have thick slices of toast for tea.'

Cass nodded mistily. 'You can stay,' she said. 'Stay the night if you want to.'

'If it snows you'll have a permanent lodger.'

Cass managed a smile of sorts. 'If it snows

I'll have a chaperon, with you in attendance, and maybe Patric will take the hint and keep away. It's awful, you know, having him living just down the road — *and* having his parents living next door to me. It's been so convenient for him to call in on me.'

'I can always keep out of the way if he calls.'

'No,' Cass said quietly. 'Don't do that. I'm finished with him. I really mean that. He's a married man, and I was a prize idiot to ever have got myself mixed up with him.'

Tam felt at home in Cass's little house. 'Give me something to do,' she said, 'while you see to those films.'

'Make some lunch,' Cass said. 'Then, if you feel like it, there's a bit more typing to do on that book of mine.'

10

In her second-floor office, Clare Faulkener waited for Craig Andrews to come to her. It was seven in the evening and the rest of the staff had all gone home a couple of hours ago; security had been given strict orders not to disturb her. As was routine at month-end, she and Craig always worked late. *He* was in his own office downstairs, checking ledger entries at the moment. Even out of working hours, it looked better if they stuck to routine. There was still security around the place, as well as the cleaners. She knew Craig wouldn't be coming up to her until he'd printed out the figures. He'd ring her, though, just as soon as he saw the cleaners leaving.

Her phone rang, and she smiled as she picked it up. Routine! How she loved it in this area of her life — the routine, the knowledge that everything worked out as it should — especially at month-end.

'They've gone.'

'And Stan Weston?' She had to be sure that the security guard had locked up and was now on a tour of the factory — a tour that would take in his supper break and a long cosy phone call home to his wife on the Despatch Office phone.

Her heart quickened a beat at Craig's soft, seductive laugh. 'Everything's going according to plan. One day, though, our Mr Weston will discover his phone calls have been logged. I'd like to see his face if you present him with a hefty bill for those nightly calls home.'

She said, 'I wouldn't be so cruel.'

'No?'

'Why should I? It gives us the opportunity to be together for a while — at least once a month.' She lowered her voice to a husky whisper. 'So, what are you waiting for? Why aren't you up here with me . . . ?'

The phone went dead, and she replaced the receiver slowly, almost immediately hearing the hum of the small passenger lift that would bring him directly into her suite.

As was their usual procedure, he came straight into the office, leaving the outer grille of the lift open. That way, nobody could summon it from downstairs. It was a safety measure that the outer grille had to be firmly closed before the lift could be operated. He placed a stack of envelopes on her desk, ignoring her as he did so, and then strewed balance sheets haphazardly across the tidy surface.

'We're *too* damned careful,' he said then, at last, as he faced her and she ran into his arms.

'We can never be *too* careful, Craig . . . ' She lifted her face for his kiss and felt a thrill of aching run through her entire body as his head swooped down and his lips fastened on hers.

There was a second desk in the large room — one that Craig often used in the daytime — legitimately — when there was no need for caution. Still holding her, and still savouring her mouth beneath his, he edged her across to it. It was relatively clear of the usual office clutter.

She felt the hard wood of the desk-top collide with the back of her thighs and he closed in on her so his body was taut and tight up against her.

'Did you have to wear such a straight skirt?' he muttered.

Her laughter was low and throaty. 'I wanted to get you in the mood — and all day you've been slobbering. Every time I've walked past you downstairs you couldn't take your eyes off my legs . . . and my body . . . '

His hands slid down the length of her body, and urgently he started tugging at the skirt. It was skintight, and resisted his efforts to raise it.

She laughed again. 'Naughty boy. Don't be so impatient.'

He tried other tactics then, as she'd known he would. Craig Andrews might have his faults, but he wasn't a brute or a roughneck. He was well practised in the art of seduction and, although he was breathing heavily, his hands were gentle as they unfastened the waistband of her skirt, then unzipped it slowly as he gyrated his hips against her and made mock thrusting movements. He eased the garment down her long legs and let it slide with a swish of its silk lining down to the carpeted floor.

She held him off for as long as it took her to step out of it, and while she did so he was giving his attention to divesting her of her long-sleeved top. He made short work of the fiddling little pearl buttons, and the blouse was soon just a scarlet splodge on the office floor.

She heard his deep, indrawn breath then, as he held her away from him, pushing her harder against the desk as his smoke-grey eyes took in every inch of her, from the scanty champagne bra to the matching lace panties under which she knew could be seen the dark sable suspender belt.

She crossed her stockinged legs and gazed at him. She was cool. She was in charge — for the time being. It wouldn't always be like this, though, and she cherished the moment while she held the upper hand and began to undress him.

He helped her — kicking away his shoes, whipping off socks and trousers while she concentrated on his top half.

'I like to see your boxers bulging,' she whispered at last.

'You're a sadist,' he said, dragging her towards him. 'They're uncomfortable as hell when . . . '

'You shouldn't get steamed up so quickly.' Her laugh was breathless.

He stripped her of her bra in one easy movement, and his hands were on her breasts then, teasing them with exquisite tortuous circlings of each rosy tip with his thumbs. Her back arched as she thrust herself forward, gasping his name. 'Craig . . . Craig . . . '

'It's been a long time.' His voice was hoarse with longing, and one hand slid down to snake round her waist, pulling her closer. 'Three weeks! Hell, Clare, we've got to get something better than this sorted out . . . '

She forced herself to be practical. 'We can't

do anything at the moment . . . '

His lips ground against hers. While he quieted her he got rid of the panties and she wriggled her ankles free of them, almost collapsing on the desk as she did so, and pulling him on top of her at the same time.

They fell together in laughter, and she was spread-eagled on the surface of the desk as he raised himself above her. 'What about the stockings?' she choked as he forced her legs apart.

'I like the stockings,' he growled. 'Leave them on.'

Laughter bubbled up inside her again. 'This desk's hard . . . '

His head was directly above hers now, and his sleek hair fell forward, almost touching her forehead. 'So — am — I,' he said.

'You don't have to tell me. Actions speak louder . . . '

He thrust into her.

Again her back arched, her nipples peaked, and she closed her eyes as, his hands free from holding her now, he began a sensuous exploration of her, coupled with a steady but controlled thrusting of his body.

She felt herself spinning in a spiral of longing. Three weeks was a long time and Patric . . . She pushed all thought of Patric from her mind. All that mattered was the here and now. All she cared about was Craig, touching her, holding her, crazily driving her mad with that deliberate holding back he was so good at. All that filled her mind, her heart, and her libidinous writhing body, were the waves of throbbing ecstasy pulsing through her, and the man — the young, virile man — above her who, with his body and his expertise, was making her young again. Young and in love with love, and eager to respond to him.

The desk was uncomfortable. She'd have bruises for a week, she knew that, but she didn't care. Patric wouldn't see them. Damn Patric . . . It had never been like this with Patric . . .

Her head jerked from side to side as the rhythm of that body ramming into her increased. She cried out at the intensity of emotion washing over her. Tears streamed from her eyes. It was so good . . . so good . . . to feel like this . . . alive again . . .

In a screaming whisper she flung her hands above her head and cried out, 'Now! Now! Now!'

He dropped his hands down onto her wrists and pinioned her to the desk. His breathing was jerky. She opened her eyes and gazed up into his face, seeing beads of sweat breaking out on his forehead.

Everything inside her reared to meet his final taking of her, and the climax burst upon them simultaneously. It was always like this — always . . .

'So good . . . ' she murmured, stretching when he'd released her. 'Mmm. So good . . . '

Softly, sitting cross-legged on the desk at her side some little time later, he said, 'Such a little word? Good?'

'Why spoil it with thinking up big words?' she said, easing up until she too was sitting, knees curled under her, facing him.

'We're great together.' His eyes were brooding. 'Why can't we make it permanent? When are you going to come to your senses and leave him?'

Guardedly, she said, 'You know when.'

'When I've made a million. Yes, you've told me before — but it's only a matter of time, so why waste *time*?'

'How long?' she asked. 'How long, Craig?'

'The matter is in hand,' he said, in an off-putting way.

'It is?'

He nodded. Enigmatically, he said, 'It's all a matter of discovering what the market wants, and then giving the market what it's prepared to pay for.'

Clare frowned. 'And which particular

market are we talking about?' she wanted to know.

'Cause and effect,' he said mysteriously. 'Give them a cause for wanting something badly enough, and they'll pay.'

'A million? They'll pay a million?' Frankly, she was amazed that he'd even started *thinking* about making his first million.

His eyes were amused. 'They'll pay,' he said. 'If they want something badly enough — they'll pay.'

His words were hard. Callous, almost. She felt a flicker of fear run through her. 'You're not into anything . . . dangerous? Not drugs? I won't have that, Craig. Nothing illegal.'

He pulled a face and shrugged his bare shoulders. 'It depends,' he said, 'on what you consider dangerous. But, no, my sweet, it isn't drugs. I can promise you that.'

'Drugs,' she said quickly, 'would scare me. Promise me you won't touch anything like that. You wouldn't be such a fool, would you . . . ?'

'Drugs!' His laughter was high and, to her mind, slightly deranged. 'Is that all you can think of? Look, I've told you, I'm not stupid — and drugs are mere peanuts compared to what I have in mind. No — I want a quicker turn-over than drugs would bring me.'

'Craig — be careful . . . ' All at once she

was worried. He seemed so sure of himself, so confident and in control. It worried her. She'd never seen this side of him before. She wondered uneasily why she had started all this.

'You laid down the conditions,' he reminded her, easing off the desk and starting to get dressed. 'You were the one who suggested a million.'

'But not if it's going to be dangerous . . .'

He made a sound in his throat that was half-laugh, half-snort. 'Did *you* get where you are today, my sweet, by backing off at the first obstacle?' he asked in a derisive tone.

'No, but . . .'

'But! *But*, my dear girl, is a smaller word than *good*! And I'm not going to let a little word like 'but' get in my way.' He pulled on his trousers, buttoned on his shirt again. He ran his fingers through his hair to tidy it, and fixed his tie and jacket so it looked as if they'd never been anywhere but hanging effortlessly on him for the past half-hour, then he straightened and said, 'Leave it, Clare. Get off my back, will you? I know what I'm doing, okay? But one thing's sure — you'll keep to your bargain. I'll make sure of that. I want you. And I'll remind you again — you made the conditions. I'll come up with the million, never fear.'

'It's you I'm fearful for.'

He shook his head, smiling. Then he walked over to her, dropped a kiss on her forehead, and tilted her head back with one finger under her chin. 'Say it,' he ordered softly. 'Say you meant it, and that you'll ditch dear Patric when I come to you with a million pounds in my hands.'

Scared now, inwardly scared and outwardly afraid of showing him she was, she said, 'The answer's yes. I meant what I said. And I don't renege on my promises.'

He grabbed at the dark hair still bunched up behind her head in its coiled, sleek roll, only slightly untidy from their romp. He jerked her head back even further as he pulled on it. And then his lips came down on hers again, hard and masterful. He was hurting her as he forced her backwards, and his mouth claimed hers in the kiss of the victor.

'That's all I wanted to know,' he said then, letting her go so suddenly that she almost toppled sideways off the desk. 'All I wanted to know, my kitten.'

And he turned on his heel and strode back across the office towards the lift, pausing only a second or two to throw her an approving glance and say, 'Get dressed, lover. Stan

186

Weston will have finished his supper by now. He'll be waiting to set the alarms for the night and lock up. And it might not be a clever move — letting him see you looking like that.

11

The postman didn't often knock at her door. Today, though, he did, and Tam was left holding a heavy flattish parcel, about eight inches square, with Mark's handwriting on the front of it.

She opened it when she got back inside the house. It was too cold to stay outside pondering what it might be. The sun was high, but there was no warmth in it yet. It was merely making steam rise up from her front fence and letting the postman's footprints leave some impression as he walked back across the frozen grass.

'A Valentine I should think,' he'd said when she'd opened the door to him.

'It's early if it is.' She'd grinned at him and signed for the parcel.

'Another three days — but you know what we love-lorn men are like where this sort of thing's concerned.' With a grin and a wave he'd left her, and hurried back to his pushbike.

Inside the house, she tore off the wrapping paper. Under the first layer was another one, this time of bubble-wrap plastic, packed round a stout cardboard box.

She balanced it in her hand. It was quite heavy — obviously not chocolates!

She was intrigued, and foraged through a mass of sticky tape, bubble-wrap, and then the box.

A heavy object slid out onto the table — also wrapped in another layer of bubble-wrap — with a crash, and she jumped back, alarmed. Then she picked it up, peeled off the plastic, and laughed.

'A horseshoe! A real iron horseshoe!'

Her lips tilted into a wide smile. 'Complete with caked-on mud,' she muttered. 'Trust Mark!'

There was a handwritten note.

> *Roses are red,*
> *Violets are blue,*
> *A card wouldn't say*
> *What I wanted to you.*

Mark then went on to explain that he knew it was corny, but he'd always been hopeless at poetry — even at school. He said he'd looked in all the shops at Rothwold, hoping to buy her something really original, but there had been nothing.

I was on my way home when I saw this thing lying in the road, and it seemed like an omen, so I stopped the car, picked it up and decided to send it to you. They throw horseshoes at weddings, don't they? This, by the way, is a proposal. One day I'll sweep you off your feet and refuse to take no for an answer. Till then, Tam, remember I love you.'

She got on the phone to him immediately. When he answered, she said, 'It's not horseshoes they throw at weddings, you nut. It's confetti.'

'I know,' he said. 'It was a deliberate ploy to get you to ring me.'

'I would have rung anyway, and thanked you for your — slightly off-beat Valentine.'

'I sent it early as well.'

She felt her face creasing into a big grin. 'I know that.'

'Have you sent me a card?'

'No. Do you want one? I don't really believe in Valentines. I think they're soppy and slushy and yuk.'

'If you don't want to send me a card, I'll get the old rose out,' he said off-handedly.

'Which rose?'

'The one you gave me on the beach up here — after you'd jumped off those shallow cliffs and given my blood pressure the fright of its life. Don't you remember?'

She laughed merrily. 'Yes, now you mention it, I do remember. I had a rose tucked into my dress. I always seemed to be wearing roses or some flower or other in those days, didn't I?'

'You gave it to me and then told me nobody else would ever have given me a rose, so I kept it, and when it died I placed it inside a book and squashed it.'

'It's called 'pressing', not 'squashing',' she said. 'Haven't you ever heard of pressed flowers? And tell me truly now — *hadn't* anyone ever given you a rose before I did?' She didn't know whether to believe him or not about the keeping it in a book bit.

'No. But it should have been the other way round. It's usually the man who gives flowers to the woman, isn't it?'

'We don't have to be conventional, do we?'

From two hundred miles away she heard him sigh heavily. 'We're certainly not that, are we?'

'Conventional's boring, Mark.' Her voice hardened. 'We don't have to do all the same old things that other couples do.'

'Like proposing marriage?' he asked mildly. 'I get the feeling that marriage is too conventional for you too — the way you keep turning me down. I'm getting a tiny bit fed up with the same negative answer I keep getting from you.'

'Why don't you think up a different screwball stratagem, then?'

'Like what?'

'I don't know.' It was true. She didn't know what it was that she wanted from Mark. Maybe she needed sweeping off her feet. Maybe she needed Mark to turn into the strong, silent type who would master her and be firm with her. In her heart, though, she knew that what attracted her to him was the fact that he was gentle, and kind, and undemanding.

'Tam!' His voice broke into her thoughts, 'Tam, tell me you're at least still interested.'

She laughed again, softly this time, admitting softly, 'I loved the Valentine, Mark. You always manage to surprise me.'

'I'm still in the running, then?'

'There's nobody else taken a hold of my heart, if that's what you're asking. But I don't want to settle down yet.' Suddenly she became serious. 'Mark — I don't want to lead you on. I'm not a flirt.'

'Can I come down there and see you? Stay with you for a couple of days?'

Did she want him down here? Tam gazed round the place, peeping through the open kitchen door at the little front room, so neat and tidy and full of somebody else's furniture. It was hers now. Hers for a while anyway. Did she want to share it? Did she really want Mark here?

'Just for the weekend?' he said, not grovelling at all, merely asking a simple question that she realized it would be boorish and perverse of her to rebuff.

'If you really enjoy being buried alive in the countryside in winter,' she said, 'come down and suffer all the inconveniences of living at the end of a track with just the marshes and the heath and a couple of dozen Brent geese for company.'

'Friday!' he said. 'I'll finish early and drive down in the afternoon. So don't do anything stupid like inviting your Cass friend over, will you? I want to see you and talk to you and eat and drink with you for a complete weekend. I want to let you know what you're missing so you'll come to believe you can't manage without me. Okay?'

'Okay!' she said. 'I'm looking forward to seeing you.'

'Take an aspirin,' he said.

Perplexed, she stared at the phone. 'Why an aspirin?'

'You must be ill,' he replied sharply. 'You never argued with me over the visit.'

On the day Mark was due to arrive, a florist's van drew up outside Herb House and Tamsin was handed a gorgeous display of daffodils, tulips and forget-me-nots arranged in a decorative basket with a huge yellow satin bow of ribbon on its handle. There was a heart-shaped card tucked in against the flowers, but it wasn't till she got inside the house that she read who it was from.

Tam sucked in her breath and muttered, 'Vaughn Herrick! How dare you do this to me?' And her cheeks burned with hot anger as she stared at the blooms, then dumped the basket on her kitchen table.

They were beautiful, there was no doubt about that, but it was a complete let down, discovering who they were from, when at first sight she'd thought they were from Mark.

'Mark!' She realized he'd soon be here. And what was he going to think when he saw flowers from Vaughn on the table? Ought she to hide them? She bit down hard on her bottom lip and looked wildly round the room. Where could you *hide* something so obvious? It was a blatant and showy display, and, thinking logically about it, why should she hide it? Mark didn't own her. She cursed Vaughn Herrick all the same, for putting her in this predicament.

In the end, she decided to leave the display

on the kitchen table. The flowers brightened the room anyway, and she wasn't going to read anything into them. Everybody — absolutely *everybody* — was sending flowers to girls this week. It didn't mean anything. She turned her back on them and walked over to the kitchen sink where, leaning up against the window pane, she'd placed Mark's battered old horseshoe. She picked it up, looked at it, and ran her fingers over its roughness as she thought about him, and knew she was counting the hours till he got here. Mark always managed to do the right thing. Mark was always there for her . . .

'To hell with Vaughn Herrick,' she snapped, putting the horseshoe back in its place, and then for the rest of the morning she tried her hardest to ignore the colourful display of flowers on her table.

* * *

She heard the car and went to the front window to look out. Mark had parked as near to the house as he could get on the little lane that led nowhere. He swung an over-large sports bag out of the back of the car, shoved a folded-up newspaper under his arm, and turned to look at the house.

Her hand flew to her mouth at the look on

195

his face. It was like thunder!

When he came into the house it was obvious to her that something was wrong. He flung the newspaper onto the table and glared at the basket of flowers, then dumped his sports bag on the floor and said, 'I won't unpack. Not yet. You might not want me to stay when I've said what I'm going to say!'

'I invited you,' she said, taken aback somewhat. 'What's wrong, Mark?'

He picked up the newspaper and found one of the sports pages, then slammed it down on the table.

'Why didn't you tell me? he said, pointing at it. 'This photo was taken more than a fortnight ago — it says so in the report — yet you never mentioned you'd been to the new Bramsdown circuit with Vaughn Herrick.'

So that was it! She glanced down at the page he'd indicated and saw the photograph — a picture of all four of them — herself, Vaughn, Patric and Clare — leaving the Bramsdown circuit restaurant. Anger surged up inside her as she asked herself what right he had to question where she went and who she went with. And why should he think she ought to have mentioned it to him?

Fighting down her rapidly rising temper, she said, 'You don't own me, Mark. I don't have to report my every move to you.'

He stared at her, then closed his eyes briefly and tilted his head back as if he were unutterably weary. When he looked at her again his manner had altered. 'Tam — I'm sorry,' he said. 'But when I saw that picture, I just saw red!'

'You're perhaps beginning to understand why I don't want to tie myself up with you,' she said in a tense voice. 'I need a life of my own, Mark. I don't want to be fettered like a dog on a leash. I'm not a pet, I'm a person, and I think it's about time you started to realize that, and treat me as an equal.'

He pulled out one of the kitchen chairs and sank down on it. 'Damn!' he said. 'Why do I have to be so crass?'

She moved nearer to him, pulled out a chair too and sat facing him. 'I didn't go to Bramsdown *just* with Vaughn,' she said. 'If you look at the photo you'll see there are also two other people there with us — Mr and Mrs Faulkener. Clare is the woman who owns Faulkener's Herbs and Spices, and Patric is a shareholder in Bramsdown. They invited me to go down there with them, and Vaughn had been staying with them so he went too. Heavens, Mark, we didn't even travel alone together, Vaughn and I. Patric Faulkener drove us, and it wasn't all that pleasant a journey. Clare spent ages talking to her office on her mobile phone on the way down. That woman is a workaholic — goodness knows how she manages to drive her own car if she always has that phone in her hand.'

Mark thumped his forehead with one clenched fist. 'And Clare Faulkener is the woman you're selling herbs to. Now I get the message.'

'She's my only source of income at the moment — I don't want to get on the wrong side of her, and when she rang up and invited me . . . well, I just felt as if I couldn't refuse.'

'Tam! What can I say?' He looked so crestfallen she actually found herself feeling sorry for him.

It wasn't going to work like that, though. She hardened her heart against him. Mark had to learn that she wasn't some meek little push-over. Taking a deep breath, she said, 'And before you read the card on those flowers in the middle of the table, I'll tell you — they're from Vaughn Herrick.'

Savagely he said, 'I guessed they would be — as soon as I walked in and saw them.'

'And of course they made you angrier than ever.'

'Something like that.' He pushed his chair away from the table and stood up, then walked over to the stove and warmed his hands at it. Without turning round to look at her, he said, 'So tell me — you're the expert on these matters — what meaning do you read into those — those . . . ' he made an impatient gesture with one hand ' . . . those yellow and red things.'

'The meaning of daffodils,' she said calmly, 'is unrequited love.'

He moved round to face her at that, his features relaxing a little for the first time since he'd entered the cottage. 'Thank goodness for that.' He actually managed a grim smile.

'Tulips,' she said, clasping her hands together on the table, 'are a declaration of love.'

The smile vanished. 'The bastard . . . '

'And forget-me-nots . . . '

'Oh, spare me the details,' he stormed, coming back across the kitchen to her. 'I don't want to know. I can guess what forget-me-nots mean, can't I? Their very name gives their meaning away.'

'Look,' she said, 'are you staying or not? And would you like a drink?'

'I'm staying,' he said, 'and you can relax. I'm not going to blow my top again — and just to show you I mean that, *I'll* make the drinks.'

She rested her elbows on the table, then supported her chin on her hands and grinned at him. 'One thing I like about you — you never stay mad for long, do you?'

He picked up the kettle and filled it with water from the tap. 'I blow up easily.' He plugged in the kettle, took two mugs out of a cupboard and spooned instant coffee into them, then came back to the table and stood watching her as she sat there. He leaned against the table, resting his hands on the hard wooden top, one either side of him. 'The flowers are nice,' he said. 'You can't blame flowers for just being there, can you?' With a wicked look at her then, he went on, 'And they're not responsible for the sod who sent them, are they?'

She picked up the newspaper, made it into a swift roll and threw it at him. She scored a direct hit, but he just laughed. It was what she liked about him. He had a sense of humour. He might be quick to anger, but he was soon over it, and he didn't usually bear grudges for long.

'Are there any flowers that mean 'I hate your guts'?' he asked suddenly as the kettle began to sing.

'Not that I know of.' She rose to her feet. 'It wouldn't be a good idea, though — sending them to Vaughn. He's tough, you know. Race-drivers are. He'd probably come over and bop you one.'

'You like him, don't you?' He swung away towards the kettle again, presenting her with his back view as he shot the question.

'Yes,' she said, coming up beside him. 'But I like a lot of people, Mark.'

She watched as he stirred each mug full of coffee. He wasn't angry any more. He glanced at her. 'Silly question, wasn't it?'

She nodded, smiling. 'I wouldn't ask Vaughn to come and stay for the weekend, though.'

Carefully he placed the teaspoon on the kitchen worktop, leaned down into the fridge and took out the milk. He topped up each cup, replaced the milk in the fridge again, then looked at the horseshoe propped up against the window. 'My horseshoe,' he said in a distinctly calculating manner, 'will outlast Herrick's flowers.' And only then did he turn to face her fully, and reach out to her to take her into his arms.

And, knowing his arms were always a safe haven, she relaxed against him, placed both her hands on his shoulders, then lifted her face for his kiss.

12

Mark helped her to tidy up the front garden of her little house the next day. It had been neglected because she'd been spending so much time on the two-acre herb garden surrounding the place.

'You really should get somebody to help you,' he said, sitting back on his heels beside a pile of weeds against her front door. A school-leaver, perhaps — or you could enquire about one of those schemes where sixth-formers do work experience.'

'I'm not yet in the league for paying out wages,' she said, squatting down beside him. 'At this time of year Clare isn't taking many herbs off my hands. Anyway, old Joshua Temple seemed to manage on his own, so why not me?'

He touched her face with a grimy finger. 'You won't give up, will you?'

'No,' she said. 'I won't — not until I've tried and failed anyway, and I don't intend failing, so . . . '

'So you're going to continue being obstinate.'

She grinned. 'Yes.'

He sighed. 'Where do you want this lot of weeds?'

'On the bonfire.'

'I thought so.' He gathered them up and stood up. 'Do you have to site your bonfire as far away as that? Right at the other end of the herb garden?'

'You know I do. I don't want a smoky kitchen.' She started to walk beside him, down the side of the house and round the back, then down the long, grassy path towards the furthermost boundary.

As they neared the bonfire pile, he said, 'Have you had any more trouble with the old church? You know — with somebody watching you from the tower?'

She shook her head. 'I can sometimes persuade myself now that I imagined it. It's been idyllic here, really. It's so quiet and peaceful.'

'But a hell of a lot of work for you,' he said, getting back to the old subject.

She hunched her shoulders. 'It's work I love, Mark. I have to be doing something with living things. Flowers were my first love, of course, but I'm enjoying working with herbs now.'

'No regrets at leaving Heronsea, then?' He tossed the armful of weeds onto the piled-up rubbish, and turned to face her.

She thought for a moment or two, then said, 'My only regret is that it's a long way from you, Mark. Sometimes I wish we lived nearer each other again.'

'I'm only a phone call away, though.'

'Two hundred miles,' she said. 'I look at the sea sometimes and think, two hundred miles — and it seems like another world.'

'Hey! Don't tell me you're missing me.' He gazed at her with disbelief in his eyes. Then they crinkled up into a smile at the corners as he said, 'Yes — go on, tell me that. It will make my day.'

She thumped him firmly in the midriff. 'Conceit is your middle name — and I'm not going to give you the satisfaction of thinking I'm missing you.' She picked up the long stick that she kept handy for poking the bonfire, and prodded it at the weeds he'd just thrown onto it.

'Aren't you going to light it?'

She gazed around her. The air was still. It was a cold day, but pleasant enough. 'I could, I suppose.'

'Want me to fetch some matches from the kitchen?'

'No.' She shook her head. 'I'll go.'

She left him happily, knowing that they were getting on well together now after an almost disastrous start last year. Last year, though, she decided, had been disastrous altogether, and it was good now to have something to look forward to — a life where she was dependent on nobody — a life where she could suit herself.

She hummed a popular tune to herself as she walked back to the house, but as she came near she stopped abruptly, and gazed at something that hadn't been there only minutes before.

'More flowers!' White ones, chrysanthemums, propped up against the green wood of the kitchen door.

Her hand flew to her mouth.

Was she imagining things, or was it . . . ?

There was a black-edged card tucked into them.

Her heart seemed to stop and her breath caught in her throat as she took a few steps nearer to the funeral tribute. She moved nearer, not wanting to read what was written on that card, but knowing she had to. She didn't need to go any further to read what it said. Under the scrolled and elaborate heading of 'In Memory of' her name was scrawled, in untidy bold and prominent letters — 'Tamsin'!

* * *

Mark heard her cry out, and spun round from tidying up the edges of the bonfire to see her racing back down the grassy path towards him. He could hear her frantic sobbing, and something primitive inside him made him start running to meet her, wanting to comfort her and protect her. She was his life, his one true love, and he couldn't bear it when she was hurt or unhappy.

'Tam!' he yelled as they collided. 'Tam — for heaven's sake . . . ' His voice was raw. He grabbed hold of her, dragged her into his arms, then pushed her away and looked for signs of injury, for blood, for anything in fact that could have upset her in this way.

She hurled herself back into his arms and her hands clawed at him, winding themselves round his waist till even through the thick jacket he was wearing he could feel her fingers digging into his flesh.

'Tam! Tam!' Her trembling was tearing his heart out, her fear so real it was making him fearful too — but for her. Only for her. 'Tam!' His arms enveloped her. 'Tam! I'm here. You're safe. What is it? Tell me. For heaven's sake. Tell me.'

Her fingers dug deeper. Her breath was coming in great sobbing gasps. She was becoming calmer, though, as he held her and tried to soothe her. At last she lifted her head and her distraught eyes sought an answer in his. 'Who would do it . . . ?' she whispered brokenly. 'So cruel . . . so cruel . . . '

'Tell me,' he said gently.

She shook her head, as if to clear it and make some sense of what she was about to say. 'Up at the house. Beside the kitchen door,' she whimpered. 'Oh, Mark. They want me dead . . . '

'Who?' His voice was urgent. He shook her a little. 'Tam — you're not making sense.'

'They must have been watching me again . . . ' Her gaze whipped away from him and over the fields towards the old ruined church. 'They *must* have been watching to know we were down here and not back at the house — or in the front garden weeding . . . '

'Who? What is it? Tam — you've got to tell me.'

At last she calmed down enough to say, 'There's a funeral tribute of white chrysanthemums propped up against my back door . . . '

With a mounting sense of dread, he said, 'It's a mistake. Somebody's made a mistake and delivered it to the wrong address surely.'

Dry-eyed now, and with a pinched

expression on her face, she said, 'It had my name on the card.'

* * *

'Things like this just don't happen,' he said as he brought her a mug of strong tea when he'd made her sit in front of the fire in her little sitting room.

She hunched her knees up in front of her, where she'd just dropped onto the rug minutes earlier, and took the mug from him with still trembling hands. 'But it *has* happened,' she said. 'And I want to know why.'

'We'll ring all the local florists . . . '

'It didn't come from a florist,' she said in a dull voice. 'Somebody made it up themselves. The plastic foam has been used before — as has that base, with the wiring. This is the work of an amateur, Mark.' She stared at him. 'I know about these things,' she insisted. 'Flowers were once my job — remember?'

'You mean . . . '

With a shaky laugh, she said, 'At a guess, I'd say somebody raided the local cemetery rubbish bin and stole a funeral tribute, stripped the old flowers from it and then beheaded a bunch of white chrysanthemums and just stuck them through the wire mesh.'

'Then delivered it here by hand.' Mark felt his agitation rising to boiling point — that somebody could do this to Tam. She'd hurt no one. She was merely trying to make a living, so why was this happening? Why, first of all, had she been spied upon? And what kind of person could do what they'd just done to her? If it was a joke, it was a sick one — to terrify a helpless girl like that. He sat down on the hearthrug facing her. She was bearing up well now — now the first shock was over.

'It was a hateful thing to do,' he said. 'Do you have any idea . . . ?'

She shook her head with vehemence. 'No! No! I haven't made any enemies. I hardly know anybody at all around here.' She lifted the steaming hot tea to her lips and took a deep gulp of it. 'Mark . . . ' Her gaze came up to rest on his face. 'Mark — why would anybody do something so horrible?'

'A grudge?' he asked. 'Did somebody else want this house, do you think?'

'No. The estate agent told me nobody had shown the slightest interest in it. That's why I was able to rent it so cheaply, I think.'

'No . . . ' He hesitated before saying, 'No man-friend who might resent *me* being here this weekend, Tam?'

She laughed, with tears springing to her

eyes again. 'I haven't had time for boyfriends, Mark. I've been so busy. Anyway, I didn't come all this way to find myself a husband. I'm not interested in that. You know I'm not that sort of girl. If I'd merely wanted a husband . . . ' Her voice tailed off miserably.

'You would have accepted me,' he said gently. 'Yes, I know, Tam. But we've got to try and reason something out regarding this sinister incident. I think we ought to inform the police.'

'No,' she said quickly. 'I don't want to make an issue of it.'

'What about Herrick?' Mark forced himself to ask. 'Would he stoop to something like this?'

'No,' she said. 'Vaughn might be an absolute rat in some ways, but this is not his way of doing things. Vaughn's straight. He'd come right to the point if he had a grievance. He wouldn't hurt me . . . '

'He hurt you when he left you pregnant.'

She gazed at him, her eyes wide and accusing. 'That's not fair,' she said. 'He didn't know about the baby — not until it was too late.'

'You won't hear anything against him, will you?' The hurt in his voice was accusing.

'There's *nothing* to hear against him,' she said, her eyes flashing a warning at him.

'Vaughn's in the clear, Mark. Vaughn would never, never do something like this.'

'Who have you had dealings with, Tam?' Mark sat forward and ticked off on his fingers the people he knew she was acquainted with. 'Cass Fairburn, Clare Faulkener, her husband . . . '

'Nobody else,' she said, shaking her head. 'There's nobody else.'

'Nobody?'

She shrugged. 'The postman! Vaughn! Clare's assistant — Craig Andrews . . . '

'Craig Andrews?'

Her dismissal of Craig was quick and to the point. 'He's having an affair with Clare — according to Cass, anyway. He's certainly not the sort of guy who would go hunting through graveyard bins, though.' She pulled a face. 'It might dirty his designer suit. He's that sort of man — you can't imagine him ever getting his hands dirty.'

'Except to top and tail Patric Faulkener's wife?' He raised one eyebrow questioningly at her.

'That's a different matter altogether. Patric too is playing away.' Her mouth snapped shut.

He knew he wasn't being fair — questioning her like this. She didn't know many people in Suffolk, and he knew her position here would be made intolerable if once she started suspecting people she knew of scaring her half to death.

Mark said, 'They seem to have their hands full with their own problems, then, those ones you know.'

'Yes.' She drank deeply of the hot, sweet tea again, then placed the mug on the heath. The fire was burning brightly, flames were shooting up the chimney. She looked up again. 'I'm getting over it,' she said. 'It was just a shock. Looking at it logically, I was a bit of a crybaby, wasn't I? Rushing back to you like that. I ought to have just picked those damn flowers up and put them in the wastebin.'

'They're there now,' Mark said. 'I did it for you — while I was making the tea. I didn't want you to have to see them again.' He'd kept the card, though, and only *he* knew that. He wasn't going to tell her. He didn't want to worry her. If there were repercussions, though, he was going straight to the police. And that card had *somebody's* writing on it. In his own opinion, however, the police ought to know about this right now. He wondered whether to broach the subject with her again, then decided against it. She had calmed down now, and seemed determined to put it out of her mind. And that was just as well, he decided, for it was Tam who had to stay here when he was gone. It was Tam who needed to make a go of Herb House. And sadly he realized that her life was her own. He had no say in it whatever.

He scrambled to his feet, picked up her empty mug and said, 'Look — I'll go and rustle up something for lunch, huh?'

She smiled up at him. 'I'll come and help you.'

He grabbed at her hand and pulled her to her feet. 'I'm an idiot . . . ' she started to say, when they both heard a car drawing up outside the front of the house.

For a moment fear flitted across her face, and he knew she still wasn't as composed as she'd have him believe.

'Hey — don't worry,' he said. 'They're hardly likely to come back, are they? And especially not in a car, for all the world to hear them.'

'No,' she said in a whisper. 'No — I expect whoever it was came across the heath. They'd have to know the place well to avoid the marsh if they'd come from any other direction except the road.'

'And we heard no car.'

'No.' She let go his hand and went hurrying to the back of the house.

Maybe it had all been a mistake, he

thought. Maybe this car was coming with somebody in it to say the flowers had been delivered wrongly. Maybe this was going to turn out to be some joke gone sour . . .

She was going out of the back door now. He raced after her. If there was going to be any more trouble, he was determined to be there to protect her.

He caught her up at the side of the house and heard a car door being slammed shut on the little lane. Then a man came into view. A slight, mouse-haired good-looking guy, slim, lithe, wearing steel-rimmed spectacles.

At his side, he heard the sharp intake of her breath.

She half turned towards him. 'It's Vaughn,' she said.

And from the man hurrying towards them came a lazy voice.

'Did you get the flowers, Tam?'

13

'I very nearly hit him,' Mark said later that evening. 'I thought he was referring to those damn chrysanthemums — and then I remembered the daffodils and tulips on your kitchen table, and stopped myself just in time.'

'You were very hostile,' Tam said as they faced each other across the hearthrug in front of the sitting room fire, where a Scrabble board and score-sheet separated them.

He glanced up at her from his tile-rack as he started placing the letters of a word on the board. 'He was a pleasant guy — that's why I was hostile. I could have taken it more easily if he'd been a bombastic, big-headed glory boy, but he wasn't, so I hated him.'

'Well, I suppose that's a good enough reason,' she said, understanding exactly what he was trying to say, and laughing when she saw the word he'd just spelled out. 'RACER?' she asked. 'Is he still playing on your mind, then?'

'Yeah!' he said. 'I'll have nightmares about him. Him and you.'

She looked down at her own set of letter-tiles, frowned and said, 'I don't have any vowels.'

'Use either the A or the E in 'racer' then,' he said. 'I don't mind sharing my word with you.'

'I'll have to,' she said, and promptly put a C above the A and an R underneath it, making CAR!

Mark let out a groan. 'Do I have to sit and look at 'car' and 'racer' for the duration of this game?' he asked.

'Just for the one.' She grinned across at him and lifted her glass of white wine to him. 'You started it.'

He filled up his own glass from the bottle on the hearth beside him, then, easing himself into a cross-legged position, said, 'Anything to do with car racing is now banned. Okay?'

'No proper names either.' She downed her wine in one go.

'And no racing car names. No Renault or Mercedes or Ferrari — right?'

She laughed. 'What about team names? Can I have Oscar-Jade?'

He leaned across at her with his glass in his hand. 'Shall I pour this all over you, my sweet?'

'Only teasing,' she said. 'I still don't have any vowels.'

The game, which she won by only two points, took up most of two hours, and it was almost midnight when they cleared it away.

Tam stood up, stretched and yawned. 'I forgot to ask you this morning — was your bed okay last night?'

'Fine,' he said, adding, 'Except it was a bed for two, and only one was in it.'

'I was so pleased with the new mattress I bought that I ordered a spare bed — just in case anyone came to visit,' she said. 'You never know, do you, just when people are going to drop in?'

'Like me.'

'Mmm.'

'I could've managed on the sofa — like at Cass's house. Do you still see her, by the way?'

'She's away on a photographic job just now. Since doing an article on Patric Faulkener's new circuit, she's been approached by a couple more new enterprises — one in Essex, the other in Northumberland. The Northumberland one isn't even built yet — the circuit, I mean — but she's been in Essex for the best part of this week. I don't think she's back yet. She hasn't phoned.'

'Tam!' He came over to her and put his hands heavily on her shoulders. 'Tam — tell Cass what happened today, will you? This morning. And if anything else like that happens . . . '

'Oh, don't,' she said. 'Don't remind me, Mark. I'd almost forgotten it and I don't want to go to bed thinking about it.'

'Liar,' he said. 'You've been brooding about it all evening. I've seen that faraway look on your face, that worried gnawing of the inside of your cheek.'

'I *am* going to forget it,' she said furiously. 'I'm not going to let a silly little incident like that take over my life.' She shrugged his hands away and moved to pick up the game they'd been playing.

'All the same — Cass lives near. Tell her. Please, Tam. It will put my mind at rest, knowing there's somebody who can be with you in five or ten minutes.'

'Twenty,' she said, pulling a face at him. 'Or nearer thirty if there's a lot of traffic around. You have to drive over that ramshackle bridge, and right round the estuary. It can take an absolute age.'

'I hate to think of you here alone at nights.'

'So far nothing's happened at night,' she said firmly. 'It's been in the daytime that I was watched, and it was in the daytime today that those flowers arrived at my back door.'

'I know that, but . . . '

'But nothing, Mark. Let's forget about it.' She moved away from him, refusing to let him know how unnerved she had been at finding that black-edged card in the flowers by her door.

At least now, though, after meeting Vaughn and talking to him, she knew that Mark didn't suspect *him* of anything underhand any more. She was glad they'd come face to face — the only two men who had ever made any sort of impact on her life. Under any other circumstances she felt they might have been friends. It wasn't possible, though. She realized that now. Mark was jealous as hell of Vaughn, and Vaughn had made it clear that he had, at one time at least, had a claim on her by talking about 'the old days,' the days when he and Rafe Thorne had been on different sides of the fence. Now it was all so different, though. Vaughn's father had died, leaving the Oscar-Jade team to Rafe, and Rafe, knowing that Vaughn's contract with a rival team had ended, had asked Vaughn to join. Tamsin knew it was a good move for Vaughn. Maybe he'd settle down a bit more now. Maybe he'd be less inclined to 'play the field' where women were concerned now he had a real chance of making something of his career.

Mark said, 'You and Vaughn — you still get on well together.'

'Yes,' she said, turning round from the dresser cupboard — where she'd put the Scrabble game away — to face him again. 'There's no point in harping on past mistakes, is there?'

'Were you in love him?' He faced her across the room and asked the question in a low voice.

She swallowed and said, 'Mark — I don't want to hurt you — but, yes, I suppose I was in love with him. I wouldn't have had sex with him if I hadn't thought what I felt was the real thing. It was a crazy mixed-up period of my life.'

'Yes,' he said. 'I know that. I was there, remember?'

'Picking up the pieces of me.' She grimaced, and went over to him. 'Where would I have been without you?' she asked softly.

'I did nothing.'

'You were *there*,' she said. 'You never held back when it came to helping me.'

'A fact that you resented sometimes.' He was standing close to her now, looking down into her face, but he didn't attempt to touch her.

'You've changed, Mark. You weren't like this when I first knew you. You were angry and touchy then, and you were an out-and-out chauvinist, yet now . . . '

'Now,' he said quietly, 'I care for somebody other than myself.'

'Me?' She raised her eyes and let her gaze rest on his face.

He bent his head and kissed her hair. 'Yes! You! Scallywag!'

'I'm getting so I depend on you.' She placed her hands on his shoulders, then linked them behind his neck and pulled his head down to hers. 'And I hate being dependent.'

He kissed her, gently, tenderly, his arms encircling her waist and holding her close to him. 'I love you,' he said simply, when the kiss was over.

'I think I know what you mean,' she whispered back.

Everything seemed so easy then. He locked up the house for her, and poured out two more glasses of wine. They carried them upstairs and halted on the landing outside her bedroom door.

'Don't leave me,' she said, looking up at him.

'Tam . . . ' He was unsure of her meaning. He glanced at the bedroom door, frowned, then said, 'I've told you, I'll always be here for you.'

'Now,' she said. 'I mean now.' She was leaning against the door. She felt behind her for the latch and opened it, then backed inside. 'Do you want me?' she asked.

He followed her inside her bedroom. A softly shaded lamp was lit in the opposite corner to the door. It gave the whole room a warm glow and brought the old wooden furniture into a new focus. He walked over to the scratched and worn dressing table and placed his glass on its top, then went back to her, took her glass out of her hand and put it on the bedside cabinet beside where she was standing.

'Come here,' he said, opening his arms to her.

She went to him and he held her. She leaned her head back and looked into his eyes. 'I feel safe with you,' she said as she steadied herself against his chest with the flat of both hands.

In a laughing whisper he said, 'Tam — that is *not* the most complimentary thing I've ever had said to me.'

'You know what I mean.'

'Mmm. I think so. I hope so. I don't want

to get this wrong. I don't want to think you need me just to chase the ghosts of the night away.'

'Do I have to spell it out?' She gave a breathless laugh.

'Do you have enough vowels to do that?'

'We aren't playing Scrabble now,' she said. 'This is a very different game.'

'I want to hear the words — complete with all the vowels,' he said.

She thought for a few seconds, then said, 'I won the game downstairs. Is it up to me to make the first move in this new one?'

He nodded. 'Afraid so. I've made all the running so far.'

'Using all the vowels, I could make three words. The trouble is — one would be a proper name.'

'We'll bend the rules,' he said. 'Just for you.'

She took a deep breath. 'Tamsin — loves — you,' she said in a very quiet voice. 'There — I've used all the vowels.'

'That's all I wanted to hear,' he said.

★ ★ ★

She woke once in the night and tried to turn over, but couldn't. And then she remembered, and saw that the lamp was still alight and Mark was beside her. He was sleeping soundly. A smile tilted the corners of her lips. She'd been right to tell him she didn't want him to leave her. It had all been so right — from the moment she'd said those words there had been no going back, and she wondered now why she had held him at bay for so long.

Mark loved her. And she cared deeply for him. It had crept up on her so slowly, the knowledge of her love, but it had been no less real for doing so. It felt good — it *was* good. He hadn't hurried her, or worried her. It had been a natural coming together, in laughter first, as they'd lain together still joking about vowels and trying to make words of love with only one vowel, then two, then three . . .

Her smile widened. It hadn't been intense at first, but it had become so . . .

She looked at him again, and his eyes were open and watching her. He turned over slowly to face her, put his hand up to her face and stroked her cheek. Her hair was tousled on the pillow. It never behaved itself.

'I love your hair,' he whispered.

She went into his arms again, to be smothered in kisses, and he said, 'I can't believe this is happening . . . I think I must be dreaming.'

'Do you want me to pinch you?' She

chuckled softly against his lips.

'You can do anything you like — I won't complain.' His voice was husky and full of emotion.

'Mark . . . ' She sighed out his name.

He raised himself up over her and gazed down into her face, and she felt the warmth of his body covering her. She dragged his head down until her lips found his, and passion flared between them.

There were no teasing words now, no making of words with vowels. Now there was something much deeper than she could ever have believed she was capable of. Her body became a vibrant flame, leaping at his caresses. He was still so very gentle with her, and took nothing for granted. With each touch of his lips, his tongue, his fingers, she became more alive. They sought, they explored, they found new ways to say 'I love you' without using words. Her hands ranged over every beloved inch of him. She drowned in the ecstasy of every delightful little pleasure as he touched and tasted her. Her senses began to soar like an eagle alongside its mate. And at the pinnacle of all sensation he entered her — not as before, earlier, when he'd been careful — too considerate almost — but with a passion that was an explosion of every sensation under the sun, a silent sound of thunder that ripped heaven from its anchor and whirled it down to earth to mingle time and eternity into one perfect, sensual aeon.

She went to sleep with her back to him, curled into the shape of his body, with his arm over and around her and his face in the hollow of her neck, buried deep in her curled golden hair.

He loved her!

That was her last waking thought before she drifted into the world of dreams, feeling safe and cared for.

14

When Mark left and went back up north Tam was restless, and felt as if she couldn't bear to be in the house by herself with just Vaughn's flowers for company.

She needed to think, to sort herself out. Two days ago she hadn't had the slightest intention of falling in love. The weekend, however, had changed all that, and now, in the cold light of another chill February morning, she knew that her life had taken a change of direction. But where was it leading? That was what she had to ask herself. Did she really want to stay here in Suffolk and grow her herbs — all by herself? The only other alternative was to return to Yorkshire . . .

Her mind shied away from *that* recourse, though. She'd always been a firm believer in looking forward, not back. But Mark was in Yorkshire — living in his lovely old house in Rothwold, and working alongside his partner Edgar Brand in the classic car business. Could she do it? Could she *ever* go back there to the memories, the heartache, and the pain of all that had gone before?

She pulled on a thick coat, wound a long wool scarf round her neck, plunged her hands into warm gloves and locked up her house. She paused at the front gate and peered up the lane towards the ruined church. The hedgerows were shrouded in mist, the silence everlasting. Long loops of spider-webs hung frosted against her fence, and her nose was beginning to feel numb from the icy air.

She turned away from the lane and headed for the heath. She'd shoved a purse in her pocket — from force of habit, she supposed. Now, though, she decided she might as well trek over the heath to Alderwood. It was hardly worth getting the car out to fetch a loaf of bread. And she might call at Cass's house and see if she had returned from her assignment in Essex.

She strode out, down what was left of the lane beyond her house, then climbed up onto the stile and jumped down the other side — the side that bordered the heath. Her head turned automatically towards the sea, but it wasn't visible today. The mist was too dense. She heard a sound and tilted her head skywards. A steady flap-flap-flapping heralded a fly-past of the geese she had come to love since moving to this isolated spot. Hardly a day went by that she didn't hear the low-voiced soft 'rhuk-rhuk' sound of the Brent at some time or other. She strained her eyes in the grey murkiness. They had no orderliness about them, not like some other strains of geese, which kept in strict V-skeins as they flew. The little unexceptional Brents flapped over her head, their wings beating, black bodies with pale grey undercarriages, in a loose flock. She listened to them until their noise died away in the stillness of the morning, and then she looked for the path that would lead her to Alderwood.

She'd been walking for some minutes when she became aware of another noise. Somebody was singing softly. She recognized the tune — an old English one — 'Greensleeves'. It was a man's voice, not melodious, not even flowing very well. Every few words were punctuated with a 'damn' or a 'blast', and then the song would start up again, getting nearer now . . .

'Greensleeves . . . was my . . . delight . . . Greensleeves was my heart of . . . Sod this blasted heath . . . Sorry, Shakespeare . . . '

Tamsin stood still, listening and smiling to herself. In another moment he'd be looming up through the mist, and he obviously thought he had the place to himself. He'd get the shock of his life when . . .

He was into *Macbeth* now. "Say, from whence you owe this strange intelligence? Or why upon this blasted heath you stop our way with such prophetic greeting . . . ?"

'Hi, there,' Tamsin called out.

'Hell-fire!' He stood in the middle of the path looking at her.

She burst out laughing. 'Vaughn! I recognized the voice. I couldn't resist it.'

'The 'prophetic greeting'! Tam — I was coming over to see you.' He grinned widely at her. He looked very young, huddled up in a thick check coat, hands buried in oversized pockets. His mousy hair was curling in the mist, his steel-framed spectacles giving him an altogether surprised look as he stared at her. 'Has *he* gone?' he wanted to know. 'That's why I decided to walk. I didn't want to announce my presence by coming in the car again — not if *he* was still there.'

'Mark?' she asked with mock demureness. 'Is it Mark you're asking me about?'

'Oh, very funny!' he said. 'Who else would I be meaning? Do you make a habit of taking in waifs and strays every weekend?'

'Not *every* weekend,' she said archly. 'And Mark is neither of those things. Mark is a friend.'

'You two looked very cosy.' Vaughn's

expression darkened into a scowl of disapproval. 'He seemed to know his way around.'

'Mark's been at the cottage before.'

'Yeah! Yeah! Yeah! Rub it in. 'Mark's a friend'!' he mocked her.

She began to shiver in the cold air. 'Why were you coming over to see me? And why didn't you ring and let me know?'

He hunched his shoulders in a shrug. 'Just thought you might appreciate some decent company — and I didn't ring because you might have said no.'

'Well, if you don't mind — I'd rather walk on into Alderwood and get a loaf of bread,' she said, in the most practical voice she could muster. 'You can't stand still on a day like this. You'll freeze to the ground if you do.'

'I thought I might get offered a cup of coffee,' he muttered.

'Sorry,' she breezed. 'I'm desperate for a loaf of bread.'

'We're only a couple of minutes away from your house . . . '

'Yes,' she said, and that was how things were going to stay, she decided.

'So why don't we go back there and get warm in front of your stove?'

'Because!' she said.

'That sounds final.'

'It is.' She grinned at him. 'Oh, come on,

old sourpuss.' She grabbed hold of his arm and turned him firmly round in the direction he'd come, and he went with her, docile as a domesticated dog.

'Did you hear me swearing?' he asked conversationally.

'Yes. To the tune of 'Greensleeves'.'

'I couldn't help it. I kept losing my footing on this tussocky stuff.'

'Heather,' she said. 'It's heather. You should keep to the path.'

'It was wet and icy. I needed to get a grip.'

'You need your rain-tyres on in this weather. Not fine weather slicks.'

'Ha-ha!' he said. 'That's right. Remind me I should be at the track right now. Testing damn tyres.'

'You should?' She glanced sideways at him. 'Why are you still at Alderwood, then, if you ought to be testing?'

'I hung on to see you. We didn't get much chance to talk the other day, did we? Not with *him* around?'

'Mark,' she said in a pleasant tone. 'He has a name. It's Mark!'

'He's no good for you, Tam. You need somebody who's a bit more of a high-flyer.'

'Like you.' Her easy laughter rang out in the stillness of the heath.

'You and I were good together. Once.' His

voice was low and cajoling.

'Forget it,' she said. 'That was one big mistake, Vaughn.'

'Mistakes can be rectified.'

'Little ones maybe. Not big ones.' Ahead of her she could just make out the blurred outlines of buildings as Alderwood came into view.

He stopped suddenly in his tracks, and as she had never let go of his arm she was jerked back too. Her hand fell to her side as she faced him. 'Now what?'

'Tam — I'm not joking.' All at once he was deadly serious. 'Tam — we could make a go of it again.'

She shook her head, wary of him now. 'No, Vaughn.'

'We *could*.'

'I don't want to,' she said simply. 'It's over, Vaughn. We had our day, but now it's over.'

'I wouldn't let you down again. I promise, Tam.'

She gave a huge sigh. 'Don't get all sloppy . . .'

He grabbed at her with both hands, pulled her into his arms and his mouth fought a battle with hers for supremacy. He was strong. His hands were clamped around the top of her arms. He had big hands. Fierce hands. As he wrestled with her, this way and that, she felt she knew how the wheel of his racing car must feel at the end of a race — bruised, battered, weary.

She stopped struggling in the end and let him kiss her. She made no response, however. She wasn't afraid of him. She knew him too well to be scared. He just had to have his own way; he had to be the victor.

She could see he was shaken by her lack of co-operation as he let her go. 'Are you really so indifferent to me?' he yelled when she made no move against him.

'Completely indifferent,' she said in a calm voice. 'I don't love you now, you see.'

He swung round so his back was towards her. His shoulders were tense bundles of muscles under the overcoat. He muttered something under his breath.

She said, 'I didn't hear what you said.'

'I still love you, Tam.' Suddenly he looked defeated.

She couldn't feel sorry for him, though. She couldn't, in all truth, feel *anything* at all for him. Friendship was out of the question after all they'd gone through together in the past. And as for love . . . She could have laughed outright, but knew that now was not the moment to do that. He didn't *love* her. He was too much in love with his own image and his chosen profession to waste strong feelings on anything except racing-cars. She doubted he'd ever loved any human being in all his life before. Again, though, this was not the time to point such a thing out to him. He'd recently lost his father — a father he'd hated and defied for most of his adult life. And just at the point when they might have made up the quarrel — Vaughn and Oscar Herrick — Oscar had keeled over and died right there in front of him. Tamsin couldn't deliberately hurt him. Not now — not at any time, really. She'd loved him once, but it seemed a long time ago now. So much had happened . . .

He spoke again. 'I feel — responsible.'

She hesitated before asking, 'About me?'

He faced her again, slowly. 'If you ever need somebody . . . '

'I won't,' she said, looking at him steadily.

'But if you do. For any reason. You'll come to me, won't you, Tam? I'd move heaven and earth for you.'

'I couldn't trust you,' she said.

'Tam . . . ' His face was stricken.

She shook her head. 'I couldn't, Vaughn. I'm sorry, but that's the way I feel.'

'I'd never let you down again,' he said in a fierce, protective way.

'Wouldn't you?' she said, and without

another word walked off and left him standing there.

★ ★ ★

Cass was pleased to see her.

'I had to come here,' Tamsin said. 'I had to get away from him.'

Cass pulled a wry face at her. 'Fancy turning your back on a famous racing-driver like that.'

'Vaughn's not famous.' Tamsin sank down onto Cass's comfortable sofa and glared at her friend.

'He might be — one day. Anyway, he's moved up from bottom of the league, hasn't he? Now he's driving for the Oscar-Jade team?'

'I suppose so. And he does have quite a following — photos, T-shirts, key-rings — that sort of thing.'

'He gets himself into the glossy racing mags quite regularly too,' Cass said. 'In fact, our Vaughn Herrick is quite a lad, if all I hear about him is true.'

'I don't read the racing mags.' Tam was tiring of the conversation.

'Well, I *work* for them, so I see what's going on,' Cass said, perching on the arm of the sofa. She tilted her head to one side and said, 'He's good, you know. A good driver. He's clean too — he doesn't try any of the dirty tactics some of them do to get themselves noticed.'

'You sound half in love with him yourself,' Tamsin scoffed.

Cass laughed — half-heartedly, it seemed to Tam. 'Half in love is all I'm going for next time round,' she said. 'The whole hog is too painful an experience to repeat. If you get my meaning.'

'Patric Faulkener? Is it really all over between you and him?'

Cass's expression was hard. 'Yes,' she said. 'Married men are definitely out. O-U-T from now on,' she spelled out. 'I was a fool, Tam. I ought never to have got involved in the first place.'

'He's a good-looking guy — your Patric! I *fell* for him too, if you remember — the first day I came down here.'

'You fell physically,' Cass said. 'Your heart wasn't involved — you just got a sore bum from landing on the High Street with Patric on top of you.'

'Hardly that.'

'You saved his life.'

'Oh, yuk!' Tam cried. 'Don't make me into some kind of martyr. If I'd known he was going to hurt you like he did, I would

237

probably have let that hooligan knife him.'

'He speaks highly of you for what you did.'

'Big deal!' Tamsin scowled. She glanced up at the wall clock. 'Look — are we going to eat? Shall we go up to the pub for a ploughman?'

Cass slid off the sofa-arm and giggled. 'The real thing — or one on a plate?'

'Do either of us want another man? Just at the moment?'

Cass considered her words for a few seconds, then said, 'I get your point. I'll settle for one on a plate.'

The pub was crowded and steamy. It had started to rain sharply, which had cleared the fog but made folks come rushing inside from their shopping with soaking wet coats. Cass had opted for a Cornish pasty, Tamsin for French onion soup.

'Why is pub food always so fattening?' Cass asked as they sat cramped in a corner at a table with a plastic carnation in a jug in the middle of it.

'Oh, no . . . '

'Yes, it is. There must be almost a thousand calories in — '

'Hide your face. Get under the table. Hell! Do something. Oh, no — they've seen us.'

'Are you all right?' Cass asked, glancing up and across the table at Tamsin.

'Vaughn! And Patric Faulkener! And they've seen us. And they're coming over . . . '

Cass's face had turned scarlet. 'No!' she squeaked. 'I don't want to see him.'

'Tell him,' Tamsin said. 'Just tell him to get lost. And to take Vaughn with him.'

'We can't . . . '

Vaughn was standing stiffly beside the table. 'Look — do you mind if we join you? There's blessed little room at the bar, and we need to eat . . . '

'And your table is the only one with two vacant seats,' Patric Faulkener said in a rigidly polite voice.

Tamsin regained her composure more quickly than Cass did. 'Help yourself to the seats,' she said sharply, making sure there was no hint of welcome in her tone. 'We shall soon be finished, so you can have the table to yourselves then.'

Cass was gulping down great mouthfuls of Cornish pasty. Patric Faulkener said, 'Please don't let us rush you.'

'You aren't doing that,' Tamsin said. She stared up at Vaughn and Patric. 'Well, sit down. We're not going to eat you. You don't have to be so obscenely polite.'

Patric squeezed in on one side of the table, being studiously careful not to touch even the sleeve of Cass's jacket, and Vaughn sat down facing him, slightly more comfortable as he smiled sheepishly at Tam.

Vaughn said, obviously trying to lighten the atmosphere, 'Anyone for square dancing? All we need do is link hands over the table and the fiddlers will strike up 'Turkey in the Straw' for starters.'

Patric was the only one who laughed.

Vaughn said, 'Sorry,' and silence descended on them all for several minutes.

Cass finished her pasty and, ignoring Patric, said, 'It's nice to meet you, Mr Herrick. I've read quite a lot about you — seen your picture too — in the magazines I've been working on just lately.'

'You have?' Vaughn was captured. Racing was his life. 'Tell me about your work.'

Cass obliged. Patric was obviously very ill at ease, and trying to melt into the background. A waiter came and brought steaming bowls of broth for both men.

Patric tried to make conversation with Tamsin. 'So — we meet again.' He gave her a well-practised smile. 'Vaughn's staying with us.'

'He seems to be making quite a habit of doing that,' Tamsin said pleasantly.

'Yes. Well, he's interested in the new circuit . . . '

'That was a few weeks ago,' Tam said

pointedly. 'I would have thought he'd be testing the new car at one of the bigger circuits by now, though.'

Vaughn had heard her words; she knew that. She saw his expression harden, but Cass was speaking to him, so he couldn't ignore her and retaliate.

'He seems to like it down here,' Patric was saying now.

'It must be the air.' Tam smiled sweetly at him.

'He says he's interested in the wildlife.'

Tam felt like laughing out loud, but wisely kept her mouth shut.

Vaughn looked up again. 'I was on the heath this morning. There was this herd of ducks . . . '

'Flock,' Tamsin corrected. 'And they were geese. Brent geese.'

Patric laughed. 'You know your geese?'

'Yes,' Tam looked at him steadily. 'I know my Brents from my Canada. Living where I do, I have geese practically on my doorstep.'

'At our old house,' Patric said, 'we had a couple of Canada geese on our pond every winter.'

Tam was interested. 'Your old house?'

'In Norfolk. The house Clare and I moved into when we were first married. We still have it. She won't hear of selling it. Yet there it is

241

— empty for most of the year — except for when Clare decides she's had enough of me for a while.' He smiled, but the smile didn't reach his eyes. 'She often goes up there for the weekend.'

'Up there?'

'Norfolk! Didn't I say? A little place called Polten Market. The house is called Lilacs — it's quite a pretty place.'

Tam decided it must be where Clare and Craig carried on their relationship, and a shiver snaked through her.

Patric said, 'Well, Clare likes it. That's why we keep it. It's nice and secluded — away from prying eyes.'

Tamsin stared at him, realizing that he must know that he was talking about Clare's love-nest. But he didn't seem to mind. In fact, he seemed quite cold about it. It was obvious from the tone of his voice that the house meant nothing to him at all.

'You don't go there yourself?' she asked politely.

'No. Never. Not now,' he said. 'I've grown out of it. It's just a memory really.' He laughed. 'Something dead — if you get my meaning.'

She felt a cold chill run right through her. 'A memory?'

'That's right.' Patric's dark eyes were

suddenly cold as ice. 'In memory of . . . ' He picked up his glass of lager for the toast.

Tam remembered the wreath at her door only two days ago. She closed her eyes briefly and felt physically sick. Patric Faulkener! No. She didn't want to believe it. Why would Patric Faulkener send her a wreath? She had no quarrel with him. But he wouldn't dare, would he? He wouldn't dare say, 'In memory of Tamsin!' Surely not . . .

'Lilacs,' he said, smiling now. 'In memory of Lilacs, that's it. The end of a dream, in fact. And when a dream is dead — the best thing to do is to bury it.'

15

Cass drove her home and dropped her at the gate of Herb House, saying she couldn't stay; she had some films to process before morning.

Tam watched her turn the car and drive back up the lane, then she went into the house and thought over the events of the past few hours.

She was worried — decidedly so. She had imagined she could put it all behind her — the white flowers and the watcher in the church tower — but now she felt that it had all been resurrected. It had unnerved her when Patric had said what he had today. And then, thinking about things afterwards, she realized that her meeting with Vaughn on the heath that morning had been the second time she'd bumped into him there. Vaughn was obviously quite familiar with the paths across the heath — and where they led. Reason told her he could easily have come across from Alderwood that way, and dumped those chrysanthemums on her doorstep. He could also have been in the church tower — watching her on the day Mark had been helping her in the garden. That flash of light she'd seen — it had looked like a reflection on glass, and Vaughn wore spectacles!

Only one thing was certain in her mind. Somebody, she knew now, was out to scare her, and with a little shiver of apprehension she made doubly sure her door was locked as the afternoon started to darken into early evening.

It was with some trepidation, therefore, that as she washed up her dishes after an early tea she heard the sound of a car coming swishing in the dreary wetness, down the lane. She stood still, poised against the kitchen table, listening, and her heart started to thump until she thought it would deafen her.

She wouldn't open the kitchen door to *anybody* she decided. She stared at it, holding her breath so desperately that she felt dizzy. She was glad she'd drawn the chintzy curtains over the window. Perhaps she could pretend she wasn't here.

'Idiot!' she scolded herself. 'Those curtains aren't thick — they'll see the light from outside . . . ' Hurriedly she shot across the kitchen and switched the light off, then fumbled her way back to the table and stood there, listening again.

All was silence now. Silence and darkness. Whoever had come down the lane in that car was obviously still inside it. There had been no sound of a door being shut, or footsteps, or anything. All was utter quiet out there.

Cautiously she made her way to the door that opened onto her small sitting room at the front of the house. As she pushed it open an eerie blue light filled the room, making her jump back in fear, and she felt the hairs on the back of her neck prickling. Then she started to panic, and crept towards the window. It was dark outside now, and she could see where the blue glow was coming from.

A police car! Her hand flew to her throat. 'Oh, no . . . '

She peered out through the thick lace curtain that was a relic left behind by Joshua Temple. Many times, she recalled, she'd been tempted to take that curtain down and leave the window clear and uncluttered. Now, though, she was glad she hadn't. With the heavy lacy pattern still hanging there, she could see out yet not be seen herself.

She stared wide-eyed at the police car parked at her gate, and all manner of thoughts went through her brain. Police cars pulling up outside your door generally meant trouble. She tried not to think about the night she'd found Ava Thorne dead at the top of the lighthouse . . .

'Mark . . . ' She was filled with dread. It had to be Mark. Something had happened to him — she just knew something had happened to him . . .

There were two figures sitting inside the car. They didn't look in any particular hurry to come in and talk to her, though; they were looking down at some papers which they were flipping over as if they were stapled together.

As she watched, the one behind the driving wheel suddenly pushed open the door and got out of the car. Tam saw then that the figure was a woman, wearing a jacket and skirt, but she was not in police uniform. She stood on the lane, looking at the house, and after a few seconds the other occupant of the car — a man, and this one definitely uniformed — joined her.

Tamsin squeezed herself tight up against the wall beside the window, and watched them. It could be a trick, she reasoned. Funny things had been happening since she'd come here — first the watcher in the church tower, and then that horrible black-edged card in the middle of the white chrysanthemums, left against her back door.

The two people suddenly started walking towards her front door, the woman first. When they reached it, she rapped loudly with the cast-iron knocker that was integrated into the old-fashioned letterbox. And Tam, even though she was expecting the noise, almost jumped out of her skin.

She fled across the room and switched on the light, then went over to the door and unlocked it. Again, she had misgivings about letting anybody enter the house, and, after making sure the chain was secure, she opened the door just a tiny little bit.

'Miss Curtis? Miss Tamsin Curtis?' a polite female voice enquired pleasantly.

Tam swallowed, then took a deep breath. 'Yes?'

A pause, then a hand holding an identity card appeared in the two-inch gap between door and doorpost. The woman spoke again. 'I am Detective Inspector Jane Goodall — Eastern Counties Police Force — and with me is Constable Alan Jackson.'

Tamsin checked the card. It looked authentic enough. She peered through the crack in the door to see if the photograph and the real thing matched up. Short fairish hair — calm and steady grey eyes — pleasant expression — yes, everything seemed to be in order.

She took the chain off its slot and opened the door, handing back the card as its bearer came into the house. They stood side by side, then she backed away into the centre of the room and looked at them with some uncertainty.

'What is it?' she asked huskily. 'There must be something wrong for you to be here. There hasn't been an accident or anything . . . ?' Again, her thoughts winged northwards to Mark — two hundred miles away in Yorkshire.

'No, Miss Curtis. Nothing like that.' Jane Goodall had a clear, calm voice. 'Look, maybe you should sit down; we've been given some information that we need to check up on . . . '

'Information?' Tamsin cut in, staring first at the woman, then at the young constable. And then, seeing him closely, she realized what this visit must be about and relief flooded over her. 'Ah — it must be the stabbing incident in Alderwood.' She smiled at the constable. 'You were there, weren't you?'

He smiled back at her, but said, 'It isn't about that, Miss Curtis. That incident is closed. But I do remember you. I remember the dreamcatcher too.' He inclined her head towards Mark's little silver trinket, which she wore on its delicate filigree chain round her neck all the time now.

'You hadn't seen one before.' Tam relaxed a little, and explained to Jane Goodall — who was looking bemused — how she and Constable Jackson had first met up. 'But how can I help you?' she finished. 'I certainly haven't been involved in any more street brawls since that one.'

'It's a little more serious than that.'

'Serious?' Tam stared at the woman, then said, 'Perhaps we should go through to the kitchen if it's to take some time. It's warmer in there than in here.'

They followed her, standing watching her as she sped across the kitchen and switched the central light on again.

'You were sitting in the *dark*?' Jane Goodall raised her eyebrows.

'Oh, no,' Tam said. 'I had the light on when I heard your car — but living in this lonely spot I don't encourage casual visitors at night. If it had been some sort of salesperson I wouldn't have let on I was at home.' She gave a little awkward laugh. 'Call me a scaredy rabbit!'

'A sensible precaution,' Jane Goodall said. 'And it's always better to be safe than sorry.'

'Can I offer you some tea . . . ?'

'No, thank you.' Detective Inspector Goodall was carrying a black leather organizer. She opened it up, looked down at it, then said, 'You were in partnership with a Miss Ava Thorne, at Heronsea, on the north-east coast last year?'

'Ava? Yes?'

'Together you ran a wedding boutique!'

'Until Ava died in November. Yes.'

'You had walked out on the partnership before then, though.'

'Only days before . . . '

'You lived on the premises.'

Tam hated the way the police always seemed to speak in statements, not questions. 'Yes. We lived and worked in the old lighthouse for a while, then I moved out into a flat, but Ava stayed at the lighthouse.'

'And Miss Thorne died there.'

Tamsin didn't want to remember how Ava had died — alone, out there on the lantern platform, in the cold and dark of a November night. She whispered, 'Yes.'

'I have to tell you, Miss Curtis, we've received a rather serious accusation against you, and as a result of that I have to ask you if you'd mind accompanying me to the police station at Alderwood.'

Tam felt all her breath seeping out of her. She stared at Jane Goodall. 'A serious accusation? What does that mean? What sort of accusation. Who has accused me of what?'

251

'We have reason to believe that Ava Thorne might have met her death in suspicious circumstances.'

Horrified, Tamsin whispered, 'What kind of 'suspicious circumstances'?'

'That's what we need to find out.'

Tam's breathing was shallow. 'You have to be joking.'

'No joke, I'm afraid.' Jane Goodall's face was impassive. 'We have to take this seriously, and ask you to help with our enquiries.'

Shock held Tamsin tightly in its grip. 'That's what they say on television when somebody's suspected of — murder!'

'We aren't on television, Miss Curtis. I am merely doing my job. You may, if you wish, contact a solicitor before you are questioned . . . '

'Ava wasn't murdered; it's just not possible,' Tamsin choked out, gripping the edge of the table to steady herself. 'So why would I need a solicitor? I've done nothing wrong.'

'We have to take this accusation seriously.'

'Tell me about it,' she said, recovering herself enough now to realize she was getting very angry. 'Go on, tell me — first of all, who has made an accusation?'

'It was an anonymous phone call to Eastern Counties headquarters. That's all I can tell you at this stage — except that it wasn't possible to identify if the caller were male or female. The voice was disguised, muffled.'

Tamsin gave a short bark of laughter. 'And you're taking notice of some crank who hasn't even got the decency to give you a name?'

'We're wasting time,' Jane Goodall said in a more kindly voice. 'Maybe we can get all this sorted out at the station — and the sooner the better.'

Tamsin stared at the bland, impassive face and realized she had no option but to do as she'd been asked. She was silent for just a moment longer, then she said, 'Is this the point where you caution me? You know? Tell me that whatever I say will be used in evidence — or whatever jargon it is you people use?' Her voice was tinged with sarcasm. This couldn't be happening, she tried to convince herself. If it weren't so serious, it would be laughable. But murder was no laughing matter . . .

Jane Goodall gave the ghost of a smile and said, 'That won't be necessary. You aren't being accused of anything at the moment, Miss Curtis.'

★ ★ ★

She wasn't under arrest, Tamsin realized, but that didn't stop her feeling like a criminal when she'd been taken to an interview room, bombarded with questions, and had everything she said recorded on tape. At the end of it all, she'd asked if she could telephone a friend and they'd agreed she could do that — and told her also that she was free to go home now.

She still sat in the interview room, however, and when Cass arrived she blurted out everything that had happened.

'They called it an interview,' she said, sitting dry-eyed and still in shock. 'The word I would have used would have been 'interrogation', though.'

Cass gazed round the cold, plain room, with the glass panel in the door, and said, 'I can guess how you're feeling, love. This place is no better than a cell.'

'I can't blame them really.' Tamsin relented a little. 'I suppose they have to take notice of such allegations.'

'I just can't take this in.' Cass shook her head in disbelief. 'How could *anybody* believe you'd kill your friend?'

'Apparently it was one of those sick phone calls.' Tamsin clenched her hands on her knees in front of her. She'd moved away from the plain wooden table and was sitting bolt-upright on a straight-backed chair against the wall. 'They say I can go home now I've told them what they want to know.'

'Which was?'

'That I was away from Heronsea for more than a week around the time Ava died.' She looked up at Cass. 'Ava and I had argued, you see. I didn't want to stay in the business with her. I just didn't know who to turn to. I spent five days in Nottingham — and the landlady of the bed and breakfast I stayed at has verified my story — but still there are areas of doubt. Two days' worth of 'areas of doubt'.'

'But why? If you have an alibi . . . '

'Cass.' Tam felt like screaming, but calmed down enough to say, 'Cass — I don't *need* an alibi. Ava's death was an accident — either that or . . . '

'Or?' Cass sat forward in the chair facing her. 'What are you saying, Tam?'

'Or suicide. There was a post-mortem at the time, and an inquiry. She died of hypothermia. They couldn't decide, though, why she should have gone out onto the lantern platform at the top of the lighthouse, or why she'd shut the door behind her. She *knew* the lock was faulty — we all did. She *knew* if she latched the door behind her she wouldn't be able to open it again without the key, yet she left the key on the inside of the door. Ava had been . . . ill, though. Oh, not physically ill. And not seriously ill. But all the same, she was a bit — unbalanced.'

'And you went into business with her? Knowing that?'

Tam shook her head wearily. 'No. I didn't know that. Not until a long time afterwards. It's a long story . . . '

'And you're whacked!' Cass stood up. 'You're coming home with me, my girl. You're not going back to that lonely house all on your own.'

'Mark might phone — and he'll be worried if I don't answer.'

'You can ring him from my house.'

Tamsin gave a shaky little laugh. 'And tell him about this? Cass — I couldn't. What would he think?'

'Mark loves you.' Cass stood looking down at her and Tamsin gazed up at her friend. 'Mark won't think anything bad of you.'

Cass crouched down and placed her hands on Tam's two which were still clenched tightly together. Their eyes were level with each other as she pulled those hands apart and said gently, 'Look at you. You're getting all upset about this, and there's no need.'

'I've been practically accused of murdering Ava,' Tam said impatiently, pushing Cass aside and getting up herself to pace the room.

'That's ridiculous,' Cass said.

'Yes.' Tam sighed. 'Yes, it might be. But there have been other things . . . things you don't know about. Things I haven't told anybody about — except Mark.'

'What kind of things?'

Quietly, Tamsin told her friend about the watcher in the church tower, and the white chrysanthemums and sinister black-edged card with her name on it.

Cass was furious. 'Somebody is trying to scare you.'

Tamsin's laugh was feeble. 'You know something? They're succeeding.'

'Have you told the police?'

Tam nodded. 'They looked at me as if I'd gone off my head.'

'But they registered it?'

'Oh, yes. Everything I said was recorded. They do that with criminals, you know. They even gave me a copy of the tape recording. Everything I said to them is on it.'

'Tam — don't be bitter.'

'But it's all true. I feel like I've done something terrible. I feel like I need a hot shower now to get the taint of this place off me.'

'But . . . '

'They say I can go now.' Tamsin looked up into Cass's distraught face. 'Do you *mind* if I

257

come back with you tonight? Did you mean what you said? I don't think I could bear to go back alone to Herb House.'

'Of course you can come to my house. I wouldn't dream of leaving you alone — not after this.'

'What does it all mean, Cass?' Tamsin was bewildered as she stumbled to her feet.

Cass stared at her. 'I don't know what to say.'

'Why are they doing this to me? I'm a stranger to Suffolk. I don't have any enemies. I hardly know anybody. So who would want to scare me?'

Cass said quietly, 'Each time — it seems as if it's getting a little bit more serious, doesn't it?'

Tamsin felt as if a cold shadow had passed over her as she replied, 'That's exactly what I was thinking. It started small — just a hint that somebody was watching me — then the white flowers and that horrible card with them, and now this . . . ' She swallowed before continuing, 'So where is it going to end? What else can they do to me, Cass . . . ? And how am I going to clear my name? There are still those two days to account for. I could still face a murder charge — or at the very least one of manslaughter!'

16

Cass drove her home again the following morning.

'This is starting to be a habit,' Tam said as they drew up outside Herb House. She was feeling slightly more at ease after a good night's sleep — brought on by Cass making her hot, milky cocoa laced with brandy the previous night.

'I feel responsible for you.' Cass grinned at her as she killed the engine. 'After all, it was me you came down here to see in the first place. Nobody could imagine that a mere visit to a friend could stir up such trouble, could they?'

'It's my own fault, though, that I decided to stay and make my home in Suffolk,' Tam said. 'The sensible thing would have been to return to Yorkshire and face up to what had happened there. I guess I was just a coward, really. There had been so much pain and heartbreak at Heronsea that I thought the easiest thing would be to run away from the memories.'

Seriously Cass considered her. 'Are you sure you're going to be okay? Coming back here on your own like this?'

Tamsin shrugged, then said in a small voice, 'Somebody's opened a real can of worms, Cass — stirring up Ava's death. It means there will have to be some sort of inquiry — and already I'm a suspect. I don't have a proper alibi for the whole of that week after I walked out on Ava. There are still two days when I *could* have driven back to Yorkshire.'

'You said the landlady of that guest house . . . '

'Oh, yes. She vouched for me while I was actually there — in my room. But I didn't stay there, Cass. I walked around Nottingham. I went shopping. I spent nearly a whole day up at the castle, for instance. And after Nottingham I drove down to Leicester and holed up again. I needed to see Ava's brother, Rafe, you see — and I knew he was racing all weekend and wouldn't be back at Oscar Herrick's house in Northampton until Monday or Tuesday. I had a whole week to kill — and for two days I didn't have an alibi. I *could* have gone back up to Yorkshire — that's what the police were hinting at last night.

'They asked if it was true that I'd had the opportunity to go back and shut Ava out on the lantern platform of the lighthouse — you know — get her up there on some pretence or other and then slam the door on her.' Tamsin was agitated; her fingernails were digging into the palms of her hands as she sat in the passenger seat of Cass's car. She stared unseeingly out through the windscreen, her mind going over and over that fateful week after she'd left Heronsea last November. 'They said that was what the anonymous caller had suggested. That I had killed Ava in that way. It was awful, Cass. Awful.'

'Those two days,' Cass said, musingly. 'Which two days exactly were they?'

Tamsin sighed. 'I told you — the day I went to Nottingham Castle, and the day I drove down to Leicester. I was on my own, Cass. I didn't want company of any kind. I just *wanted to be on my own.*'

'Let's go over those days. Right from the minute you got out of bed in the mornings.'

'It's no good, Cass.' Tam was full of impatience with herself. 'I didn't see *anybody* who knows me. I didn't talk to anybody either. I just wanted solitude — that's why I went to the castle. It stands high up on a rock. I just went up there and wandered around the gardens, and sat on seats.'

'You must have eaten. *Where* did you eat?'

'I bought a packet of sandwiches out of a machine in town.'

'Oh, Tam!'

Tamsin raised her eyes to the roof of the car and slid down in her seat. 'Yes. You might well say, 'Oh, Tam!' But I didn't know then that I was going to need an alibi, did I?'

'You went into town as well, then? As well as going to the castle?'

Tam let out a long sigh. 'A department store, a book shop . . . several stores, in fact. I needed some make-up. I left Heronsea in such a spectacular rush that I forget to even put a lipstick in my bag . . . '

'Maybe a shop assistant would remember you.'

'I doubt it. You know how impersonal credit card transactions are — the assistants are so busy with those little zippy machines they don't have time to even look at you, let alone remember you several months later.'

Cass sat forward. 'But if you paid by credit card you've got your alibi. Your card receipt will be dated.'

'It won't tell the police I didn't drive back up to Yorkshire *after* I'd paid for the stuff, though.'

'Did you take your car into Nottingham?'

'Yes.'

'You parked it?'

'Yes.' Tamsin shot up in her seat at that. 'In a multi-storey . . . '

'Your ticket would be dated and timed, then.'

Tamsin's face took on a defeated expression. 'The ticket, though. I need the ticket.'

Cass was already halfway out of her car. 'Come on,' she yelled.

Tamsin scrambled out of her door and ran round the car. Cass was already yanking open the garden gate and running towards Tam's car, which was parked on the overgrown drive at the side of the house.

Cass turned round, jigging up and down, holding out her hand. 'Your keys,' she yelled. 'Quickly now. Give me your car keys.'

'Are you crazy?' Tamsin handed over her keys. 'Cass — what's the point of this?'

'You haven't cleared out that glory-hole of a glove compartment, have you?'

Realization dawned at last. Tam drew in her breath and then squealed, 'Cass! You're an angel! I never thought of . . . '

'The mess you leave your car in?' Cass asked briskly.

'Oh, Cass . . . '

Tamsin could have thrown her arms round Cass and hugged her when she found the ticket in question, screwed up, but intact.

Cass gave a whoop of pure joy. 'It was even one of those new ticket machines, where you have to key in the actual numbers on your registration plate so the ticket can't be transferred to another vehicle. Tam, you are one lucky girl.'

Tam clutched the small ticket and gazed at it. The time on it showed that she had parked at twelve-forty-eight.

'I didn't leave the guest house till after a late breakfast — I couldn't possibly have driven to Yorkshire and back before lunch-time.'

'And you didn't leave the car park until . . .'

'Five-thirty-one! See — it's there on the ticket. At the time I was impatient with the whole idea of checking in, keying in my car number and then having to put the ticket back into the machine when I left the car park. Now, though — I'm really glad they installed those machines in Nottingham. And,' she said, 'what's more to the point, I was back at the guest house for dinner at half past six.' Tamsin closed her eyes and offered up a silent prayer. Then she opened them, looked at Cass again and said, 'But there's still the Sunday to account for.'

'The Sunday you drove down to Leicester?'

Tamsin nodded, and she felt a moment's despair as she said, 'I left Nottingham at around ten in the morning, arrived in Leicester less than an hour later and went to an address the woman in the Nottingham guest house had given me.'

'And booked in for the night?'

'Yes.' Tamsin stared at Cass. 'I had Sunday lunch there, then stayed in watching television all afternoon.'

'So somebody knew you were there?'

Tamsin nodded, then her face fell. 'I went out later on, though.'

'No more car park tickets?' Cass asked eagerly.

'I walked.'

'You couldn't have driven back to Yorkshire then, could you? Not if you'd left your car at the guest house.'

'I don't have an alibi for my car. It was just street parked — away from the B & B I'd booked into. I had one hell of a job finding a space.'

'Where did you walk to?'

Tam thought back to that fateful day, and remembered. 'I needed some money. I went to a bank machine — a hole-in-the-wall cash dispenser.'

Cass dived back into Tamsin's car and brought out all the rubbish they'd recently rummaged through again. 'Come on,' she said. 'It must be in here, mustn't it? The slip for the cash. Dated and timed. And the address of the bank? You never throw anything away, do you?'

They searched through everything, but could only find a petrol receipt for the following Monday morning.

Tam stood back, gazing at her car.

Cass said, 'Go inside the house and phone your bank. See if they can come up with something. They must have proof somewhere that you took that money out of your account.'

It was all too much for Tamsin. She pressed one hand firmly against her mouth to stop her lips trembling, and tears poured down her cheeks. Cass, she knew, had saved her from a whole heap of trouble. She could now account for all her movements on those two days, and the police would have to believe her.

She howled. And Cass hugged her and got her inside the house and made her a strong cup of tea.

'I don't know how to ever thank you . . . ' Tam said, after blowing her nose and mopping up her tears.

'What are friends for?' Cass said, grinning.

The news hit the headlines in the local early evening newspaper, and Tamsin was devastated as she read it. "Helping police with their enquiries," she muttered to herself, for Cass had gone now, leaving her to phone the police that afternoon and tell them that she could, in fact, account for her movements on those two days that she'd been questioned about. They were sorry, of course, that the story had gone to press. Detective Inspector Goodall tried to placate her, telling her that her name would definitely not be mentioned.

Wearily now, she pushed herself up from the kitchen table where she'd sat reading the newspaper, rested her hands flat on either side of it and looked down at the picture of Herb House that stared back up at her. No — they hadn't mentioned her name in the newspaper, they'd merely said '*a young woman who has recently come to live in the area has been helping police with their enquiries into a suspicious death in the north of England*'!

Her phone started ringing, making her head jerk up. She went over to it, stood staring at it anxiously for several seconds, then picked up the receiver. It was Cass.

'Tam! The newspaper picture of your

house! How could they?'

Tamsin said, 'I know. It sickens me. Somebody obviously put two and two together, and now everybody in the damned area will know it's me.'

'Where did they get the photo of the house?'

Tam gave a shaky laugh. 'They could have come down here and just taken a picture, couldn't they? Or the estate agent . . . he had one.'

'Tam — what can I say?'

Tamsin said quietly, 'Thanks for ringing me, Cass. But there's nothing I can do, is there? They didn't print my name, but it will be obvious I'm under some sort of suspicion.'

'I'm sorry, Tam. I wish there was something I could do. I can, of course, make some enquiries at the local printers and see who was responsible for putting the picture of the house in the newspaper . . . '

'No,' Tam said. 'It doesn't matter — really, Cass. People will get to know eventually that I had nothing to do with Ava's death. At least I wasn't arrested in connection with it.'

'Call me, love. Please. If there's anything I can do.'

'I will. And Cass . . . '

'What is it?' Cass asked.

'Thanks. Just that. I really appreciate you

looking after me last night — *and* helping to clear my name this morning.'

Cass laughed softly. 'I told you,' she said. 'I'm your friend.'

★　★　★

The phone rang again — two minutes after Cass had rung off. Clare Faulkener sounded really irate.

Tamsin explained, as diplomatically as she knew how, what had happened, and why the picture of Herb House was in the newspaper.

'It won't do your reputation any good,' Clare said haughtily.

'I didn't ask the police to take me in for questioning,' Tam pointed out. 'Until yesterday Ava's death had not been treated as a suspicious incident.'

'I realize that, but . . . '

'But you don't want to continue doing business with me? Is that it?' Tamsin came straight to the point. She realized that she had to. Clare was not a woman who would put her own livelihood in jeopardy.

'I didn't say that.'

'I didn't kill Ava Thorne,' Tam stated. 'I can prove now that I didn't. I wasn't within a hundred miles of Yorkshire when Ava died.'

'You can *definitely* prove that?' Clare's voice was shrill.

'Yes. I have done. Today. It was just bad luck the press got hold of the story beforehand.'

'We-ell . . . '

Tamsin said, hating herself for pleading, 'Look, Clare, just give me a chance, will you? I haven't let you down yet, have I? And I promise you — there will be no mud sticking to my name by the end of the week.'

'You can guarantee that, can you?' Clare's response was far from friendly.

'Yes,' Tamsin said, 'I can!' And with that Clare agreed to speak to her again at the end of the week, then rang off.

Less than ten minutes later she heard a car drawing up outside the house, and her heart turned over at the thought of it being the police again. Then she scolded herself, 'You have nothing to hide. Nothing to be scared of.'

But it didn't work, telling herself that. She *did* have something to be scared of. Somebody had made an allegation to the police about her, and so far nobody knew who had done that. Somebody, too, had spied on her from the church tower, and somebody had sent her a funeral wreath. The police knew all about those former incidents now, but it was like they said — there wasn't much hope of catching the culprit. She ought to have informed them sooner, Detective Inspector Goodall had told her.

Tam had asked her when she'd said that, 'And what would you have done?'

The reply had been cautious. 'We could have examined the flowers — and made enquiries as to where they'd been bought.'

'They were probably stolen,' she'd said.

'Then it would have been our job to find out by whom,' Jane Goodall had answered.

'And would you really have bothered going to all that trouble for a few flowers?' she'd come back at the woman.

'If time had been available.'

She always had an answer!

Footsteps were coming down the side of the house now. It wasn't too dark outside yet. It was barely four o'clock and it had been a bright, sunny day, cold, but cheerful all the same.

Tamsin went to the kitchen door and pulled it open just as Vaughn came round the corner of the house. She might have guessed! Probably Clare had sent him over to try and find out more than what was reported in the newspaper.

He stood outside her door and looked at

her. His face was pinched and worried-looking. His hands, as usual, were thrust into the deep pockets of his hideous checked jacket. 'Can I come in?'

She nodded. 'I was half expecting you.'

'You were?' He followed her inside the house and slammed the door shut behind him.

'Clare's obviously sent you.'

His face registered nothing but blank surprise. 'I'm not Clare Faulkener's errand boy, Tam.'

'Okay!' She held up one hand and said, 'I'll make us a drink.'

'Don't bother,' he said. 'Not for me. I won't be staying long. I had to see you, though.'

'You've read the newspaper.'

'Yes.' There was a dull red flush in his cheeks. 'You might have told me, Tam. It was one hell of a shock reading the headlines, and seeing the photo of your house on the front page of the *Echo*.'

'What ought I to have told you?' She spun round to face him, the table between them.

'About the suspicions. About Ava Thorne's death. I thought it was an accident.'

'It was.'

'Then why . . . ?' He spread his hands out

towards her. 'Why were you taken in for questioning?'

'Somebody rang the police and told them I was involved.'

'Somebody? Who?'

'I don't know. The police don't know either. It was a malicious phone call. Somebody obviously doesn't like me.'

'Tam . . . ' He came striding round the table towards her, grasped hold of her shoulders and shook her. 'Tam — you're talking in riddles. What's going on?'

'Take your hands off me,' she said, wriggling away from him and dashing his arms away with her own hands. 'And don't talk to me like that. You sound as though you think I'm guilty . . . '

'Guilty of what?' he snapped, his eyes bright and piercing as they gazed at her from behind those steel-framed spectacles.

'Murder — if you must know.' Even as she spoke the dreaded word she felt her knees going weak. She took herself in hand and grabbed hold of the back of a chair to steady herself. She wasn't going to crack. She was determined not to let this get at her any more. She had a good friend in Cass, and she remembered what Vaughn had said to her only the other day, about him being there for her if ever she wanted him. She had two

273

friends at least who she could count on . . .

'Why didn't you tell me?' he asked, and now there was a hard edge to his voice, and he didn't try to touch her again.

'It's not something you shout from the house-tops, is it? And anyway, I've only been home since this morning . . . '

'They kept you overnight?' His voice was raw. 'At the police station? In a cell?'

'No,' she almost screamed at him. 'I wasn't arrested. I stayed overnight with Cass. I couldn't face coming back here — not when somebody had made such an allegation about me.'

'You must know who your enemies are . . . '

'I don't have any enemies. I haven't been here long enough to make enemies.'

'I don't trust your darling Mark Langham,' he sneered. 'He'd do anything to get you back in Yorkshire. You know damn well he would.'

Her eyes widened and she stared at him in horror. 'Mark wouldn't do this to me. Not in a million years, he wouldn't.'

'Have you asked him if he was the informer?' he snarled.

'No! And I never would. Mark isn't like that. Mark . . . '

'Mark! Mark! Mark!' he ground out. 'Hell, Tam, can't you see what he's after? He wants

274

you at any price. He wants you to go running back to him. He wants you to — '

'Shut up,' she yelled, covering her ears with her hands. 'Shut up, Vaughn. You don't know what you're talking about. You don't know Mark at all.' Suddenly her hands fell to her sides and her shoulders drooped. She walked over to the stove to warm herself. All at once she felt incredibly cold. She faced him from the other side of the room. 'What's happened to your promise, anyway?' she asked quietly. 'I seem to remember you telling me you'd never let me down. You said I could come to you if I ever needed somebody.'

He couldn't meet her gaze. He looked down at the floor and muttered, 'I didn't take into account at the time that I might be speaking those words to a girl who could be accused of murder.'

She drew in a long, slow breath, then exhaled it even more slowly before replying, and her words were short and to the point. 'Get out,' she said. 'Get out, right now, Vaughn.'

His head jerked up. Those cold eyes stared at her. 'This changes everything, Tam. Can't you see that?'

'I am not a murderer,' she said in a flat tone.

'I have my career to think about.'

She managed to keep her temper in check, but only just. 'Get out,' she said again.

'You do understand, don't you, Tam.'

For some reason he reminded her of a little boy who had been caught stealing apples. 'Just go, Vaughn,' she said, hardening her heart against him.

'Maybe when this is all over . . . '

'No,' she said.

'Aw, Tam. Don't be like that. You must know that I can't go on seeing you with this hanging over you.'

'Please Vaughn. Just turn round and walk out of my life, will you?' Inwardly, she was seething. She clenched her hands at her sides and fought down the urge that was making her want to scream at him, run across the kitchen and batter him unmercifully with those hands.

'I'd never let you down . . . ' Those words rang in her ears, deafening her with their insincerity and their utter hypocrisy.

She turned her back on him and held out her hands towards the stove. She didn't want to look at him. She never wanted to see him again. She was alone and frightened in this alien place, and he hadn't uttered one word of sympathy or offered one iota of help.

She heard his footsteps going out of the kitchen, then muffled as he went down the path at the side of the house. And then his car engine sprang into life at the front of the house, and she heard the squeal of tyres on gravel as he turned and raced away from her up the long lane.

And she knew she had been right to doubt him that day on the heath. Her own words came rushing back to taunt her, and she recalled how she'd doubted him.

She stared at the door he'd gone through. 'I always knew it. I couldn't trust you, Vaughn, and now I know for certain that I never will.'

She made up her mind swiftly then. There was only one thing left for her to do now.

17

She sat in her car in darkness on the sea front at Heronsea, gazing out at the midnight sea. The promenade was deserted, and through the windscreen, up ahead of her, she could see the stark white column of the lighthouse rising from the headland. The lighthouse was in darkness, except for the one red light right at the very top. It was a signal to low-flying aircraft that a high building was there, and had to be avoided.

It was a clear night. Tam recalled she'd set out before nine that night and the roads had been deserted. The latter half of February was turning out to be milder than the first part had been. There was a sharp frost, though, so she'd packed her warmest clothes and dumped her suitcase on the back seat of the Beetle for the drive north. She didn't know how long she would stay in Yorkshire. It all depended . . .

She bit hard on her lip and stared even harder at the sea. The car engine was still running to keep her warm, but she realized she couldn't stay here all night. There was just one more thing to do, though — before she drove the extra ten miles to Rothwold.

She drove slowly up to the headland and parked in the shadow of the lighthouse. Her teeth were chattering together as she got out of the car and walked towards the towering white building. She stood in front of the securely locked door and stared at it. Across one of the windows a 'SOLD' notice had been plastered. She was sorry to see that. She hadn't wanted it to be sold. She'd wanted it pulled down and hurled into the sea, stone by hateful stone. It was a dreadful place.

She walked right round it, her shoes clattering on the paving stones. The town was quiet, but still well lit, with street lamps behind her now. When she reached the seaward side of the lighthouse, she leaned her back against the cold white wall and wrapped her arms round herself. The tide was fully in below the great concrete sea wall on top of which the lighthouse stood. Spray was being tossed up forty and more feet as the waves crashed and thundered below her. She eased herself away from the tower and walked to the smooth iron railings on top of the sea wall, taking a firm hold of them as she looked down into the swirling dark waters that were hurling themselves with a foaming fury at the mighty sea defence. She could feel the force of the ocean shuddering up through the structure and through her whole body. She turned and looked up at the very summit of the lighthouse. It was up there that Ava . . .

She swallowed the lump in her throat and refused to turn her eyes away from the high lantern platform so far above her. It was up there also that she and Vaughn Herrick had made love for the last time . . .

At that thought she did turn away. She flung round and faced the angry sea again, but in her mind she was living again those days in the not so distant past when she had laughed and been happy here, and worked here, and loved here. There were ghosts to get rid of tonight, though, and it was something that had to be done. If she faced up to what had happened in the scariness and darkness of night, she knew she might well be rid of those ghosts for evermore by day.

She tried to be charitable. She tried to reason within herself that Ava had been ill. In her heart, though, she knew that Ava had been to blame for a lot of things. Tamsin cast her mind back to the night when she herself had fallen down the lighthouse stairs and had lost Vaughn's baby in a miscarriage. It had been no dream that had sent her hurtling down those stairs. It had been no ghost either. It had been Ava.

Tamsin realized as she stood there that it wasn't Ava's death she'd been fighting all these months; it was Ava's life. It was her mistaken loyalty to her one-time business partner that was making her so she couldn't think of Yorkshire as her home any more. She'd blamed herself constantly for not being more understanding, not having the same ambitious interest Ava had in the business, and lastly for not realizing what Ava was capable of.

It hadn't been an accident, she realized now. Ava's death. It had been deliberate. Suicide had been the one sure way Ava could punish her, leave her with a heart full of guilt and a life full of regret. And it had worked. Until now.

Slowly, Tamsin walked round the base of the lighthouse and back to her car. She slid behind the wheel and looked at the dashboard clock. It was well after midnight now.

And Mark, ten miles away, would be in bed.

★   ★   ★

Mark stirred restlessly in his sleep. Rain was beating at the window, and he pulled the quilt up and over his head to shut out the sound. Normally he could sleep through anything, but this must be one heavy downpour to be making such a racket.

The pattering at the window kept on, and on, and then he thought he heard a voice. Tam's voice.

'Idiot,' he muttered sleepily to himself. 'She's never off your mind. Never will be. You should get out and start living — meet somebody else.'

Not in a storm like this, though. Rain was pelting his bedroom window now, with more force than he'd ever known before. Then it stopped. As suddenly as it had started, it stopped, and all was quiet. He was wide awake now, though, and he hauled himself up in bed and looked over to the window. There was a bright moon shining, he could see. And stars. Stars and rain didn't usually go hand in hand. Cloud accompanied rain, and cloud blocked out the stars. He grimaced at the window.

And then the telephone at the side of his bed started to ring.

'Damn!' He rolled over to it and snatched it up before it impinged any more on his consciousness. He'd never sleep tonight now.

This was all he needed — Edgar getting him up for a call-out. Some motorist who'd been caught out in that storm and now had a stalled engine somewhere out in the wilds of the East Riding.

'What *does* it take to get you out of bed? Dynamite?'

A woman's voice. He held the receiver away from his ear and looked at it. Then cautiously he returned it to his ear and listened again.

'Mark! Have you answered the phone in your sleep?'

He sucked in his breath. 'Tam?' he asked cautiously. He peered in the darkness at his bedside clock. 'Tam!' He was wide awake now. She wouldn't ring at this time unless something was wrong. 'Tam! What is it? It's way after midnight, for heaven's sake . . . '

'Hey! You're there. Let me in, will you? I've been slinging gravel at your window for ages.'

'Where are you?'

'Just down the road. I remembered there was a phone box. It works better than the gravel.'

'Tam! Do you know what time it is?'

'Yes. You just told me. Way after midnight.' A pause, then, 'Twelve-forty-six, if you want it exact!'

'Yeah! Midnight — twelve-forty-six. What's wrong, Tam?'

'Are you going to let me in? I'm running out of ten pence pieces.'

It struck him then. She was out there in the dark. Alone. But why?

'I'm coming. Get back in your car. You never know who's around these country lanes at night.'

'If you peep out through your bedroom window, you'll see my car is parked neatly against your front door,' she said with a little laugh.

'Tam — for goodness' sake — stay where you are. I'm coming for you.'

★ ★ ★

'When you asked me if I'd like a drink, I expected cocoa — or hot milk,' she said teasingly, her hands clasped round a small glass half full of golden liquid.

'Whisky's the best cure for February.' He sat facing her across the hearth, both of them in comfortably deep armchairs with soft cushions. Mark felt relaxed, but he could see that Tam *couldn't* relax for some reason; she was perched on the edge of her chair, looking into the open fire where he'd just lodged two logs from the log-box by the side of the hearth onto the dying embers. They were already crackling and spitting, and in another few minutes he knew they'd flare into vibrant life.

She looked up at him. 'Since you let me in, you haven't asked me why I'm here,' she said softly.

'It's enough that you are here. I also haven't whipped you up into my arms and carried you off to bed,' he said, 'because obviously something's wrong, and you'll tell me about it in your own good time.'

'It's going to be hard to tell you.' She took a deep gulp of whisky, then placed her glass on the hearth beside her chair.

'So, take your time,' he said, hiding his impatience from her because he knew that was how it had to be. She was here. She had come to him. And it must be something serious, something important, because all she had wanted to do a few weeks ago was leave Yorkshire and never, ever return to it again.

He wasn't going to rush her, though. He didn't care what it was that had brought her back. She was here, and that was enough for him. He realized he had changed a lot in the past year. At one time he would have been full of disquiet and intolerance with her. He would have demanded an instant explanation; he would have rushed in asking questions, wanting answers. Not now, though. He'd learned how to handle her. She wouldn't be rushed or pushed; she'd dig her heels in if he treated her as anything less than an equal. He realized that not so long ago he'd been turning into what a few years ago women would have called a male chauvinist pig. But then he'd met Tam, and she had changed all that.

She linked her hands loosely together in front of her and said calmly, 'The police took me in for questioning over Ava Thorne's death. Somebody, it seems, has it in for me. An anonymous phone caller told them I'd killed her.'

★ ★ ★

'We should get married,' he said next morning, when he'd cooked breakfast for them both and they'd sat on opposite sides of the table and eaten it.

Surprised, she asked, 'Why should we get married?' And, without waiting for an answer, she got up from the table and started clearing it of the breakfast things.

He followed her to the other side of the kitchen and put his arms round her as she stacked the dishwasher. 'Because I love you,' he said.

She turned round in the circle of his arms to face him. 'Did you take in *anything* I told you last night?' she wanted to know. 'Did you realize that for a couple of hours at least I was suspected of being a murderer?'

'I heard what you said,' he said, nuzzling her cheek with his unshaven chin. 'And I'm not in the least concerned that you might be a murderer. If you are one, I'll write my memoirs — something along the lines of 'I slept with a . . . ''

He winced as she jabbed her slippered heel down hard on his bare toes. 'Ouch! That hurt.'

'Be serious, then,' she said, laughing and looking up into his eyes, and loving him for his consideration and care of her.

'I am being serious. You could no more kill somebody than fly to the moon.'

She ignored that. 'You need a shave. Your chin prickles.'

'You didn't complain earlier.' He lowered his voice to a sexy whisper.

Seriously she looked at him and said, 'Did you expect me to complain about bristles when I was desperately in need of someone to hold me, and kiss my fears away, and love me . . . '

'I'm holding you now.'

'You don't mind about me being accused of . . . '

He placed a finger on her lips. 'Don't,' he said. 'Don't say it and don't even think it. You wouldn't even be capable of killing a butterfly. You know darn well that you won't even swat a wasp — you'd sooner let it sting you.'

Her laughter was tremulous. She felt very weepy, which wasn't like her at all. To get things back on an even keel, she decided a change of subject would be a good idea. 'Vaughn Herrick came over to see me,' she said. 'He was worried I might harm his career.'

'You've been seeing him?' Warily he held her away from him and looked into her eyes.

'Not 'seeing' him in the sense you mean. I met him a couple of times on the heath when I was walking into Alderwood, and when Cass and I went for a pub meal he turned up with Patric Faulkener.'

'So 'not seeing him' means . . . ?'

'He means nothing to me, Mark,' she insisted quietly. 'I don't hate him, but I could never trust him again. I just feel — empty of him now. Is that a good thing, do you think?'

'I'm glad about that.' She knew he believed her by the way the taut muscles alongside his jaw relaxed. He said, 'Did you tell the police about the watcher in the church tower, and the white chrysanthemums that were delivered to your door with the 'In Memory of . . . ' card?'

She nodded. 'They didn't think either thing was important in itself. I got the feeling they were more concerned that I might start running amok with a hatchet or something. They were there, on the ball — knocking on my door — only an hour after they received that vile phone call about me.'

'And they're satisfied now that you had nothing to do with Ava's death?'

'They seem to be.'

Taking her face in his hands, he bent his head and kissed her lips, then said softly, 'Why did you come to me, Tam?'

She hesitated for a moment, then, 'Panic, I guess. I'm only hanging onto Clare Faulkener's contract by the skin of my teeth, and I began wondering what was going to happen next. I suppose it was instinct that made me run to you. There was also the fear inside me that you might read about me being taken in for questioning if one of the big newspapers picked up the story.'

He was quiet for a while, holding her gently, then saying hesitantly, 'I wonder if that's what the phantom prowler wants you to do? To run? To get out of Suffolk?'

'He doesn't know me very well if he thinks I'll do that.'

'But you have done it — you've run to me, Tam.'

'It's not a permanent arrangement, though — me running here. I just needed a breather. I had to get away, but only for a short time.'

'You said 'he' too,' Mark said quietly. 'What makes you think it's a man who's doing this to you?'

She lifted her shoulders in a shrug. 'Do you think a woman could be behind it, then?'

He sighed. 'I don't know. But I don't like what's happening. I think it might be best if you don't go back straight away.'

She gazed up at him. 'But then they'll have won, won't they? If I do what we think they want me to do?'

'Better that than . . . '

She heard the note of fear in his voice and knew he was scared. Scared for her, and for what might happen to her. 'They haven't resorted to physical violence,' she reminded him.

'It's such a lonely spot, though — where you live. I hate to think of you there alone. Anything could happen . . . '

'Hey! Don't make remarks like that.' She reached her hands up to his shoulders and said, 'Don't worry, Mark. Nobody's hurt me.

They're just trying to frighten me, I think. But for what reason, I just don't know.'

'Don't go back,' he pleaded. 'Stay here. You'll be safe here.'

'Safe! Wrapped-in-cotton-wool safe? Mark — I can't live like that.' Her eyes were troubled.

'You're living looking over your shoulder all the while now, Tam. Is that any better?'

She shook her head. 'I don't know. I just don't know, Mark. I don't really know why I came here, except . . . '

Viciously, he said, 'Except that Herrick hurt you by what he said to you. Did you think that I might take the same attitude — not want my name linked with yours because of the suspicion you'd been under?'

'No,' she cried. 'It wasn't like that. I've told you — I didn't want you to pick up a newspaper and read about me. I don't care about Vaughn. He can't hurt me. I don't care enough for him to hurt me any more. It was something more than that which made me drive up here. I went to the lighthouse at Heronsea last night. I was there at midnight. I had to lay a ghost or two. If I hadn't been determined to do that, I wouldn't have ever come back to Yorkshire.'

He let her go. 'You went to the lighthouse? Last night. Tam — are you crazy?'

'I had to.' She pushed past him and began clearing more stuff off the table and putting things away in cupboards. Eventually she stood still and looked at him again. 'Don't you see? It was blocking the way for me coming back — what happened at the lighthouse.'

'And now?' he asked.

'Nothing very startling happened last night. I guess I just came to terms with my life, and realized that no matter how far away I go from Heronsea nothing is going to change the past. It happened. And life went on.' She lifted her shoulders in a helpless little gesture. 'Places aren't important, are they? It's people who matter, not places.' Her hand flew suddenly to the neckline of the warm wool shirt she was wearing over leggings. Her fingers touched and then held onto the pendant she rarely went anywhere without nowadays. She glanced down at the little silver filigree charm she was holding on its long, slender chain. Softly she said, 'People who think enough of me to chase my bad dreams away.'

'Tam!' He had her in his arms again in seconds. 'Oh, Tam . . . ' His voice was husky with emotion. He bent his head and she was warm and willing, and waiting for his kiss. She wanted to stay with him then — stay, and never have to go back to Herb House.

She couldn't turn her back on Stratton End, though — or on the people she'd left behind there. She had a contract with Clare Faulkener. And Cass would be worried out of her mind when she discovered she wasn't at home. There was somebody else too — somebody as yet unknown to her, but who was nonetheless real because of that. The watcher in the tower was a threat, but she wasn't seriously afraid of him — or *her* — she amended in her mind.

'Stay here,' Mark was saying. 'You'll be safe here.'

Her hands were on his shoulders, she looked up into his face. 'I'm safe in Suffolk,' she insisted. 'Somebody is intent on stirring things up, but I believe that's as far as it will go. Maybe it's somebody who had a grudge against old Joshua Temple. I've been wondering if Joshua had promised to leave the house to somebody when he died and then went back on his word. I keep going over and over in my mind what the reason could be to scare the pants off me.'

'I worry about you all the time, Tam . . . '

'Don't,' she said quickly. 'If you worry about me, then *I'll* worry about *you* worrying, and we'll just go round in ever-decreasing circles — worrying. It's unnerving, I must admit, when I feel somebody's watching me. It was a bit scary too when those white chrysanthemums arrived. But I've got to sit this out, Mark. Try to understand — I *need* to know why I'm a target for somebody's paranoia like this.'

'It's dangerous, Tam.' Mark's jaw tightened like stone again.

'No,' she said, 'I don't *feel* I'm in danger. I feel as though somebody is playing silly games with me. And I want to know why. I *need* to know why. And that's why I'm going back to Suffolk . . . '

'Not right away?'

'No,' she said gently, tiptoeing to kiss him again. 'Not today. I'll stay till the weekend. Will that satisfy you?'

★ ★ ★

It was Friday, and she was out in Mark's vast garden, hacking at weeds and pruning long tendrils of prickly rose hedging, when he came out to her and suggested — for her last day with him — that she might like to go out for a meal instead of enduring his bachelor-style cooking.

'Tonight? That'd be lovely.'

He stood, arms folded, watching her as she snipped the rose tendrils into short lengths and dropped them in a sturdy plastic garden waste-bag. 'You're never happier than when you're working with those things, are you?' His soft laughter was deep and attractive.

'I love being out of doors. I could never sit in an office all day.' She sheathed the secateurs she'd been using, shoved them into the pocket of her jeans, and then peeled off her thick gloves. 'Don't you ever see the beauty in this glorious garden of yours?'

He grimaced. 'In summer maybe, when it's a mass of colour. Not now, though, when everything's drab and waterlogged.'

'This is when the work needs doing, though,' she said. 'I think I'll spend the afternoon giving you lessons on pruning and ground-clearance.'

He groaned. 'And there was I thinking we might have a run out onto the moors, or do something madly exciting like walking on a deserted beach somewhere and being romantic and alone together.'

In a practical voice, she said, 'Your roses need attention.' Relenting a little then, she added, 'But a tramp across the moors would be lovely.'

'I was thinking more of a *drive*,' he said. 'A civilized drive on well-marked roads.'

'We could start off that way.' She scrambled past the clutching arms of rose bushes and went to him, standing in front of him and lifting her lips to his. She felt his response deepening, and darted away from him to stand, hands on hips, laughing at him. 'We could park the car, though — and then go tramping across the moors and the heather. How about that?'

His face relaxed into a wide smile. 'You always get your way, don't you?'

'No,' she said, 'this is a compromise — you get your drive and I get my tramp.'

Inside the house a phone started ringing. He swung away from her and loped back to the building, disappearing inside the kitchen door while she stood there and watched him. She'd enjoyed the last few days, and she knew it was going to be hard to leave him tomorrow. She made a promise to herself to come up to Yorkshire more often from now on. She'd cleared the first hurdle; it wouldn't be so difficult next time. In fact, it wouldn't be at all difficult next time. Here was where she wanted to be. She realized now that her headlong flight into the unknown on New Year's Day had been a mistake. She wasn't going to abandon all her plans, though — it would take time to tie up the loose ends down in Suffolk. The lease on Herb House still had several more long months to run; her contract with Clare Faulkener had a similar amount of time due on it. And Cass? Cass needed her friendship now that the affair with Patric Faulkener had fizzled out like a duff firework on a rainy Guy Fawkes' Night.

She heard Mark yelling her name, and then he was there in the doorway, waving to her. 'Phone, Tam!'

She ran up to the house. 'Who is it?'

'Cass,' he said. 'She sounds in a right old state.'

She raced inside, picked up the phone and said breathlessly, 'Hi, Cass!'

'Tam! Thank goodness you're there. I've been worried out of my mind.'

'Sorry! I've been meaning to ring you to let you know where I was . . . '

'I guessed when you weren't at the house — but Tam — you've got to come back. Something's happened . . . '

'Cass — what is it?' She drew in a deep breath, knowing instinctively that something was very wrong for Cass to have taken the trouble to track her down here.

'There's been a fire,' Cass said, obviously trying to keep calm. 'Tam — there's been a fire. They say it's an arson attack. I think you should come home at once.'

18

Clare Faulkener knew only too well that her driving suffered when she was engrossed in what was happening back at the office in her absence, and she could feel the tension mounting in Craig Andrews — sitting beside her in the car — as she finished the conversation with her despatch office, switched off her mobile phone and handed it to him.

'You're going to kill yourself one of these days,' Craig snapped, snatching it from her. 'You do know, I suppose, that it's illegal to use a mobile phone when you're driving a car?'

She glanced across at him when he slammed the phone down on the padded leather dashboard. 'Temper, temper,' she taunted. 'And what business is it of yours whether I kill myself or not — or,' she asked pointedly, 'if I bend a few road rules regarding phone calls? I had to make sure that consignment of cinnamon products for

Paris had set off for France. Now I know for sure that it will arrive on Monday morning, I can relax for the weekend.'

'You'll relax only until something else at Faulkener's Herbs and Spices takes your attention,' he grumbled. 'Honestly, Clare, I'm beginning to think that nothing else matters to you except that damn factory of yours.' He scowled at her, and shuffled down in his seat in an attitude of mulish resignation.

Clare knew she should have more patience with him. If she were honest with herself, however, she would have to admit he was beginning to bore her — at least where work was concerned. He just didn't have the same interest in it as she did.

'Don't sulk,' she retorted, jamming her foot hard down on the accelerator and speeding up to what she knew herself was an unacceptable speed for the road ahead of them. 'And get off my back, will you? You've done nothing but complain about one thing or another ever since we set off this morning.'

'Don't you mean this *afternoon*, my sweet?' he sneered. 'We didn't leave Alderwood until one o'clock — and that was hours later than we'd planned to be on our way to Lilacs.'

'What's the hurry?' she chided. 'It isn't a matter of life and death that we reach Polten Market to a strict time limit. Our little love-nest will still be there even if we don't arrive until midnight.'

He made a great show of looking at his watch and said, 'It's ten minutes to three now, Clare. I sat waiting for you for two hours in my flat, and I was going crazy with worry that you'd had an accident or something. I didn't dare ring your home number in case *dear* Patric answered the phone, and I couldn't ring the office either because somebody there might have put two and two together and made . . . '

'Oh, don't be such a whinge,' she said, her head jerking round to look at him. 'Let people think what they will. I'm getting thoroughly fed up with this hole-and-corner stuff. I think Patric suspects something anyway.' Her attention momentarily taken off the road, she glanced round only in the nick of time to swing round an 'S' bend, and slew both herself and Craig sideways in their seats.

'Look out!' he yelled. 'For pity's sake, Clare . . . '

'I'm perfectly safe,' she said 'I knew the bend was coming up.'

'You're a maniac when you get behind the wheel . . . '

'I was talking about our future,' she said, composed again now. 'I wish we could come out into the open and let the world know we're having an affair.'

'Why don't you admit it, then? Admit it to *dear* Patric, and then you and I can be together for always.'

In a pitying way, she said, 'And live out our days in that dreary little flat of yours? No thank you.' Her foot was hard down again.

'Slow down,' he yelled, then, when it became apparent she wasn't taking any notice of what he was saying, he followed it up with, 'We could live at Lilacs if you left Patric, and made a clean break away from him.'

'No!' She kept her gaze on the road but did decrease the speed at which they were travelling a little.

'Why not?' he argued. 'We both like the house.'

'But it's *my* house,' she said fiercely. 'I don't want to share it with you — or anyone else on a permanent basis.'

Craig laughed softly. 'But we *do* share it — on the weekends you manage to get away.'

'We don't *share it*,' she insisted. 'You are a visitor. The house belongs to me, and only to me. When will you get that into your head, Craig?'

'Well, thank you for those few kind words,' he drawled. 'I never realized I was just a visitor. I always thought that visitors were

301

given their own bedroom when they came to stay.'

'You know what I mean.' A sigh jerked out of her, and she came down to the proper speed limit now he was no longer trying to control the way she was driving. 'Why do you have to be so argumentative?' she asked. 'Why do you always have to try and be so clever, Craig? You know what Lilacs means to me. You know I could never let you have any part of it for keeps.'

'I don't get part of anything *you* own — for *keeps*', he muttered. 'I just get tossed the scraps — as if I'm a scrounging mongrel begging for tit-bits.'

She stole a glance at him. 'I gave you a key to Lilacs — and that's something I've never done with anybody else,' she pointed out.

Inside she was seething; she regretted giving him that key now, but didn't feel able to ask for it back. There were times when she actively disliked him, though. Then she thought of those other times, the times when he made her clamour for his caresses, and at those times she knew it was she who begged for favours from him, she who became the cowering bitch on heat, avid, excited, and burning for him to make love to her. Marriage to Patric had never had the urgency, the thrill, that Craig could awaken in

302

her. In that moment though, embarrassment poured over her like a shower of molten lava, and not for the first time she wished she had more control over her feelings for Craig.

In an attempt to hide her confusion, she said airily, 'How dare you talk about scraps and tit-bits? I pay you a damn good wage — a lot more than you'd get anywhere else.'

'You pay me peanuts for what you get out of me,' he snorted. 'I ought to make you pay extra — maybe a retainer — or a stud fee — for services rendered *outside* office hours.'

'You know the conditions,' she said in an icy voice. 'Before I settle to anything more permanent with you, I must know that you're reliable. We agreed on a million pounds . . . '

At that moment her phone began to ring again.

Craig snatched it up before she could let go of the wheel, and held it just out of her reach. The car swerved and skidded as she tried to grab it out of his hand.

He yelled at her, 'Pull in to the side of the road — then you can have it. I'm not risking my neck again.'

She braked hard, and suddenly, flinging him forward, his seat belt catching him and making him grunt painfully. The handbrake grated as she snatched it on. Behind her a car horn blasted out because she'd stopped so abruptly without warning. As the overtaking car passed her stationary one, she fumed, 'Roadhog!'

Craig closed his eyes, but handed over the still-shrilling phone to her, then leaned back in his seat, his head against the head-rest as he listened to her talking, this time to her sales manager.

'Okay, Harry,' she was saying. 'Will do. I've brought the contract with me. I'll go over it during the weekend.'

'Like hell!' Craig muttered, glaring at her.

The conversation over, she slipped the phone into the door pocket on her side of the car and said, 'I'll take care of this from now on. You had absolutely no right to try and stop me taking that call.'

Craig said, 'If you're keeping the damn thing where you can answer it, then get out of the driving seat and I'll do the next stretch.'

'This is my car. You can't tell me what to do . . . '

He grasped her wrist as she made to turn on the ignition again. 'No, you don't,' he snarled. 'I'll drive, Clare; that way we might just get to Polten Market without the help of paramedics.'

Her eyes blazed at him. 'You are an alarmist,' she stated, fighting him furiously to get her hand free of him. 'You always think you know best, don't you? You're so damned perfect — in your own eyes.'

'I don't want to die,' he said calmly. 'I value the life I have.'

'I'm a safe driver. I have *never* had an accident.' She yanked on her hand but he held it fast.

'There's always a first time — and the first accident could be your last.' He had the ignition keys in his other hand now, and he let her go so suddenly that as she pulled away from him her wrist cracked on the steering wheel. She let out a little scream of pain and temper.

'You . . . you . . . ' Tears of fury sprang to her eyes. 'You fool! You could have broken my wrist . . . '

He leaned towards her, examined her hand, moved it gently this way and that. 'Not broken,' he said then, glancing up at her face. He smiled, then laughed softly. 'I must remember not to bind you up with silken scarves in bed tonight, though, my love. You're going to have one hell of a bruise there.'

A tingle went right through her at his easy words. He knew her weakness. All anger left her as she relaxed in her seat, stared lazily back at him and said in little more than a whisper, 'I still have another wrist, Craig. I

305

won't complain at silken scarves being used on that one.'

★ ★ ★

Clare was sated. Completely naked, she lay in her lover's arms in the sumptuous bed that Craig liked to describe as 'cavernous', and stared up at the beamed ceiling. Pink-shaded lamps, cream-washed walls, dark panelling and a soft ivory-coloured carpet added an unusual touch of homeliness around the burgundy satin sumptuousness of the bed.

Softly she spoke. 'I can't believe that this can last. That one day we'll be together, just you and me.'

'It's all in hand,' he said. 'I'm on my way to making that million pounds we bartered about, my sweet.'

'Maybe I could help you make that million.' With her forefinger she traced a line right down his body from mid-breastbone to navel, and she would have travelled still further if his hand hadn't shot out, descended on hers and grasped hold of it, holding it immobile.

He twisted his head towards her. 'No way,' he said. 'I'm not going to let you into the secret of making a million pounds in one fell swoop.'

'But even you can't do that. It takes some planning to make money — even to eke out a decent standard of living nowadays. Unless,' she said slyly, watching for the effect her words would have on him, 'unless you're somebody like Vaughn Herrick, the racing-driver who Patric often invites over for weekends now.'

Craig was not going to be drawn; she knew that instinctively when he said, bestowing his most charming smile upon her, 'I'm good at planning. And, though I do know the kind of money racing-drivers make, my love, I'm not aiming to become one of them myself. I can think of easier ways of making a living than hurtling round a track at two hundred miles an hour in one of those little hell-fire motors.'

'Some of those racing-drivers are very attractive.'

'Their *bank balances* are attractive. I rather think that's what you mean, isn't it, my darling Clare.'

She shrugged her bare shoulders. 'Vaughn Herrick *is* attractive, though. You can't get away from that — with those gorgeous bluey-grey eyes of his and his big, capable hands ... ' She gave a delicious shiver. 'I wouldn't say no to him.' Softly then, and making it sound almost an afterthought, she said, 'He was here, last weekend, at Lilacs.

307

You didn't know that, did you?'

'You kept that very quiet.' Craig's fingers tightened round her wrist.

She gave a little breathless laugh. 'Are you jealous?'

'Should I be?' His voice was almost imperceptibly hostile.

'Don't answer my question with another question,' she said.

'Does he excite you?' he asked.

She gave the question a few seconds' thought before replying, 'He's . . . different, somehow.'

'You were here with him?' His voice hardened.

She laughed, her vanity satisfied by his reaction. 'No. He came here alone. I told him he could use the house for the weekend.'

'Did he sleep in this bed and make love with the gorgeous and tantalizing Tamsin Curtis?' he wanted to know.

Her hackles were up. 'Tamsin Curtis?'

'They had something going between them — a few months ago,' he said. 'Didn't you know? She was expecting his kid. Something happened, though — she had a fall and lost the baby.'

'I knew she had met him before — knew there'd been *something* between them at one time — but how do you know all this background stuff about her?' She loosed herself from his grasp, leaned up on one elbow and looked down into his face.

'I made it my business to know. I made enquiries.'

'Why?'

Seductively he said, 'You were going into business with her, my sweet. I didn't want you being conned or anything like that.'

'You did it for me? You had Tamsin Curtis investigated? For me?'

'Who else but you?' He made a casual movement with his shoulders as he lay watching her.

'You cared enough to do that?'

'You know I care for you.' His voice held a vibrant warmth, yet she still couldn't tell if he were teasing or not. It was so unlike him — putting somebody else's feelings first.

'Did you have to pay for your information? About Tamsin and Vaughn?'

'It was very — discreet,' he said. 'But you have to pay dearly for discretion.'

She sank back against the pillows and lay there, looking up at the ceiling again, then said, 'Tell me more about our friend Tamsin, then? Was I right to trust her? To enter into that contract with her?'

'She is — or was — something of a mystery. For all her air of self-confidence I get the feeling she could easily be manipulated — by the right man. She's had a bit of a traumatic past. She's imaginative, though — artistic people usually are — and I found out she was a bit of a whizz with flowers. Apparently she can do wonders with growing things — plants, flowers, that sort of thing. Artistic people, though, can sometimes take things a bit too much to heart, and apparently there was some trouble with the woman she was in partnership with.'

Quietly, Clare said, 'She told me about Ava Thorne. She was quite open about what happened.'

'Tamsin had bad dreams, though. Did she tell you about those?'

Clare turned her head on the pillow to look at him. 'Everyone has bad dreams at some time or other in their lives.'

'She seems like somebody who scares easily, though. I found out she lost the baby when she fell down some stairs, trying to run away from a dream she'd had.'

Clare felt suddenly cold. It was as if melting icicles were drenching her. 'You had no right to go prying into her private life.'

'I did it for you,' he said simply.

'But I didn't ask you to.' She was suddenly sharp with him.

'Didn't you?' He stared at her, his eyes

hard and calculating.

'Of course I didn't . . . '

'One day you might understand.' He averted his eyes.

'I don't like prying. It's underhand. It's monstrous not to respect somebody's private life.'

'You'd rather be left in the dark about somebody you're doing business with?'

'No. I didn't say that . . . '

'She could have been anybody. Just anybody. You knew nothing at all about her.'

'But you obviously do *now*.'

'I know she was deeply involved with Herrick at one time. I think there's still something there, some undercurrent of feeling.'

'And what good will it do you? Knowing that?'

'You never know,' he said. 'You just never know. One thing did become clear in my investigations, though. Vaughn Herrick could give you that million pounds you're always going on about. Racing-drivers are extremely rich people.'

'But I don't want Vaughn to give me a million,' she said. 'I want *you* to prove to me that you really do want me. That you can care for me and give me the things I need. It would be easy — too easy — for me to keep footing the bills. I have to know that you love me enough to . . . '

'I have to prove myself. Is that what you're saying? That this is some sort of test? If I can make one million, why not two, or three, or . . . ?'

'Yes,' she broke in. 'I want a man who can look after me. I don't want a wimp who depends on me for everything.'

'You aren't interested in Herrick, then?'

'I told you — I find him attractive.'

'I'm ten times the guy Herrick is — in bed.'

She laughed and rolled onto her side to look at him. 'How do you know that?'

'Racing-drivers spend all their time looking after number one. They wouldn't give you the things I can give you. They have to keep off women and sex before a race.'

'He obviously didn't keep off sex with the delectable Tamsin.'

That seemed to throw him, but only for a moment. 'It happened when he was disqualified from some of last year's races,' he said. 'You can't blame him for bedding the girl, can you?'

'It might be . . . interesting,' she said lazily. 'Finding out if Vaughn Herrick's more of a man than you are.' She gazed at him from under lowered lashes, then, as he reached out and grabbed at her again, she cried out, 'Hey — that hurts.'

He said, 'Don't cry wolf, my darling. This isn't your injured wrist.'

'I'm not the only one who lies,' she said.

'Meaning?'

'You're kidding me — telling me you're on the way to making that million.'

'Am I?'

'You know you are.'

'I'm right for you, though. One day you might just acknowledge that.'

'Mmm.' She let out a long, low sigh. 'So right. I ought to have met you before I married Patric. Maybe things wouldn't have been so difficult then.'

'I'd have been twelve years old,' he teased, 'when you met Patric.'

Her face darkened. 'Don't talk like that.'

'You can't stand the thought of growing old, can you?' His voice held a cruel taunt.

'I won't grow old. I won't let myself.'

'When I'm fifty-two,' he said, 'you'll be sixty.'

She laid into him, beating him with both hands and clawing at him. When he caught hold of her hands she flung her head down onto his chest and bit into the fleshy part of his breast above the nipple.

He yelled in pain and flung her to the far

side of the bed, but she was up and at him again, her arms flailing, legs kicking out at him.

He caught her in a bear hug, squeezing her to him until she had no breath left to lash out quite so ferociously. She still fought him, though, with any bit of her that managed to escape his wrapped round arms and legs. They thrashed about all over the bed, and it was inevitable that in the tangle of sheets and pillows and quilt they would come unstuck.

They rolled off the edge and onto the floor, Craig landing first, with Clare on top of him. Angry tears of frustration were wet on her cheeks. She had never been so furious with him before in all her life.

'Pig!' she screamed. 'I hate you.'

'Male chauvinist or the other kind?' His laughter rose higher than her screaming, and he started making pig noises against her ear then, 'Oink, oink, oink.'

She began to laugh, but was near to hysteria. She prided herself on being able to take a joke, but jokes about her age were inexcusable. He knew where to hit her hardest, she realized. And where it hurt.

He released her hands, and then on his hands and knees went after her, head down, grunting away again like a pig.

She scuttled away, squealing.

'Pigs squeal,' he said, laughing helplessly as he chased her round the bedroom. 'So — you squeal, huh? And I'll grunt. You be pig-woman. Me — I'm big pig. Illustrious pig.'

Clare, at last, rolled onto her back, completely exhausted with laughter. He leaned down, one hand either side of her shoulders, then straddled her and gazed down at her.

'How shall we do it this time?' he asked, his voice soft and seductive.

'Any way you want me,' she breathed, and then she moaned as he lowered his head and his mouth found her taut nipple, hardening at the merest touch he bestowed upon her.

19

Tamsin stood and surveyed the charred remains of the out-house that had been burnt almost beyond recognition. She was dazed that this could have happened in the short time she'd been away — dazed and bewildered, for it was obviously no accident.

She turned to Cass, who was standing beside her. 'There was nothing stored in here that could account for this — no paraffin, no matches. All I kept in here were cuttings from the plants. They were all in plastic trays — dozens of them. And the only tools I lost were small ones — bedding out tools and a metal watering can.' She stared down at the heap of rubble, and at the can in question, twisted by the heat of the inferno into something unrecognizable.

Cass said, 'You were lucky it didn't spread to the main house; it was so near too. A stray spark and it could all have gone up in smoke.'

'With me inside it,' Tam said with a little

shudder. 'I wonder if that's what somebody intended?'

'No,' Cass said. 'They would have known you were away from home. Your car had gone. I don't think anyone meant to harm you personally.'

'A month's work — nurturing and tending those cuttings — doesn't harm me *personally*?' Tamsin gave a strangled little laugh.

'It doesn't, though — does it?' Cass said in a reasoning tone. 'If you'd been here, you would probably have been hurt. I know what you're like, love — you'd have fought the blaze yourself, and then you *might* have been hurt.

Tamsin turned to face her friend. 'Just what are you getting at, Cass?'

'Whoever is behind all this — I don't think they're out to hurt you. The watcher in the tower, the person who left those flowers at your door, and whoever it was who made that accusation to the police about you being involved in Ava Thorne's death. Don't you see? Somebody is out to undermine you, but that somebody hasn't hurt you — not physically.'

'They've hurt my house.'

'It's scare tactics, Tam. I'm convinced of it. Somebody wants to scare you.'

'But why should they want to do that?'

317

'I don't know. Maybe they're doing all these things to judge your reaction to stress or something.' Cass made a useless little movement with her hands. 'Can you think of anybody with a warped sense of humour? Somebody who might be a bit malicious towards you — for whatever reason?'

'Cass! This is somebody sick in the head.' Tamsin at last turned away from the fire-damaged out-house and said, 'Let's go back inside the house. I can't stand the sight of this place.'

In the kitchen of Herb House, as Tam lugged her suitcase — which she'd brought from the car to the house — into the front room, she heard Cass putting the kettle on. When she went back into the kitchen, Cass said, 'Sit down. You've had a shock. I'm sorry I had to phone you like that, but I thought you ought to know what had happened.'

'When did it start? The fire?'

'Some time in the early hours of this morning. Luckily the alarm was raised when somebody saw the glow in the sky from across the heath. It was an anonymous caller who alerted the fire brigade by all accounts . . . '

'Cass . . . ' Tamsin was staring at her friend, her eyes troubled.

'What is it, Tam?'

'An anonymous caller? That's what you said — and it was an anonymous caller who rang the police and intimated I was involved in Ava's death . . . '

Cass stared at her. 'It's coincidence, Tam. It has to be.'

'We don't know that.'

'Tam, I know you're upset, but . . . '

'Cass! I'm convinced of it. Two 'anonymous' phone calls — it can't just be coincidence.'

'Check with the police and the fire station,' Cass suggested. 'Check to see if gossip is correct or not before you start jumping to conclusions. It was just hearsay I was going by — honestly, my heart turned over when I learned while I was out shopping that it was *your* house. I thought you'd be here, you see, and, as you hadn't phoned me to tell me about the fire, I went down to the police station to try and find out if you'd been injured.'

'Cass! I ought to have told you I was going up north to see Mark.' Tam shook her head worriedly. 'It was so late at night, though, when I decided to go, and I was upset . . . ' She paced the kitchen as Cass made the tea, then left it in the pot to brew before leaning her hands back against the work-top and watching her.

'You were upset?'

Tamsin nodded, shrugged off her coat and threw it onto a chair then said, 'Vaughn had been here to see me that day.'

'Vaughn Herrick! He's nothing but trouble.'

'Yes.' Tam's laugh was unsteady. 'I'm beginning to think so too.'

'You think he did this? Set fire to your out-house.'

Tamsin shook her head. 'No! Vaughn wouldn't do that.'

'You said you were upset, though . . . '

Tamsin gave a great sigh, walked over to the cupboard and took two cups and saucers out of it. 'He came to tell me he didn't want to be associated with me while all the furore about Ava's death was going on. He said the gossip might harm his career.'

'The bastard!' Cass walked over to the table and sat down heavily on one of the chairs there.

'He was scared I'd had a hand in Ava's death. You can't blame him really.' Tamsin took over now, fetching the teapot to the table and pouring strong, hot tea into the cups.

'I'm the one who should be doing that.'

Tamsin grinned at her. 'Let's go out for a meal, shall we?' That's what Mark had planned for me tonight — if I'd still been at

Rothwold. He went mad at me when I wouldn't let him come back here with me. But what would have been the point?'

'Oh, Tam — I am sorry to have dragged you back — *and* to have caused any trouble between you and Mark.'

'Don't blame yourself, Cass.' Tam managed a laugh of sorts. 'But how did you guess where I was?'

'I couldn't think of anywhere else to try except Mark.' Cass shrugged, then picked up her cup of tea and drank heartily of it.

'No,' Tamsin said. 'I wouldn't go to anyone else, would I? Not when I needed a shoulder to cry on. Mark's the one I always fly to when I'm in any sort of trouble.'

With a wry grin, Cass said, 'You could have flown to me, you know. I was nearer than Mark.'

'You have troubles enough of your own, though.' Tamsin grimaced. 'You don't need mine adding to them.'

'Patric! You have to be referring to Patric Faulkener, I suppose?'

'Yes,' Tamsin said. 'Whatever you say, you know darn well you're still in love with him.'

'But it's a hopeless situation,' Cass said, sighing. 'He'll never leave Clare.'

'So what will you do?'

'I've been thinking,' Cass said, 'of moving

away from here. Right away. Somewhere I'll never have to bump into him again. I think it's the only solution.'

★ ★ ★

On the following Saturday morning Patric Faulkener pulled his car up outside his parents' house at Stride Common and got out. He was just about to walk up to their front door when he stopped, then stared at both houses in front of him — the one belonging to Jack and Dorothy Faulkener, and the other one where Cass Fairburn lived.

Then he drew in his breath, swung back towards Cass's house and stormed up to her front door instead of going straight to see his parents. He banged heavily on her door with his fist, waited a few seconds, then hammered again.

The door opened. Cass was in her dressing gown, he saw — a blue Paisley thing that was ages old. He knew it well, and he loved seeing her in it. Cass had been wearing it for years, and had turned down numerous offers from him to buy her a new — and more fashionable — one. He wished that this morning she hadn't been wearing it, though. It brought back too many precious memories. He wished she'd been fully dressed. Seeing

322

her as she was now, with her hair all mussed up from sleep, and in *that* dressing gown, he wanted to put his arms round her as he'd done countless times before, and hold her. He wanted to protect her . . .

She blinked at him and pushed one hand through her thick fair hair in an attempt to straighten it, protesting, 'What time do you call this?' And she scowled darkly at him.

'A few minutes after eight,' he said. Then, without giving her a chance to say another word, he stormed, 'But what, *may I ask*, do you call *this*?' and he flapped his hand at the noticeboard fastened to the front of the little house on a stout wooden pole.

'You can see what it is. It's a board saying my house is up for sale,' she said in a stony voice.

He felt anger rising within him, but managed to hang onto his temper enough to fling at her, 'You never told me you were going to do this, Cass. You never gave a hint that you'd be moving.'

'I don't have to tell you *anything*,' she said, tossing her head back and giving him a sullen stare.

'You *should* have told me,' he insisted. 'After all we've been to one another, I think you're being very unfair.'

'You don't own me,' she said quietly.

'Look — let me come inside. We've got to talk.'

She said quickly, 'You can't. What will people think? They'll have seen me answering the door to you in my dressing gown and . . . '

'And they can all go to hell,' he ground out, pushing her aside and striding into the house. 'Now,' he said, turning to her, 'shut that damned door and tell me what's going on.'

'I'm getting out,' she said, facing him in the tiny vestibule and leaning her back against the now firmly closed front door. 'I think it's for the best.'

'The best for whom?' he enquired politely, holding himself stiffly so as not to touch her in that confined space.

'Oh, come on into the sitting room,' she said, pushing him aside as she passed him. 'And for heaven's sake sit down, and stop looking so pained and self-righteous.'

Patric, from years of experience of avoiding hitting his head on the lintel, stooped slightly as he followed her into the front room of the small cottage.

She said, 'I love how you always do that.'

'Mum and Dad's house is the same design as this one, remember?' he said in a tight voice. 'I grew up with doorways that never had enough headroom for anybody over five feet ten inches.'

'Sit down,' she said again, and she folded her arms and waited until he did as she'd asked him, before perching herself on the edge of an easy chair facing him.

She took a deep breath then, and said, 'I'm moving out because there's no future for either of us, Patric. I'm going away because seeing you like this — every time you come next door to visit your parents — is tearing my heart out.'

'*Where* are you going?' he asked, his face drawn and pale. 'At least tell me that. I think I have a right to know.'

'I don't know. Not yet. Maybe I won't buy any property outright until I've finished these two assignments I'm working on. I've almost finished the Essex one, but I still have that contract to fulfil in Northumberland — the new track that's being constructed there.'

'The house might not sell.' He was stony-faced.

She lifted her shoulders in a shrug. 'I can't force anybody to buy it, can I? And really, it doesn't matter how long it takes. The people in Northumberland are arranging accommodation for me for the time I'll be spending there.'

Knowing he was merely clutching at

straws, he said, 'It *will* sell, though. Won't it?' He lifted helpless eyes to her. 'It's a nice little property. Somebody will snap it up — probably for a holiday home. It's in a good situation and it has character.'

'You sound like the man who came to value it,' she said, forcing a strangled little laugh.

He clasped his hands in front of him, bowed his head and said, 'I'll miss you, Cass. You don't know how much I'll miss you — how much I depend on you always being here. I have nothing left now except you.'

To his relief she didn't attempt to throw cold water on what he said, or to placate him with mindless platitudes. 'Yes,' she said. 'I know.'

Slowly he lifted his head and looked at her. 'Would you marry me?' he asked. 'If I were a free man?'

'But you aren't free,' she said softly.

'I could be.'

'You'd have a great deal to lose if you split up from Clare. Don't talk like that. Don't even think about it.'

'*It*?' he said, his eyes watching every futile movement of her hands, every painful expression on her face.

She hugged her dressing gown closer round her, and tucked her bare feet into its folds.

'Divorce,' she said. 'It's not for you, Patric. For one thing, it would go against all your beliefs, and, for another, you have too much to lose. You and Clare are tied up in more than a marriage. There are the two businesses — Faulkener's Herbs and Spices, and now the racing circuit at Bramsdown. Both your worlds would crumble, and you'd both blame me for the crash that would inevitably follow such a break-up.'

'Clare might welcome it,' he said, making himself believe it was true. 'And I know I would. I want you, Cass. I don't care if I lose everything else. I want you.'

'It's over,' she said gently. 'Patric — I told you before, it's over. I couldn't live with myself if I thought I was responsible for splitting you up from Clare. And I know, too, that in your eyes marriage is for life. Even if you divorced Clare, you would probably never feel free.'

'She doesn't care about me. And we have no marriage to speak of.' He held out a hand to her. 'Come here, sweetheart. Don't lock yourself away from me behind that tight reserve. Come here and let me hold you.'

'No,' she said, wrapping her arms more tightly around her body and shaking her head. 'I've made my mind up, Patric. I'm going to get away from here. It was wrong of me ever to have encouraged you — I know that now.'

Patric felt a deep sense of regret, but knew she was taking the only way out that was possible in the circumstances. She was right when she said that his beliefs about marriage were strong ones. It was how he'd been brought up. And when he'd first met Clare and married her he'd never imagined it could all end like this.

'It will be a terrific wrench for you,' he said. 'You shouldn't feel you're being forced into this. It's me who should be moving away. Maybe if I left Clare and set myself up in Cambridge — somewhere near the Bramsdown circuit . . . ?' He looked up into her face, wanting her to suggest some means — other than moving herself — as a solution to what they were both facing.

She seemed not to have been listening to him, however. She gazed almost absently around the little room. 'I think it will be good for me to have a change of scenery,' she said. 'Do you know — since Mum died last year, I haven't been able to bring myself to clear a thing that belonged to her out of this place? There are still all her clothes in the wardrobe upstairs, and in the loft there are my old toys — the toys I had when I was a child — toys, and boxes of letters that Daddy sent to Mum when he was working on the rigs all those years ago ... and photographs ... ' Her voice tailed away while she got a grip on herself, then she continued, 'It's time I took stock of everything and had a damn good clear-out.'

'I'll divorce Clare,' he said, his voice suddenly ringing out dramatically as he made the only decision he knew he could make in the circumstances. 'I will, Cass.'

'Then,' she said softly, 'come to me when you're a free man, if you're so determined to free yourself. But don't do it *because* of me. People change, Patric, and we neither of us are the same people we were a year ago — or even a month ago. If you do this for the wrong reasons, you'll end up hating me — and I couldn't bear that.'

'I know.' Pushing himself wearily to his feet, he stood and faced her. 'I do realize that some of the magic has gone out of our relationship. It will come back, though. I know it will,' he said fiercely. 'I care for you, Cass. I love you and I want to spend the rest of my life with you. Just tell me one thing. Tell me you feel the same way about me.'

'I do,' she said, seeming to retreat into herself as she huddled in the old armchair and made herself into a small, blue Paisley bundle with her knees up under her chin.

'I've never in my whole life met anyone who means so much to me as you do.'

'Then let me see you again . . . '

'No,' she said, and her voice was firm. 'I don't want to open up all the heartache again. I want to get over it and start afresh.'

Stiffly he said. 'If that's your last word, I'm wasting my time . . . '

'Yes,' she said in a quiet voice. 'Today's not a good day. You're getting angry again, and soon we'll both be saying things we'll regret if you stay any longer. It would be best if you left now. Your mother will have seen your car outside the house. She'll be expecting you.'

20

Mark surprised Tamsin that weekend, by driving down to Suffolk and turning up on her doorstep. By then, though, there was little evidence left to show the extent of the fire damage.

'I cleared it all away,' Tam said, standing on the blackened area of ground which had once been the outhouse. 'It wasn't a very big place — barely ten by eight — the size of a small garden shed.

'It was brick-built, though.' Mark looked worried. 'It must have been some fire to destroy it completely.'

'I just want to forget about it.' Tam hated seeing him so upset about what had happened. 'It was only bricks and mortar, for goodness' sake. There was no real harm done.'

'What do the police say?' he wanted to know.

'They took away a petrol can. But what *can* they say?' She spread her hands. 'Whoever set fire to the place made damn sure they didn't leave any other clues; it was all destroyed and it was so pointless.' She gave a heavy sigh. 'Look — I just want to put all this behind me. And before you say anything more — I'm taking you out for some lunch.'

'Why can't we have it here?' His gaze drifted towards the house.

'I'm not the world's best cook.' She grinned at him.

'A can of soup would do . . . '

'Mark! There's a handy pub two miles up the road.' She didn't tell him she'd been lying low this past week, and hadn't even been out to refill her larder or cupboards. At the house, she felt safe. If she went out anywhere, it meant coming back alone, and going back into the empty building was scary in the extreme. She never knew what she was going to find. The fire had unsettled and frightened her. Peeping Toms and funeral flowers she could deal with. Even the accusation of murder had backfired too. The fire was a different matter altogether, though. Fire was dangerous. She wasn't going to let Mark know how fearful she was, however. He'd start getting tough with her if she did, and she was determined to stick this out alone.

Mark looked searchingly at her. 'It's getting

to you, isn't it?' he said, reaching out a hand to her.

Her answer was deliberately sharp. 'No! What nonsense. I'm not worried. The police know what's been going on, and although they can't keep a twenty-four-hour surveillance on the house, they told me they'll keep sending somebody round just to see that things are okay.'

'Yeah,' he said with a note of bitterness in his voice. 'That's right. They'll send somebody round in a ruddy great white police car — a car that anybody out to do you harm will spot a mile off. Do they really think that's going to help?'

Lamely she said, 'It's better than doing nothing.'

'Tam!' He grabbed both her hands and pulled her towards him. 'Tam — I hate to think of you being here alone.'

'I'm not alone now.' She laughed up into his face. 'You're here! For two whole days.' She couldn't hope to hide the relief in her voice.

'Why don't you go and stay with Cass at nights when I'm gone?' he said, linking his arms round her waist now and holding her very close.

'I can't do that. Cass has put her house up for sale. She won't want my clutter around the place.'

'Cass is leaving Alderwood?' he asked, sounding dismayed.

She nodded. 'She hasn't made any definite plans yet, but the affair with Patric Faulkener seems to have fizzled out. At least I think that's the reason behind her selling up.'

'What a mess,' he said. 'You'll miss her.'

'Yes,' she said, bending her head and resting her forehead against the thick wool jersey he was wearing. 'It is a mess. It usually gets that way when you tangle with a married man.'

Softly he said, 'All the more reason why you should settle down with me. I'm young, free and single.'

Amused, she lifted her head and looked into his face. 'You needn't worry that I shall get mixed up with a married man. I don't know any that I fancy anyway.'

'You manage to get into enough trouble without married men confusing the issue,' he said in a sober voice. 'You need somebody to look after you.'

'Don't be boring,' she said, raising herself up on tiptoe to kiss his mouth. She was alarmed, however, when he moved his head aside and avoided her kiss.

'Tam! We can't go on like this,' he said.

'I've had enough. I need some answers. I've asked you to marry me so many times . . . '

'Don't go getting all serious,' she teased, knowing that a discussion about marriage was more than she could take at the moment.

'For me — it *is* serious. I need to know I'm not wasting my time.'

More impatient with herself than with Mark, she said, 'If you have better things to do . . . ' and pushed him away from her, moving *right* away from him before turning to face him again.

He was standing quietly where she'd left him. She thought he might have followed her and tried to hold her again, but he didn't. After a silence that was almost unendurable he said quietly, 'I won't ask you to marry me again, Tam. Not ever.'

She tried to laugh, when all she really wanted to do was cry. She didn't want it to end like this. She needed Mark as she'd never needed anybody in her life before.

'That's right,' he said. 'Laugh. That's all you do when I try to get serious with you. You always . . . '

'Not *always*,' she broke in swiftly. 'Not when . . . ' Suddenly she found she couldn't utter the words, for words were useless, intransigent things when you tried to form a relationship out of them. And she and Mark had a good relationship — in one area of their lives at least. She tried to blank out of her mind the memory of his lovemaking. It had been so perfect, and it had seemed so right. She knew there was, and always would be, an unseen bond linking them together. It had been there, right from the start, right from the first day she had met him, when she had made herself so objectionable towards him. He'd been different in those days, though, a year ago almost. He'd given the appearance of being aloof; he'd bandied his brittleness like a banner for all the world to see — though even then she supposed she'd known that he was going to play a big part in her life. He wasn't a man you could ignore. At the time she'd thought he wasn't a man she could ever love either, but all that had changed . . .

He gave a harsh laugh. 'So — I'm okay in the bedroom department, huh? But not husband material, is that it?'

He was able to read her innermost thoughts, and she was alarmed at the way the conversation was going — and a little scared too. Mark had always been so dependable. 'I don't want us to quarrel,' she said, subdued by his attitude.

He pushed his hands into his pockets and hunched up his shoulders as he gazed at the garden, not at her any more. 'Tam,' he said, still not looking at her, 'you're taking this all too lightly — these threats against you. And I feel so damned helpless.'

'There's nothing you can do,' she said, walking over to him.

'There is! I can give you a home. You don't have to bury yourself down here. I just can't understand you any more.'

Anger flared briefly inside her. 'You never could,' she said, regretting the hasty words as soon as they'd left her lips. She snapped her mouth shut, determined not to argue, not to say anything more that he might put the wrong interpretation on.

He was facing her now. 'I understood you a lot better than you ever knew,' he said, and there was a sadness to the words. 'You were always headstrong, though. And you just never trusted me enough, did you?'

'How did we get into this conversation?' she said. 'Mark . . . ' She seemed in a daze, 'Mark — I was so glad when you turned up today, and now we're fighting.'

'You shut me out,' he said. 'Always you shut me out when I try to help you.'

'No,' she cried, 'I don't.'

'You refused to let me come back with you last weekend after Cass rang you about the fire,' he stated. 'I begged you to let me bring you back but you'd have none of it. You just had to prove you could cope without me.'

'You seem to forget,' she said, 'that you have other people depending on you. Edgar Brand, your partner, for instance.'

'It was Friday,' he said. 'I had the whole weekend free.'

'So you've been storing up your resentment against me all week! Is that it?'

'Not resentment,' he said. 'My *fear* for your safety. My *dread* — every time the damned telephone rang this past week — that something had happened to you. Do you think I can turn my concern off when you're out of sight? Out of sight, out of mind? Is that it? Can't you understand what I've been going through?'

'Is this what marriage to you would be like?' she asked, appalled. 'Would I have to answer to you for my every movement? Would I need your permission to drive the car, walk on the beach, take a shower?' She shook her head. 'I don't understand you all of a sudden, Mark. I don't need a minder. Give me some room in my life, will you? Give me some credit for taking charge of my life. Don't slap a 'bimbo' notice on me and behave as if I don't possess an ounce of common sense.'

'Okay!' He held up one hand. 'Okay, Tam. Let's cool it, shall we, before things get out of hand?'

'You've already said things . . . '

'Yes,' he said. 'But from now on, I won't. I meant what I said earlier, though. I shall *never* ask you to marry me again. Is that clear?'

'You want to wash your hands of me?' Suddenly the thought of him doing that was almost more than she could bear. She didn't want to be rid of him. She wanted him there. Always. But some things had to change — his attitude for a start. She was determined — always had been, from the start of this venture — to show him she wasn't like other women. She wanted him to be proud of her, wanted him to treat her as an equal. She wanted so many things, but most of all, and she'd always known it in her heart, in the end she would want *him* more than any of them.

'I wouldn't do that.' His jaw tightened. 'I would never wash my hands of you.'

She turned and walked into the house. He didn't follow her. She went upstairs to her bedroom and looked at herself in the mirror and tidied her hair. And still he didn't come to her.

She went back downstairs and he was in the kitchen.

'Your car or mine?' he asked.

'I'll drive if you want a drink with your lunch,' she offered with a smile.

'I don't want a damn drink. I want to be in full possession of my senses.'

'So you drive,' she said. 'And I'll have a drink myself. I'd be quite glad to be stoned out of my mind for a while, but we'll take my car, if you don't mind. I need to fill up with petrol.' She grinned, glad the conversation was on safer ground now. 'I always do that on Saturdays. You might not believe it, but Alderwood's only petrol station doesn't open on Sundays.'

'What a place,' he said, but there was a smile touching his lips.

*   *   *

They had lunch at a quiet pub on the sea front in Alderwood, then Mark suggested a walk on the beach, so they left her car in the car park and did that.

'You really meant it about that petrol, didn't you?' He linked his hand in hers as they trod the smooth, firm sand at the edge of the sea. 'I saw the opening times pinned up on that forecourt. Till then I thought you were kidding me. I can't believe that petrol stations don't stay open seven days a week down here.'

'It's only the Alderwood one,' she said. 'It's such a sleepy little place for most of the year that I doubt they'd get any customers in winter. They do open up for a couple of hours on Sunday afternoon in July and August — or so Cass tells me.'

'We didn't come here to talk about petrol stations, though, did we?' he said when they were well clear of the seafront houses and all that was ahead of them were untidy sand dunes, matted with coarse grass and straggly gorse bushes. In the near distance was the marsh, and beyond that, inland, the heath.

She stood still and faced him. Their hands were still linked. 'We didn't come here to argue either, Mark.'

'I don't intend to,' he said. 'Let's just talk about us, shall we?'

'Us?' It was the last subject on earth she wanted to tackle just at the moment, but she knew it had to be faced.

With a sigh, he said, 'We're all washed up, aren't we? Maybe it would be best if I stayed away for a while — just till you get your life in order. You know where I am if you do ever want me, but ... ' He paused to give the words their fullest meaning. 'But, Tam, I don't think you will do that, will you? Not really want me, I mean.'

Shock hit her squarely and coldly, just as if the biting North Sea alongside them had suddenly reared up and doused her in a tidal wave. She stared at him, hardly believing she'd just heard those words he'd uttered. There was no guile in his face, though, no hint that he was winding her up. He just looked unhappy, even though he was trying now to smile but not quite making it.

'How can you say that?' Her voice was a mere whisper. 'Oh, Mark — how can you think I don't want you?'

'Don't look so tragic,' he said, pulling her towards him, putting one arm round her shoulders and giving her a hug. 'We can still be friends.' He started to walk alongside the sea again, pulling her with him, supporting her when she stumbled because her eyes were blurred with unshed tears.

In a practical tone of voice, he went on, 'Look — I think it might be better if I went back up north today, don't you?'

'No . . . ' she choked out. 'No!'

'No?' He stopped walking and she jarred to a halt as he pulled her round to face him again. 'Tam?'

'I — I don't want you to go back.' She sniffed and tossed back her golden curls, which were blowing haphazardly across her face. She blinked and sniffed again.

'You're cold,' he said. 'Your face looks so pinched and white. Why didn't you say? We could have gone back to that pub and sat in the warm.'

'I'm not cold,' she yelled at him.

'Your nose is red; your eyes are watering,' he said with a little laugh. 'You are damn near frozen.'

'I'm bawling my eyes out,' she said, feeling her face starting to crumple and her lips to tremble.

He pushed her away from him, placed both his hands on her shoulders and bent his head to look at her. 'Hell!' he said, with surprise written all over his face. 'Hell! What have I done, Tam?'

She felt a tear trickling down her cheek and smacked at it with an angry hand, then tore herself out of his grasp and began running back along the water's edge, the way they had just come. As she ran she grew more despondent and yet more furious with him. And he'd had the temerity to ask what he'd done!

He'd brought her to her senses! That was what he'd done! The words pounded in her brain . . . ' . . . we're all washed up . . . ' He was giving up on her. And she knew why.

A hand grabbed her shoulder and brought her crashing round and into his arms. The collision knocked them both off their feet and had them tumbling down onto the damp sand where the retreating tide had left a scummy line of foam and strings of wet seaweed. Their legs were tangled together, but before they landed he twisted himself so that she fell onto him, and he broke her fall.

She found that her hands were clinging onto him and her face was very near to his.

'You're not hurt, are you?' He was flat out on the sand as he stared into her eyes.

She bowed her head over him, then raised it to say, 'I'd have had a softer landing if you hadn't been under me. Your body is very hard. You're all muscle!'

'You're not crying any more.'

She gave a hard laugh and said, 'No. I seldom cry. You caught me at the wrong time of the month, I guess.'

'I didn't mean to hurt you.' His hands relaxed on her now. 'I thought I was doing the right thing — saying the right thing too.'

'About going back up north today?'

He eased them both into a sitting position, but she didn't attempt to move away from him. She just sat staring at the sea, her knees hunched up in front of her, sand clinging to her black ski-pants, her boots and her jacket, but she didn't care how she looked any more. He was sitting beside her in much the same position she'd adopted, and that was all that mattered — that he *was* there.

'What's wrong, sweetheart?' A careful hand was tucking the stray curls back behind her ear.

She flung her head round and glared at him. 'I don't want you to give up on me, Mark.'

He was silent while half a dozen waves washed lazily onto the shore a fair distance away from them. Then he said, 'What is it you're saying, Tam? You see, I don't want to jump to the wrong conclusions again. I don't want to read something into this friendship if . . . '

'Friendship!'

'Relationship, then.' He lifted his shoulders in a tiny shrug.

'You keep on telling me you love me.' Her face was set into a stony expression.

'I've never lied to you,' he said quietly.

'You just want to walk away and . . . '

He broke in fiercely, 'I don't want to walk away. I want something back from you.'

Deliberately misunderstanding, because she was feeling so fragile, so hurt, she snapped, 'You want to go to bed with me again? Is that it?'

He grabbed her and shook her in a none too gentle manner. Then he tapped a finger on her forehead and said, 'I want something in here to *feel* something for me.' His voice

345

was ragged. 'I don't just want your body. Hell — haven't I made that clear to you in the past? Tam — I want us to build something together — a relationship — a life. I want you there, beside me, sharing that life. The way we're doing things now is a sham. It means nothing to either of us. There's no continuity.' He let go of her and scooped up a handful of sand, then let it drizzle through his fingers. 'This just about sums it up. We grasp at something and it trickles away. We build on sand and when the next tide comes in, it's all swept away again — and I want something more than that, Tam. I want commitment. I'm thirty-one. I have a decent home, money in the bank, and security. What I don't have, though, is *you*, so all the rest means nothing.'

'You *do* have me,' she cried.

'Not this far away,' he said, rolling away from her and standing up. 'Not two hundred damn miles away.'

She scrambled to her feet too and stood a few paces away from him. Neither of them seemed aware of the sight they must look, with rotting seaweed clinging to them, and sand embedded in their clothing.

'I have a life too,' she said sullenly.

'We both have a life — two hundred miles apart from each other,' he said, and he sounded incredibly weary. 'What do you want me to do, Tam? Sell up my share in Brand Motors and move down here?'

Vigorously she shook her head. 'Don't be silly . . . '

'I wouldn't do that,' he said. 'So what do you suggest as an alternative?' He bounced the ball of contention neatly back into her court.

She didn't need to think very hard for a solution. It was obvious. *She* could move. He couldn't. Soon, she'd be on her own down here in Suffolk. The only friend she had — Cass — would be moving away, and the contract with Clare Faulkener wasn't bringing in the amount of money she would have liked. On top of that, Clare had been decidedly cool with her just lately, and the fear was in Tam's mind that her contract might not be so readily renewed next year.

Her head jerked up and she looked him straight in the eyes. 'I wanted to make a success of my life before coming to you,' she said. 'Instead, though — things haven't worked out the way I intended them doing.'

'So it's pride that's bothering you.' His eyes narrowed. 'You're letting pride get in the way of something much more precious.'

'Give me a bit more time, Mark.' Suddenly

she was pleading with him. She needed to get things into perspective. She had plans, but they couldn't be rushed.

'Give *me* one good reason why I should do that,' he said in a curt voice.

She didn't answer. She just stared at him, knowing she was in real danger of losing him now.

He waited long minutes for her reply, but it didn't come. The beach was deathly quiet except for the far-off waves lapping the shore, and a solitary seagull circling them and uttering piercingly mournful cries.

'It's over, Tam,' he said at last. 'I'm going home.' And he turned and started walking slowly away.

She watched him getting further and further away from her, but there were no words she could utter to stop him. She began to follow him, not hurrying. There was no need for hurry. Her mind was whirling with thoughts and words. But she couldn't find the words that would make him stay with her. And did she really want him to do that? she asked herself.

'No!' Sadly she said the one little word that over the centuries had been responsible for breaking hearts and shattering nations. No — she didn't want him giving up his life for her. She wouldn't respect him for doing that.

At the same time, though, she knew that she couldn't give up her own hopes and dreams either.

There was no alternative. She would have to let him go.

21

She hadn't caught him up by the time he reached the pub car park again, so she began to hurry. Across the small yard, with barely a dozen vehicles in it, she saw him suddenly stop as he reached her car. He seemed to be staring at something, and then he spun round and came sprinting back to her.

Something was wrong, that much was obvious, and she began to run too — towards him, her heart pounding, her mouth dry.

'What is it?' She was panting as they met. She stared into his eyes. 'Mark what's wrong . . . '

'Your car.'

'My car?'

He nodded. 'Looks as if somebody's hit it with a ten-ton steamroller.'

'Oh, no . . . ' She felt the breath draining out of her. 'No — not something else! First the fire and now this . . . '

'It *looks* like a genuine accident, Tam.

Don't go jumping to all the wrong conclusions until we know for sure.'

'It's easy for you to say that,' she blazed. 'It's not happening to you, is it?'

Quietly, he said, 'Isn't it? Don't you think it's hurting me? Seeing what somebody is doing to you?'

She pushed her hands through her hair. 'Mark — I'm sorry . . . I didn't mean . . . '

'It's okay,' he said, putting his arm round her shoulders and steering her towards the car.

Tamsin stared at it. The front was caved in, windscreen shattered and glass all over the place. She was devastated, horrified that events had taken such a turn, and so soon after the fire at Herb House.

Before she could say anything, though, a man came out of the pub and hurried across the yard to them, a piece of paper flapping in his hand. She recognized him as the landlord who had served them lunch earlier. He wore a worried expression.

'Sorry about this, love.' The familiar soft Suffolk tone of his voice calmed her instantly as he went on, 'It was an accident — the sort we get used to in my kind of business. Some folks will drink and drive, see! No matter how much anybody tells them not to . . . '

'You know who did this?' Mark cut in.

351

The man held out the sheet of paper. 'He's a local feller. This is his name and his insurance details. Oh, and the names of three witnesses. He admits, though, that it was his fault — there's no harm in him really. He just wasn't looking as he reversed out of his parking spot.' He gave a subdued sort of grin. 'If it's any consolation, the back of his car looks much the same as the front of yours.'

Tam let out a long indrawn breath that until then she hadn't been aware she was holding. It really was a genuine accident, then, and not a deliberate ploy to undermine her still further. The relief was instant. She looked at the name on the paper Mark was holding. It meant nothing to her, but she knew there was a street of the name stated in Alderwood. And if the licensee knew the man . . .

'There shouldn't be any trouble.' The man gave her a grim smile. 'Not for you, anyway, Miss. *He'll* get away lightly, though — his insurance will cover him when he ought by rights to be facing a stiff sentence for drink-driving. It might not have been a car he ran into, if you see what I mean. Next time it could be a pedestrian.'

Tam shuddered. She was happy with the situation as it was, though. At least this wasn't malicious damage. She would be without a car, however . . .

Mark said, 'We'll have to see about car rental to get you through the next couple of weeks. I'll take the Beetle up to Yorkshire and do the repairs myself.' He turned to the pub landlord. 'Look — I should be able to get this car moved by six o'clock-ish tonight. Will it be okay to leave it here till then?'

The man replied, 'Sure! I'll tell the regulars in there to keep clear of the broken glass till I can get it cleared away.' Then he hurried off back to the pub and went inside.

Softly, she said, 'You're not deserting me altogether, then?'

'Tam . . . ' His expression softened. He leaned forward and kissed her forehead. 'I'm not saying we should split up and never see each other again.'

'You might meet somebody else,' she said, every word cutting into her soul.

'So might you.' He was standing very still, looking down into her upturned face.

'It's not what either of us wants . . . ' She made a useless little movement with her hands.

'No.' The one word was emphatic. 'Not what *I* want, anyway.'

'Nor me.'

'Look,' he said, 'we should be thinking of

getting back to your place. Can we call a taxi?'

'Alderwood doesn't have a taxi.'

'Hell!' He threw his head back, then started to laugh softly. 'I might have known.'

'We can walk back over the heath. It'll only take about twenty minutes.'

He took out his mobile phone. 'I'll ring Edgar and get him to send Jack-O down with the transporter before we go.'

She stood beside him while he spoke to Edgar Brand and arranged for the man who worked for them both to come and fetch her car. He turned to her then and said, 'Jack-O should be down here in about three hours, so we'll have time to go back to Herb House for a couple of hours before I have to come back here to meet him around five-thirty. Is that okay?'

She nodded. 'Thanks, Mark.'

'Come on.' He linked his arm through hers, and sighed. 'Come on, let's start walking, then, shall we?'

★ ★ ★

'You could have just driven home and left me,' she said when they were back at Herb House.

'That's how things were working out,' he

354

said soberly. 'It's what I would have done by now too, if your car hadn't been smashed. I fully intended going back to Yorkshire as soon as we got back here.'

'Oh, Mark . . . ' She went across the little sitting room to him and he took her in his arms and kissed her.

When the kiss was over, she looked up into his face and said, 'Some good has come out of my car being rammed, then?'

'It depends,' he said. 'But, yes, I suppose it's given us a bit more breathing space — I can't leave you on your own here without a car, not until we can sort something out for you on Monday. Maybe it's fate giving us a hand, huh? Fate telling us not to be too hasty.'

'I talked to Cass a couple of days ago,' she said.

'Don't you talk to Cass most days?' He still held her, and she made no attempt to move away from him.

'About my herbs. I need new outlets, Mark.' Worriedly she flicked a glance at his face again. 'Clare Faulkener seems to be cooling off me a bit. I get the feeling she likes to do business with men — not women. Being taken in by the police for questioning didn't do my reputation much good either. Word soon gets round in quiet country places like this.'

Mark frowned. 'What are you saying, sweetheart?'

'I told you — I need more outlets. Somewhere else to sell my herbs. Cass has offered to help; she's going to take some photographs of them, and then I shall send out a price list and some advertising material to various other places that use herbs.'

'What kind of places?'

She lifted her shoulders. 'Cosmetic manufacturers and candlemakers. Then there's the aromatherapy business. There are various other outlets besides herbs and spices. I've already looked for likely industries in the business directories in Alderwood library.'

'It sounds like a good idea — and with Cass to help like that . . . '

Tamsin was enthusiastic. 'She's a first-class photographer. She has to be — it's her job. I'm going to take some cuttings of various species of herbs and let her have them tomorrow. Cass suggested a photograph of a huge vase with all different herbs, and then having an identical sketch to accompany the picture with the names of the herbs in the appropriate places. It wouldn't cost as much as smaller but individually labelled photographs. I'll need about fifty for a start, you see, and — '

356

Mark cut in, 'Fifty's pushing it a bit, isn't it? Could you manage fifty more outlets?'

She laughed. 'No! Of course I couldn't, not with just the couple of acres I have here. But if I send fifty brochures and letters of introduction out, by the law of averages not all of them will reply favourably. Cass reckons I'll be lucky to have even ten enquiries. But — ' she shrugged ' — I've got to try and sell the herbs, Mark.'

'Even though flowers have always been your speciality? Are you sure you're doing the thing you really want to do, Tam?'

She eased away from him and walked over to the window that overlooked the front of the house, and gazed out at the still and silent heath. She was quiet for a few seconds, then she turned and faced him. 'I like working with living things. It doesn't really matter whether it's herbs or flowers — though flowers were, of course, my first love.'

'You were so good with them.' He came across the room and stood in front of her. 'You can't be quite so artistic with herbs, can you?'

'Beggars can't be choosers.' She pulled a comical little face at him.

'You aren't exactly a pauper, though — and I could help if you wanted to go back into flowers, or the wedding business again.'

'Is this a bribe? To get me back to Heronsea?' Her head jerked up sharply. 'If so . . . '

He held up a placating hand. 'No,' he said. 'It isn't a bribe. I'd help you no matter where you decided to start up again. I just don't like this place — especially after all the trouble you've had here. It's so damn lonely, Tam. I'd like to see you settled in a better area — one that isn't in the back of beyond, surrounded by marshes and heaths and with such spooky — almost evil — surroundings.'

Her heart went out to him. 'Mark,' she said gently, 'I know what you mean. And I also know that this isn't an ideal place to live — not when I'm alone. But honestly, most of the time it's okay.'

'It's *not* okay, though, is it?' he said, his voice tense and with a note of anger in it. 'It's not okay when you're spied on, and sent funeral flowers, and have your house set on fire, and you're accused of murder!'

Inwardly, she went cold at his words, and had to admit to herself that, no, it wasn't okay. There was an enemy out there somewhere, but she just couldn't turn her back on all she'd planned and walk out. She'd taken on the lease of Herb House for a year, and that year wasn't a quarter of the way through yet. She had a commitment to Clare Faulkener too, and she wouldn't let Clare down — on that point she was adamant. She said all this to Mark, but he dismissed her logic impatiently. She knew that only one thing mattered to him, and that was getting her back in his own world where he could look after her — back in Yorkshire. Somebody else seemed intent on pushing her back there too. Somebody as yet unknown to her — the watcher in the church tower, the sender of those white chrysanthemums, the police informer, and the arsonist who had set fire to one of her buildings.

'I just can't imagine who would hate me enough to do all those things,' she said. 'Nobody knew me before I came to live here.'

'Except Cass,' he said thoughtfully. 'Cass knew you.'

She shook her head. 'Cass wouldn't do anything to hurt me.'

'Would she tell anybody about you? Tell them about your life before you came down here? Could anyone else have known about Ava Thorne's death — and the circumstances surrounding it?'

'We-ell . . . ' She thought for a few minutes, then said, 'I *did* tell Cass what had happened — in a letter. That was when she invited me down to stay with her.'

'And Cass was *very* friendly with Patric Faulkener.'

Her eyes widened as she stared at him in horror. 'Patric? But why would he want to hurt me. Heavens, I saved his life on the day I arrived here — I told you about the street brawl, didn't I?'

He nodded. 'So we can rule out Patric — as well as Cass,' he said.

'Of course we can. There was never any question of it being either of them who were putting the frighteners on me.'

'Patric could have talked to his wife — Clare — about you.'

'I don't think they *talk* all that much.' She grimaced. 'I don't think they have anything left in common now. Clare is too preoccupied with Faulkener's Herbs and Spices. And besides that, what would Clare get out of scaring me?'

'Vaughn Herrick, then,' Mark said. 'Vaughn knew all about Ava's death.'

'Vaughn is all right, Mark. I know you don't like him, but . . . '

'*Don't like* is putting it rather mildly, Tam. Vaughn stole you away from me. If it hadn't been for Vaughn Herrick, by now you and I would probably be married.'

She gave a faint laugh. 'I don't think so.

You and I never hit it off in the old days, did we?'

'Vaughn is the only one I can think of who would want to stop you and me getting together, Tam.' Mark swung away from her and paced the room. Spinning back round, he said, 'That could be it. He wants you back. He wants you to go running to him. And you're in the right place to do that — he's always staying with the Faulkeners just lately, isn't he? He could be behind all this — *and*,' he pointed out, 'every time something has happened here — the watcher in the tower, the flowers, the accusation, *and* the fire — *he's* been staying in Alderwood.'

'We — we don't know that . . . not for sure,' she faltered, her mind whirling and then shying away from the fact that it could be Vaughn who was behind all the trouble that had been caused recently.

'Then find out,' Mark said quietly. 'Make enquiries. It shouldn't be difficult. Cass could help. She could ask Patric Faulkener to give her the exact times that Vaughn Herrick has been out of the house while he's been staying with them.'

'No,' she said, shaking her head, and feeling slightly sickened by the suggestion. 'I can't do that. I can't be so devious. It's like spying — being an intruder,' she shivered. 'I can't go making wild accusations . . . '

'All those things have been done to *you*,' Mark said. 'Spying, intruding, accusing.' He went over to her and, placing his hands on her shoulders, shook her gently. 'Wake up, Tam,' he said. 'You can't let him get away with it. It's obviously Vaughn Herrick who's behind all this. He's jealous. He still wants you. And he's trying to make you run straight back into his arms.'

She felt herself go rigid in his grasp, and looked him straight in the eye as his words hit home. There was somebody else who wanted her to run straight into his arms too, she realized. She glanced up into Mark's stern face and said, 'Do you realize that in describing Vaughn just now, you've overlooked the fact that you too want the same thing as you're accusing him of? You have, in fact, just described yourself.'

22

His hands fell away from her. 'You seem to forget,' he said in a cold voice, 'I was here in the garden with you when you were first aware that you were being watched from the church tower, and you and I were together again when the fire-bug struck — we were *together*, Tam, two hundred miles away in Yorkshire, for heaven's sake.'

She knew it was ridiculous to suspect Mark of anything underhand, but neither could she reconcile herself to the fact that Vaughn Herrick would stoop so low as to frighten her the way *somebody* was doing. The fact remained, though, that things had happened and somebody was to blame. She walked away from Mark, turned on a small table-lamp and then swished the curtains shut, for the afternoon was darkening and it had become a habit, now, to draw all the curtains and closet herself away from the outside world when daylight faded. She walked across to the door of the little sitting room and turned to say, 'You see how stupid it is? For *me* to blame *you*? But it's what you're doing to Vaughn. You're condemning him without even knowing him.'

'And you *do* know him, I suppose?' There was the light of battle in Mark's eyes as he spun round to face her again.

'Of course I know him,' she cried. 'I had an affair with him, didn't I?'

Callously, Mark shot out, 'An affair which he walked away from when it suited him.'

'That's a risk we all have to take when we love somebody,' she said. '*You* threatened to walk out on me today, don't forget.'

She saw him swallow, seeming at a loss for words. He couldn't meet her gaze for some moments, then slowly he looked up at her and said, 'That was different.'

She shook her head. 'No,' she said. 'It wasn't different. *You* would have walked out on me just like Vaughn did.'

'It wouldn't have been permanent in my case, though.'

'No?' She tilted her head on one side and observed him critically, possibly, she thought, for the first time ever. 'You would have come back to me, then?' she asked quietly.

'You know damn well I would.'

Wanting to hurt him, as his threats had

hurt her, she said, 'I wouldn't have had you back.'

'Tam . . . ' It was a cry of anguish, and one which she hardened her heart against. A hint of fear stared out at her from those eyes that would forever remind her of the sea on a lazy summer day.

'I don't trust people who walk out on me,' she said, making her voice hard. 'I don't forgive easily, Mark.'

'I didn't go,' he said at last. 'So does that make me a genuine walker-out or not?'

She let go of the door handle and went back to him. She put her hands on his shoulders, leaned up on her toes and kissed him firmly on the mouth. 'You'll probably regret not walking out,' she said. 'I can be a real bitch when I put my mind to it.'

'Tam . . . ' His arms were round her, fastening her to him in an embrace that threatened never to let her go ever again. 'Tam . . . ' he said huskily. 'Forgive me.'

Slowly she began unstudding his jacket and pushing it back over his shoulders. Reluctantly, it seemed, he freed her only long enough for his arms to shrug off the jacket and let it slide to the floor. Then he pulled her to him again, and his head descended to hers, and his kiss was filled with a passionate brutality from which she emerged shaken, bruised, but with her heart racing, her whole being wanting him so much it was almost a physical pain.

'You want me, don't you?' she whispered as his hands seared up and down her body and then tangled in her hair, twisting her head this way and that so he could smother her face with kisses.

'I want you. I want to touch you and hold you and feel you all over. I want to be so close to you that we'll melt into each other and never come apart in a million years,' he said, his voice husky with desire.

'I'm here,' she said, and there was urgency in her voice. 'I need you too, Mark. We fight when we're together, but we can't survive apart, can we? Love me. Love me here. Love me now.'

'Here?' He raised his head only slightly to indicate the room.

'It's warm enough. The fire's still glowing.' She grinned up at him and flung her arms round his neck, and brought his head down towards hers again. And while their lips were locked together they stripped each other of their clothing, scattering the garments, tossing them aside as of no consequence, before tumbling down onto the floor and wrestling and rolling on the crimson thread-bare carpet in front of a dying fire in the black-fronted grate.

Her need of him was desperate; she had no time to wait for preliminaries now — not like the previous weekened at Mark's house, when their lovemaking had been passionately languorous and repeated several times over. She was still smarting from his threat to leave her *now*. She needed to rid herself of the remembrance of his hurtful words to her that day — 'we're all washed up' — 'I shall never ask you to marry me again' — 'it's over, Tam . . . '

Those last three little pathetic words were etched into her brain. And no matter how much he told her he loved her — as they lay there on the carpet, as he leaned over her, as he kissed her, and as he thrust into her — those words would *not* go away. She closed her eyes tightly, squeezing back the tears as her body responded to his touch and to the feel of him inside her. The joys of heaven, the perils of hell — they went hand in hand with the uncertainty of love, she thought wildly as she climaxed and dug her fingers deeply into the flesh of his body, and she wanted him to stay there, locked inside her, for ever, to keep her safe — and to stop him from leaving her.

It couldn't last, though, that closeness, that binding together of soul and spirit, or whatever it was that passed for the ultimate and death-defying fragment that lived on through all eternity. It always seemed so real to her at the time of consummation, and it *was* real for a few glorious moments — until proper, down-to-earth actuality came floating back into focus and forced itself into the now conscious mind, reminding the sated body that nothing lasted for ever.

She gave vent to her feelings with flippancy as they lay side by side. 'Somebody should have found the secret of making an orgasm last longer.' She twisted her head to one side to look at him. 'Don't you think?'

He leaned up on one elbow to look down into her face. He touched the little silver dreamcatcher pendant that lay awry against her throat on its silver chain. 'It's like dreams,' he said. 'You can't catch them and hold them, but some of them are good to remember afterwards.'

'Are you glad you didn't walk out on me?' She reached up a hand and let her fingers slide through his thick fair hair.

Gently, he leaned over and kissed her — a light, yet lingering kiss on her lips. Against her lips, he muttered, 'I'll never be able to let you go. You do realize that, don't you?'

She began to laugh softly. 'So you'll stay with me tonight?'

'Try to stop me.'

'Don't forget Jack-O,' she teased. 'You said you'd meet him at the pub car park this afternoon.'

'No problem,' he said. 'We still have more than an hour left before I have to leave for dear old Jack-O.'

★ ★ ★

Vaughn Herrick strode out of the back door of the pit lane garage into the paddock and, impatient with himself and all that had happened that afternoon, flung up the boot lid of his car and hurled his driving gear inside.

Patric Faulkener hurried after him, stood beside him, looking down at the rumpled mess of clothing that had been slung haphazardly into the rear of the car, the distinctive Oscar-Jade Nomex suit, the helmet and boots lying there in a pathetic heap. 'Don't take it so badly,' he said. 'You weren't to blame for that patch of oil on the track.'

Vaughn rounded on him. 'I was to blame for not seeing it. I *should* have seen it. It's my job to see things like that.'

'The car isn't a write-off though.'

Vaughn threw back his head and laughed. 'Tell that to my boss, huh? Did you hear the language he hurled at me? Hell! I must be going soft — letting the damned car dance around like that — and then smashing it against the Armco barrier. One second I took my mind off the damn track. One second! And that happened.'

'It was an accident.'

'Yeah! Tell Rafe Thorne that.' Vaughn jerked his head back towards the garage and the pit lane. 'I tried to, but he let all hell loose at me. Bastard's my middle name now, because I wrecked the test car so we can't use it tomorrow. Hell and damnation — even the tyres were ripped to pieces.'

A glimmer of amusement lit Patric Faulkener's eyes. 'The tyres were the least of your troubles. Tyres only have a very limited life anyway.'

'Yeah, yeah, yeah. Rub it in.'

Patric sobered instantly. 'Look — don't take it quite so much to heart. These things happen.'

'Yeah! Cars bend in the middle every day of the week.'

'It didn't do that.'

'No, it split in the middle.'

'So — forget it. It was only a car.'

'Expensive!' Vaughn said, glaring at him. 'More than expensive. It's not your average Mini, you know.'

'Get off home, man.'

'I don't have a home.' Vaughn stared morosely at the pile of clothing in the car boot again, then slammed the lid down. 'I've had it with motor racing,' he said. 'I'm jinxed.'

'Look — stop feeling sorry for yourself and get yourself over to Alderwood. Clare's expecting us back. You can take things easy for what's left of the weekend. Go and see your old girlfriend if you like.' Patric grinned. 'She'll probably be glad of the company, living where she does in that Stratton End backwood.'

'Tam's not interested in me any more — and I can't say I blame her. I've behaved like a prize fool towards her. She'll never want to set eyes on me again if she lives to be a hundred.'

'She's crazy, then. You're a good catch for any woman.'

'I let her down. Badly. I let everybody down.' Vaughn glowered again.

'Go and see her. Look — call on her on your way back to Alderwood. Something's got to lift you out of that gloom. Just go and see her and tell her you're sorry for whatever it is you've done.'

'I intend to *try* and see her,' Vaughn said, glancing at his friend again. 'I've been intending to for the past few days, but I feel such a jerk. I really did do a stupid thing, Patric . . . '

'We all do pretty stupid things at times,' Patric stated. 'But women are wonderfully forgiving people — *if* you just make the right noises.'

'Tam's not like that. She'll probably call me a patronizing bastard and throw something at me.'

Patric said with a deep sigh, 'Faint heart never won fair lady . . . '

Vaughn said, 'Yeah! Yeah! I've heard all that before.' He stood back from the car and looked thoughtful. 'Maybe I'll give her a call, though . . . '

Patric gave a satisfied laugh. 'That's right. She'll probably invite you over for supper — so maybe we won't be seeing you tonight. Just give us a phone call and tell us not to wait dinner for you, huh?'

Vaughn's natural good spirits started to return. 'I'll do that.' He walked round to the driving side of his car, opened the door and slid inside.

As he started up the engine in the dying light of the afternoon, he heard Patric yell, 'And good luck!'

Vaughn laughed back through the side window, then muttered under his breath, 'With a girl like Tamsin, I need more than luck.' And with a furious revving of his engine that wasn't absolutely necessary he shot away from the paddock, the car screaming as he swung up and over the bridge that spanned the track.

He raised his hand to the gate-keeper as the main road came into view. He was speeding; he was being reckless and he knew it. He reached the main road at the end of the driveway, and had to sit there waiting for passing traffic. His impatience mounted. He had to see Tamsin. He had to try and win her over again. He'd grovel. He'd tell her he couldn't live without her. His spirits sank. Tam would see through it. She wouldn't have forgotten how he'd hurt her. It had been a damn stupid thing to do — telling her he didn't want his career put in jeopardy when she'd been taken in by the police for questioning over Ava's death. But there just had to be a way of making her see sense. His foot jammed down on the accelerator again as the car sat idling in neutral. He revved the engine continuously, cursing the stream of traffic holding him up. He was anxious and jittery. It had been a bad day.

How to handle the apology, though — there was the question. He knew in his heart that an apology wouldn't be enough. He'd hurt her, and badly.

He'd get her, though. He'd win her back from that damned Yorkshireman who was pursuing her. Determined on that point at least, he realized that drastic measures might have to be taken. If such action got her back, though — nothing else mattered.

23

Tamsin towelled herself dry after her shower. Mark had been gone twenty minutes now. A smile touched her lips. He'd said he wouldn't be long — depending, of course, upon the transporter arriving on time from Yorkshire. She'd have time, though, to gather some of the herbs that Cass had asked for from the garden, and stack them in a sinkful of water in the kitchen until she could take them over to Alderwood the next morning.

She padded through to the darkened bedroom and went over to the window, dragging on her clothes — jeans and a warm sweatshirt — as she looked out at the garden. The light wasn't good out there, but she had a high-voltage security light fixed to the back of the house. It flooded the whole area with brightness so she'd easily be able to work in the light from it. She'd done it before — several times.

Downstairs the phone shrilled, and with her trainers still unfastened she raced down the stairs, lodging the phone between her ear and shoulder as she hopped first on one leg and then the other to tie up her shoelaces.

It had to be Mark. 'Hi,' she said. 'Did Jack-O arrive on time from Yorkshire?'

The voice that answered her wiped the smile from her face. 'Tam — I have to see you . . . '

'Vaughn!' She recovered from the shock of hearing *him* on the phone, and said, 'Sorry — Mark said he'd ring me . . . I thought it was him . . . ' She stopped trying to explain anything. There was no point in going over what had happened to her car; he wouldn't be interested anyway.

'You're still seeing him, then? Mark Langham?'

In the background, on the other end of the phone, she could hear the frantic revving of a car engine. 'Are you at the circuit?' she asked.

'No. I'm sitting in a lay-by — phoning you on the mobile.'

'Is that your car I can hear?'

'Yes,' he snapped. 'Is that a problem for you?'

'No,' she said, keeping her temper with difficulty. 'But if you're impatient to be off, don't let me stop you.'

'I'm impatient to *see* you,' he said in a surly voice.

She sighed. 'Sorry. Mark's here for the weekend — and even if he wasn't, I still wouldn't want you to come here, Vaughn. The past is done with . . . '

'Like hell it is! I need to see you.'

'What for?' she asked, making her voice pleasant.

'To talk.'

'Not now, Vaughn. I've told you . . . '

'Langham's not with you now. You thought it was him on the phone when I rang,' he said, an accusing note in his voice.

'He's just gone into Alderwood. He'll be back at any time.'

'How long is 'at any time'?'

'Vaughn — I don't want you coming here.'

'I said . . . '

'I heard you, but I am not going to answer that question because I don't know exactly how long Mark will be. All I can say is that you won't be welcome if you turn up here. In fact, I won't even answer the door to you.'

'Okay,' he said in a belligerent tone, 'I get the message — but I'm not going to be put off, Tam. I warn you — '

She put down the phone. Threats she could do without. Vaughn was a hot-head. He couldn't bear it if he wasn't getting all his own way. She chewed worriedly on her bottom lip, hoping against hope that Vaughn would take notice of what she'd said. Her new-found peace with Mark was very fragile. She didn't want anything to upset that peace. She didn't want him coming over and making trouble.

But Vaughn, she knew, was a law unto himself.

★ ★ ★

Clare Faulkener opened the door of her Alderwood seafront home after the doorbell had been repeatedly attacked by whoever was out there.

'Craig! What the hell are you doing here? For heaven's sake — I've told you never to come here . . . why didn't you phone . . . ?'

'It's something urgent,' Craig said, pushing her aside. 'Get out of the way, will you? Let me come inside and explain.'

She peered left and right up the road. 'Where's your car?'

'Parked — discreetly — up the next side-street.' His voice held a leering note as he added, 'Don't worry yourself, my sweet — *darling Patric* won't see it if he should come home unexpectedly.'

'He *is* coming home, you idiot.' Clare was furious with him. 'You shouldn't have come. What's he going to think if . . . ?' Craig was leaning on the wall in the passage as she slammed the door shut and whirled round to him. 'Well? What is it? What's so damned important that you have to come swanning over here to . . . '

'I'm going away,' he said, folding his arms and watching her closely.

'For the weekend?'

'Maybe longer than that.'

'You can't,' she said sharply. 'I need you at the office on Monday.'

'No can do, my sweet. I've been summoned to Scotland.'

'Scotland?' She stared at him, her mouth dropping open slightly. 'What in the world are you going to Scotland for?'

'You remember me telling you about my old granny?'

She shook her head. 'You never told me about an old granny.'

'I didn't?' He pulled a face. 'She's not important anyway,' he said. 'But she's dying — or so some old biddy of a hospital sister told me on the phone an hour ago.'

'Your grandmother is dying!'

'That's just about it, honeybunch.'

'You sound really worried,' she came back at him with sarcasm.

'I can think of things I'd rather be doing than sitting at a hospital bedside for the next

379

few days,' he taunted. 'Things like ripping your clothes off and . . . '

'Your granny's dying,' she reminded him. 'Ought you to be talking like that?'

'She's a right old hag,' he said, looking up at the ceiling as if he were bored by the whole subject of his grandmother.

'So why go? She can die without you there, can't she?'

'You aren't available this weekend,' he said. 'And granny has a soft spot for me. She's been asking for me. I have to go.'

'Are you sure this 'granny' doesn't wear a mini-skirt and exotic perfume?' she asked archly.

He made the sign of a cross on his chest. 'Cross my heart,' he said. 'My gran is dying in a hospital in Stirling, and I have to go to her because she's loaded.' He gave her a sly grin. 'Remember that million pounds? Well, Granny Andrews has always promised me she'll leave everything she has to me.'

Clare looked at him through narrowed eyes, as if she couldn't make up her mind whether he was lying or not. But this granny was a complete newcomer on Craig's scene. She couldn't remember him ever mentioning any relative he had before.

'And your granny has a million pounds to dispose of, does she?' she asked him in cool, disbelieving tones.

He gave a nonchalant shrug. 'She was — apparently — the only daughter of one of these Scottish lairds they talk about in the history books. You know — something along the lines of *Braveheart* or *Macbeth* — or,' he added with a twinkle, '*Ben Hur.*'

The joke fell flat. '*Ben Hur* isn't anything to do with Scotland.' She was furious with him. She liked to keep him on a tight rein — and Scotland was a hell of a long way from Suffolk. Too far to keep tabs on him!

'I'm probably thinking of Ben Nevis, then. He's some guy in Scottish history, isn't he?'

'He's a mountain — not a man,' Clare said, beginning to tire of the conversation. 'Don't act the fool, Craig. It doesn't suit you.'

'Just joking, sweetheart. I do know my history books.'

'And you're seriously going up to Scotland? Tonight?'

He nodded and pushed himself away from the wall to lean over and kiss her forehead. 'Sorry about work on Monday — I can't hope to be back by then.'

'But when *will* you be back?' All at once, Clare was worried. She couldn't manage without him indefinitely, either in the office or out of it.

He shrugged again. 'Who knows? I just

need to be there. There's a lot at stake.'

'If she's already made the damned will in your favour — what's the hurry?'

'Women are notoriously fickle,' he said. 'Gran could change her mind even at the eleventh hour. I want to be there so I know what's going on.' His tone became more cajoling as he reached out to her and stroked a sensuous finger down her cheek, 'Just think of it, sweetheart — I'll probably be coming back to you with that million you asked for. A cool million.' He gave a low little whistle. 'And then we shall see the sparks start to fly, shan't we? When you tell *dear Patric* you're leaving him for little old me.'

'Your gran might not die,' she said, hardening her heart as well as her voice.

'She's ninety-eight,' he said.

Her heart sank. 'How can I reach you?' she asked. 'I might need to ask your advice on something — workwise.'

'You can't reach me, lover.'

'I may need to . . . ' Her voice rose on a shrill note. 'Craig — I have to be able to talk to you.'

'I don't have the hospital phone number on me,' he said. 'I'll ring you when I get there, huh?'

'Wait!' She hurried away, and went into a room along the corridor. She came back seconds later, holding her own mobile phone. 'Take this with you,' she said. 'That way I can get in touch with you wherever you are.'

'Wow! Aren't I the honoured one, then? This is your precious phone I have in my hand,' he said, taking it from her.

Drily she said, 'Cut the sarcasm, Craig.'

'I shall ring you as soon as I cross the border,' he said. 'I shall have a piper play 'The Campbells are Coming' over your very own mobile to you — just to prove I am in Scotland, of course.'

'We could have been at Lilacs,' she said angrily. 'If only Patric hadn't decided to bring that racing-driver, Herrick, back here.'

'Next week — or the one after that, sweetheart.' Craig stopped his teasing now, and took her into his arms. He kissed her long and hard, then put her away from him, and, his face serious, said, 'Don't go to Lilacs without me. Promise me that. I couldn't bear to think of you there without me.'

She tossed her head. 'I shall do as I please.'

'If you do that,' he said, his jaw tightening, 'I shall do as *I* please too. In Scotland. Life can, I imagine, get very boring sitting waiting for time to pass in a Scottish hospital, but,' he said, with meaning edging his every word, 'I expect there are some gorgeous nurses up there if I should get too lonely.'

Clare's anger flared instantly. 'Don't you dare . . . '

Smoothly he said, 'If you are going to be at Lilacs without me . . . ' and left the sentence hanging.

'I won't go,' she said, her heart-rate soaring to a dangerous level. 'You know I won't go. Not without you. Believe me, Craig — *please*, believe me. I couldn't bear to go to Lilacs without you.'

'That's a good girl.' He stroked her hair, kissed her one more time then looked at his watch. 'A quarter past five! I have to go.'

'I'll miss you . . . '

'Hey,' he said, laughing down into her face, 'know what happened earlier?'

Puzzled, she shook her head.

'I was in the pub,' he said. 'And dear little Tamsin Curtis's car got a real walloping from some guy who was obviously over the limit.'

Interested in spite of herself, she asked, 'Was she hurt?'

He shook his head. 'She and some guy she knew from Yorkshire were on the beach at the time. The landlord said Ms Curtis's car was being taken up there for repair — some time late this afternoon by her friendly Yorkie. Told us all to avoid the glass and debris scattered over half the car park.'

'Poor old Tamsin,' Clare said loftily, with

no real feeling in her voice.

'Yes.' Craig kissed her forehead again. 'I feel really sorry for her.'

She stood at the door and watched him leave her then, his long legs carrying him effortlessly down the promenade, and soon he was lost to view as he turned into a side-street some distance away.

Did he really have a grandmother? she wondered. And after a few moments' deliberation she decided he must be telling the truth. He must have known all along that the old lady was in failing health too. That was why he had talked so glibly about making a million. That was why he had been so convincing. He'd known all along he was going to inherit his grandmother's wealth, and when that happened . . .

Clare suddenly shivered and went back inside the house, closing the door firmly behind her. Things were moving quickly. Too quickly. But she'd made him a promise, not ever thinking he would ever have money of his own when she'd done so.

She gazed at herself in the hall mirror. Could she give up everything for him? She stared hard at her reflection, then a smile tilted her crimson lips and she whispered softly to the face that stared back at her, 'Promises were made to be broken,' before moving away and starting to sing softly to herself.

★ ★ ★

Tam looked at the watch on her wrist. The time was ticking away steadily towards six o'clock, and she wondered idly if Jack-O and the transporter had turned up at Alderwood by now. It was a long way to have to come just to pick up her old Beetle, and, thinking logically about it, she supposed she ought to have let the local garage look at it first. They would probably have scrapped it, though; the damage was extensive. On the other hand, Mark had all the right equipment up in Yorkshire to make a first-class repair. It was his job, restoring old cars, and he was good at it.

She looked down at the garden trug against her feet. It was overflowing with herb cuttings. She'd taken most of them from the base of the plants, and some of them were eighteen inches or so in length. Her clothes smelled strongly of rosemary and cotton lavender. The trug was a mass of mainly greenery, for the flowers would come later in the year. She was well aware that March wasn't a good time for photographs, but Cass had told her she was confident about the way she was going to tackle the advertising material.

Tam gathered plants that looked good for the time of year. March had been warm so far, and a strong sun had been out today. The garden was coming on well, she decided, pleased with the result of all the work she'd put in during the colder winter months. She was ready for spring now. She clipped at the hedges, adding sprigs of new hawthorn to the pile already gathered, seeing in her mind's eye the brilliant effect the bright green tightly rolled leaves would have if they were set off against a display of the darker, more fleshy angelica. She went along the pathways, adding lily of the valley leaves, tansy, ferny camomile and fennel. A spray of golden elder joined the other plants in the trug, and then she came to the dense, bushy, herb of grace — the rue — which she knew she had to take care in handling because of her former allergy.

She was wearing thick gardening gloves, and had come prepared with a plastic bag in her pocket. She shook out the self-sealing bag, clipped a few stems and dropped them into the bag, being careful not to crush them. Airtight in the bag, they would stay fresh enough, she knew. She pushed the bag carefully into the jumbo pocket that ran along the front of her hooded sweatshirt with its zipped neckline. Sealed in plastic as they were, the cuttings wouldn't harm her there.

She turned back towards the house and then stopped, drawing in her breath. There was a light on in the bedroom over the kitchen. *Her* bedroom! Surely she hadn't left it on. She frowned. No! She distinctly remembered getting dressed in the semi-dark after her shower. As she looked at it, wondering how it could be — it suddenly went off.

Mark must have returned, she decided, though she hadn't heard his car, and the old Porsche did kick up quite a racket coming down that bumpy lane. She walked slowly back up the garden's grassy pathway, not unduly worried about seeing the light in the bedroom window, but a little apprehensive because it wasn't in Mark's nature to spring surprises — and he *must* have seen her in the garden when he returned. So why hadn't he called out to her? In the light of everything that had happened recently he might have known she'd be a bit uneasy at a presence in the house she had thought to be unoccupied.

She went into the kitchen, took off her gardening gloves and perched the over-full trug on the end of the table. She was about to walk through to the foot of the stairs then, when for some reason she hesitated, tilted her head towards the ceiling and listened. A floorboard above her creaked, startling her so that she moved silently across to the window and picked up the iron horseshoe that Mark had sent her for St Valentine's day. She weighed it in her hand, then laughed softly at herself. What on earth would it look like if she walked into the bedroom and confronted Mark with a weapon in her hand? Still, it was better to be safe than sorry, she thought. And the worst he could do would be to laugh at her. Sobering, she knew he *wouldn't* laugh at her. He would say she was perfectly right to think about her own safety . . .

At the foot of the stairs, she called out, 'Mark! Is that you?'

There was no reply.

She called out in a sharper tone, 'Mark! Don't play games. I know you're up there.'

Still there was no reply, but overhead a floorboard creaked again.

She poked her head into the front room and tiptoed in there, lifted the edge of the curtain and peered out of the window. It was very dark out on the lane after the brightness of the back garden, with the high-voltage electric light flooding the place. She just caught sight of a gleam of chrome beyond the little fence and privet hedging round her front garden, though, and she let out a relieved sigh. Of course it was Mark. It had to be Mark, even though she couldn't be absolutely sure it was the Porsche out there.

Back at the bottom of the stairs, she flicked on the landing light. It was a two-way switch that could be operated either from upstairs or down. When she was halfway up the stairs the light clicked off, and she was left in total darkness.

For a second, she froze in terror, then, 'Mark,' she yelled, 'stop being so stupid . . .'

She raced up the rest of the stairs, transferring the horseshoe into her left hand as her right one stretched out in front of her to find the electric light switch on the landing wall. She never found it, though, because before she could do that, something barred her way. It was like a solid shadow, moving silently out of the bedroom and for a second letting a glimmer of light escape. A glimmer she recognized as reflected light from the outside security lamp, which was still flooding the garden with its brightness. It was gone in a second as the door swung to again, and Tamsin, too late, realized she had been a fool to come up here alone.

She was spinning round to the stairs again then, her breath coming in great gasps of terror, aware all the time that she was shut in the absolute darkness of the heart of the house with something that was evil. Before she could even find the top step of the stairs, though, a hand snatched at hers. It was cold, hard, and leather-gloved. It hauled her away from the switch on the wall, and away from the safety of the stair-well. It dragged her then, silently and menacingly — as she fell onto her knees in an effort to prevent it — into the back bedroom.

The dim light was back again, reflected from outside as the bedroom door swung shut behind her. She staggered to her feet, her wrist still locked in the hand of her assailant. The scream she wanted to utter stuck in her throat. It was like a nightmare where you couldn't run away. But this was no nightmare. This was reality. Struggling to her feet, she gripped the iron horseshoe in her left hand and had the sense to keep it hidden against her thigh as she waited for her chance to use it. Her right hand, almost devoid of sensation now, was still held firm in that merciless grip.

She was facing the unknown figure now, seeing it clearly for the first time. And in ever-mounting horror she stared at what confronted her. It looked, silhouetted as it was against the window, like a giant black ant.

It couldn't be real. Her mind asserted itself, though, and told her it *was* real. A whimper of horror escaped her lips, and it was some seconds before she rationalized what it actually was.

A driver! A racing-driver!

The tall figure was dressed in dark motor racing gear — soft driving boots and a quilted fireproof suit that covered him from heel to chin. Her eyes, getting accustomed to the dimness now, saw that his face was obscured by a motor racing helmet — shiny, black and ominous, with the darkly tinted visor pulled down so it was impossible to make out any features.

She knew only one racing-driver.

'Vaughn?' His name, a mere whisper, broke from her lips.

No! She wouldn't let herself believe that Vaughn could do this to her. Terror was mounting and the scream broke loose at last. Not one scream, but scream after scream, piercing the still air, echoing in her brain, adding to her terror. Screams and terror went hand in hand . . .

The figure grunted. Then its free hand swung up and cracked her across the jaw. Pain shot through her head. The whole room went dark as she felt herself spinning into oblivion. She fought to stay conscious, but lost the battle as her legs crumpled beneath her.

And she sank into absolute blackness.

24

Mark paced the car park, then looked at his watch for what seemed like the hundredth time in the past half-hour. Where was Jack-O? He'd said half past five and now it was well after six. He took his mobile phone out of his pocket and wondered whether to ring Edgar Brand up in Yorkshire, but decided against it. Jack-O could be held up for any number of reasons, he knew, and it would do no good to go worrying Edgar.

As he held the phone, and stood looking at it, it suddenly started to ring, and with relief he answered it.

Jack-O had been held up.

'A puncture!' Mark relaxed. 'Thank goodness it was no more than that.'

Jack-O said, 'Sorry, mate. I'll be with you before seven. I'm still on the A1, though. Quite some distance away.'

When Jack-O had rung off, Mark quickly dialled Tam's number, pacing up and down, and cursing when there was no answer.

Eventually he gave up trying and pocketed his phone again, not worried unduly, as he knew what Tam was like when she got into her beloved garden. All the same, even though the day had been relatively sunny for March, it was turning cold now, and she ought to be inside the house. She'd had a list in her hand of all the herbs she wanted to gather for Cass when he'd left her, though, and, knowing Tam, she'd be hunting round the garden for the best samples she could find. There was no hope of her hearing the phone ringing if she were at the far end of the garden.

He blew onto his hands to try and warm them. Tam often said she'd buy him a pair of gloves, but he detested gloves. They stifled him. He only possessed one pair and hardly ever wore them — they were so old now. He was used to the cold north winds; he had to be in his job. The garage where he, Edgar and Jack-O carried out their restoration of classics was situated right on the seafront at Shorecross, the little coastal village a few miles from where Mark lived — inland — at Rothwold.

He walked across the car park towards the sea now, then turned round to look at the pub. The building was in darkness; it didn't open until seven. 'What a place this is!' He sighed. Anywhere else in the country, pubs were open all day — but not at Alderwood. The little tucked-away village hadn't caught up with the twentieth century yet!

A figure was hurrying along the far side of the car park, where the road to the village centre ran. The figure seemed familiar somehow. He stared hard at it. Then he recognized it, and yelled, 'Cass! Cass! Wait!' And he started to run across the deserted car park towards the low wall that bordered it on its far side.

She spun round at the sound of her name. Street lamps were lit now, and he could see her peering across at him as he neared her. Then her face lit up with a smile as she saw who it was.

'Mark! What a surprise! Where's Tam?'

He stopped on his side of the wall. 'At home. Gathering herbs to bring to you in the morning for their photo-call.' He grinned. 'I've just tried ringing her but she's obviously still in the dratted garden. There was no reply.'

'What are you doing here?'

He jerked his head in the direction of Tamsin's car, just visible a few yards away, and explained what had happened that afternoon.

'Oh, poor old Tam. She relies on that car so much.'

He nodded. 'Yes, I know. And now Jack-O's been held up — probably for another hour.' He glanced at his watch again. 'I suppose I'd have time to go back to Herb House and tell Tam myself, but . . . '

'You'd barely get there, and if you did you'd have to turn straight round and come back,' Cass pointed out. 'It takes almost half an hour to get to Stratton End by road.'

'I wish she'd answered the damn phone, though.' His brow drew into a frown. 'I worry when she's there on her own.'

'Look,' Cass said, 'why don't you come back to my house and have a hot drink while you're waiting for your mechanic. You can keep trying to ring Tam from there just as well as here — and you'll only be a couple of minutes away. You can keep popping back to see if the transporter's arrived if you want to.'

'Cass! You are an angel.'

She grinned at him as he vaulted over the low wall. 'You should wear gloves,' she said. 'Your hands are red-raw.'

'Can't bear the things,' he said with a grimace. 'Tam's always on to me to get some, though.'

'Your coat looks cosy.'

He fell into step beside her. 'It is. We'd been to the pub for a meal at lunchtime, and then took a long walk on the beach.'

'And it was then — when you came back — that you found out what had happened to Tam's car?' Cass asked conversationally.

'Yes. We walked back to Herb House across the heath — and that is some creepy, cold place.'

'I suppose I'm used to it.' Cass laughed. 'I grew up with it.'

'You've always lived here?'

They'd reached Cass's house by now. She put the key in the lock and turned it, pushing the door open. 'Uh-huh. I wasn't born here, though. Dad worked on the North Sea oil rigs and he and Mum lived on the Scottish borders when they were first married. I was born up there, but Mum suffered with bronchitis so they moved south when I was two or three years old. I don't remember anything else but Alderwood, though. My life seemed to start here. There were no photographs of me as a baby either, or as a toddler — not until Alderwood. I think it was the first place my parents had ever put down roots when they bought this house.'

'Won't it be a big wrench? Selling it — as you're hoping to do now?' he asked quietly as he followed her inside the house.

She switched on the light as she went through to the small front sitting room. 'I still don't know if I'm doing the right thing.' She frowned.

He closed the front door, then went and stood in front of the fire and watched Cass as she went through the archway wall and into the kitchen. She switched on the electric kettle, spooned tea into a teapot, reached two mugs out of a cupboard, then took off her warm winter coat and came back to him.

'Sit down. Make yourself comfortable. Would you like something to eat too?'

'No, thanks. Tam will no doubt have got something ready for when I get back. A hot drink is what I need.'

She made the tea, brought his through to him, then perched herself on the arm of an easy chair across the hearth from him, nursing her own mug between her hands.

'What will you do if you get a buyer for the house before you've made up your mind whether you want to sell it or not?' he asked.

She gave a little shrug. 'I'll sell. I don't like messing people about. And something seems to be telling me I need to move on from here.'

'You're lucky that you can do your job from any part of the country.'

She smiled. 'Yes. I realize that. I enjoy seeing new places. I'm looking forward to the Northumberland job later in the year.'

'Have you enjoyed the Essex one?'

'Mmm. I suppose so. I like being near the sea, though, and it was strange being in a big town.'

'I feel the same way. I've always lived near the coast — although my house is a mile or two inland, I work with the sea on my doorstep.'

'You don't like Alderwood, though, do you?'

'Does it show?' he asked in a wry voice. 'I thought I kept it remarkably well hidden — my hatred of the place that's taken Tam away from me.'

Cass said, 'Take things one day at a time. Tam cares for you, but she's not the sort of person you can push into things.'

He gave a sober little laugh. 'Tam? Being pushed? It hardly bears thinking about.'

Cass looked sympathetic. 'Give her time, Mark.'

He looked down at the tea in his mug and said, 'How long does it take, Cass?' Then he looked up at her. 'She's got commitments down here now. This business with Clare Faulkener, and the year-long lease on the house.'

'She needs more than this, though,' Cass said quietly. 'She misses the contact she used to have with people before; I do know that.'

'She does? Has she told you that?'

Cass said, 'Not in so many words, but sometimes you don't need words to know what a person's thinking, do you? And she spends a lot of time thinking about you.'

'She does?' Mark asked, his voice wary. He felt vulnerable at that moment, and didn't think he could bear it if Cass were merely humouring him. He had to be sure that Tam really wanted him. Thinking back to that afternoon, though, he knew for certain that what he and Tam had shared, back there at Herb House, had been real enough. They were well suited. Making love to Tam was . . .

Cass cut into his thoughts. 'Do you want to try and phone her again?'

He glanced at his watch again. 'Six-forty. Yes. I ought to, shouldn't I? And then I'll get back to the car park. Jack-O must be almost here by now.'

Mark tried on his mobile to get in touch with Tamsin, but there was still no reply. Cass said, 'Maybe it's your phone playing up.' And she tried on her own telephone, but the result was the same. Tamsin didn't answer, and they both stared at each other, not daring to voice their concern.

'Maybe she's taking a shower,' Cass said at last.

'I have this awful feeling . . . '

'No!' Cass said sharply. 'Don't start

imagining all sorts of things. There's got to be a perfectly reasonable explanation.'

Mark stood up. 'If Jack-O isn't there when I get back to the car park, I'm going back to Tam,' he said. 'There's something wrong. I just know there is. She wouldn't *not* answer the phone on purpose.'

'I'll go over there while you see to the car,' Cass said, already marching through to the kitchen, putting the mugs on the draining board and getting into her coat again. She unhooked her car keys from near the back door, then spun round to him. 'Don't argue,' she warned. 'And don't try to stop me. I'm going over to Herb House right now, so you just get that car of hers loaded onto the transporter and then follow me. Okay?'

Mark nodded, his face tense. 'Thanks, Cass. You're a lifesaver — as always.'

'Hardly that.' She grimaced as she led the way out of the front door again. Her car was parked a few yards up the street where the road was wider. She hesitated for just a moment. 'Don't worry,' she said. 'Tam knows how to look after herself. In another half-hour or so we'll be laughing about how worried we both are right now. Just you wait and see.'

'I hope so.' Mark's jaw was set. 'I sincerely hope so.'

The lane was in darkness, and as Cass drove down towards Herb House a feeling of dread steadily began building up inside her. It grew stronger as she neared the place, and was soon churning her stomach and making her feel physically sick.

'Idiot,' she scolded herself as she passed the site of the burned-out church and tried not to look in its direction. 'You're hungry! You've missed a meal! That's what's making you feel like this.' She thought with anguish of the piece of fresh salmon still sitting in her fridge, just waiting to be poached. 'Mark Langham,' she muttered, 'you are a pain in the neck.'

She pulled the car to a silent halt outside Herb House. The front of the house was in darkness, but the back was well illuminated with the bright security light she'd persuaded Tam to have fitted. Surely Tam wasn't still working out in the garden, though. Not at this time of night. Cass saw that her dashboard clock showed it was fifteen minutes past seven as she opened the door, then switched off her main-beam headlights, and got out into the cold, still night.

She forced herself not to panic as she walked down the path at the side of the house and round to the back door. It was wide open, she saw as she approached it. And there was a light switched on in the kitchen.

She went inside, calling out, 'Tam! Tam! It's me — Cass!'

The kitchen was quiet and deserted. On the floor was an upside-down garden trug, and all around it were scattered cuttings from herbs. The trug had obviously been placed on the edge of the table and had then either fallen or been knocked off. Cass crouched down. Under the table were more herb cuttings. She reached out to them — an automatic response to clearing up something that was untidy. Then her hand drew back. Wouldn't it be best to leave things as they were and concentrate more on finding Tam?

She stood up, went and looked in the front room. One curtain was caught up at a corner — as if somebody had been peeping through onto the lane outside. She gave a little shiver, went to the foot of the stairs and called out again, 'Tam! Are you there?'

Only silence greeted her! She switched on the light at the bottom of the stairs and, taking a deep breath, went up to the landing. All the three bedroom doors were open, and all the rooms were in darkness. She went into the back bedroom. There was some light in there from the one that was still shining outside. She switched the central light on for good measure, though, gazed round the room, saw nothing untoward, and then went to the remaining two bedrooms and put lights on in both of them as well. Nothing was disturbed.

She walked out onto the landing and saw the bathroom door, still firmly shut, and her heart turned over as all manner of things went through her mind. Tam could have slipped in the shower. She could be wedged behind that closed door with a head injury. Or she could have fallen in the bath and . . .

'No! Oh, please, please, no . . . ' She ran at the door and hurled all her weight at it. It opened without a problem. She jerked on the pull switch and blinked at the brightness that flooded the tiny room. Towels were arranged neatly. There was a delicious scent of expensive shower gel permeating the place. There was, however, no sign of Tam.

Cass retraced her steps and was halfway back down the stairs when she heard the sound of Mark's car roaring down the lane. She ran outside to meet him, and tell him as he leapt out of his car, 'She's not here, Mark. There's no sign of her.'

'She *has* to be here,' he ground out between gritted teeth. 'Where the hell else would she be? She hasn't got a damn car to go anywhere.'

'She walks across the heath if she wants something from Alderwood . . . '

'Not at this time of night surely?' He stared at her. 'Nobody in their right senses would walk across that heath at this time of night.'

'If she wanted you — and without a car — she would . . . '

He closed his eyes briefly. 'Oh, no . . . '

Cass shook her head. 'No,' she said. 'She wouldn't leave the house open, would she? And the back door wasn't locked — it wasn't even shut.'

He pushed past her and raced down the path at the side of the house, barging into the kitchen as Cass followed and caught up with him. She saw him standing looking down at the mess the fallen herbs had made on the floor there.

He spun round to her. 'Did you knock this off the table?'

'No.' She shook her head. 'It was like that when I came in.'

'Like somebody left in a hurry and caught it as they passed the table and knocked it off onto the floor?'

She nodded. 'That's what it looked like.'

'Why would she leave in a hurry like that?'

'I don't know,' Cass yelled, fear taking hold of her.

'Have you looked upstairs?'

She nodded wildly. 'Yes. Of course I have.'

'And . . . nothing?'

'Nothing as far as I could see. She's definitely not here, Mark.'

'She has to be.' He strode outside. Every bit of the garden was illuminated by the outside security light. 'The sheds,' he muttered. 'And the greenhouse.'

Cass raced after him, already knowing in her heart that the search would be futile as he flung open the out-houses and went inside each one in turn. She stood on the grassy path, shivering with cold and fear and hugging her arms round her body in a self-preservation attitude.

They returned to the house together, hurrying and saying nothing. Mark's face was grim and unyielding as they entered the kitchen again. He went through the house then, downstairs first, then upstairs, and again Cass followed. In the back bedroom he stared at the bed, and said suddenly, 'There was a throw-over on the bed. Now it's gone.'

Cass stared at him. 'A throw-over?'

He made a dismissive little gesture with his hands. 'You know — one of those old-fashioned things — Tam found it in one of the drawers when she first moved in. It was old and faded, but she fell in love with it. She washed it and put it on the bed on top of the quilt. She said it was cosy.' He glared at Cass. 'Well, say something. You *do* know what I'm talking about, don't you?'

'A bedspread?'

'Tufted. In stripes. With a pattern of roses in the middle.'

She nodded. 'It's called *candlewick*,' she said. 'What colour was it?'

There was exasperation in his voice as he said, 'Does it matter?'

'The police will want to know,' she said. 'Mark — we've got to inform the police about this.'

He stared at her. Then he said slowly, 'Yes. Of course. But will they take it seriously? I mean — I was only out of the house for a couple of hours. They won't treat her as a missing person, surely . . . '

'They will,' she said. 'They'll have to. They know already about the scares she's had here — the feeling she was being watched, the white flowers . . . '

'Yes.' Mark's voice was subdued. 'When they took her in for questioning over Ava Thorne's death she told them, didn't she? But they said there was nothing they could do. Hell! If only they'd taken her seriously then . . . ' His face was strained and pale. 'What if that black-edged card was more than a threat . . . ?'

'Don't talk like that.' Cass grabbed hold of his arm. 'For heaven's sake, Mark. Don't start getting all morbid.'

'That candlewick — or whatever you call it — is definitely missing,' he said. 'It was there today. I saw it when we . . . ' He hesitated, then went on, 'When I brought my weekend bag upstairs.'

Cass deliberately disregarded the catch in his voice. She'd guessed, of course, that they were sharing a bedroom — that they were lovers. But it was no concern of hers. Gently, she said, 'Let's go downstairs and see if anything else is missing.'

In the kitchen, Mark stooped down and started gathering up the herbs and putting them back into the trug. Cass looked round the room. It was growing cool in there. The stove obviously needed stoking with more coal. She could see, though, that Mark wasn't concerned about such a triviality. He was crouching there on the floor amid the spilt greenery, and just staring into space. Her heart went out to him. She went over to him.

He pointed across the room, to a chair. 'What's that?'

She bent down, saw what it was he was looking at. 'A sheet of paper, I think,' she said. 'It probably blew off the table in the draught from the door. Tam had a list of the herbs she wanted photographing. It must be that . . . '

'No,' he said. 'That was a screwed up bit of a thing. This looks like a letter of some sort.'

Cass went across the room and fished the paper out from under the chair.

Without looking at it — in case it was something private — she handed it to him.

He stood up, holding what had looked like a sheet of plain paper, muttering, 'Oh, no. No. I don't believe this . . . '

'What is it?'

He seemed unable to speak. His face held a haunted expression. He stared at her and just handed the letter over to her. 'Read it . . . ' he croaked.

And Cass took the paper from him, still convinced at first that it was just a blank sheet. And at first sight that was what it appeared to be — until she read the message typed neatly across the centre of the page in minute lettering.

She sucked in a deep breath, then read it out loud, ''*If you inform the police — she's dead!*''

25

Without opening her eyes, because her head hurt so much, Tam just tried to lie as still as possible — which wasn't easy because she felt as if she were being jolted around in a food mixer.

Something cuddly and warm was wrapped round her; it covered her head too. She knew this because she could feel her stiflingly hot breath close around her face. It couldn't escape — the breath she was breathing out — it was packed like a layer of soft padding around her cheeks and her chin, and her nose and her forehead. She was stiff and cramped, though, and when she tried to move her arms they wouldn't budge.

There was something hard locked in the fingers of her left hand. It had a rough surface that was digging into her palm. She managed to move one finger across its surface. There were little indentations in it.

The horseshoe! Mark's horseshoe!

Memory came filtering back through the

layers of hot breath. She jerked her head backwards and it hit something hard that brought stinging tears of pain to her eyes and made her gasp. Wherever she was, there certainly wasn't much room. It smelled of rubber and oil and petrol. Suddenly she was scared. Petrol! She remembered the fire at Herb House. Whoever it was doing this to her — he couldn't be going to set fire to *her*, could he?

She tried to scream, but the sound was deadened by what felt like a heavy blanket that was covering her completely. She tested moving her arms again, but they were fastened to her sides. She wriggled and attempted to get her legs free. Like her arms, though, they were held firmly together. Banded round with something. She moved her face, pushed out her tongue — the only bit of her that didn't seem to be shackled. It touched something fluffy. She breathed in deeply. The smell coming off her covering was familiar.

Washing powder! The same brand she used herself.

She managed to open her eyes. At first everything was dark, then she made out a hint of pink. Pink. Fluffy.

'Candlewick,' she gasped. 'My bedspread.'

It was bound round her tightly, she found

out, as she experimentally tried to disentangle herself from it, but discovered to her frustration that bonds which felt remarkably like leather suitcase straps were wrapped round the outside of the fabric, holding her arms and legs immobile. She lay still again, exhausted by her struggles, coming to realize slowly, though, that she was in a moving vehicle — but not in the most comfortable of seats!

It wasn't a *seat* at all, and the engine noise seemed a long way away from her. Then there was that worrying smell of rubber and oil. She inched her feet around in the confined space, and realization dawned — she was in the boot of a car. She lay back, eyes wide, but seeing nothing because of the covering that was stifling her now.

How long? she wondered. How long had she been unconscious? There was no way of telling. She forced herself not to panic. Try to get some kind of bearings, she told herself firmly. Lie still and concentrate. If she was being taken to Alderwood, she'd know when they passed over the river bridge. Her own car always rumbled and shook when they went over the bridge.

She could make out nothing, but then, suddenly, the car seemed to be slowing down. She felt the wheels jolting over uneven ground and then veering to the left. There was a crackling sound under the car. Panic coursed through her and she began to struggle. 'Not fire . . . ' she whimpered. 'Please God, not fire . . . '

The car stopped. And after an eternity that was entirely made up of seconds, she felt a lurching sensation as somebody got out of the driver's side. Footsteps — hushed footsteps — came round the side of the car, and Tamsin tried to curl herself up and make herself small and inconspicuous. She wouldn't let him know she was awake . . . she'd pretend to be still unconscious . . .

The sound of a key grated very near to her head, and then a gush of fresh air blew through the coverlet she was wrapped in.

Somebody was standing there, gazing down at her. She held her breath. The back end of the car creaked. He was leaning on it — leaning inside the boot — looking at her, listening to her.

'Damn!' The voice was muffled, distorted to her ears. It was a man's voice, though. She was sure of that.

He prodded her, and she stiffened.

'You're not dead then.' The voice was a hissed whisper how, completely unrecognizable. 'I thought I'd better check before we went any further.'

414

She stifled a sob.

'Are you going to co-operate with me?'

She groaned.

'Was that a yes?'

'Let — me — out . . . ' she begged. 'I — I'm suffocating . . . '

A hand grasped at her neck and she tried to scream, squirming away from it. She felt something growing tight around her throat, and started choking. The tightening continued as her captor dragged her into a sitting position. She began to cough as something cut into her throat . . .

'No . . . ' she panted. 'N-o-o-o . . . '

He jerked her head back and something snapped so she could breathe more easily again. She realized in that moment what it was. Mark's little silver pendant — the dreamcatcher. Its silver chain had been pulling tight round her throat, and now it had snapped. If only . . . she thought desperately. If only she could throw it out onto the road where somebody might find it . . . they'd know which way he had taken her then. She had to try and do it, but how? Her arms were fastened to her sides; her legs were strapped together and full of cramps. And she was completely enveloped in the coverlet taken from her own bed at Herb House.

'Please . . . ' she begged in a choking

whisper. 'Please ... get me out of here ... my legs ... '

He slid an arm under her knees, another round her shoulders, and hauled her out of the car boot. She still couldn't see a thing because the bedspread was doubled over her head, and not even a gap had been left to let in a little light.

She was being lowered to the ground, however, propped upright against the back of the car. He still held onto her tightly, though, and she tried to wriggle away from him. Her movements only made his fingers dig into her all the more cruelly. Only one thing was reassuring — the crackling noise she'd heard was now explained. It wasn't fire, as she'd feared, it was dry twigs and leaves underfoot. A lay by? Or could it be a clearing in a wood?

'Leave — me — alone — ' she gasped. But blood was circulating more freely in her legs now, and with it came the pain. She cried out as the muscles of her legs seemed tied in knots. She would have overbalanced if he hadn't supported her.

'Why ... ?' she stammered almost incoherently into the depths of the enveloping blanket. 'Why are you — doing this ... ?'

She was jerking this way and that — not merely to wrench herself out of his grasp, but

416

also to try and dislodge the little dream-catcher pendant that she could feel lodged in her bra, where it had slipped after the chain had broken. She was sobbing with frustration when he said, 'That's enough. Back inside now.'

'No . . . ' she screamed. 'No . . . '

He grasped her shoulders and shook her harder than she'd ever been manhandled in her life before. And she felt the silver pendant start slithering down her body under her sweatshirt, felt rather than heard it chink against her shoe as it reached the ground, and her sobbing then was of relief that at least she had managed to leave a clue as to the way she was being taken.

'Don't give me any grief, lady.'

'Please . . . ' she begged. 'Not in there again . . . '

'It's the only way.' The muffled voice was harsh. It was somehow familiar, too, but she couldn't quite place where she'd heard it before.

'Vaughn . . . ?' she whispered.

A laugh, quietly derisive, greeted this question. 'Wouldn't you like to know?'

'Vaughn — you — wouldn't . . . '

'Wouldn't I?' The voice was menacing.

'No . . . Oh, please, no . . . '

She heard a smothered sort of oath, and

417

then she was swept off the ground again and dumped without ceremony back inside the boot of the car. She heard the lid slam down, and she cringed inside her covering and cowered as far away from the lock as possible as she heard the key being turned once more.

★ ★ ★

Cass lay exhausted, curled up on the sofa in Tamsin's small sitting room early the following morning. When Mark took a cup of tea in she shot up with a start.

She rubbed her eyes and pulled the quilt firmly up to her shoulders — even though she was still fully dressed — and, staring at him, her face pale and pinched, she asked, 'Any news?'

He shook his head and perched on the sofa just below her knees, which were bent up almost to her chin under the thick, downy coverlet.

'No! You should have gone home last night. There was absolutely no need for you to stay.' His voice was curt.

'I wanted to stay. I wanted to be here if . . .'

'If what? If they brought her back? Do you think that's likely?'

'There might have been another message.

They're going to get in touch with you again, aren't they? They have to. There must be some point to all this.'

'A ransom note? Is that what you're expecting?' he asked her dully.

She nodded slowly. 'It has to be that, doesn't it? Why else did they leave that note?'

'I don't know.' He handed her the cup of hot tea. 'Here, drink this. And for heaven's sake don't cower away from me like that, Cass. You surely don't think I have anything to do with Tam's disappearance, do you?'

She sipped at the tea. Then she said, 'I couldn't sleep for hours. I just kept thinking and thinking until my head was aching.'

'Thinking what?' he asked.

She stared at him, and tried to stop her hands trembling. Could she tell him? Dared she tell him?

In a husky voice she said, 'You were the last person to see her.'

'No,' he said. 'The other guy — or guys — were the last to see her. Whoever it was who left the note — they were the last.'

'You know what I mean.' She took a deep gulp of tea.

'Why did you stay?' he said, his eyes narrowing, 'If you thought *I'd* done away with her.'

419

'I — I didn't think that. Not — not at first . . . '

'When did that thought hit you, then?' he asked.

She couldn't lie to him. She couldn't meet his steady gaze either. 'About three o'clock this morning.'

'About the same time it hit me,' he said. 'At least — that's what everybody is going to think, isn't it? That Tam and I had a fight? That I hit her — just a little bit too hard? Is that what's been going through your mind?'

'You can't blame me for exploring every . . . '

He lifted his shoulders in a helpless kind of shrug. 'No — I can't blame you.'

'No, no, no.' She leaned off the sofa and clattered the cup and saucer onto the floor beside her, then sat up again and faced him. 'I don't believe that, Mark. I know you love her . . . '

'I don't have a typewriter,' he said. 'I couldn't have written that note.'

She stared at him. 'Tam has one,' she said in little more than a whisper. 'She's been typing up the notes of a book I'm writing.'

'My fingerprints won't be on it,' he said. 'I haven't even seen it.'

'She keeps it on top of the wardrobe.'

'And there it's staying,' he said. 'I might need an alibi.'

'Don't,' she whispered. 'She might be . . . ' Her face crumpled and tears cascaded down her cheeks.

Quietly, Mark said, 'Do you think I haven't thought that too?' And his face was grim now, grim and grey, and she could see he hadn't had much sleep — if any.

'What are you going to do?'

'You read the note yourself. What can I do?'

'You have to go to the police, Mark.'

'No,' he snapped. 'You saw what it said. They'll kill her. We must wait.'

'And the longer we wait — the more likely it is that we'll never see her again,' she said angrily, mopping at her tears with her hand. 'We have to take that chance.'

'No. I won't take chances where Tam's concerned. That note was a warning. We don't know what they're capable of doing.'

'Yes, we do,' Cass said. 'They're ruthless — they have to be to have hounded her these past few weeks like they've done — and the fire . . . '

'Yes,' he said. 'I've gone over it all during the night. The spying on her, the funeral flowers, the murder accusation, and then the fire. None of it makes sense.'

With a sudden burst of insight, Cass said, 'Maybe it's not meant to.'

He stared at her. 'What do you mean?'

'Just that. Perhaps it's to put us off the scent — all those little things. Red herrings — just to confuse the issue while they get to the heart of the matter.'

'The heart of the matter?'

'Something entirely different — not just petty nuisance.'

'You call it 'petty'? Scaring somebody half to death?'

'It is, though, isn't it? No real harm was done. Not like this . . . kidnapping.'

Mark put his hands to his head and pushed his fingers through his hair. 'I've been trying to avoid that damnable word,' he said.

'I know,' Cass said gently. 'I know. But it had to be said, Mark. At least now we're beginning to admit what we're up against.'

26

'Come on. Time to get you out of there.' The voice was still disguised, still muffled. It was also authoritative, and Tamsin guessed it wouldn't take kindly to being ignored.

'Go to hell!' In her mobile prison, she curled herself up tighter than ever and refused to move. The car had come to a halt several minutes ago, and she'd listened to someone walking over gravel, putting a key in a lock, throwing open a door. She knew what was coming next — another confrontation with her captor — but as she was powerless, and unable to get free, she could do nothing to avoid that particular situation developing.

She'd gone beyond those first bleak feelings of terror by now. During what must have amounted to more than an hour's long drive she'd exhausted herself by her efforts to loosen her bonds, and her mind had given up trying to discover — by sound alone — where he was taking her. She would know soon enough, she decided, and with that thought she had managed somehow to come to a sort of acceptance of what was happening to her — though not without tearful frustration mingling with fear of the unknown at times. There had been no tell-tale sounds to convince her they were going back into Alderwood over the little river bridge, and, judging by the time it had taken to reach the destination they were at now, she knew she must be a considerable distance away from Alderwood.

He spoke again — a hollow, faraway sound. He must still be wearing that driver's helmet, she thought. The words were spoken sharply. 'Don't make me get rough with you.'

She shivered. That voice was completely lacking in any sort of human emotion. He wasn't going to get things all his own way, though. If he made things rough for her, then she'd strive to make them equally rough for him in any way she could — she was determined on that score.

She felt hard hands grabbing hold of her and dragging her out of the car boot. She struggled and tried to kick out at him, but her legs were still firmly fastened together, and for the time being she had to admit to herself that he was in charge of the situation. He couldn't keep her trussed up like this, though. Not indefinitely. Could he? She flinched at his touch, at his rough handling of her.

'You're not being very clever, considering your situation,' he muttered as he slung her effortlessly over his shoulder and she heard his footsteps on the gravel again as he spun away from the car with her.

She tossed and twisted and screamed at him to let her go, but it was all to no avail. Not being able to see anything because of the covering over her head, she suddenly sensed that they were no longer out in the open air, and assumed they were inside the building he'd unlocked. She wondered uneasily what sort of place it was. Outside, she remembered now, she'd heard trees rustling overhead, and an owl hooting. There had been no sounds of traffic. It must be dark . . . no street-lamps, obviously, because they would have penetrated the blanket that was covering her. She felt herself dumped onto the floor in a heap, and it wasn't a cold, hard floor. It was carpeted. Carpet! Not some derelict warehouse, then, she thought. No! It was warm in here, and the floor underneath her was definitely soft. She rolled herself around, pushing her bunched-up feet outwards to try and touch something that might give her a clue as to what sort of place this was he'd brought her to. For a moment she relaxed. He'd dumped her and left her. But, no — his muffled footsteps were coming back to her. She tensed up and held her breath, knowing the exact moment he was standing over her, watching her.

'Are you comfortable down there?' A kind of amusement filtered through to her from the helmeted voice.

'Bastard!' she yelled.

'Tut-tut! What a naughty girl you are.' The voice was above her. Easily six feet above her. Or five feet six above her, or five feet ten above her. Which one? How tall was he? How broad? How old?

Not old. He couldn't have carried her so easily and effortlessly, slung across his shoulder, if he'd been old. She searched her memory for some clue as to his identity. She'd caught only that one fleeting glimpse of him in her bedroom at Herb House, though, and it wasn't enough. Vaguely, she supposed she'd registered that he was tall and slim. The driving helmet would have added inches to his height, though. She remembered too, her first fears — the 'giant ant' theory, and then the realization that he was wearing the gear of a racing-driver which, in the semi-darkness, had given him a sleek, clear-cut image. Was it Vaughn? Playing games with her? She tried to convince herself that Vaughn wouldn't have used physical violence on her *or* have trussed her up like a sack of potatoes, as this man had.

Fit? Yes! He must be fit because he hadn't even been breathing heavily when he'd lifted her out of the car and carried her in here.

Racing-drivers were fit! Vaughn Herrick was fit. But again she refused to believe it could be Vaughn. Maybe, though, if she pretended to herself that it *was* Vaughn, she wouldn't be quite so frightened. That's a crazy notion, she told herself. That's not facing up to reality.

'You don't scare me,' she flung in the general direction of where she thought he might be standing. She struggled to a more comfortable position, and thought how stupid she must look, enveloped in a pink candlewick bedspread with not even her head sticking out of it.

'I *shall* scare you — if you don't do as I say.' The words were casual, yet ominous.

Inside her cocoon, she forced herself to keep calm. If once she panicked, it would be the finish of her, she realized. He'd know then that he'd won. Know too that he could dominate her and scare her into submission. 'You're *trying* to disguise your voice,' she accused.

'I am *succeeding* in disguising my voice.' He laughed, and for some reason the laughter struck a chord, somewhere deep in her subconscious. Before she could start to analyze it, though, he said, 'I wouldn't try making any wild guesses if I were you.'

'But it means that you're known to me,' she said. 'You wouldn't try to disguise your voice if I didn't know you.'

Complete silence greeted this little speech. Feeling bolder now, she asked, 'Am I right?'

Her ears caught the sound of a movement, and then he was picking her up so suddenly and unexpectedly that she squealed at the surprise of it. He tossed her over his shoulder again, and after a few seconds she felt herself being carried up some stairs. Then she *was* scared.

'Where are you taking me?' she yelled, with candlewick tufts almost stifling her as the cover pulled tight across her face with her struggles.

'Upstairs.'

'I know that.'

'Don't ask silly questions, then.'

Again, she realized he was not the slightest bit out of breath carrying her. She could feel something hard against her shoulder. 'Are you still wearing that stupid helmet?' she muttered scathingly.

'Would the Phantom of the Opera be more

acceptable to you?' he asked, following it up with, 'Speaking for myself, I feel a mask would be slightly *too* theatrical in this situation — hence something you're more familiar with — a racing-driver's helmet.'

'What do you want with me?' she gasped.

'*Not* what you think. *Not* what's making your little heart go all pit-a-pat just because I'm taking you upstairs. Does that put your mind at rest?'

They'd reached the top of the stairs now. All the floors were carpeted, she decided, quite thickly carpeted too, because she couldn't hear his footsteps.

'Where am I?' Her heart was hammering inside her like a mad thing. She began to panic again. 'You've got to tell me . . . where am I?'

He dumped her onto something soft. 'In bed,' he said.

She tried to roll off the bed, but found he'd sat down beside her, facing her, when a quick hand shot out and stopped her moving.

She swallowed and tried to make her voice normal, but even to her own ears the terror was apparent. 'What — what are you going to do?'

His voice was soft. 'Chain you to the bed, I think.'

Panic again. 'No . . . ' She threw herself at

429

where she guessed he'd be, hoping to dislodge him from the bed. Not really knowing what she would do if she managed it.

His hands were gripping the top of her arms now, holding her immobile. 'Look — I've got to fasten you up *somewhere*. Here is as good a place as any.'

'I need the bathroom,' she said, her mind working fast.

'You can have the bathroom — afterwards,' he said.

'Afterwards . . . ' Fear made her heart lurch crazily and her voice rise at least an octave higher than was normal for her . . .

'Listen to me.' He shook her hard, then. 'Listen, will you? It's like I said, I don't want you for sex — so for heaven's sake relax.'

The words hit her like a bucketful of cold water being poured over her. But they reassured her only fleetingly. He'd say that, she reasoned. He'd say *anything* to stop her struggling and fighting and trying to get away from him. She couldn't trust him. There was no way she was going to believe anything he said to her. He was dangerous.

He was pulling the bedspread away from her now. Carefully, starting at the bottom of her, near her feet, he was tugging it free of the shackles that were binding her legs together.

He worked upwards and she wriggled her body to help him as the fabric came away from her hands and arms and was then lifted off her face and head. At some point she managed to ease the horseshoe she'd been gripping so tightly under the edge of the pillow. At least it would give her a certain measure of reassurance. It wouldn't be very effective as a weapon, but, she decided, it was better than nothing.

When she was completely free of her covering, he let it slide onto the floor at the side of the bed. The brightness of the light made her blink. She glanced up at the ceiling and saw a centrally situated glass chandelier-type fitting. The whole room had been tastefully and professionally decorated in muted shades of dusky pink and cream; the furniture and fittings were sumptuous in the extreme. Her gaze came back to rest on him as he sat watching her.

She was still fearful, and still not trusting him. It was unsettling, having such a menacing figure so close to her. The dark-coloured visor of the black racing helmet perturbed and frightened her. It was daunting, having to talk to, and look at, someone without a face, knowing they could look at you and see all your emotions laid bare on your own face. She couldn't hope to keep up the pretence that she wasn't scared of him. She was. She was helpless too, with her arms still bound tightly to her sides and her legs banded together. She'd been right about the leather straps. Though they didn't feel so tight now the bedspread was out from under them, they were nonetheless holding her immobile. That thought unnerved her more than anything else. He could do as he pleased with her and she was in no position to fight back.

Inside, she was a churning mass of fear and apprehension. Her bonds might be looser, but she was still his prisoner, and, panicking again, she started struggling to get her hands free, but all her efforts were to no avail.

The feeling of utter dependence on him angered her. She hated the way he was watching her too, through that dark visor. Close up now, she could just make out his eyes through the perspex. He was taking no chances of her recognizing him, though, she realized, for under the helmet, obscuring all other features, was a white balaclava of the type racing-drivers wore under *their* helmets as a fire precaution.

She struggled in vain, then, losing control altogether, she screamed at him, 'Let me go. For God's sake, unfasten me. I can't stand this . . . ' And the words ended on a sob, for which she cursed herself roundly. It was what he wanted — for her to lose control and be scared to death of him. He was cool and calculating. He could afford to be like that. *He* wasn't trussed up like a Christmas turkey. He wasn't feeling threatened and helpless. She'd had enough. She huddled up against the carved wooden headboard, trying to get as far away from him as possible, and still he just sat there, still as a corpse, watching her — just watching her.

'Let me go,' she pleaded as her gold curls, free of the confining blanket now, cascaded around her face. 'Please — just tell me what you want of me. But let me go. Don't do this to me . . . ' Tears were streaming freely down her face now. She shook her hair back impatiently from her face. She was scared, terrified, and once all that pent up fear had broken loose there was no way of stopping it.

He stood up slowly, walked over to a run of mahogany wardrobes down the other side of the room. She watched him with distraught eyes, her dread of what was happening making her heart thump far faster than was normal for it. Beside the wardrobes was a wide window with crimson curtains drawn across it to shut out the night. The bedcover she was sitting on was crimson too — a heavy linen. She saw all this at a glance, whilst never taking her eyes off him for a single second.

He closed the wardrobe door and walked back to the bed. Horrified, she tried to back away still further as she saw what he was carrying. He dropped the long length of fine, but strong chain on the bed. Fastened on either end of it were handcuffs . . .

'No . . . ' she whimpered, petrified now as her gaze moved from the chain to his visor again.

He stood over her, reached up both hands to her face and turned her head towards a door, not three feet away from her, directly opposite where she sat shivering on the bed.

'That's the *en-suite*,' he said, in a slightly derisive tone. 'No home should be without one!' It was intended to be a joke, she realized. It didn't make her want to laugh, however. 'When I've made you secure, you will able to move about. Understand? It will be possible for you to get to the bathroom, but not to the window or the bedroom door. Do I make myself clear?'

Numbly, she nodded, even while the thought of being chained up like an animal appalled her.

The bedroom door he spoke of was at the far end of the large room, and at an angle to the window which was directly facing the bed.

'Your only means of escape is through that door,' he said, the visor moving as if he were following her gaze. 'And I shall be on the other side of it.'

She said a silent prayer of thanks for that bit of information at least. With him on the *other* side of the door she might be able to compose herself and channel her thoughts in a more coherent direction. As if he could read her thoughts, he said, 'At least, I'll be on the other side for some of the time.' And at that her spirits did a downward swoop. Despite what he'd said about not wanting her for sex, she couldn't bring herself to believe him entirely on that score. It came, she supposed, from her mistrust of men in general. Men had, in the main, let her down, starting first with her father abandoning her, and then Vaughn Herrick . . .

'Why are you doing this?' she whispered, cowering away from him.

With irritation lacing his words now, he said, 'For heaven's sake, don't keep shrinking away from me. I'm not going to hurt you.'

Tremulously she said, glancing again at the long length of chain on the bed, 'Do you seriously expect me to believe that . . . '

'I insist that you believe it,' he said. 'You are merely a means to an end. When I have what I want — and believe me, I *will* get it

— then you can go back to your man and live happily ever after.'

His voice sounded hollow and unconvincing to her. She made a movement to get off the bed, but he held up one hand and said, 'No. Tamsin — I have to do this first.' And he spun round on his heel, picked up the chain and locked the handcuff around her right wrist.

'No . . . '

He made no more attempt at conversation, but fastened the other end of the chain round the sturdy wooden bedstead and snapped a lock to secure it there. Still without speaking, he unfastened the straps that had secured her, the one round her arms first, and then the other, which had cramped her legs so much.

Relief made her sink her head into her hands and sob uncontrollably. After a moment or two she became aware of the silence in the room and realizing that tears were not going to help, she looked up. He was standing over by the bedroom door, which was open.

'I'll leave you,' he said quietly. 'My staying here is only unsettling to you.'

The door closed, and she was alone. He'd gone and left her. She sat and listened for any sound that might mean he was coming back to her, but there was none. Her tears started drying on her face. It was a long time since she'd shed tears like that, and she knew she must look horrendous. She glanced at the door he'd told her was the bathroom, and carefully crawled to the edge of the bed and tested her weight on her feet when she'd lowered them to the floor. The cramp in her legs was wearing off. She remembered the horseshoe then, and swiftly fell onto her knees beside the bed, foraging under the pillows and breathing a great sigh of relief when she saw it was still there. He hadn't found it, then — not when he'd been fastening that hateful chain. She pushed the horseshoe further under the pillow. It wouldn't do for it to fall out onto the floor.

She rested her arms on the bed as she knelt there, then her head fell forward again and another wave of despair crept over her.

'Mark,' she whispered brokenly. 'Oh, Mark — come and find me. Come and take me away from this awful place . . . '

27

Mark and Cass had spent the last half-hour arguing, and in the end Cass had agreed to wait a couple of hours before doing anything drastic, to see if the phone would ring with a message about Tam. She still maintained that the best thing would be to contact the police, but Mark was adamant — he wouldn't put Tam in any danger, he insisted.

An uneasy peace had settled between them, and Cass was washing up the breakfast things and Mark was raking out the dead ashes in the fire grate when they heard the sound of a car coming down the lane.

'Tam . . . ?' Mark raced to the back door and Cass followed him.

Vaughn Herrick rounded the corner of the house, saw them standing there outside the kitchen door and demanded, 'I want to see Tam. Where is she?'

Mark — after a few seconds and a brief glance at Cass — said, 'You can't see her. She's not here.'

Vaughn glared at him, then transferred his gaze to Cass, who inwardly shrank away from that venomous stare. 'What's going on here? What are you two doing together? Where's Tam. I have to see Tam.' He thumped one clenched fist into the palm of his other hand and raved, 'Just get her, will you? Tell her I want to see her. I have to see her.'

Mark began, 'I just told you — she isn't here . . . '

Vaughn's eyes narrowed. 'What is this? What are you trying to say, man?'

Mark looked helplessly at Cass again, and Cass said wearily, 'Mark — we can't keep this to ourselves . . . '

'Are you two having an affair? Does Tam know about this?' Vaughn's tone was contemptuous.

Cass said quickly, 'It's nothing like that.'

Vaughn levelled a gaze at Mark and said softly, 'You bastard. You utter bastard. Tam trusted you . . . '

'You've got the wrong idea altogether . . . ' Mark was shaking his head worriedly. 'You don't understand. Look — come inside the house. I'll try to explain if you'll just come inside.'

Before Vaughn could refuse, or make any other comment, Mark was striding back into the kitchen and Cass followed him. She took up her stance at the kitchen sink as Vaughn entered, and, for want of something to do, picked up a teacloth and started drying the mugs and plates they'd used that morning.

Vaughn, Cass could tell, was incensed by the scene of domesticity he'd interrupted. She knew, though, that he couldn't even begin to guess at the inner turmoil both she and Mark were suffering. His lip curled as he drawled, 'Oh! I see the lie of the land pretty thoroughly. Cosy. Very cosy. Is this a case of 'while the cat's away, the mice will play'?' Giving Cass a vicious stare, he went on, 'I assume you were here for breakfast.'

Cass flushed furiously and snapped, 'It's not what you think.'

'What the hell have you done with her?' Vaughn marched across the kitchen to confront Mark. He thumped the table beside him and yelled, 'What the devil have you done with her?'

'We don't know where she is,' Mark yelled back at him. 'Just cool it, will you? We're just as eager as you are to find her.'

'Find her? Do you know what I've got here?' Vaughn fumbled in the pocket of his windcheater and slammed a sheet of paper down on the table. 'A ransom note. Is this some sick kind of joke? I came straight over as soon as I opened it. I couldn't rest till I knew she was safe. And now you're telling me she's *not* here, so where the hell is she? Somebody's got some explaining to do.'

Mark moved over to the table and picked up the notepaper. His eyes raked over it.

Cass felt the teacloth slide out of her nerveless fingers. She gasped, 'What does it say?' She ran across the room to Mark, leaned over his arm and read out loud, "*I've got the girl. Tamsin. If you want to see her alive again, have one million pounds ready to hand over in exchange for her within the next twenty-four hours. I shall be in touch!*"

Cass took the note from Mark and gazed at him.

Mark went over to the dresser, opened a drawer and came back to Vaughn with the similar note he and Cass had found on the kitchen floor the previous night. Without uttering a word, he handed it to the young racing-driver.

Vaughn took it, read it, then stood as if stupefied before looking up, his face tense and pale. 'What is this?' he asked hoarsely. 'What the hell . . . ?'

Mark said, 'The two sheets of paper are identical. Both taken from the same note-book. Even the typeface is the same.'

Vaughn leaned heavily back against the table now, half sitting on its edge. 'Who,' he asked, dazed, 'would do something as crazy as this?'

'When did you get *your* note?' Cass asked faintly.

'This morning.' Vaughn turned his head towards her. 'It had no postmark; the Faulkeners have one of those outside letter-boxes, the lock-up kind. God only knows how long the letter had been sitting there. Patric brought it in with this morning's papers.'

'Whoever put it there knew you were staying with the Faulkeners, then.' Mark came up to him.

Vaughn nodded. 'I often stay with the Faulkeners. I'd been testing yesterday at the Bramsdown circuit. I phoned Tam last night, on my way back to Alderwood.'

'You phoned her!'

Cass noticed that Mark's hands had clenched themselves into fists. She went over to him, laid a hand on his arm and said, 'Mark . . . calm down. It's pretty obvious Vaughn had nothing to do with Cass's disappearance.'

Mark shook her hand away and repeated, directly to Vaughn, 'You phoned Tam. Why?'

'I wanted to come over and see her. I'd had a lousy day . . . ' Vaughn shrugged. 'Is there any law against me seeing an old girlfriend?'

Mark's fists bunched even more tightly at his sides. Cass could see he was keeping his temper with the utmost difficulty.

'And you came here and *saw* her, then? Last night? While I was away attending to her wrecked car?'

Vaughn glared at him. 'Look — I don't know what you're getting at, but, no, I didn't come *here*. I phoned her on the way back from Bramsdown and there were harsh words exchanged. She told me I wouldn't be welcome. Is that what you want to hear? That she didn't want to see me?'

Mark was breathing heavily. 'What I want to hear is the truth. Is *that* the truth? That Tam wouldn't let you come here? That she didn't want to see you?'

Vaughn nodded, then said, 'I got the feeling it was a *permanent* brush-off. She might just as well have said she never wanted to see me again.'

'So you didn't drive over here last night?'

'No, man. No way. I don't need to push myself onto a girl. I can get any girl I want . . . '

'Except Tam,' Cass said quietly.

Vaughn looked downcast. 'Point taken,' he said. 'But what about this damn note? Both these notes. What are we going to do?'

'We're going to the police,' Cass said firmly.

'No!' Mark yelled, rounding on her. 'It's too dangerous. You know what the note said.'

Vaughn said, 'We've got to take this seriously.'

Cass said, 'The police will take it seriously. There's nothing *we* can do on our own . . .'

'No!' Both men rounded on her then, dinning the same word into her ears.

She stepped back a pace or two from both of them. 'I think you're wrong,' she said. 'I think the most sensible thing to do would be to take both these notes to the police.'

'No! We can't risk it.' Mark's jaw was set, his lips fixed into a stern, straight line.

Quietly, Vaughn said. 'I agree with you. I think we should take that threat seriously. I can start raising that million pounds.' He sighed. 'Heck — what does he think I am, though? I'm not in the top league of drivers who could afford that kind of money at the snap of their fingers. It's going to take time.'

'Time's something we don't have on our side,' Cass argued fiercely.

Vaughn, completely losing his temper, shouted, 'I'll move heaven and earth to get that million.'

'And I'll help you,' Mark said in a sober voice. 'I'll sell everything I have, if necessary.'

'You are talking out of the tops of your stupid heads,' Cass said. 'You can't just get your hands on a million pounds in less than twenty-four hours.'

Mark had a desperate look on his face. Vaughn said in a slightly less vindictive tone than he'd used previously, 'I can get it. I *will* get it. Make no mistake about that . . . Tam — that poor kid — wherever she is, she must be absolutely petrified.'

There was a sound outside the house, and all three heads swivelled in unison.

'A car,' Cass said, springing towards the door.

Mark raced after her and pulled her back inside the house. 'Don't rush out there. He's dangerous. Whoever he is — if he's got Tam, he's dangerous. He could be armed.'

She spun round to him. 'The kidnapper is hardly going to come walking up to the door to confront us, is he?'

Mark went to the door as they heard footsteps coming down the side of the house.

'God, no!' he muttered as the uniformed figure rounded the corner.

Cass was standing behind Mark. She drew in a sharp breath and felt light-headed. She tried not to think of what the police officer was going to say, but words were going round and round in her head. 'An accident . . . '

— 'I'm sorry to have to tell you . . . ' — '*Did* you know a Miss Curtis . . . ?' She couldn't stand it. If anything had happened to Tam . . .

Vaughn pushed past her. 'What the hell is this? What's happened. For God's sake — tell us what's happened . . . '

Constable Alan Jackson looked suitably impressed by the reception committee. He grinned, then said, 'Don't get all worried, sir. I just called to have a word with Miss Curtis . . . you see, we found this . . . ' He pulled something small and silver out of his pocket and let it swing from his fingers in front of them. 'It was found in a wooded lay-by about five or six miles outside Alderwood. And I recognized it as being like the one Miss Curtis usually wore. At least, if it isn't hers then it's very similar to the one belonging to her.' He searched their faces, one by one. 'Do any of you know if this *is* the actual one? I couldn't be sure, of course, but . . . '

Cass elbowed her way forward. She stared at the object dangling from Constable Jackson's hand. 'It's Tam's dreamcatcher,' she said in a dull voice. Then, looking Mark squarely in the eye, she said, 'I think we should ask the constable to come inside, don't you? I think there's something we ought to tell him.'

* ★ ★

Tam was sitting almost as far away from the bed as she could get when she heard footsteps coming up the stairs. She didn't move from her cross-legged position on the floor against the dressing table as the door opened.

'The Driver', as she'd christened him in her heart, closed the door behind him and stood looking down at her.

'Are you sulking?' He glanced at her, then pulled the curtains back from across the window, letting in the golden light of morning sun. He went over to the door again and switched off the electric light.

She refused to answer him. She just turned her head away from him, painfully aware of the long length of metal chain that snaked across the carpet, anchoring her to the hated bed.

He crouched down in front of her, and she could tell he was amused. 'You didn't sleep there? On the floor? Did you?'

'I didn't sleep. Full stop.' Her eyes were accusing, her voice flat. 'Did you expect me to?'

'Why not? What kept you awake?'

'Bastard!' she hissed. 'Get away from me.'

'Don't keep calling me that name,' he said.

'I'm perfectly respectable. I had a mother *and* a father.'

'Pigs!' she shot at him. 'To breed something like you, they must have been pigs, or rats, or vermin of some kind . . . '

His gloved hand shot out and fastened round her free wrist. 'Stop it,' he said quietly, but with no malice in his words. 'This kind of talk won't get you anywhere.'

She twisted her hand in his grasp, but he wouldn't let her go. 'I'll bring you some food,' he said. 'What would you like?'

'Nothing!'

'You have to eat.'

'I'll starve sooner than eat anything *you* give me,' she said, sullen in her defiance of him.

She thought he would start arguing with her, but he just shrugged and said, 'Okay. I'll bring you a cup of tea. Why don't you get up off the floor and sit somewhere more comfortable?'

She averted her head.

'Are you managing to get around okay?'

Slowly she turned her head to face him again. Adopting a sarcastic attitude, she said, 'The room is delightful! The water in the bathroom piping hot! But can I settle the bill now and leave?'

'You still have a sense of humour,' he said

drily. 'I admire that in you — after all I've put you through.'

'I hate you,' she flared.

'I know.' He still crouched there, looking at her through that dark-tinted visor. 'It doesn't worry me, though.'

She flung his hand away from her. 'Get out,' she snapped. 'Get out of my sight.'

He stood up, sighing. Then, hands on hips, he gazed down on her again and said, 'Do you want to be on your own all day, or are you going to try and come to terms with this?'

'What is 'this'?' she asked brutally.

Quietly, he said, ''This' is kidnap, Tamsin.'

'Why?' she cried. 'Why? What do you hope to gain by it?'

In a calm voice, he said, 'I've asked for a million pounds for your safe return.'

Her breath caught in her throat; for a few moments she couldn't bring herself to speak, then she laughed unsteadily and said, 'I'm not worth that much to anybody. You're crazy. I don't even know anybody who has a million pounds to spare.'

'He's the crazy one, not me. Crazy for you. He'd do anything for you. He'll pay up.' His voice was filled with confidence.

She tried to laugh, but the situation didn't merit it. 'He won't,' she said. 'He doesn't have that kind of money.'

'Racing-drivers,' he said softly, 'are rich people.'

'He's not . . . ' She shook her head. What was he talking about? Mark wasn't a racing-driver.

'I know what he's worth — don't try to play me up that way. He splashes money around all over the place. Do you think I haven't seen him doing that? Even dear Patric's taken in by him, but he just wants the Faulkener brass — sponsorship, I believe they call it. The Faulkeners are rolling in it. Herrick will get more than just a few pretty pennies out of them.'

'The drivers get nothing out of sponsorship,' she said, staring at him now. 'And Vaughn isn't anywhere near the top of the league. He doesn't have the kind of money you're asking for.'

'A nice try,' he said softly, coming down to her level again, crouching in front of her and reaching one gloved hand out towards her. 'It won't work, though. I know what I've seen and heard about lover boy . . . '

Faintly, and not really wanting to know the answer to her question, she had to blurt out the question all the same. 'What will happen to me if he *doesn't* pay up?'

'Don't ask,' he said in a low voice. Then, on

a complete change of subject, he stared hard at her and said, 'You have something in that pocket across your waist. What is it?'

'Nothing!'

'It's bulging. Why didn't I see that before?' His eyes, she could see through that dark visor, were hard.

'Maybe you were too full of your own importance to look at me,' she snapped back.

'Give!' he said, his gloved hand still reaching out to her. 'Come on — take it out — whatever it is, and give it to me.'

Slowly she pulled out the plastic bag with the sprigs of rue inside it. She handed it to him, and hoped he wouldn't notice what she'd left behind in the pocket — the iron horseshoe that she'd retrieved from under her pillow after she'd splashed her hands and face with hot water in the dream of a bathroom earlier that morning.

He held the plastic bag — she size of a small supermarket carrier — and frowned at it.

She explained, 'I was in the garden when you broke into my house . . . '

'I didn't *break in*,' he said. 'The door was open. I knew you were alone, though. Knew that your Yorkshire friend had gone to Alderwood.'

'How did you know?'

'I heard about your car.'

'So you decided on the spur of the moment . . . '

'No,' he said. 'I've been planning this. Just waiting for a suitable opportunity. Your car getting smashed up gave me that opportunity. I was in the pub when the landlord came in and told everyone to watch out for broken glass outside. I got talking to him when I realized it was your car, and he even gave me the time that your friend would be coming back to Alderwood to meet the pick-up truck. So you see, I knew you'd be alone.'

'I might have decided to go into Alderwood with Mark . . . ' Tam was trying to keep him talking. That way, she reasoned, she might be able to put a name to that heavily disguised voice.

'That was a risk, I must admit.' He laughed.

Again, the laugh reminded her of some-body. She said, 'I never heard anyone come down the lane to Herb House — yet you had a car . . . I was out in the garden gathering herbs.'

'I freewheeled the car down the last bit of the lane so you wouldn't hear it.' He peered in the bag at the herbs, then said abruptly, 'They're wilting. Are they important?'

'They need water and fresh air.'

'I'll put them in water, shall I?'

'You can throw them in the bin for all I care,' she said.

'No,' he said, getting to his feet. 'You can't deliberately kill them.' He walked to the door and went out of the room.

She fastened her teeth on her lips in an effort to stop them trembling. She sat there, not daring to move, and after a few minutes he came back to her, a Wedgwood blue vase in his hand with the herbs sticking out of the top.

'I can't bring you flowers,' he said, teasing her, 'so this is the next best thing, huh?'

'How kind!' The sarcasm was there again in her voice. He stepped over her outstretched legs and placed the vase on the bedside table. Then he came back to her.

'I'm not all bad, you see.'

'I'll recommend you for an award. Kindness to herbs,' she said.

He perched on the edge of the bed and looked down at her. 'You really are a bitch, aren't you? Yet you have the look of an angel.'

'Do you want me to say something nice about you?' she asked, her words tinged with acid. 'Do you want me to say that you're a perfect gentleman? That I just love your outfit?'

'You could try saying *something* complimentary,' he said. 'I doubt if you know the meaning of the word, though.' He sounded bored. He got up from the bed and walked over to the window, keeping his back towards her.

'Maybe if I could see your face I'd be able to say something nice about you. But you won't let me do that, will you? You have no face, and your voice isn't your real one. It's all an act, isn't it? I don't know who you are,' she said in a husky voice. 'I don't know where you've brought me. You could easily let me go and I wouldn't be able to tell the police a thing about you.'

He spun round, 'Could I? Let you go? Just like that?'

She couldn't tell if he was teasing or not. That voice was so brittle, so faint and hollow-sounding, coming as it was from behind the helmet — and the balaclava underneath the helmet.

'You know you could.' She scrambled to her feet and, forgetful of the chain that was holding her, leapt towards him. She gave a little scream as the chain pulled tight and almost yanked her off her feet. 'Please,' she begged in little more than a whisper. 'Please — let me go. This is madness.'

'It's the only way,' he said.

'You don't need the money — not with a nice house like this. You must be quite well off — I mean — all this luxury — it . . . it's . . . ' Her voice broke off.

'It doesn't belong to me,' he said.

She felt every bit of strength she possessed draining out of her. Hardly able to speak, she whispered, 'There's . . . somebody else . . . involved in this?' and her eyes were wide and terrified. What was happening? she wondered in horror. Was it some sort of syndicate which was answerable for her predicament — her kidnapping? Did responsibility for what happened to her rest not just with this man but with a whole lot more? The thought terrified her. She sank down onto the floor again, kneeling this time, kneeling and burying her face in her hands and rocking back and forward, silent now in her dismay.

She never heard him move away from the window, that was why she let out a scream and tried to avoid his hands when she felt them fasten on her shoulders. He was down at her level again, crouching, facing her. 'I won't hurt you,' he said. 'I give you my word.'

'I don't believe you.' She stared at him through eyes that were full of hatred and loathing.

He stood up, pulling her up with him. She

tried to wrench herself out of his grasp, but his fingers only dug into her shoulders all the more when she struggled. At last she stopped fighting him, and faced him.

'Don't,' he said. 'Don't start crying again, will you? I never thought it was going to be like this . . . '

'What did you think it would be like?' She tossed her head back to look up into his eyes — the only part of him that was visible. 'Did you think it would be like a game?' she spat out. 'Did you think people would be falling over themselves to pay you your million pounds?'

'No,' he said. 'I just didn't think you'd be so scared of me.'

'Maybe I wouldn't,' she said, 'if you had a face and a voice.'

'You can see my eyes,' he said, dragging her closer to him and thrusting his face down towards hers. 'They're not the eyes of a killer, are they?'

'I never met a killer before,' she said, beginning to shake all over. 'I don't know what killers' eyes look like.'

'Stop it,' he ground out. 'Stop being like this. I never had a woman scared of me in the whole of my life before.'

She tried to laugh, but the laugh came out as something between a sob and a hiccup.

'You keep chains in your bedroom and you can say that?'

'It's not *my* bedroom. I told you that.' He shook her lightly, more exasperated, she could tell, than angry with her.

'You knew where to find the damn things, though.'

'I have been here before,' he said, his voice silky soft now. 'Chains don't always have to be objects of terror, Tamsin. Haven't you ever experimented . . . ' His voice tailed off, and he said, 'You *did* have an affair with Herrick you *did* get pregnant by him, so don't come the innocent with me.'

'You're weird. You know that, don't you?' she panted.

'It's the games people play,' he said, and she could hear the smile in his voice. 'Tamsin Curtis — some people actually *enjoy* kinky sex sessions.'

'Leave me alone . . . ' She tried to pull away from him. 'I want no part of your games.'

'You're safe with me. I told you that before. Why don't you believe me?'

'Safe!' She laughed harshly. 'Safe?' She pulled herself away from his hands, then held up her wrist with the chain hanging from it. 'Safe? How can I feel safe like this?'

'It won't be for long.' He backed away from

her, then lifted his hands, palms facing her, in an attitude that was meant to tell her he wasn't going to use violence on her. 'Okay,' he said. 'Let me put it another way — I don't need *you*. I have a woman. I don't need *anybody* except her. I don't *want* anybody except her.'

'Let me go, then,' she whispered. 'Let me go and then you can get on with your life again.'

'I have no life,' he said. 'If I lose her, I have no life.'

Bewildered, she had to ask, 'So why are you doing this?'

'You have a right to know,' he said. 'It's the money. It's a test. I have to prove I can do it.'

Realization came slowly to Tamsin. The woman, whoever she was, had set him up. She looked at him as he dropped his hands to his sides in an attitude of utter weariness. 'You're doing this for *her*?'

'The money,' he said. 'She doesn't know how I'm getting it. I just have to get it some way or I'll lose her.'

'You don't need a million,' she said quietly. 'To set up home with a nice girl, you don't need that much money.'

'But I do,' he said. 'It's not as simple as you'd like to believe.'

'So tell me more,' she said, hoping he

458

would and that she'd get another chance to identify him.

Slowly and deliberately he shook his head from side to side. 'I can't do that,' he said. 'It's best if you know nothing about me, and I've already said too much. I'll fetch you that tea now.' His arrogance was back again as he challenged, 'And you're having some food too. You will eat and drink if I have to force the stuff down your throat myself. From now on you will do as you are told, *Ms* Curtis!'

28

The police had cordoned off the lay-by the time Mark, Cass and Vaughn got there.

The three of them had spent the last two hours 'helping the police with their enquiries', which involved answering hundreds of questions and laying bare all their private lives with regard to Tamsin.

They couldn't go beyond the taped-off area, so they stood and watched, together with Detective Inspector Jane Goodall, who explained what was happening now.

'They've taken photographs of tyre tracks, and there was a reasonably good footprint in mud that we were able to take a cast of, right at the spot where the silver trinket was found. Luckily, this is a pretty quiet stretch of road, and not many cars use it. I suppose that's why the kidnapper came this way.'

Vaughn said, 'We don't know where he went from here, though, do we? There must be hundreds of little roads like this leading to who knows where.'

'If we get anything from the tyre tracks we can plot the way he's gone,' Jane Goodall said. 'This won't be the only lay-by we're interested in. If he stopped two or three times . . . '

Mark broke in, 'Why would he do that? Why didn't he just drive straight to his destination? This lay-by is only twenty minutes' drive out of Alderwood. *Why* did he stop here?'

Goodall looked at him. 'We think Miss Curtis was in the boot of the car. It's possible she was knocked unconscious. I don't suppose she went willingly with him.'

Mark groaned. 'Oh, no.'

'He stopped, we believe, to check she was all right.'

'How do you know that?'

'Dust particles on the ground — similar to what might be expected from inside a car boot — against the footprint. Fibres from something pink. Probably the candlewick bedspread that went missing. At a guess, I'd say he tied her up and wrapped her in it.'

Mark swallowed. It was all so clinical, so technical. To them, Tam wasn't real flesh and blood like she was to him. She was a 'missing person' — made up of fibres and dust particles and all manner of 'clues'! To them, he realized, she was probably already dead. To

461

him, however, that thought had to be ignored, pushed to the farthest recesses of his mind. He had to keep telling himself she was still alive. He *had* to believe that, and keep a tight hold on his reason. Without Tam, his world would crumble.

Vaughn, at his side, said, 'They'll keep her alive. They need the money.'

Cass's head jerked up. 'We ought to get back to the house,' she said.

'We ought to get back to Aldwich House — the *Faulkeners'* house,' Vaughn replied. 'That's where the kidnapper will try to get in touch with me again.'

'The police have gone there.' Cass stated the obvious. 'They're bugging all the phones — at my house, at Tam's, *and* at the Faulkeners'.'

'Clare will be going scranny.' Vaughn managed a grin. 'Clare can't live without a phone.'

'She won't be without it,' Mark said. 'But the police said they don't want anybody making outgoing calls. They want all lines left open so the kidnapper can get in touch.'

'Do you think he'll do that?' Cass was sceptical.

'Yes,' Vaughn said in a tight voice. 'That ransom note leaves me in no doubt at all about that.'

* ★ ★

Ms Curtis, he'd called her! Tam's head was swimming. Only one person in the whole world had ever called her *Ms* Curtis in such a derisory tone of voice.

She sat where he'd left her, on the bedroom floor, wondering how she could have been such a fool not to have known who he was. She should have recognized him, she realized now. The height of him, the breadth of him, even the voice now she came to think about it — all those things gave him away. He might try to disguise the inflections in his voice, but he had a certain way of saying things — imperiously, high-handedly. He was haughty and proud. He was a man who made an impact on women; he didn't need to do this. He could have had any girl he set his mind to getting, with his good looks and his bearing. He didn't *have* to run circles round Clare Faulkener and do her every bidding.

Would she have been as scared of him in the beginning if she'd known who he was? she wondered. Yes, came the answer, she *would* still have been scared of him, because he was cold and calculating, and he'd have no mercy. She'd known that from the first moment she'd met him. On the surface he might seem pleasant enough, but underneath he was

463

hard. He knew what he wanted. And Clare Faulkener was the prize!

She heard him coming back up the stairs. She mustn't let him know she'd guessed . . .

The door opened and let in the delicious smell of grilled bacon. He brought a tray of food over to her. Bacon, mushrooms, tomato! She was hungry. There was coffee too, and toast.

He placed the tray on the floor beside her. There was a spoon, but no knife or fork. He'd already cut the bacon up into bite-sized pieces.

'I feel like a dog — chained up like this and eating off the floor,' she said, looking up at him. 'And why don't you trust me with a knife or a fork?'

'Knives and forks are dangerous things.' His voice was harsh. 'You could do some damage with them.'

'To you?' she asked mildly. 'Or to myself?'

'Only you know that.' The reply was enigmatic. 'Eat it,' he said.

To her relief he didn't stand watching her. She didn't think she could have borne that indignity. He went over to the window and looked out. In between spoonfuls of mush-rooms and bacon, she asked him, 'What can you see out there?'

There was the hint of a smile in his voice. 'Norfolk!'

'Which bit of Norfolk?'

He half turned towards her. 'The bit I like best.'

'It's like that game, where you ask questions to get clues, isn't it?' she said, realizing he knew what she was up to.

'You won't get any clues out of me, Tamsin.'

He came back to her when she'd eaten and had drunk the cup of coffee.

She said, 'Thank you. That was nice.'

'You've changed your tune,' he said. 'Where's the sarcasm?'

Seriously, she said, 'I was getting nowhere with it, was I?'

'Wise girl.' He picked the tray up and carried it to the door.

'Don't go,' she said. 'Stay and talk to me.'

He placed the tray on a chest of drawers and came back to her. 'Which game is this one?' he asked.

'No game.' She drew her knees up almost to her chin. 'If you go, though, and leave me here, I'll start all sorts of wild imaginings. That's why I couldn't sleep.

'There are dark shadows under your eyes,' he said, perching on the bed above her.

'Why did you do all the other things?' she

465

said. 'Why did you watch me — then put those flowers and that horrible black-edged card against my door? Why did you tell the police I killed Ava, and why did you burn my out-house? Are you such a power freak that you need to scare your victim half to death before your final strike?'

'They were all things that couldn't be laid at my door,' he said. 'This is what I intended all along — that nothing should connect you with me. I watched you closely for a couple of weeks. I climbed into that old church tower near your home.'

'I saw you,' she said.

His head came up sharply.

'Not *saw* you close up,' she said. 'I caught the glint of the sun on glass one afternoon.'

'When you had a visitor at the house. The guy from Yorkshire.'

'Yes,' she said. 'I saw the sun glinting on your spectacles.'

'Binoculars,' he corrected. 'I don't wear spectacles . . . '

'So,' she said softly, 'that lets Vaughn out of the running, doesn't it? If you don't wear glasses.'

'You know damn well I'm not Herrick, don't you? I want that million pounds from him — and anyway, I'm a good eight inches taller than he is.'

She nodded. 'Yes,' she said. 'And Vaughn wouldn't treat me like this.'

'So — we're back to that again, are we?'

She lifted her wrist to him — the one with the chain attached to it. 'Take this off,' she said. 'It's not needed, is it?'

'I think it is.'

'Why? What could I do against someone as strong as you are?'

He lifted his shoulders slightly. 'Jump out of a window? Hit me over the head with something?'

She was beginning to feel more able to cope now she'd had something to eat. She spread her hands wide, 'What, in this sumptuous room, would be hard enough to crack your skull? Or to crack that driving helmet? Isn't it uncomfortable? Having to wear that — and the Nomex — all the time?'

'The suit?' He inclined his head slightly to look down at himself. 'It's cumbersome,' he allowed, 'but there's no alternative when you're around.'

'You're dead set on collecting that million pounds, aren't you?' she said.

'Yes,' he said. 'I've been planning it for some time.'

'Did you know me before I came to Suffolk?' she asked archly.

He stared at her for several seconds before

replying. 'It's better if I don't answer that one.'

To try and put him off the scent, she said, 'Your girlfriend — did she work for Ava and me, up north? Is it someone with a grievance against me?'

He hesitated. 'Maybe,' he said, but she could tell the lie didn't come easily.

'Why?' she asked. 'What have I ever done to her?'

'You ask too many questions — Tamsin.'

'Most people call me Tam.'

'*I* shall call you Tamsin.'

She was slightly unsettled at the sound of her name on his lips. 'Why did you try to get me arrested over Ava's death?'

'Another little ploy. You might have flown the nest if you really were guilty of murder. And you might just have flown straight into my arms — if I'd been around to catch you — as I intended I should be. The time wasn't right, though. I hadn't made enough plans.'

'You have a twisted mind,' she said, but there was no venom in the statement.

He laughed. 'I would have had my million by now if I could have got hold of this place to bring you to earlier.'

'And *I* would be a fugitive. *If* I'd killed Ava.'

'Your love life would have been nil,

though,' he said. 'If Herrick had been bamboozled out of a million pounds and then you turned up and didn't know a thing about it. You wouldn't have dared to bring the police in, would you? Either of you? Not if *you* were on the run from them.'

'I *didn't* kill Ava, though.'

'So — my plot backfired. There was plenty of time to hatch another one.'

'Will you really let me go when all this is over?' All at once she was scared again. Could he let her go? *Would* he let her go?

He pushed himself up from the bed. 'Don't go getting all upright again,' he said. 'The police aren't involved in this, and if Herrick's got any sense they never will be.'

'How do you know that?'

'I *know*. Believe me — I know.'

'I had a visitor at the house. I have a friend too in Alderwood. They'll be missing me.'

'Yes,' he said. 'I left them a message.'

'Have you threatened them?'

He gave a small laugh. 'In a manner of speaking.'

'Money or — my life?' Her throat felt constricted.

'Wouldn't you like to know!'

She went back to the original subject. 'It was dangerous — setting fire to my out-house.'

'No,' he said. 'There was no danger to you. You had gone away. I wouldn't fry my golden goose, would I? Anyway, I alerted the fire service as soon as I got back to Alderwood.'

'You didn't have to send me the flowers with the black-edged card, though,' she said. 'That was ghoulish.'

'All those things,' he said. 'They didn't really matter. They were just to make you uneasy. You began to be just a little bit too careful. You didn't know what to expect next, and you stayed home a lot. It was easy to plan when to snatch you then, because you always kept close to home. You would either be at old Herb House, in the safety of your beloved garden, or you would be walking on the heath. You did both those things quite a lot, so you made my job a lot easier. You became conditioned to looking over your shoulder — and people who are scared stay where they think they're safest.'

'So what happens now?'

'We wait,' he said. 'I have all the time in the world.'

'Wait for what?'

'For the answer to a phone call I shall make . . . ' he glanced at the bedside clock ' . . . in a little while from now.'

29

The Faulkeners' phone started to ring. Patric spun round from the window and said, 'Let it ring four times, Clare. You know what Inspector Goodall said.' With the words, he glanced across at Jane Goodall, who nodded in agreement.

'We mustn't let him know the police are involved — better to let him think everything's normal here — and the normal thing would be for your wife to answer the phone.'

Four rings were almost as much as Mark could bear. Vaughn too was tense as Clare picked up the phone.

She listened, gave a little gasp, then, her voice unsteady, said, 'I'll get him.' She handed the phone to Vaughn.

Jane Goodall stood up and lifted a hand. 'Count to ten,' she whispered. 'We need to trace the call.'

Vaughn obeyed. Then, steadily he said, 'Vaughn Herrick, here.'

'You have a mobile phone?' Craig asked on

the other end of the line.

Vaughn, without thinking, said, 'Yes.'

Goodall, some distance away across the room, mouthed the words, 'Keep him talking!'

Vaughn nodded at her.

'Give me the mobile number. And be quick or I'll ring off.'

Vaughn fired off a number and the phone went dead.

Jane Goodall said, elated, 'Twelve seconds for the call — ten for the time between Clare handing over the phone and you replying. Long enough to trace the call.'

'He threatened to ring off,' Vaughn said. 'I daren't stall any longer. I couldn't risk Tam's life by cutting contact with that bastard.'

'Okay!' Jane Goodall got up and went to the window, where she took out her own phone, clicked in a number and got an instant response.

'She means nothing to you,' Vaughn stormed. 'Absolutely nothing! How can you be so damn cool and collected?'

'Keep calm,' Jane Goodall said, covering the mouth-piece of her phone. 'It does no good, getting abusive.'

Mark stood up, hands clenched at his sides as the detective inspector carried on a muted conversation with the boys who were monitoring all calls to the Faulkener house. 'Herrick's right,' he stormed. 'It's just another case to you.'

Jane Goodall's face was impassive as she faced the others again. She'd finished her call now. 'I'm *trying* to do my job. And my job is to get this girl back safely.'

Mark knew she was right, he realized, too, that the woman was good at her job. It had been a frustrating morning, though — a morning that had deepened into afternoon — and now it was four o'clock and this was the first contact they'd had with the kidnapper. 'How would *you* feel,' he grated, 'if it were *your* daughter, or *your* sister, or somebody close to *you*?'

'I'd feel as you do,' she said. 'I'm not made of stone.'

Mark swung away. It had been a long night and a long day. Tam had been gone for nearly twenty-four hours now, and they hadn't got a clue where she was or who she was with. Cass had gone home. She had a job to do, and she wasn't closely connected to Tam. Not as close as he was, and with every second of every minute, and every minute of every hour, his hope of ever getting Tam back was fading.

'They usually make contact within twenty-four hours,' Jane Goodall said, just as if it was an everyday occurrence.

'Is this a stereotype personality we're talking about, then?' Mark snapped back at her. 'Is it the *average* kidnapper we're looking for? Is there really such a person as an 'average' when it comes down to something like this?'

Clare Faulkener burst into tears then, and ran from the room. Mark was startled.

Patric said quietly, 'That's completely out of character for Clare. Usually she's the very model of self-control.'

* * *

Craig Andrews walked quickly away from the phone box in the foyer of a well-known supermarket near the centre of Norwich, got into his car and drove out into the mainstream of traffic again.

He was a good hour's drive away from Lilacs, and who knew what the girl would be up to? Not that she could get up to much — not still shackled as she had been when he left her. She'd pleaded with him *not* to leave her, though, and he'd nearly been swayed to stay with her. That wouldn't solve anything, though. He had to see this little charade through to the bitter end now, he realized . . .

'Something might happen while you're away.' Her pinched little face had been colourless with worry over her ordeal. Her big grey eyes had pleaded silently with him.

He'd been instantly reassuring. Being cooped up with her now for almost a day, it was becoming commonplace to constantly try and put her mind at ease. 'Nothing can happen to you,' he'd promised.

'The house could catch fire. And I'm helpless up here.'

'That won't happen, Tamsin!'

'I'm scared.'

He'd wanted to hold her, to touch her golden hair and tell her he wouldn't let anything hurt her. He'd never felt like this before, not about a girl. He'd always been so sure that Clare was all he wanted. Clare never needed reassurance. Clare could take care of herself.

'Don't go. Please — don't go.'

He went over to her, sitting forlornly on the edge of the bed. He bent down and took hold of her hands. 'I'll be away for two hours. No more. I promise you.'

'If you have an accident while you're away — anything could happen, and I'd be left here for weeks and weeks . . . '

He had to smile at that. Clare wouldn't let 'weeks and weeks' go by without coming to her beloved Lilacs, he knew. All the same, he realized what Tamsin was going through. She was bound to be frightened.

She pulled her unshackled hand away from his and thrust it into the large pocket on the front of her sweat-shirt. The shirt was pale green and over-sized. It dwarfed her small frame. He'd been almost overwhelmed by the need to take her in his arms and tell her everything was going to be all right, but he'd known if he did that she would put the wrong interpretation on it and be even more fearful of him.

'Look,' he said, 'I'll bring you some food and drink up before I go. I can't ring Herrick from here, though. I have to go at least forty or fifty miles away — they might have informed the police, and the calls could be traced.'

'Money! Is that all you care about?' Her eyes were stormy as she raised them to pour scorn on him.

'No,' he said. 'But now I've come this far I'm not going back. I'm within an inch of every damned thing I've ever wanted in my life.'

He caught the glint of tears in her eyes, and saw her fumbling in the big pocket in front of her. He bent his head and tried to think of something comforting to say to her. He glanced up, and there was something in her hand, which she'd drawn back against her head, and it was descending now, aimed at his neck — at the gap between driving helmet and his shoulder.

He dived to one side, still hanging onto her other hand, and the weapon came down in a glancing blow on his shoulder. She was sobbing now, and raising her hand again, smashed away at his helmet, at the visor, at anything she could get near to.

They'd both fallen off the bed and onto the carpeted floor in the skirmish that ensued, and, having his wits about him again, he'd grabbed at her hand, torn the horseshoe out of it and flung it into the farthest corner of the room. He soon had her subdued and lying flat out on the floor, pinning both her hands at the sides of her head while she writhed and kicked at him.

Over the first shock of her attack, he was breathless, and leaned over her, panting, 'Don't you know these helmets are built to withstand head-on car crashes? Don't you realize you had no chance at all of knocking me out?'

'Let me go,' she whispered.

'No chance!'

You're hurting my hands.'

Slowly, he eased the pressure off her wrists, but still held her there. 'Don't try anything like that again,' he warned softly.

She lay still. Only her eyes moved, searching his face as she spoke. She seemed confused. 'You're not angry . . . ' she said. 'I had the horseshoe with me all the time, but I was scared to use it . . . '

'I wouldn't hurt you,' he said, knowing that he couldn't be angry with her ever again — no matter what she did. The passing hours had changed all that, and he bitterly regretted now all the things he'd done to her in the past few weeks. They'd been stupid, childish things, and now he knew her better he felt absurdly ashamed of himself. Clare Faulkener was receding to the innermost regions of his mind too. When he was here, with this girl, nothing else seemed to matter.

He'd eased himself up from the floor and backed away from her.

And she'd lain there, never moving, and watched him with accusing eyes as he left her . . .

He accomplished the drive back in less than forty-five minutes, pulled the car onto the drive at Lilacs and raced into the house. There was no sound from upstairs and his heart began to pound. He had a nagging feeling that something was wrong — 'Hell — if anything's happened to her . . . '

He threw off his outerwear and scrambled into the driving gear again. He'd be glad

478

when all this was over. He couldn't take unnecessary risks, though. He took the stairs two at a time and burst into the room.

She was lying on the bed, facing away from him. She was lying very still.

'Tamsin!'

She didn't answer, and slowly he walked across the room and stared down at her. He could see she was breathing; he looked round the room. There was nothing she could have harmed herself with. Tension began to drain out of him.

He said her name again, quietly, 'Tamsin!'

He didn't want to touch her. If he touched her, he wouldn't want to stop touching her. She was soft and fragile, and if somebody had told him right then and there that he would never see Clare Faulkener again, but he could have this girl, he would have believed he was in heaven. 'Tamsin!' His voice was harsher now, and she moved slightly and groaned.

At once he was concerned. He leaned over her, and rolled her to face him so he could see her.

Her eyes were wide open, but her face . . .

He gasped and took hold of her shoulders. Her face was a mass of red blotches and weals, and she was burning up when he felt at her forehead. He looked down at her hands; they too were red and swollen.

'Tamsin — for God's sake — what happened?' He was taking in great lungfuls of air, trying to control the panic that was fast taking hold of him. 'Tamsin — what's wrong?'

She held up her wrist. The handcuff was cutting into it, it was so swollen.

'Can't . . . breathe . . . ' she panted.

He let go of her hands, brought a small key out of his pocket and unfastened the handcuff. He flung it, and the chain, away from the bed. 'You're free,' he said. 'Tell me what to do.'

'Get — a — doctor,' she whispered. 'Hospital . . . '

'No.' Frozen with shock, he stared at her. 'I can't do that.'

'You *must* . . . '

'What is it, Tam. Why are you like this?'

She started to cough, a heavy rasping sound that seemed to be tearing at her throat.

'Tell me. For God's sake tell me what I can do?'

'Allergy,' she muttered, her eyes starting to close.

'An allergy? To what?'

'Rue,' she whispered.

'Rue?'

Her hand made a movement towards the side of the bed. He saw that the vase of herb cuttings had been knocked over. Sprigs of the green stuff were scattered all over the bedside tabletop. He hadn't noticed it before; he'd been too concerned about her to notice anything except her inert body on the bed.

'You're allergic to that stuff? Did you know that?'

She made a little movement of assent with her head.

He sank down onto the bed and looked at her. He felt helpless. 'Why?' he wanted to know. 'Why the hell had you got it with you, then?'

'Photographs,' she whispered. 'Cass was going to photograph some of my herbs.'

'Photographs . . . '

'Publicity — I need more outlets . . . ' Coughing racked her body again and she curled her legs up and her shoulders shook.

'And I — I took those damned herbs out of their plastic bag and put them there — right at the side of the bed. God! Tamsin — why didn't you tell me?'

She drew in a deep breath. 'Wouldn't hurt me — not there. Not till I touched them . . . ' The exertion of talking was making her breathless.

'You touched them? Deliberately *touched* them? Knowing this would happen?'

Again, that movement of her head.

481

'Why? In the name of . . . '

'So you'd have to — let — me — go . . . '

'You deliberately made yourself ill . . . ?'

She nodded vigorously this time. Her breath was rattling in her throat.

Incredulous, he asked, 'You hate me so much you would put your life at risk?'

She made no response at first; she just lay back against the pillows taking great gasping breaths of air, then she spoke, and her voice was a hoarse whisper. 'I don't . . . hate you. I just . . . want to go home . . . '

He despised himself then, for what he'd done. 'This has happened before?'

She nodded again.

'What did they do for you?'

'Hospital . . . ' she said faintly.

He hardened his heart against her. It was difficult to do that, but he forced himself to say, 'Out of the question, Tamsin. I can't take you to a hospital.'

'Allergy!' she said again. 'Medication for allergy, then . . . '

'Which consists of?' He was frowning. He was panicking too. 'Tell me — I could go to a pharmacist and get you something.'

'Hay-fever . . . travel sickness . . . ' She made an attempt to smile, but it was too much for her; she closed her eyes and lay back, exhausted.

His mind worked swiftly. Clare had caught a bad cold the previous summer, he remembered. She'd insisted it was hay-fever. She'd bought some little pills from the local chemist. Without a word he raced from the room, back down the stairs and into the kitchen. Clare kept all manner of things in a kitchen drawer. Aspirin, paracetamol, sticking plaster, cotton wool, wasp-sting spray — though to his knowledge she'd never been stung by a wasp in her life. He'd laughed at her little drawer. She'd said that it was common knowledge that most accidents happened in the kitchen, so there her 'life-saver' was staying. He recalled she'd only taken a couple of the hay-fever pills and had complained they made her drowsy. He rummaged through the drawer and found them.

Back in the bedroom, with a glass of water, he supported her with one arm round her shoulders and made her take two of the pills. She gulped the water down. She seemed calmer now, and leaned against him. He stayed with her, and half an hour passed and she fell asleep. He lay her gently back down on the bed and, holding her hand, felt for a pulse in her wrist. It was steady. She was cooler too.

He cleared away the herbs and took them

downstairs. He didn't bother to lock the bedroom door. The million pounds ransom meant nothing to him any more. He removed the driver's helmet and its underlying balaclava, and then his gloves. What use were they to him now? He'd been a fool. A complete and utter fool.

He busied himself in the kitchen, creeping silently upstairs two or three times during the next couple of hours to check she was all right. She was sleeping though, and the redness was fading from her cheeks a bit more every time he saw her. Her hand had been flung out at her side the last time he went up. Where the handcuff had been was a thin red angry line, right round her wrist. He swallowed, hating himself and despising the woman who had forced him to take such drastic measures against the girl. It wasn't Clare's fault, though, he reasoned silently. Nobody was to blame but himself. He'd allowed Clare Faulkener to become an obsession with him.

He went downstairs again and placed a pan of soup on the hob to simmer. He put coffee into Clare's latest fad — an elegant glass cafetière — and switched on the kettle. At some point the phone rang, but he ignored it. Nobody knew he was here. Nobody would be expecting an answer. In his heart, he knew it was Clare on the other end of the line, and he just couldn't be bothered with her. She'd recognized his voice when he'd rung the Faulkener house, he knew. There had been that little gasp when he'd asked to speak to Vaughn Herrick. She wouldn't let on to them, though. She wouldn't want to be implicated in something as sordid as this.

He looked at his watch. More than three hours had passed since he'd come back to Lilacs from making that call in Norwich. He walked into the hall, still wearing the driver's suit, but without the disguise of the helmet now. His foot was on the bottom stair when he looked up and saw her.

Tamsin was halfway down the stairs; the redness of her skin had paled and her breathing was normal.

'You forgot to lock the bedroom door, Craig.' Her voice still had a slight huskiness about it.

'I *didn't* forget,' he said quietly.

'You forgot to wear the helmet too.'

Again, in a low voice, he said, 'I *didn't* forget.'

'You were coming up to me?' Her head tilted slightly in an enquiring manner.

'Yes. I wondered if you were ready for something to eat.'

'Without the helmet!' Her voice wavered.

'Damn the helmet. And damn the million pounds.'

'You mean that?' She sank into a sitting position on one of the stairs and stared, wide-eyed, at him.

He nodded, then held out his hand. 'How long have you known it was me?'

'Since you called me *Ms* Curtis.'

'Do you know where you are?'

She stood up again and took a few steps down the stairs towards him. 'At a guess — Lilacs — Clare Faulkener's house in Norfolk. I heard Canada geese outside my window a while back, and Patric once mentioned there were Canada geese on a pond here.'

He said simply, 'I'm glad you know.'

She went down the remaining stairs until her face was on a level with his.

'So what happens now?' she asked in a quiet, resigned voice. 'What are you going to do now I know who you are, Craig?'

30

At Aldwich House, the atmosphere was tense, made more so when Clare walked in some hours after the phone call and said, 'I'm not staying here.'

'It would be best if you did,' Jane Goodall said, standing up at once.

'It's not my damned home any more, and I deeply resent this intrusion into my privacy.' Mark saw that Clare was obviously furious — and who could blame her? he reasoned silently to himself.

'I am *not* staying here,' she went on. 'This kidnap affair is none of my making and I don't see why *I* should suffer.'

Patric went over to her side. 'It can't be helped, Clare. This is where Vaughn can be contacted. The kidnapper knows that. The police have to be here.'

'But I *don't* 'have to be here'.' She mimicked him unkindly, shooting a malevolent look at Jane Goodall, 'And if *you* — madam — want to keep me at Alderwood, you will have to put me under arrest. I've had enough.'

Jane Goodall said, 'I can't keep you here. I am merely suggesting that you stay.'

Patric pleaded, 'Be reasonable, Clare.'

Quietly she said, 'I don't feel reasonable. There's nothing I can do here. I'm going to Lilacs until all this has died down.'

Patric looked round at the others. Vaughn shrugged; Mark said, 'I agree with Clare, Patric. She shouldn't have to put up with all this in her own home.'

'Okay!' Patric sighed.

Without another word, Clare left the room, and within minutes they all went quiet as her car was heard, revving up outside the house and then driving away.

'Lilacs?' Jane Goodall asked Patric from her side of the room.

'The house we lived in when we were first married,' he said, walking over to her and standing looking out through the window at the sea. 'Clare loves the old place. She won't hear of us getting rid of it.'

'And Lilacs is . . . where?'

Patric smiled, fished a cigarette case out of his pocket and said, 'A little place called Polten Market — it's near Norwich.'

'Norwich!'

Mark said, 'That phone call Vaughn had

was from a Norwich phone box.'

'There can't be any connection,' Jane Goodall said. 'Unless . . . ' She stared at Patric. 'Unless you can think of one?' Her eyes narrowed.

Patric didn't light the cigarette he was intent on smoking. 'How could there be any connection?' he asked in surprise.

'An empty house,' the woman said. 'Convenient, don't you think, for somebody with something to hide? Who knows about this Lilacs place?'

Patric glanced round the room. 'Just the people here, my parents, and probably Clare's assistant at work . . . ' He stopped suddenly, then said, 'No — that's too ridiculous to contemplate.'

'Nothing's ridiculous,' Jane snapped. 'A girl's life might be at stake, though.'

At that moment the phone shrilled again, and Mark sprang to answer it. Jane Goodall came over to his side, her eyes anxious.

'Tam?' Mark drew in his breath.

'Keep her talking.'

Mark wasn't listening to Jane Goodall. Tam was there, talking to him from goodness knew where, and that was enough for him. She was alive.

'Tam — where are you?'

She told him. Mark glanced at Jane

Goodall and nodded his head. 'Lilacs,' he said. 'You're sure, Tam? You're certain that's where he's taken you? Okay — we'll be right over . . . and Tam . . . ' Not caring that everybody in the room was listening to him, he said, 'Tam — I love you.'

★　★　★

Clare Faulkener's temper was at boiling point by the time she reached Polten Market. 'Damn him! Damn him!' Her foot was hard down on the accelerator as she swung into the drive at Lilacs and saw his car there in front of her.

In the kitchen they'd obviously heard her brake-squealing arrival. There were two soup plates on the table, two cups of coffee, her glass cafetière still three-quarters full of rich brown liquid.

Craig was on his feet, facing the door. The girl had her back to the wall by the side of the window.

Clare stood in the doorway, breathing heavily, and stared at them both. Her voice was steel-hard as she said, 'Are you mad? Are you completely mad — bringing her here?'

'It was the only way.' Craig Andrews squared up to her. 'You wanted the money.

How else was I to get such an amount?'

'What are you going to do with her?'

He stared at her as if she'd lost her senses. 'Do? I'm giving myself up. Something like this would never have worked. Anyway, I found I couldn't go through with it. Call it conscience, if you like. Whatever it is, I find I don't have the heart for it any more.'

'You've chosen a rotten time to discover that,' Clare said. 'All hell's been let loose in Alderwood. They traced that call you made — to Norwich. The damn house is overrun with police — they're like a swarm of ants around there. And you — you have the audacity to bring her *here*! To *my* house. To implicate *me* in this filthy little scheme of yours. I can't believe it.' She threw up her hands in a theatrical gesture, and, screeching at him now, went on, 'You didn't even have the sense to keep her blindfold, you fool. Look at her . . . ' She flung out one hand, forefinger outstretched. 'Look at *both* of you — you were actually eating a cosy little meal together, as if you hadn't got a care in the world . . . '

Tam moved into the centre of the room. 'Don't . . . ' she begged. 'Don't go on like this, Clare. Craig didn't let me see his face at first — and he disguised his voice . . . It *could* have worked, and *you* would have had what you wanted . . . '

'Craig?' Clare gave a scream of laughter. 'Craig, is it? We're on first-name terms with a damned kidnapper, are we? Are you sure you weren't in this with him from the start?'

'No,' Tamsin cried. 'Why would I have done that?'

'Maybe he wanted that million so he and you could go off together.'

Craig said, 'Clare! Be reasonable.'

'I'm past being reasonable.' Clare's voice turned ugly. 'You lied to me. You gave me that cock-and-bull story about your dear little grandmother . . . ' She was panting heavily now, and her face was distorted with rage. 'I believed you — I even gave you my mobile phone so you could keep in touch with me from Scotland . . . ' Glancing wildly round the kitchen, she saw the phone on a work-top and strode over to it, picking it up and shaking it in his face. 'You rat! You spineless rat! How could you do this — to *me*! You won't get away with it. I'm warning you . . . '

'I've no intention of getting away with it.' Craig glanced across at Tam. 'Tamsin phoned the house — on my instruction — ' he glanced at the kitchen clock ' — it was forty minutes ago. You must have already left

492

Alderwood or you would have known about it. They're on their way here. They can't be more than ten minutes behind you — I expect they'll arrest me.'

'They *know* you're here?' Clare's eyes widened in horror. 'At *my* house?'

Craig nodded. 'Clare,' he said simply, 'I won't implicate you in this, I promise, but from now on we're through. You and me — this is the end.'

Scathingly, Clare replied, 'You can bet your sweet life it is.'

'I'm sorry.'

'You will be.' She swung round, plunging her phone into her pocket as she ran out of the house.

Tamsin caught at the edge of the table and swayed. Craig was beside her in seconds, his arm round her shoulder. 'Don't worry,' he said. 'You'll be okay.'

'She'll slaughter *you*.' She looked up into his face, worried for him.

He laughed softly. 'I don't think so somehow.'

'Go and tell her you're really sorry.'

'I'd better go and see if I can cool her down. She ought not to be driving in a state like that. Are you sure you're all right, though? I thought you were going to keel over just now.'

'I'm okay.'

'You're a great girl, Tamsin.'

'I'm glad you're not calling me *Ms* Curtis any more.' Suddenly she was serious.

'I won't do that again. I've learned to have some respect for you.' His arm fell away from her.

She caught at his sleeve as he would have left her. 'Craig — take care.'

'Care?' he asked, his eyes serious but a smile playing round his lips.

'I don't trust her . . . '

'I can handle Clare Faulkener.' He grinned at her. 'And you're the last person in the world who should be concerned about me.' He went out of the kitchen and left her standing there. Already, she could hear Clare's car revving up outside on the drive.

★ ★ ★

Clare saw Craig walking down the drive towards her, weaving past his own car, then setting off at a jog as he realized she was trying to reverse off the drive.

It was dark outside, except for the headlights of her car.

Clare saw him clearly in their beam and she was furious. Incensed. He needed teaching a lesson.

In a deliberate action, she took the car out of reverse and put it into forward gear, hardly knowing what she was doing her rage was so intense.

He was standing at the back of his own car now, shouting something to her — probably he was yelling at her to stop. Well, she wasn't going to take orders from *him*! She'd show him . . .

She juggled the accelerator and clutch, keeping the car stationary on the bite point and revving the engine until it was screaming, then in a final burst of fury she lifted her left foot off the clutch and jammed her right one hard down on the accelerator — aiming the car directly at him.

★   ★   ★

Patric was driving ahead of the police car containing Jane Goodall. Mark was sitting in the passenger seat and Vaughn was in the rear of the car.

As Patric swung into the drive at Lilacs, Mark yelled, 'Stop!'

They pulled up within inches of Tamsin. She was sitting on the cold ground, cradling something in her arms. In the light from the headlamps Mark saw what it was, and his stomach turned over.

He pushed open the car door and raced towards her. There was blood soaking into the green of her sweatshirt and her golden hair was tumbled over her face.

Mark knelt down and took a lifeless hand in his and felt for a pulse. There was none.

Gently, he glanced up, pushed her hair back from her face and said gently, 'He's dead, Tam.'

She nodded. She was shivering and her teeth were chattering together. 'I know.' There were no tears on her face. Just a hopeless expression of grief stared out at him from her eyes.

Patric and Vaughn were standing watching. She glanced up at Patric. 'Your wife . . . ' she said. 'She's insane, Patric. For heaven's sake don't get in her way. I thought for one moment she was going to kill me as well, when I ran out to see what had happened. She backed up and drove away, though.'

'Clare did — this . . . ?' Horror filled Patric's eyes.

She nodded.

Another car screeched to a halt at the bottom of the drive. Several figures came running.

Mark was on his knees beside her now as they came up. His arm was round her shoulders, holding her safe. She eased herself away from the body on the ground, took one last look at it as Mark drew her to her feet and, still holding her close to him, edged her away from Craig's body and slowly turned her round to face the house again.

Jane Goodall was assessing the situation, Mark saw as he glanced back. She had her phone in her hand now, was issuing orders to the local police to stop and apprehend the driver of . . .

'The number of your wife's car?' she rapped out to Patric Faulkener.

As if in a daze, Patric told her.

'We have to do this.' Jane Goodall's voice was practical as she faced Patric after she'd relayed the information, and asked for an ambulance to be sent.

'I know.' Patric's shoulders sagged. Mark saw him walking back to his car, switching off the headlights. He walked swiftly towards them then.

'Take Tamsin inside the house,' he said to Mark. 'We might as well all go in there and wait.'

Tamsin's head turned just once to look at the bundle on the ground. It was in shadow now. She gazed up at Mark, then down at her sweatshirt and back at his jacket. 'We have his blood on us,' she whispered.

'Better that,' he said, 'than him having *your* blood on *his hands*.'

'It would never have come to that,' she said. 'He was only a man in love — but with the wrong woman.'

31

Clare Faulkener drove hard. Headlights coming in the opposite direction kept blinding her, and making her swerve in towards the grass verges at the sides of the country roads. She headed south, back towards Alderwood. There was nowhere else to go! The enormity of what she'd done was slowly sinking into her brain. She hadn't intended to hurt him — frightening him would have been enough. But, as usual, her temper had got the better of her.

The girl had screamed at her. 'You've killed him! You've killed him!'

Tamsin Curtis could have been hysterical, though. He might *not* be dead. In her heart, though, she knew that what she had done was unforgivable. She hadn't stopped to reason it out, but now it was being forced upon her.

Craig had done what he'd done because of her. She'd thrown out a challenge: 'Bring me a million pounds!' He could have done it too. Patric, Vaughn and Mark Langham had spent most of the day raking up the money, from bank accounts, from investments, from anywhere and everywhere, and she knew that in a couple of days Craig could have come to her with that million pounds.

Not now, though.

She swerved again in the darkness, and a passing truck blasted its horn at her.

A road junction was coming up ahead of her. She knew she'd have to turn now and go across country towards the coast — and Alderwood. She'd wait for them there. They'd come and arrest her. Her world was falling apart. How was she going to face Patric after this? How could she live without Craig . . . ?

The road was quite busy with late-evening traffic. She was constantly slowing down and then speeding up again, having to be ever watchful of vehicles behind and in front in the darkness. She drove mainly by instinct — her mind was elsewhere.

She was glad when she came to the estuary. Not far now. Alderwood was safe — maybe for a few short hours. Who knew how long it would take them to come knocking on the door . . . ?

Craig filled her thoughts. She couldn't have killed him, she reasoned. She loved him. The girl, though — Tamsin — she had screamed, 'You've killed him . . . ' and there had been

Craig's blood on her as she'd crouched there on the drive at Lilacs — holding him so carefully, as if he was a baby who'd had a tumble . . .

What did Tamsin know anyway? She wasn't a doctor or a nurse. Mistakes were made even by those who were professionals. Craig wasn't dead. Craig wouldn't leave her like that — not when he'd been at such pains to get that million pounds for her . . .

Traffic Lights Ahead! The moon was throwing its clear, cold light onto the waters of the river as it snaked away towards the sea. The mud-flats gleamed darkly alongside the road.

Road Narrows! She cursed under her breath. 'Damn!' She slowed right down. *Single File Traffic* . . . Always, whenever she drove either in or out of Alderwood, she cursed this stretch of road. 'This damned bridge! Will they never get round to widening it?'

She tapped the steering wheel impatiently with her fingers. She could see nothing on the other side of the bridge. Why wait for the lights to change? She could make it . . .

Foot hard down, she sped forward past the red light.

The speedometer read sixty . . . Headlights were coming towards her . . . She pressed hard on the accelerator. Seventy. Seventy-five . . . She *could* still make it.

On the seat beside her, her mobile phone started bleeping.

She picked it up. 'Patric! This is a fine time to ring me.'

She was doing over eighty. The phone was a nuisance. It left her only one hand to steer with. She was weaving all over the road. Exhilarated with the speed. The headlights in front of her didn't worry her. They were on the other side of the road.

Single File Traffic . . . There was no 'other side' to the road. She was still on the bridge. The huge headlights in front were blinding her now. They were coming straight for her. It was big. A truck . . .

She panicked. The phone spun out of her hand. She let go of the steering wheel, pressed her hands up to her face. Her feet jammed down hard on brake and clutch simultaneously . . .

The car went into a skid. The lights were on top of her. The truck couldn't stop. And neither could she. The lights came at her. Metal screeched on metal. Pain shot through her. Her legs were trapped; she couldn't move them. She could hear Patric's voice coming out of the phone as she crashed through the parapet of the bridge — her car and the truck, locked together.

'Clare! What the hell's going on! Clare — speak to me . . . '

Slow motion now. Silence too. The smell of petrol! And pain! More pain than she could bear.

There was a splash, and a gentle rocking movement. Every inch of her body was searing, agonizing pain, and closing in on her brain was a blackness like she'd never known before . . .

* * *

Tam was quiet on the way back to Herb House, and Mark didn't push her to talk. She held tightly onto his hand in the back of the police car. Jane Goodall was in the front with a driver; Tamsin tried not to listen to the news relaying back and forth on the radio about Clare Faulkener and her supposed whereabouts. What Clare had done completely sickened Tamsin.

She whispered to Mark, 'I wish they didn't have to talk all the time like this, about what happened at Lilacs.'

He slipped an arm round her shoulders and pulled her closer to him in the darkness. 'It can't be helped, Tam. They've got a job to do. It sounds from what they're saying as if they've got the whole of the eastern counties police force on the look-out for her.'

'It won't make any difference to Craig now, though, will it?' She raised her eyes to look at him as street-lamps illuminated the interior of the car briefly when they flashed past them.

'He had it coming to him.' Mark's voice was hard.

'Nobody deserves to die like that. He wasn't an evil man.'

'You can forgive him? For what he did to you?'

'It was worse for *you*,' she said quietly. 'Having to sit through my interview with Inspector Goodall back at Lilacs, and hear how Craig kept me prisoner there.'

'You didn't have to make the statement there,' he said in a soothing voice. 'I could have taken you to Alderwood police station tomorrow morning.'

'I had to get it all out in the open,' Tam said. 'It was fresh in my mind, and I just had to talk to somebody or I would have gone mad, I think. I didn't want to have to go to sleep tonight with it all bottled up inside me. It was best this way. The police know what happened now — and, more importantly, so do you.'

'I've cursed myself a thousand times over for going back to Cass's house when Jack-O rang me to say he'd be late turning up for your car,' he said.

'It wasn't your fault.' She rested her head against the hollow of his shoulder.

'I should never have left you,' he said savagely. 'I keep thinking of what might have happened — '

She broke in gently, 'Nothing happened to me. Craig didn't hurt me. It's Clare Faulkener I can't forgive, for giving him that ultimatum. She ought to have known that he'd move heaven and earth to get that money for her. And now . . . ' Her voice petered out, and she turned her face into his jacket. 'I just want to try and put it behind me,' she said, her voice muffled. 'I shall never forget, though, that I was instrumental in causing a man's death.'

'Hush,' he said. 'You're not to blame in any way.'

'I told Craig to go after her and apologize to her . . . '

'He would have gone after her anyway.'

'We'll never know,' she said, 'whether he would or not. He'd told her that he was through with her. He'd come to his senses about her earlier than that, though, I think. That was why he allowed me to make that phone call to you — telling you where I was — the call that brought you hot on her tail.'

'Inspector Goodall was just putting two and two together,' he said. 'I think her suspicions were aroused when Clare marched out of the house and said she was going to Lilacs.'

'Craig wanted to put things right,' Tamsin insisted. 'He was devastated when he realized what the consequences could have been if those pills he gave me hadn't worked.'

'I dread to think of those consequences too,' Mark said.

'I took a risk there.' She sat up straight again. 'I felt pretty rough, and I wished I hadn't handled and rubbed those rue cuttings on my face — afterwards.' She laughed shakily.

'You forced his hand, though — and your plan worked.'

She nodded silently, then said, 'It was only a matter of time before he'd have let me go, even if I hadn't done that. Craig Andrews might have been a conceited and supercilious sod, but he wasn't all bad.'

'It's easy to say that now,' Mark stated. 'You must have been terrified at the time, though.'

'Yes,' she said softly. 'I was. But in his way, he was kind to me. I can't say otherwise — and I wouldn't, not even if he were still alive and having to stand trial for kidnapping me. He wasn't a monster. He treated me with respect.'

'I wish you could be as soft-hearted about *me*', Mark said. 'I've almost given up hope of you ever wanting me on a permanent basis.'

She lifted her head and stared into his face. 'You know that I want you,' she whispered. 'Mark — what would I do without you?'

'When it suits your purpose, you want me,' he reminded her. 'But are you ever going to come back to Yorkshire to me? Will we ever enter into something more lasting than what we have now? Those are the questions that plague me. I need you, Tam. And not on a part-time basis.'

'You said you would never ask me to marry you ever again,' she said.

'I'm not doing that. I want to take care of you, though. Damn marriage. If you don't want a ring on your finger, just let me care for you — no lasting commitment required on your part — I promise.'

'That wouldn't be fair on you.'

They were speeding towards home when the radio crackled again and Jane Goodall began speaking to one of the cars that had been alerted to pick up Clare.

'An accident?' She repeated some information to the driver. They heard her mention Alderwood, and the Borda River bridge.

The message ended, and she turned round to them. 'Sorry about this — we have to make a slight detour.'

'You said something about an accident,' Tamsin said.

Inspector Goodall said briskly, 'I have no details yet, but, yes, Clare Faulkener's car's reported as being involved in an incident of some sort on the bridge this side of Alderwood.'

Mark said, 'Can't you drop us off first . . . ?'

'Sorry!'

'Look — just let us out. We could get a taxi or something . . . '

Jane glanced at the back seat again. 'We have to go straight there,' she said.

Mark's voice was tense. 'Don't you think Tam's gone through enough without this?'

'I can't just abandon you in the middle of the damned countryside,' Jane Goodall said heatedly. 'And I can't spare the half-hour drive across country to Stratton End; just bear with me, will you?'

Beside him in the car, Tam started shivering. She'd thought it was all over — the trauma and the bloodshed — but it seemed there was more to come.

★ ★ ★

They finally made it to Stratton End around eleven o'clock.

When Jane Goodall let them out of the police car, Tam could hardly stand, she was so tired.

In the house, when Mark had locked the door securely, she stood in the middle of the kitchen, stared down at her sweatshirt, with the great uneven stain of Craig's blood that had dried upon it, and suddenly she started trembling uncontrollably.

Mark went to her as she held her arms away from her body and stammered, 'T-take it off ... for pity's sake ... take it off me ... '

Gently, Mark rolled up her shirt and eased it over her head and arms.

'Burn it.' She shuddered. 'Put it in the stove and burn it.'

Mark didn't argue. He did as she asked him to do, pushing her shirt inside the kitchen stove — which was barely alight but still had a faint glimmer of heat coming from it — and poking it with a rake until flames consumed it.

She stood with her hands crossed over her chest, watching him. He took his own blood-smeared jacket off, took his phone and wallet out of its pockets, then pushed that into the stove before turning back to her.

'Let's get you upstairs,' he said.

'A sh-shower,' she said, her teeth chattering. 'I need to wash it off me — his blood.'

'I know,' he said, leading her to the stairs and keeping one arm firmly round her as she stumbled up each step.

He took off his own clothes while she stepped out of her jeans, pants and bra, then went into the shower with her and scrubbed her with a scratchy sponge and plenty of suds before washing himself. She kept very close to him, tilting her head back and closing her eyes as he soaped her hair and cleansed every part of her.

There was nothing sexual in the actions they went through. Sex was the last thing on either of their minds. When they were both soaking wet from head to toe, and the last bubbles had dribbled away down the drain, he said, 'Is that okay?'

She clenched her teeth tightly together and nodded her head with vigour. 'Yes,' she managed to mutter. 'I feel clean now.'

He wrapped her in a bath sheet and towelled her dry, and rubbed at her hair till it was no longer streaming water down over her shoulders, but was frizzing up in its natural state and would soon be curling softly round her face again. She reached for a fragrant body spray as he dried himself on the same towel he'd used for her.

In her bedroom, she pulled on a plain cotton nightshirt that reached to her knees, then went and switched off the light. Mark was already in bed, waiting for her. She made her way over to him.

He'd turned the covers back, and, still shivering, she crept in beside him and crawled to his side. He never wore a stitch in bed, and he was warm as she cuddled up against him. Some of the heat began transferring itself from him to her own body.

If she could have stopped her teeth from chattering she would have said, 'Hold me,' but he did that without being asked, seeming to know instinctively it was that which she needed. He held her close, with her head just under his chin and his arms right round her. She twined her legs round his, laid her hand on his shoulder. She was warm now; she was home, and nothing was going to hurt her again. Mark would see to that.

She tilted her head back in the darkness and said, 'Love me, Mark. Make love to me. I need to feel normal again.'

32

Cass heard a car pull up outside, and then footsteps came hurrying up towards her door. It was after midnight, and she had just decided there was going to be no news about Tam, so she might as well go to bed and try to get some sleep.

A sudden pounding on her front door, though, had her grabbing at the back of a chair as all the breath seemed to gush out of her body. It could only mean one thing.

She hurried to the door and flung it open.

Patric Faulkener said, 'I have to talk to you,' and his face was grim.

She pressed a hand to her thudding heart and said, 'Patric — what is it? Is it bad news . . . Tam . . . ?'

'Tam's okay,' he said. 'She's with Mark — back at Herb House. She's okay, Cass.'

'Thank God.'

'Can I come in? I don't want Mum and Dad next door to see I'm here just yet. I shall have to go there later, but . . . '

She held the door wide. 'What's wrong?' One look at his face, then, told her to expect the worst.

'It's Clare,' he said.

'Clare!'

She made him sit down in the cosy little sitting room. He sat with his head bowed, his hands clasped between his knees, and she dropped on her knees in front of him and said, 'Tell me.'

'There's been an accident. A terrible accident.'

'Clare? You mentioned Clare,' she said.

'She jumped the lights on the river bridge — and it was my fault. I'd just phoned her. I heard it all.'

'Oh, no!'

'She hit a truck. Head-on.'

Cass held her breath. 'And . . . ?'

He looked up at her slowly.

Cass let out a slow breath. Inside, though, she felt as if a weight was being lifted off her. With Clare out of the way, there was a future for them . . . She hated herself for thinking that, though. She mustn't think it. It was horrible. 'She's — dead? Is that what you're trying to tell me?'

Even more slowly, he shook his head.

She wanted to weep with relief. She wanted to thank providence, or God or whatever or

513

whoever was responsible, for saving Clare. She must have been mad in those few moments when she'd hoped that Clare had died in the accident. In a voice devoid of emotion, she said, 'You must be thankful for that, then.'

'Thankful?' His eyes burned into hers. 'Thankful?'

'If she's alive . . . '

'They amputated one leg at the scene of the accident . . . after they got her out of the river.'

'Oh, no . . . '

'I've just come from the hospital. They say there's serious damage to her head, and her spine.'

Cass sank down onto the rug and curled her knees up under her. Her gaze never wavered from his.

'They saved her life. She can't move, though. She can't speak.'

'They can do marvellous things nowadays . . . '

'Shut up,' he snapped. 'We both know what this means, don't we?'

Her eyes were downcast now. She murmured, 'Yes.'

'No divorce,' he said.

'You would never have gone through with it.' Her words were flat. They were true, though. She knew that much. It would have gone against everything he believed in to divorce Clare.

'And that's not all . . . ' Slowly and painfully he told her what had happened that day. 'If she survives, she could face a manslaughter charge for killing Craig Andrews,' he finished at last.

Cass let the words sink in. 'You've had a hell of a day,' she said.

He looked up at her. 'I came off lightly,' he said. 'I keep thinking about that poor bugger, mangled up on the drive at Lilacs!'

'And poor Clare too,' she said. 'You've got to think of her now.'

'I hate her,' he said. 'I loathe the selfish bitch. But what can I do?'

'You've got to care for her. You know that, deep down, don't you?'

'Care for her?' His laugh was harsh and uncaring.

'You're all she's got,' she said in a strangled voice.

'Yes,' he said. 'That's what I keep telling myself.' He pushed himself wearily to his feet. 'Cass . . . ' He held out his hand. 'This really is goodbye, you know.'

She nodded. 'I shall clear everything out of the house,' she said. 'I shall leave it up for sale and put all the furniture — all Mum's belongings — into storage, Patric, and move right away from here.'

'Yes,' he said. 'You have all your life ahead of you.'

'All my life?' She gazed deeply into his eyes as pain seared through her at his words. 'All my life? Without you?' she whispered.

He said, 'It has to be that way.'

And in her heart she knew that what he said was true. From now on she must look to the future, because there was no way she could return to what was past.

* * *

Mark woke just after eight the next morning and saw that the bedroom curtains had been pulled back, letting in a watery sun — and *she* was gone from his side. He knew she wouldn't be far away. He got out of bed and went over to the window, chewing pensively on his lips as he watched her down there, outside in the garden, tending her beloved herbs. He went to the bathroom, cleaned his teeth and shaved. Back in the bedroom, he knelt beside his weekend bag and pulled out a navy blue tracksuit. It wasn't new, it was just an old shapeless thing that was comfortable, but it would do, he decided, realizing that wearing anything resembling the clothes he'd had on yesterday wouldn't be a good idea. He combed his hair, went back to the window and looked out. She was still there, plunging a small garden trowel into the dew-damp soil and digging out the weeds.

Silent in his trainers, he walked down the grassy path towards her. No matter how quietly he moved, though, she heard him, and looked up when he was about ten feet away from her.

There was grime under her fingernails and she plundered the weeds relentlessly, placing them in a neat pile beside her. As he reached her, he went down on his haunches.

'Do you want some help?'

Her hair was gleaming in the early-morning rays of the pale sun; a bit of colour had returned to her cheeks. She looked as she'd always looked in the past; down to earth and practical in jeans and a serviceable work-shirt.

'You could make me some breakfast.' She grinned up at him.

'I'm ready for some myself. I just realized, I haven't had a thing to eat since lunch-time yesterday.' He watched her carefully for some kind of reaction to his mention of the day before. It was no good pretending yesterday had never happened, he told himself.

'I had some soup ... ' She stood up,

dusting her hands down on the sides of her jeans. A magpie swooped down onto a tree branch and started up a noisy, clamorous chattering. In a deliberate and precise voice, she said, 'Craig Andrews made me some soup — before he died,' and she didn't waver as her gaze met his.

'Was it good?'

She nodded her head. 'Yes.' She turned her head and looked at the magpie. 'One for sorrow,' she said. 'That's how the old saying about magpies goes, isn't it?'

'I guess so.' He, too, rose to his feet now.

'Do you think the police will want to talk to me again today?'

'Maybe.' It was more than likely they would, he knew.

She dragged in a deep breath of fresh air, then blew it out slowly. 'I wish we'd not had to go with the police to that accident last night. Clare's car . . . ' Her voice broke momentarily, but she recovered herself quickly and went on, 'It didn't even look like a car when they'd hauled it out of the river, did it? I wonder if she's still alive.'

'We could phone the house and see what the news is. Patric will probably be expecting us to enquire.'

She thought about that for a second or two, then she nodded and said, 'Maybe we should — we owe it to Patric. He can't be held responsible for Clare's actions, can he?'

'Are *you* okay this morning?'

She gave him a level stare. 'Yes,' she said. 'I'm all right, Mark. I'm tough. I'll get over it.'

'Do you want me to stay longer? I could phone Edgar Brand and explain what's happened. Trade's slack at the garage just at the moment; they could manage for a couple of weeks without me if they had to.'

'No,' she said. 'I have to deal with this in my own way.' She looked down at the pile of weeds. 'This helps.'

'I'll make that breakfast, then?'

She managed a smile that turned into an unsteady laugh as the magpie flapped away over the garden. 'He'll be back!' There was a bleak note in her voice. Then she turned to him. 'I think I'll come and help you with that breakfast,' she said.

33

Tamsin was more lonely than she'd ever imagined it was possible to be when, a few days later, Mark went back to Yorkshire.

His presence had been comforting after all that had happened, and his friendship, she realized now, was the one sane and good thing she could count on, no matter what happened. That they were lovers had been a bonus; and she constantly counted her blessings for having Mark around at all the worst possible times in her life. The knowledge worried her that at times in the past she had treated him dreadfully, and consequently their relationship had suffered. That relationship was very precious to her now, as, alone again, she couldn't get him out of her head, and found herself wishing constantly that he was back with her — either that or else she wished she'd gone back with him.

In the space of a few days — not with a fanfare blast or an explosion of fireworks, but merely by listening quietly to the voice of her heart — came the realization that she loved him beyond all reason.

The harassment of the past weeks was over for good she'd had one or two favourable replies to the advertising material she and Cass had concocted between them, and life, she found, was going on as usual. But she couldn't settle at Herb House; there was an emptiness in her life, a presence she missed, and her usual natural exuberance for living was at a low ebb. With Mark gone, her enthusiasm for her work had disappeared. Those last days he'd been with her had taken on a new meaning. It had been right, somehow — them being together. And now two hundred hated miles were separating them, and to Tam two hundred miles might have been the distance between her and the end of the earth, it seemed so final.

Clare Faulkener was still fighting for her life twenty miles away in hospital. Cass rang Tamsin regularly, giving her up-dates on Clare's condition, but it was becoming obvious that Clare would never fully recover from her dreadful injuries.

In Alderwood, and the surrounding villages, the events in which Clare Faulkener had played a major part had become a nine-day wonder, and it was rumoured that

Patric Faulkener was now throwing himself into his own design work at the new racing circuit near Cambridge, and had no interest at all in Faulkener's Herbs and Spices.

Cass was worried as to how Tam was coping.

'I'm fine.' Talking on the phone to her friend nearly three weeks after her kidnap ordeal, Tamsin hoped her voice conveyed more confidence than she actually felt. 'I'm missing Mark terribly . . . ' Her voice broke off, and she felt that a good old howl on somebody's shoulder might make her feel better.

'Tam — I wish I had more time I could spend with you, but the Essex job is running on longer than I'd anticipated.'

'Mark offered to stay with me a bit longer,' Tam said, 'but I couldn't ask him to do that. He does have his job to think about. He said Edgar could manage without him, but Mark *is* a partner in Brand Motors. He has a right to be there, not here, mollycoddling me.'

Cass said, 'Clare's in a bad way. Patric's mum, who lives next door to me, told me there doesn't seem to be much improvement — except that Clare is breathing on her own without the ventilator she was dependent on at first. So I suppose that's something to be thankful for — if thanks are indeed appropriate where that woman is concerned.'

'The accident's the talk of the whole area.'

'If Clare survives, she'll never walk again. Her spine was crushed — not surprisingly, really. Patric said she hit that truck at eighty miles an hour. I can't find it in me to forgive her for what she put you through, though, Tam. Nobody would blame you if you hated her.'

Tamsin made no attempt to inject any false sentiment into her words. 'At the moment, my feelings are mixed, love. I can't honestly say that hate is one of them. She's paying dearly for what she did. In my heart I try to forgive her, but . . . ' Again she couldn't finish the sentence. The memory of that night, when she'd held the dying Craig in her arms, still haunted her, and she couldn't rid herself of the feeling that she was in some way to blame herself. *If* she hadn't come to Suffolk in the first place; *if* she'd never set eyes on Herb House; *if* she'd not met Clare Faulkener . . .

She pushed the recriminations away and said, 'I'd have broken my contract with her after all that's happened rather than have any more dealings with her.'

'I'm sure you would have been within your rights, love — the repercussions of that night are affecting all of us. *You* because you'll lose your prime source of income when Patric sells the business, *me* because with events as they are he couldn't even think of leaving Clare, and *Mark* because his commitments are hundreds of miles away so he can't be there for you . . . Oh, it really is a mess, isn't it?'

'Oh, Cass . . . I've been so wrapped up in my own problems . . . ' All at once Tamsin felt guilty for selfishly thinking only of her own worries. 'I never really considered what the implications of Clare surviving — but being totally dependent upon Patric — would mean to *you*.'

Cass gave a weary little laugh. 'Clare Faulkener *is* a survivor,' she said. 'Make no mistake about that. Clare will have the last laugh on all of us. This is the one way she can keep him all to herself.'

After Cass had rung off, Tamsin knew she couldn't put off the inevitable any longer. If she intended making something of her life, it was definitely not going to be here, she decided — two hundred miles away from Mark. She hated having to virtually admit defeat, but, being honest with herself, she knew her heart wasn't in her work any longer. The first enthusiasm she'd been fired with when she'd had those encouraging replies from her advertising material somehow didn't matter any more. She decided there were more important things that needed her attention — and Mark was the top of the list of priorities.

She went upstairs, had a quick shower and put on a suit and smart sweater, then set off for the small town of Halesworth in the hire car she was using until her own was repaired. Her destination was 'John Chambers — Estate Agent'!

★ ★ ★

He didn't seem in the least surprised to see her.

'I need to know,' she said, 'if I have to stay on at the house. I realize there are still another eight months to run on the lease, but circumstances are forcing me to rethink my original idea of living there and . . . '

He held up one hand to silence her, then smiled kindly at her. 'As a matter of fact,' he said, 'I was going to get in touch with you, Miss Curtis. You see, I have two clients who are showing an interest in the old place — one has even made an offer to purchase Herb House, and its two acres of land.'

Tamsin was surprised. 'But nobody showed any interest when it was up for sale previously. And surely no one would buy it without seeing *inside* the house first?'

'Suddenly, everybody wants to buy Herb House,' he said. 'As I say, I have had *one* very good offer, and another gentleman who seems interested but is thinking it over at the moment. The first party — the one who has made the firm offer — has my vote, though. And he doesn't need to see the house before buying it.'

Suspicious, she asked, 'Is this because of the newspaper stories? Because of what happened to me, I wonder?'

He shook his head. 'Not entirely. Although it will, of course, attract a certain ghoulish interest. Inevitably — in a case like this that involves kidnapping, manslaughter and then that ghastly accident Mrs Faulkener suffered — you get what I personally call 'ghoulish gawpers', Miss Curtis. They don't go so far as wanting to buy the house, though. They merely want to 'gawp'!'

'But you *have* had a serious offer . . . ?'

'That's right. It was made a week and a half ago — before all the publicity you have subsequently received, my dear.

'A really good offer?' she asked.

He named a colossal sum of money that staggered her. 'Maybe I shouldn't be telling you this, but for a quick sale can I make a considerable profit. It's a property developer you see. A consortium, actually. They've already acquired the land the old church stands on at Stratton End. They intend building three hundred and sixty semi-detached dwellings, I believe, and if they purchase Herb House, they would build even more than that on the land.'

Tam stared at him, aghast. 'So — if I stay there . . . '

'At a guess, I'd say you'll soon be surrounded by about six hundred *near* neighbours — but your lease would run out in January next year, and it most definitely would not be renewed. I have a duty, you see, to sell — not to lease, if at all possible.' He closed his eyes momentarily and shuddered. 'For myself, the thought of six hundred near neighbours would be a living nightmare — I like my solitude, Miss Curtis.'

'I was getting quite used to the solitude myself,' she blurted out, horrified at what he was telling her.

'Can I take it, then, that you *won't* be entirely heartbroken if the lease on Herb House is not renewed next year?'

Tam's thoughts moved swiftly. This was the end. If she'd needed her mind made up, this was the thing that was going to do it. 'I've already decided to go back to Yorkshire,' she said.

'A wise move — in the circumstances.' John Chambers stroked his chin thoughtfully. 'If you had wanted to stay in this part of Suffolk, I could have suggested several similar properties I have on my books. You could have moved your herb business too, but — '

She broke in swiftly, 'I don't want to stay.'

'That,' he said, 'could be an advantage to both of us.'

'You mean I can get out of Herb House immediately, then . . . ?'

He said, '*If* I can settle the deal with the consortium without delay . . . ' He gave her a twinkling smile. 'I would, of course, make it worth your while. I would refund a generous part of what you paid to take out the lease.'

A little niggling voice was telling her she was taking the easy way out. She hesitated. 'Can you give me a week to think it over?' she asked.

He leaned back in his chair. 'Of course I can,' he said. 'Just get in touch with me when you have decided on the course of action you wish to take.'

She was being stupid and indecisive, her brain told her. And it wasn't like her at all. Usually, once her mind was made up, that was it. In her heart now, she knew what she *had* to do.

Cut your losses, conscience was telling her.

Go to Mark, reason was insisting.

And in her heart she knew that a week wasn't going to make any difference to the outcome. She was still going to feel the same way, and if she dithered now that consortium might just pull out, and then where would she be?

She didn't have to ask herself that. She knew well enough where she'd be — left high and dry and with six hundred neighbours clustered right up to her boundary. The thought made her shudder. She made her mind up on the instant.

'I don't need that week,' she said. 'I'll move out, Mr Chambers — just as soon as you want me to. You can sell to that consortium.'

'I'll need your signature to that effect, Miss Curtis.' He looked at her over the top of his owlish spectacles. 'If you could just wait ten minutes while I get a letter of consent to quit before your lease is up typed out in the back office?'

She nodded, and settled herself down to wait for his typist to do what was necessary. A sense of excitement gripped her. This wasn't the end. This was the start of something else. And when she had signed her name, and agreed to vacate Herb House, she knew a sense of infinite relief that this chapter of her life was almost over.

Back at Herb House, she packed a suitcase and headed north. She'd surprise him, she decided, as, at the wheel of her little hire car, her spirits began to lift. The sun came out, turning the wet road in front of her into a gleaming silver highway. It was a good omen, she decided. It was taking her in a new direction. There just had to be something good waiting at the other end of it.

★ ★ ★

Her optimism flowed like a river in full flood. She sang as she crossed the border into East Yorkshire. The rolling green wolds welcomed her, and the roads were quiet and almost devoid of heavy traffic as she headed towards the coast. Seagulls circled and flocked round a ploughman and his tractor. The soil he was churning up was dark and rich and moist. The sun glinted wetly on it. She let the window beside her slide down and took deep breaths of the fresh earthy perfume of another springtime. Already she could detect the scent of the sea too. A smile settled on her lips. She was going home . . .

At Heronsea, she parked on the seafront and walked up towards the headland — to the lighthouse. There were still ghosts she had to confront. That gaunt, white, silent sentinel had overshadowed her life for too long. Those shadows had to be sent packing. The past was a closed chapter in her life.

A young woman with three noisy children — two of school age and one in a baby-stroller — ran past her. She stopped and watched them making for the lighthouse. They hurried inside. A man came out, dressed in white. White jacket, white pants. He was carrying something. A board. Slowly she began walking again. He'd gone inside now and left the board outside. From here she could just make out the words at the top of it — *'Light-Bite Cafe'* — she was intrigued, and went forward.

At the door — which was propped wide open, — several plaques were fixed to the wall. *'Light-Bite Café'* was just one of them! Out loud, she read the others.

' *'Bev's Hi-Lites!' 'Skylight Travel'!'* She gazed up at the tall tower. From inside came the sound of voices — laughter. The Ivory Tower had never rung to the sound of laughter in the past. Ava — if she could see what was happening to it — would be having kittens!

Tam went inside — tentatively at first, wondering what she was going to find. There were workmen there — she'd noticed one or two cars and a large van parked. Inside, on the ground floor — in the exact centre of what had been her and Ava's wedding dress boutique — a large circular area had been screened off. She went over to one of the men. She was inquisitive as to what was happening behind those screens.

'What are you doing?'

'Installing a passenger lift, love.' He grinned at her. 'This place is going to have all mod-cons, see?'

She glanced towards the stairs. 'Can I still go up there?'

'Course you can. Go and see Bev.' He winked. 'She's my girl. Hairdresser. Second floor.'

Slowly, Tamsin climbed the stairs. With the noise of cutting and grinding machinery making a din down below her, and the voices above, came also the smell of food — a smell reminiscent of the snack bars and seafront cafés she remembered so well from the days when she'd been here last year.

It had all been so different then. The lighthouse — the Ivory Tower — had been a world apart — a world of satin and lace, of flowers and luxury. A world that had disappeared now that the elegant wedding dresses had all gone and Ava was dead . . .

And in its place — this. Workmen — a passenger lift, the man had said. Where her and Ava's powder room for ladies had been, two notices down there on the ground floor had proclaimed in stark black and white lettering — 'Guys' and 'Gals'. Yes — Ava would certainly be having kittens!

As she reached the first floor, Tam felt a wide smile forming on her face. Where the wedding dress storage area had been there was now a high counter round two halves of the lighthouse. There were chrome and leather mustard-coloured high stools, mirrors and bright lights, microwave ovens and a grill. People were sitting round eating burgers and drinking coffee and fizzy drinks out of plastic cups. The man in white who she'd seen downstairs putting the board outside looked foreign. Italian, maybe, she thought. He had dark curly hair; he called out, 'Can I help you, luv?'

Laughing, she said, 'I was looking for Bev.'

'Next floor up. Hairdressing.'

She thanked him and climbed the next set of stairs. Up here, it smelled of scent and soap. She popped her head inside the door. This had been Ava's living room once. It bore no resemblance to it now, though. Mirrors again glass, pretty coloured bottles, no carpet — fresh, clean blue tiles. Tam held her breath and went inside.

Bev wore a brooch with her name and a

black cat on it. She was obviously the one in charge. There were two girls busy shampooing customers' hair at pristine white bowls.

Bev came towards her. 'You have gorgeous hair.'

Tam laughed again. 'I used to live here.' Her gaze flew to the ceiling. 'Well, — up there, anyway.'

'Take a look round.' Bev smiled. 'You'll notice a big difference, I expect.'

'What else is there here?'

'Not much at the moment. A travel agent near the top. Two floors still vacant, though — if you're interested. We're trying to give everything a snappy sort of title. We feel — all of us here at the moment — that the old lighthouse deserves a bit of happiness. It seems to have got a reputation for failing at everything, and a lighthouse shouldn't be like that, should it? It should give hope and light, and life. It should be positive.'

Tam's smile faded. 'What a lovely idea,' she said, feeling a lump forming in her throat and tears springing to the back of her eyes.

'Hey! Come on in and have a cuppa. You look all in.'

Tamsin shook her head. 'No,' she said. 'I've just had an idea.'

'You have?' Bev grinned at her.

'You said there were two floors still vacant

— but what about the ground floor?'

'Vacant too — as far as I know. Or it will be when the workmen have finished.'

'I wonder . . . '

'What business are you in?'

Tamsin stared at her. 'Flowers.'

'Hey — that would be great — lots and lots of flowers down here, to welcome folks inside. What's your name, by the way?'

'Tam!' Tam said. 'Tamsin Curtis.'

'"Tam's Flower Tower"!' How does that strike you?'

It was too much. The homecoming. Everyone's friendliness at the old Ivory Tower. Tam's tears overflowed.

Bev led her away from the main body of the salon, sat her down and said, 'You're going to have that cuppa. I insist.'

34

At Rothwold, Tamsin had another shock. Turning her car into the drive at Mark's lovely old house, she was devastated to discover the house was up for sale.

'No!' She pulled on the brake, killed the engine, and just sat staring at the huge board a local estate agent had erected just inside the open gate.

She got out of the car, ran up to the front door and battered on it. There was no reply. She peered through the windows; the house still looked lived in. Everything was just the same inside. She sighed with relief.

But why hadn't he told her? How could he dream of doing something like this and not tell her about it?

Something was wrong. She knew that instinctively. Mark would *never* take a step such as this without telling her — or at least talking it over with her. She felt as if she'd been given a heavy, gut-wrenching blow. How could he do this? What did it mean? Why was

Mark thinking of leaving his home? And where was he going?

It became obvious — as she traipsed round the outside of the house and alternately called his name and inwardly berated him — that he was not there. She took a last look round the gardens, at the roses in their new spring greenery, and the hawthorn hedge sprouting fresh, unblemished shoots. The white limestone paths were weed-free, the borders of flowerbeds neatly clipped. He'd always been so proud of the old house, so genuinely attached to it.

So what had happened?

She ran back to her car and reversed out of the drive. It was only a short distance to Shorecross and the garage where he and Edgar were in partnership — rebuilding and restoring classic cars.

Less than ten minutes later, she spun into the forecourt of the garage in a cloud of wet gravel, parked up and then got out of the car and marched up to the wide doors which were partly open. She stormed inside.

A pair of blue-denimed legs were sticking out from under a jacked-up Jaguar.

She walked over to the legs and demanded, 'What the hell do you think you're playing at?'

Jack Orgill slid out from under the Jaguar

and stared up at her.

She took a step backwards. 'Heck! I'm sorry! I thought you were Mark.'

Jack-O grinned. 'Me legs must be still in good shape, then — if you thought I was 'im.'

She hadn't really taken note of the shape of those legs, she realized. As usual, she'd just barged in and opened her mouth before connecting voice to brain.

She gazed round the place. A radio was blaring away at the far end. 'Is he here?' She looked down at Jack-O again. He was sitting up now and watching her.

'No,' he said. 'He's taken a day off.'

'An auction?' she asked. 'Has he gone somewhere with Edgar Brand?'

Jack-O shook his head. 'Just said he was taking a day off.' He grinned. 'I don't ask no questions, love. I just get on with me work. Them two's the boss — Mark and Edgar. I just does as I'm told.'

She could have shaken him. 'Would Edgar know where he's gone, do you think?'

'He's taken the day off as well. Business, he said.'

'Hell!'

'No, love. Heaven,' Jack-O said. 'Heaven for me. He's been like a bear with a sore head just lately.'

'Edgar?'

'Mark.'

'Oh! I'm sorry.'

Jack-O grinned again. 'Maybe he'll start to laugh again — now you're back.'

She went back to her car and headed to Edgar Brand's house. There was nobody there. She stood outside on the road, wondering what to do next. It was getting late. If she didn't find him soon she'd have to book into somewhere for bed and breakfast.

She decided to go back to the house and wait a while there.

She sat in her car on his drive, gazing at the house, then growing cold as the daylight shadows deepened and the clock crawled round to four o'clock.

She foraged in the glove compartment and found a notebook she always kept there. She wrote him a note, telling him she was going back to the garage and then on to a pub in the village to take a room for the night.

She pushed the note through his letterbox and drove again onto the seafront at Shorecross, parking on the garage forecourt, popping her head into the garage, seeing Jack-O's legs once more, this time underneath a Mini. She didn't disturb him. There was no sign of Mark's Porsche, and it would have been there if *he* was there.

She needed to talk to him. Why wasn't he

here? Mark had always been there when she'd wanted him before. She was restless and impatient. She walked to the edge of the low-lying cliffs and looked over onto the beach at the sea rolling in.

It would soon be dusk. She gazed back down the coast — back towards Heronsea.

The coastline was ragged and uneven. The winter had been severe and, as was inevitable in this part of Yorkshire, great bites had been taken out of the land by the winter tides. Up and down the coast, the cliffs had eroded. There were miniature mountains of boulder clay heaped up on the beach, and there were wide ledges of green grass halfway down some of the cliffs, where the land had slipped and made a plateau, hanging there between the sea and the sky. Little tables, they were, looking so solid and unruffled. They might hang there like that for a month, a year, a century, being host to nobody but the seagulls. But then one day they'd be gone, and they would finish up like the rest of the land had finished up — another miniature mountain, another heap of boulder clay.

And the sea would claim it, and carry it away.

It felt so good — being back!

She scrambled down the low cliffs and started walking against the stiff breeze blowing inland off the sea. Waves were curling and foaming on the incoming tide. She loved to hear the crash they made when they hit the smooth, clean sand. There was something very relaxing about the sea, she found.

She walked nearer the edge of the surf and gazed out over that wide expanse of water. The sky was darkening but the sun was still bright behind her, setting as it was in the western sky.

Her long shadow stretched out before her on the waves. And then another shadow joined it.

He'd come up silently behind her. 'Sorry I missed you,' he said, grasping hold of her arm and spinning her round to face him. His head swooped down and his lips touched hers. 'What brings you here?' His eyes searched hers while his hands and hers clasped.

'I'm coming home,' she said, knowing there was no point at all in prevaricating.

'Home?'

She nodded.

'What happened?' His voice was guarded, then, before she could answer, he said, 'No! Let me tell you what I've done first of all.'

'Your house,' she said. 'Why the hell are you selling it, Mark?'

'A long story. It involves a girl.'

She drew in a sharp breath. 'A girl?'

'She wouldn't marry me,' he said. 'She's a terror. Completely out of my reach, of course. She's got this bee in her bonnet about being independent.'

'I hope,' she said, 'that you're talking about me.'

'Who else could I be talking about? She's forced me into an intolerable situation,' he said, still holding her hands and still looking down into her face. 'She's made it so I can't exist — two hundred miles away from her.'

Shock registered at last. 'You're not selling up because of me?'

In a practical sort of voice he said, 'I've invested in another quarter-share of the garage. That means I own half of it now, and Edgar owns the other half. It means, also, that Edgar can afford to employ somebody to take my place there, and I'll still be a shareholder. Like that girl, I want to be independent, you see. I want an income of my own. I couldn't let her keep me, could I? Not off the income from her herbs.'

'You think that's what she wanted?' she asked softly.

He thought about her question for some moments, then said gently, 'No, Tam, I don't think that's what you wanted. But I came to my senses at last and realized that things couldn't go on as they were doing. Two hundred miles away from each other is two hundred miles too many. I'm coming down to Suffolk. I'll get some sort of a job down there so I can be near you.'

'No,' she said, 'you can't do that.'

'Try and stop me.' He grinned. 'The house is up for sale. I've got people interested in it.'

'This is madness,' she cried. 'I don't want you to do this, Mark.'

'Too late,' he said, with a tiny shrug of indifference, 'I've already talked to your Mr John Chambers — Estate Agent, down in Suffolk. I'm putting in an offer for Herb House as soon as my own house sells.'

'Herb House is already sold,' she said. 'Or as good as. A consortium is buying it to pull it down and use the land for new houses.'

His face mirrored his disappointment. 'No!' he said. 'I don't believe this.'

She nodded. 'It's true. I'm leaving Herb House, Mark. I'm going to live here — in Yorkshire. *I* want to be near *you*.'

'Near me?'

'At Heronsea. It's not so far away, is it?'

'You're crazy. You hated Heronsea. It holds nothing but bad memories for you.'

'You're crazy too — thinking of giving everything up — your job, your lovely house — for me.'

'That's different.'

'*This* is different,' she said. 'I'm going back to the lighthouse, Mark.'

'You can't . . . '

'I can. I have done. I agreed to all the terms and conditions at a property developer's office in Heronsea this afternoon. I'm being checked out for credit worthiness right now. It won't be a problem, though.'

Speechless, he stared at her, his face a picture of disbelief.

'I'll have the ground floor — the floor that used to be the wedding dress showroom when Ava and I lived there.' She pulled a wry face. 'I'll get used to the passenger lift going up the middle. I suppose it's what you might call progress! The ground floor will be ideal for my purpose.'

'Your *purpose*,' he said faintly, looking slightly askance at her.

'Flowers,' she said. 'Bev — the girl who has the hairdressing salon — suggested I call it 'Tam's Flower Tower'.'

He said, 'I bet you felt like hitting her.'

'No,' she said. 'I did a totally silly thing — I burst into tears and thought it was a wonderful idea.'

'Tam,' he said, pulling her into his arms, 'Oh, Tam, my darling girl. Are you sure you're doing the right thing?'

'Bev made me a cup of tea.' She lifted her

head and looked into his eyes. 'She's nice. They're all nice. She introduced me properly to the girls who work for her, and to Tony, who runs the café on the first floor, and to Jane and Matt in the travel agent's upstairs. I think I'm going to be happy there.'

'You really are going through with this?'

She nodded her head. 'Yes,' she said. 'I'm tired of running away. I couldn't let that old lighthouse get the better of me, could I?'

'It has so many bad memories.' He was still worried, she could tell.

'Memories can't hurt me.' On a different subject now, she said, 'There's no living accommodation there, though. I'll have to find somewhere . . . '

'Come and live with me. There's no point in me selling the house now, is there?'

She kissed him on the lips, then said, 'I was hoping you'd suggest that, but I'll only come on one condition.'

'And that is?' His arms were linked round her waist now. He was holding her close and there was amusement playing round his lips.

'I want to marry you.'

His voice was guarded. 'Tam! This isn't some kind of joke, is it?'

'Do I have to get down on one knee and propose to you?' she asked solemnly. 'Is that the only way you're going to believe I'm serious.'

He considered her words and then said, 'Going down on one knee is the *usual* way to propose marriage, I believe.'

She threw her arms round his neck. 'Have you ever in your whole life known me to do anything in the *usual* way, Mark Langham? Will it do if I just ask you nicely if you'll marry me?'

'It'll do,' he said mockingly. 'And I accept your proposal, Miss Curtis.'

He kissed her hard and long and passionately, and when the kiss ended she broke free of him and raced down to the sea, threw her arms wide and spun round to face him.

'I am so happy, Mark,' she yelled.

He stood where she'd left him, a few yards away.

She saw him reaching into his pocket, fishing something out, and then he yelled, 'Can you catch from there?'

She nodded, and asked, laughing, 'Is it another horseshoe?'

He started to laugh too, then sobered and said, 'No. Nothing new this time. I just had the catch repaired on the chain. If I throw it — can you catch a dream?'

He tossed a tiny box to her. She caught it

deftly and opened it, knowing before she looked inside what it would be. She slipped the box into her pocket, then reached up and fastened the dreamcatcher pendant around her neck.

She went to him then, and held out both her hands to him.

'Take me home, Mark.'

'You're home already,' he said softly, latching onto her hands and drawing her into his arms.

THE END

We do hope that you have enjoyed reading this large print book.

Did you know that all of our titles are available for purchase?

We publish a wide range of high quality large print books including:
Romances, Mysteries, Classics
General Fiction
Non Fiction and Westerns

Special interest titles available in large print are:
The Little Oxford Dictionary
Music Book
Song Book
Hymn Book
Service Book

Also available from us courtesy of Oxford University Press:
Young Readers' Dictionary
(large print edition)
Young Readers' Thesaurus
(large print edition)

For further information or a free brochure, please contact us at:
Ulverscroft Large Print Books Ltd.,
The Green, Bradgate Road, Anstey,
Leicester, LE7 7FU, England.
Tel: (00 44) 0116 236 4325
Fax: (00 44) 0116 234 0205

DEAD FISH

Ruth Carrington

Dr Geoffrey Quinn arrives home to find his children missing, the charred remains of his wife's body in the boiler and Chief Superintendent Manning waiting to arrest him for her murder. Alison Hope, attractive and determined, is briefed to defend him. Quinn claims he is innocent, but Alison is not so sure. The background becomes increasingly murky as she penetrates a wealthy and ruthless circle who cannot risk their secrets — sexual perversion, drugs, blackmail, illegal arms dealing and major fraud — coming to light. Can Alison unravel the mystery in time to save Quinn?

MY FATHER'S HOUSE

Kathleen Conlon

'Your father has another woman'. Nine-year-old Anna Blake is only mildly surprised when a schoolfriend lets drop this piece of information. And when her father finally leaves home to live with Olivia in Hampstead, that place becomes, for Anna, the epitome of sinful glamour. But Hampstead, though welcoming, is not home. So Anna, now in her teens, sets out to find a place where she can really belong. At first she thinks love may be the answer, and certainly Jonathon — and Raymond — and Jake, have a devastating effect on her life. But can anyone really supply what she needs?

GHOSTLY MURDERS

P. C. Doherty

When Chaucer's Canterbury pilgrims pass a deserted village, the sight of its decaying church provokes the poor Priest to tears. When they take shelter, he tells a tale of ancient evil, greed, devilish murder and chilling hauntings . . . There was once a young man, Philip Trumpington, who was appointed parish priest of a pleasant village with an old church, built many centuries earlier. However, Philip soon discovers that the church and presbytery are haunted. A great and ancient evil pervades, which must be brought into the light, resolved and reparation made. But the price is great . . .

BLOODTIDE

Bill Knox

When the Fishery Protection cruiser MARLIN was ordered to the Port Ard area off the north-west Scottish coast, Chief Officer Webb Carrick soon discovered that an old shipmate of Captain Shannon had been killed in a strange accident before they arrived. A drowned frogman, a reticent Russian officer and a dare-devil young fisherman were only a few of the ingredients to come together as Carrick tried to discover the truth. The key to it all was as deadly as it was unexpected.

WISE VIRGIN

Manda Mcgrath

Sisters Jean and Ailsa Leslie live on a small farm in the Scottish Grampians. Andrew Esplin, the local blacksmith, keeps a brotherly eye on the girls, loving Ailsa, the younger sister, from afar. Ailsa is in love with Stewart Morrison, who is working in Greenock. Jean is engaged to Alan Drummond, who has gone to Australia, intending to send for her when his prospects are good. But Jean shocks everyone when she elopes with Dunton from the big house . . .

BEYOND THE NURSERY WINDOW

Ruth Plant

Ruth Plant tells of her youth in a country vicarage in Staffordshire, a story she began in her earlier book NANNY AND I. Together with the occasional dip back into childhood memories of a nursery kingdom where Nanny reigned supreme, she ventures forth into a world of schooldays and visits to relatives, the exciting world of London and the theatre, the wonders of Bath and the beauties of the Lake District. She travels to Oberammergau, and sees Hitler on a visit there. On the threshold of life the future seems bright and war far away.